MOONLIGHT HELMSMAN

Robert Smalls' Amazing Escape

This is a work of fiction. Some names, characters, places, and incidents either are the product of the author's imagination or are used fictitiously, and any resemblance to any persons, living or dead, business establishments, events, or locales is entirely coincidental.

Moonlight Helmsman
Robert Smalls' Amazing Escape

ISBN: 978-0-9984937-0-1

MOONLIGHT HELMSMAN

Robert Smalls' Amazing Escape

A novel by
Richard Maule

To unsung heroes of every color
who took life's helm and changed history

Prologue

At the end of his earthly life, northern newspapers wrote that Robert Smalls' achievements would be forever remembered as a glorious stanza of our national epic. They weren't. Like so many people of color, the memories of Smalls' exploits were allowed to fade, the written records systematically buried by whites who were eager to erase such a remarkable chapter in our history. It is unfortunate that African-Americans have learned to expect such treatment.

Great stories like Smalls' cry out to be told, not so much because of the hero's race but because of his greatness. The events of his life, even viewed in broad strokes, are amazing. He rose from servitude to become a ship's pilot – called a wheelman because the word helmsman was reserved for whites. During the Civil War, he masterminded a brilliant conspiracy whereby he and a group of Charleston slaves stole the Confederate's flagship. Honored for bravery in the Union cause, Robert Smalls became the first black man to command a warship in the United States Navy. After the war, he went on to become the first African-American congressman from South Carolina, serving five terms in the United States House of Representatives.

It was Robert's misfortune to be born into a time and place that robbed him of the title *hero,* another designation he richly deserves. What brief mention he receives in books is almost universally relegated, indeed *segregated,* to the far corner of our libraries reserved for "Black History." Even on those shelves, the record of Smalls' life and exploits has been overshadowed by the more familiar stories of Harriet Tubman, Frederick Douglas, and Dr. Martin Luther King, Jr.

Though it should sadden us that his achievements are not well known, we can find comfort in the knowledge that Robert Smalls did not do brave deeds in order to be famous but to be free. It is this quest for freedom that elevates his story above other accounts of military bravery. His deeds impress us, but it is Robert's passion for freedom that inspires us. His story endures, not just as an amazing tale of escape, but as the saga of an oppressed human being who seized life's helm. Transcending the fences of Beaufort and the fortressses of Charleston Harbor, Robert Smalls became much more than a freedman. He became the *helmsman,* teaching us to embrace the dignity of our human nature – born for dominion and created in the very image of God. May his story motivate us to celebrate every sacred opportunity for our mortal hands to grasp the helm of our greater destiny.

A Special Note

This volume is presented as a novel, a work of fiction. It doesn't seek to manipulate history, but rather to bring it to life. I've done my best to present an account that, where possible, matches up with the facts as we know them. Some events and characters have been added or embellished to assist the writer's artistic vision and the deeper meanings of the story. Astute readers will find a few historical anachronisms (like the early inclusion of the *CSS Hunley* in Chapter 27) and occasional modernizations of 18th century language. The actions and words attributed to historical characters are speculation, and any resemblance to other persons, real or fictional, living or dead, is unintended and coincidental.

While I have tried to use terms for African-American people that were common when Robert Smalls lived. Designations like *Negro, African,* or *colored* are ones he himself used. I make no apology for my avoidance of one particular word, one so repugnant that I personally refuse to speak it or put it into print. Readers craving this level of historical accuracy will have to look elsewhere.

My hope and prayer is that this book brings honor to the amazing life and legacy of its hero.

Richard Maule
2016

Chapter 1
The Helmsman

Robert Smalls did his best to live as a Christian, but there were times he wanted to kill every white man in South Carolina. He restrained himself of course. Neither the Lord nor his mother would have been pleased for his heart to be ruled by vengeance. Robert simply resented anything, or anyone, who stood between him and freedom, and it was the blue water of the Atlantic that offered him that prize.

White sailors had long embraced the notion that a slave could never make a good helmsman. Blacks were, they thought, created for physical labor, but in 1854, when Captain John Simmons put Robert Smalls behind the wheel of the schooner *Lone Kestrel,* they said he would never be *more* than a helmsman. In truth, this was fine with him, for he had never aspired to be anything more, or anything else.

At age six, he had caught his first glimpses of the boats along the waterfront in Beaufort, South Carolina. As salty breezes stroked his face, Robert inhaled deeply, as if it had been his first life-breath. The year was 1845, and from that moment, he was entranced and beckoned by the water.

"Get back from there!" whites would shout angrily as he walked atop the sea wall, "Black boys had best stay clear of the water."

But Robert didn't get back. The ocean inspired him. At times he dreamed of being a great ship captain, but at other times its infinite expanse of the Atlantic could make him feel wonderfully tiny and anonymous, a lone brushstroke silhouetted against the panorama of swirling tides and distant horizons. It was the closest thing to intoxication a young boy could experience. Robert came to embrace the sea as his dearest friend, and in time, his most formidable adversary. In the course of God's plan, it would offer him an open door to freedom.

During those tender years in Beaufort, he stole every opportunity to marvel at the water. Sneaking before dawn to the wharves along Bay Street, Robert welcomed the unfettered promise of each sunrise over Ladies' Island, watching it glisten off the bright-capped waves as the night breezes waned.

To white folks who strolled the boardwalk, the little brown boy who stood opposite the South Pier became a familiar sight, a fixture of sorts. Some supposed Robert might be deaf or feeble-minded because he so rarely spoke, even when addressed, but his mother Lydia knew better and she always knew where to find him. Her clearest memories of his childhood were the conversations they had at those wharves on Bay Street. But *conversation*, in the singular, would have been the better term for it, for their words were always pretty much the same.

"Where on earth have you been?" she would ask.

"Where else?" he would always reply. "Where, *always?*"

"Daydreaming," she said, shaking her head.

"Not dreaming," he said, "Looking."

"Looking is dreaming," she said as she put her arm around him, "and dreamin' don't bring nothin' but trouble."

"Looking… is nice," he said, "and so is dreaming."

"What you staring at?" she asked. It was the same question every morning, and his answer was always the same.

"Nothing, just the river." At that, she would pull him by the arm, shaking her head and then she would give him a stern talking-to all the way home.

Lydia should have known the water was enough for him. It was Robert's connection with the world, one of the few ways a slave boy of six might find to connect. Her son might be the wild child at church, but here he sat quiet and still, almost reverent. The waterfront inspired him more than any human sanctuary. He calmed himself at this sea wall the same way his mother contemplated the faded lithograph of *Jesus in Prayer* that hung on a nail over her bed. Open water was his deepest longing and his greatest reward, the storehouse of whatever milk and honey this life might have to offer.

"'Tain't time to daudle around lookin' at nothing," she would say.

But it wasn't nothing. As Robert grew, he would describe in detail all that he saw and heard. There were birds, crabs, and of course, big fish, and these he would talk about all the rest of that day. He also eavesdropped on the roughs and stevedores who worked the docks. And at night, Robert would share with his mother the fantastic stories and profane words he had heard that day, soon discovering that she was not fond of either. She would have washed his mouth with lye soap if they'd had any.

But over time, he began to focus on something else. Amidst the familiar backdrop of the river scene, his eyes were particularly drawn to the ships. Though he was curious about every detail of the shore and the docks, it was the tall clippers that took his breath away. Their towering oak masts, harvested from the forests of New England, were taller than any tree in Carolina's Low Country. Some of the newer boats were driven by steam, but Robert liked the clippers best. These square-rigged ships traveled thousands miles on the quiet strength of the wind alone. The biggest of them were as long as a city block, imposing islands of freedom in God's big ocean.

On these vessels a peculiar brotherhood of men endeavored to live, work, and travel to every corner of the world. Robert watched the sailors' every move, as they climbed the rigging, knotted ropes and smoked their long briar pipes. Their eloquent cursing and joking were as musical to him as were their songs. Their stories were fantastic concoctions, but filled with lessons that could ring as true as scripture. These sailors were oft prone to bicker like enemies, yet when pressed, they would defend one another to the edge of death itself. In the taverns of Beaufort, they might blacken each other's eyes, but on the ship each crew member was respected and treasured.

Each man, of course, entrusted his life to the others. From the captain on down, each man was assigned his list of duties. One man might plot their course, while others lifted heavy burdens or mounted the rigging to the top of the mainmast. Their respect for one another transcended rank for every one's work was of concern to all. To neglect the tiniest of tasks was a shameful thing, for the proper execution of any duty might serve to save or sink the boat.

Positioned at the bridge of every ship was a special man whose hands gripped the wheel – the helmsman. Robert studied closely how each of these wheelmen plied his trade. At times the lone figure might not move at all, but at the captain's shout, he would spring to life. First to starboard, then to port he would spin the spokes of the wheel in a graceful, soundless blur, his face like carved stone and his eyes always locked on what was ahead.

Unlike the gears of a grist mill or the squeaking machinery of a cotton gin, a ship's wheel was smoothly and artistically worked. Fondled warm in the hand, the spokes' movements were organic and living, with movements as silent as the strokes of a dove's wings. As rhythmic as the rising and falling of a mother's breast. Thus turned, the helm could cause a boat to tilt precariously back and forth as it negotiated the river's maze of sweetgrass islands and shoals all the way out to open water – beautiful and inscrutable sorcery.

Robert was amazed at how, when underway, only the slightest movement of the helm was sufficient to direct a boat. Any gesture, perhaps just the twitching of one spoke, could urge the rudder, followed by the gradual, sweeping movement of the boat in its course. He had heard that cocking the wheel just one finger-width could decide whether you would drop anchor in London or Calais, wherever those places were. Robert marveled that God had condescended to put such power into the hands of mortal man, and all his life he longed to be such a man, a helmsman.

'One day I'll command my own ship,' he thought, 'even if I have to steal it.' Even as a young boy, Robert was wise enough to realize the danger of mentioning his notions to anyone else, even his own mother. He hid these dreams deep in his heart until it finally came true on a moonlit night in May of 1862 when he took the helm of the *CSS Planter* and sailed off to freedom. But that part of his story would have to wait till later.

As a child in antebellum South Carolina, such freedom, or any freedom for that matter, was a blessing reserved for a privileged circle of men, rich white men. These masters controlled the plantations, the slaves, and had the say-so over just about every area of life in Beaufort County. Many of them were altogether mean and selfish, while others showed themselves to be of more benevolent temperament. But good or evil, they reigned as masters, owners and patriarchs. It was wise for women, children, and slaves to obey them, and it was risky to do otherwise. Ruling over others was the masters' lot in life, and their greatest delight. Everyone else in South Carolina had to tiptoe around with nervous steps.

Still all in all, the Low Country was peaceful, a place of awesome natural beauty. Long before the first colonists or slaves arrived, a divine hand had painted the skies over Hilton Head with white and pink cloud-strokes which continually moved inland from the Atlantic. Their clusters arrived in a silent and constant rhythm, luminescent against a blue sky without texture. Below them, the steady cadence of waves struck the shores of the Sea Islands like the eternal ticking of heaven's own clock. It had always been thus, and most folks here were content in the knowledge that it always would be so.

Day after day, the tides brought tall-masted Yankee and European ships to the wharves along Bay Street, exchanging manufactured goods for Southern cotton, sugar and indigo. Incoming cargos were quickly unloaded from the boats on to pallets and wagons for delivery inland. Funds, in checks and gold, changed hands at the exchange office downtown while each ship's hold was emptied and cleaned.

Along the wharves, stevedores chattered and slaves sang as they worked, loading boxes and tying cotton into tight bales. A handful of dock bosses shouted orders, threats and poetic profanities to the "pea-brained Micks, half-wit imbeciles, and black bastards" that sweated along the busy piers.

Goaded or not, the loading process always ended up taking about a day and a half. The largest of the men could swing huge burlap sacks of rice, two at a time, onto their shoulders to stagger up the gangway. To be a 'two bag man' was a point of pride. On board, the supervisors and crews bickered over how every inch below deck could be most efficiently filled, and the owners would tell you it was never stacked tightly enough. The sound of the loading, shouting and grunting along the wharves rose into a surf-like roar, and could be heard from the farthest ends of the waterfront. With full personnel and favorable breezes, a morning arrival might be back out to sea in three days or less. The turnaround of cash and cargo mimicked nature's rhythmic delivery of the waves below them and the clouds above.

From heaven, the buildings of town and the plantations that surrounded it must have appeared small and inconsequential. Unlike the grand Old World cities like London or Paris, these columned homes must have seemed provisional and makeshift, the flimsy edge of civilization. But in the eyes of Beaufort's 5,961 white citizens and 32,000 black slaves, the mansions of the plantation owners stood as symbols of blessing and privilege.

Their great grandfathers had first brought civilization here. The indigenous peoples who had inhabited the area for almost 4000 years, had been gradually driven out by successive settlements of Spanish, French, English and Scots beginning in 1514. Having come from older colonies in the West Indies, the first settlers in Carolina's coastal region established a plantation economy to resemble the system they had known in the islands. This led to the enslavement of the native tribes followed by the importation of thousands of Africans to provide labor for the plantations where rice, sugar and indigo were cultivated. As early as 1720, these people of color formed the majority of the population of the region, and upon their strong backs, Beaufort became a growing hub of wealth and commerce.

The early explorers, nobles and Indians gave their names to towns and islands – William Hilton, Captain Johannes Fripp, and the Edisto Indians. A growing trade in crops and raw materials attracted investment by wealthy Englishmen like Henry Somerset, the second Duke of Beaufort, for whom both the city and county were named.

Because of its dependence on commerce with Britain, there was divided loyalty in the Carolinas when the Revolution came. Some plantation owners like Thomas Hayward, Jr. sided with the Colonists and signed the Declaration of Independence. Similarly, the 30 families on Hilton Head Island aligned themselves with the cause of independence, but nearby Daufuskie Island became a gathering place for Tories loyal to the crown, and it became a British stronghold during the war. After peace came, all sides were gradually united under the new banner of the United States and under the irresistable spell of commercial progress.

Before the War Between the States, their little corner of creation seemed to them an immutable and prosperous paradise, a vibrant and nearly perfect masterpiece. It was the world their forefathers had dreamed of and built, and their expectation was that their children's children would drink from the same wellspring of blessing. But somewhere, far past the sun-drenched horizon, storm clouds were gathering, brush strokes of a darker hue.

Chapter 2
Moonlight Boy

From the upper windows of the John McKee house, an observer could observe all that was done in the yard and down Prince Street toward town. New Street led toward the water, down to the collection of townhouses and businesses they called *the port*. From there one could travel up the dusty gravel of Center Street through Beaufort proper.

Once north of town, the road roughened and narrowed to become what was generously called the Turnpike. As everyone knew, it ran a few miles inland, as then straight as a plowed furrow, all the way up the coast to Charleston. Only a few of them had ever traversed the full measure of it. *The big town,* as Charleston was called, was more quickly pleasantly reached by boat.

Sipping sweet tea from the upper balconies of their homes, white townspeople could see where the highway and its few travelers disappeared into the blurry distance, where the manicured meadows of Beaufort met the unmeasured grayness of the marshes. It was said there were pine forests a mile or so out of town, and small farms beyond that. Before Sumter was fired upon in 1861, no one imagined that soon, almost every white citizen of Beaufort would travel that road, many never to return.

Life along this coast had remained unchanged for as long as any of them could remember. Continuity was not their aspiration, it was their unquestioned assumption, for none of them considered the prospect that change would, or even could, occur. The events of the coming years would shake the very foundations of their universe, and men like Robert Smalls would be the instigators of such events. While the facts of his birth were not noteworthy, from the beginning, his presence made ripples, and eventually waves, in the long-quiet stream that was Southern life. The troubling of the waters began on April 5, 1839.

The sounds of the dawn floated through the open windows of the McKee house as the songs of night insects melted into those of the morning birds. The clack of wood chopping echoed across the backyards of Prince Street as black women moved quietly about, stoking fires and gathering eggs to prepare breakfast for the white folks who were just now waking in the mansions. There was always much work to do, and none of them even looked up as the cries of 43 year old Lydia Polite rose above the gray shacks known as the servant quarters. The baby was coming.

When her groaning suddenly ceased, everyone stopped in their tracks as an abrupt silence fell over the yard. Even the birds seemed to stop their songs mid-verse, leaving only the hushed hiss of the breeze blowing in across the marshes. After the squawk of a newborn cracked the stillness of the dawn, the natural symphony of morning sounds began to slowly return, the birds resuming their songs as slaves went back to their work.

Few of them noticed when after a few minutes, Leena, a middle-aged midwife, emerged from the small cottage. "A boy," she muttered to herself, but loud enough to be heard by all, her words spoken with no particular tone of celebration. It was as if she had remarked about the weather. A second time she announced, louder this time, "A boy," but by then everyone was back to their tasks. The birth of another Negro man-child represented no particular cause for rejoicing, except perhaps as an addition to the already considerable wealth of the McKee family. The whispering would only start later.

Word quickly spread that this baby was yet another *moonlight child*. In the parlance of these Swonga slaves, this was a delicate way of referring to a slave child of mixed parentage. The lighter skin of half-white newborns was poetically, and politely, attributed to the effects of the moon's rays, but it was known by all that such a child was the result of some white master's lust. Though half-white in color, such a child would be designated as colored, and in any case, a slave. The folks of the town might refer to him as a mulatto, but most would probably say nothing at all. Gentlefolk would be similarly reticent to credit any particular white father by name.

So it was that for the first years of his life, the slaves on Prince Street referred to Robert Smalls as *Moonlah-bai,* which in the Gullah language means moonlight boy. His paler shading would constantly confirm that the whispered stories of his origin were based on more than idle rumor. The deference shown him by the Henry McKee family left little doubt about who Robert's father was.

It wasn't long before Jane Bold McKee was told that her servant

Lydia had given birth to a half-breed child. Mrs. McKee began to see the boy running around among the darker youngsters in the yard outside the slave quarters. She had wanted to tell herself that one of the white field hands or visiting tradesmen had violated her girl Lydia, but her own eyes, and the whispers around the plantation, told her that young Robert Smalls belonged to her husband Henry.

Jane resolved never to disclose her awareness of her husband's dalliance. Henry had not touched Jane since July, when he had learned she was expecting their first child, Elizabeth. Even before her impregnation, Jane's own response to Henry's romantic advances had already begun to grow colder and more distant. What vestiges remained of her womanly passion had become as bleak and motionless as a winter sky. Of course she had never once withheld herself from him; she was after all, still a Christian wife.

Even though she rendered Henry McKee the service expected of a righteous wife, Jane had come to dread his very presence. And his disgusting presence could seemingly fill a room, a large house, or at times the whole of Beaufort County. Although he stood only slightly above five and a half feet in height, everyone was inclined to think of him as tall. This perception pleased him greatly, of course. Whether sitting, standing, or riding his gray stallion, Mayor, Henry presented himself to the world with the perfect uprightness of a Southern gentleman. A master.

He existed as something like a painting to her. Henry would often stand motionless for long minutes, usually gazing at some far off person or object over which he was pleased to have control. From a distance his posed silhouette might easily have been mistaken for a statue, or perhaps one of the erect fence posts that dotted the plantation grounds. His clothing, always light colored, was kept clean and well-pressed, and when viewed from across the vast yard, he presented an elegant picture of manhood. In truth, most people liked Henry McKee best when they could regard him at a distance.

Inside the house, the master's arrival was usually preceded by the sound of brusque commands barked from outside or perhaps from the next room, and it was command, not conversation that provided the consistent theme of his communication with others. Though piercing and not quite manly, his was a voice that demanded obedience. For the family and servants, it began every day at dawn with the demands for clothes, shoes and tea as he shouted from his bedroom. For Jane, it began long before dawn, in the darkness of her bed.

Their expressions of romantic love, if it could be called that, were expressed with perfunctory regularity, like the gathering of eggs or the frying of breakfast sausage. Jane supposed that Henry found her attractive, since his amorous advances had remained somewhat consistent over the eight years of their marriage. But their intercourse was usually silent and brief. Though she always did her best to respond to him in the fitting manner, these carnal visits were universally burdensome to her now.

The experience was perplexing rather than painful. Her Protestant training had taught her that sufferings were to be expected in life, but it was impossible for Jane to view Henry's nightly visits as anything consistent with the Christian religion. And though Saint Helena's rector referred to such intercourse as marital love, to equate this with affection was unfathomable to her. It was not love but duty, and a grim one at that. There was no choice but to play along of course, and night after night, the unfathomable was endured, and her wifely function was performed in the spirit of Christian submission.

Over time, Jane had come to recognize that God made women to be ruled by two great passions, the first being their natural attraction toward masculine strength. Their second passion, and often the more enduring one, was the mothering instinct. Over the span of their marriage, Jane had incrementally abandoned the former to give herself to the latter. Every good Southern woman came to recognize and adapt to this divinely ordained plan for male and female. What began with the fires of nature, soon turned to the arms of nurture. Maidens evolved into mothers, and strong men, over time, became needy little boys.

Jane could recall that in the first weeks after their wedding, she had been embarrassed by her own thirst for his amorous assaults. He had brought her poems and flowers by day and was insatiable in their bed by night. With the arrival of Elizabeth in 1839, and later William, the passions of womanhood had been gradually replaced by matronly urges, and bit by bit her heart and energies were transferred to the little ones.

Such was the unfolding plan of heaven, she reasoned – mothering thus becoming her passion – if such could be called a passion. Even her relationship with Henry became more maternal in character, with less frequent intercourse and more frequent moments of comforting him in his troubles. But in all her experience, Jane resigned herself to the truth that women were ever destined to be servants of one passion or the other. Men might present themselves to the world as brash stallions or helpless infants, and both of these in their ugliest forms. God had equipped women with the gifts to cope with either, and eight years of marriage were sufficient to teach Jane Bold McKee that men were generally a grotesque mixture of both.

Things were not at all simplified with the arrival of little Robert. Jane had first taken note that her girl Lydia was with child back in the fall of 1838, but she was reluctant to say anything. It would not do for Jane to ask Lydia about the child's parentage, for neither the truth nor any lie would have constituted an acceptable answer to the question. Would it not be a horror if this slave woman should clearly name Henry as her violator? But it would have been even more painful to force Lydia to soften the situation by fabricating some lie to lay blame on some other man. By Christmas of that year, something had to be said.

"You're with child?" Jane had finally said, more as a statement than a question.

"Yes, ma'am," Lydia replied with her eyes lowered. "Been so five months now."

"And the father?" Jane asked. "Do we know him?"

"Ain't my place to say," she answered. "Wasn't something I was prayin' for."

"But we know him?" Jane said, determined to press the issue.

No longer cowering, Lydia raised her face. Her dark eyes glowered coldly at her mistress. "Oh we knows him all right," she said. "Just wouldn't do for me to say nothing. Wouldn't do for you neither, Missy." This, of course, told Jane McKee everything she needed to know, and hated to acknowledge. The child was Henry's.

The thought that her husband had vented his lust on a Negress was distasteful, and only reinforced Jane's opinion that the conjugal act was bereft of any spiritual or romantic meaning. 'He's a pig,' she thought to herself, 'and all this while I carried his child.'

"Will that be all?" Lydia asked.

Jane could think of nothing else to say right then, but there were a number of more difficult questions on her mind. What, if anything should be said to her husband? What, if anything, should be done with this mongrel child? Would the members at Saint Helena's assume that Jane had been disobedient in her duties as a wife? Jane hoped the discussion of these things might be avoided as long as possible, but such discourse, and the ensuing gossip, could not be forestalled forever. As she mused over these issues, she became aware that Lydia was still waiting for her answer.

"I suppose that will have to do for now," Jane said. "Once again a man has left the women to pick up the pieces."

"Yes'm," Lydia said. "'Nuff pieces for all of us, I reckon. You gonna send me and the baby away?"

The thought had never crossed Jane's mind. "I can't see my way to let Henry off so easy," she said. "He needs to do right by the child."

"Robert," Lydia said. "His name is Robert." Jane turned to walk back toward the house, then turned back to Lydia for a brief moment.

"I'll keep you in my prayers," she said. "I'll have to talk to my husband about all this, but I'm not sure how."

"Then," Lydia said. "I suppose I should pray for you too." As Jane walked away, Lydia could almost see the wheels spinning in her mistress' head.

To Jane McKee, the hurdles seemed insurmountable. First she would have to let Henry know that she was aware of the child's origins. This point would have to be made with delicacy, as it would not do for a wife to confront her husband with accusation, even a true one. Jane wrestled with thoughts and slept poorly almost every night until spring, when events finally forced her hand.

The presence of a light-skinned infant in the slave yard was neither a surprise nor a welcome sight to Jane, but in any case, it meant that the time to talk had come. Everyone would have to show their cards. It would have to be brought to Henry's attention that such a child had been seen among his servants. Then the question could be asked, "How do you suppose that such a thing could come about?" This would allow Henry to propose an explanation less offensive than the truth.

Jane spent an hour in prayer that morning, arming her heart for Armageddon. Lydia happened upon her mistress in the garden. "I'm going to have the conversation," Jane said. "You'd best say a prayer for me."

Lydia just nodded and lowered her head at first, but then found words to reply. "Good luck, Missy," she said. "If he raises a hand to you, you cry out now."

Two houses down, a hound was heard barking as a small cat suddenly came bounding across the McKee's backyard. With the clatter of wings, the birds in the bushes flew up to the safety of the higher branches of the trees, and Lydia went back to her chores.

The steps between Lydia's cottage and the big house were not sufficient for Jane to compose herself entirely. "Guard my words, Lord," she whispered to herself.

She found Henry sitting in his customary place between the

fireplace and the front window of the parlor. Next to him on the side table was a cooled cup of sugared tea, and a volume of poetry was spread, for appearance sake, across his lap. When he glanced up at her, their eyes met and he could sense that she was possessed of some question. Jane never looked him in the eye unless there was a question.

"Have you walked the grounds lately?" she asked, beginning the conversation with a stupid pleasantry. She had seen Henry walk the property twice a day for the past eight years.

"Yes, of course," he said politely, "Just this morning." Her husband sensed accurately, that she had some other question in mind.

"You've no doubt seen that the servants have had a conspicuous addition among their young?" She referred of course to young Robert, whose paler skin stood out among the other slaves.

Incredulous that his wife was capable of such a frontal assault, Henry knew there was no possible path of escape. He sat quietly for a moment, considering the best way to return her volley. "I have seen the child you speak of," was all he could think to say. Then, feigning a look of scientific interest, he asked, "What do we know of its origins?"

'My God, he's a weasel,' Jane thought, yet doing her best to hold back any appearance of sarcasm or derision. 'Do we know?' she laughed to herself. 'Are you surprised that others can discern the obvious?' Rejecting every sarcastic response available to her, Jane chose to leave Henry twisting in a minute of painful silence. Then, she finally offered in clear and measured words, "What would *I* know of his origins? I imagine one of the bad men of the town ventured upon our property, in drunkenness perhaps."

"You're likely correct," Henry said, somewhat relieved at her explanation. "I've heard that ruffians, foreigners, and even Jews have been known to pay such visits to slave women... with shameful results."

"Shameful in the eyes of God," Jane said, and then added a dagger. "But I would doubt that a godless man would feel much shame." She looked him straight in the eye as a moment of jagged silence fell between them. "A godly man, would repent, wouldn't you think?"

Henry's heart began thumping as he averted his eyes from hers. She knew. As she moved closer to get his attention, he stepped away toward the front window, feverously scanning the farthest corners of the horizon for some object, any object.

"It was that infidel Moses Goldsmith, no doubt." Henry said, blaming the only Jew that Jane was likely to recognize by name.

As silence again fell upon the room, she offered no words to mollify his uneasiness. She hoped the pause would hit him with painful force, a force he could never physically experience from her hand. Finally, all Henry could offer was, "What's done is done, I suppose."

"Done... but not done.," she replied, as she audibly exhaled. "What's to be the fate of the child?"

"Fate? What fate could it have but to be a slave?" Henry asked. "He'll have to be what he is born to be."

Jane wondered what exactly is he *was* born to be. Henry's evasive simplicity was not enough. She had no doubt that both she and her husband would be forever haunted by persistent feelings of responsibility toward this unanticipated offspring. The child's very existence was both a tragedy and an embarrassment, but the most painful fact was that the brown boy in their slave yard was a blood relative of the McKee family.

Despite Robert's ordained position of servitude, he was, in the end, family, or at least partly so. It seemed appropriate that his treatment might differ, indeed should differ, from that of the other slaves. He was of better blood, his life should be especially nurtured and preserved. Robert must be assisted in rising above the state of his African companions. He should be given certain advantages, perhaps even be educated.

Henry of course would not welcome the notion that a slave should, or could be schooled to any extent. He had, on occasion, delivered tirades on the subject. Henry, of course, had no conviction that the black race was somehow sub-human or incapable. A lifetime on the plantations had taught him that a black man could have a quick mind and hold memories there as long as a white could. But to educate a slave was to upset the entire social order upon which Southern life was built. It would invite the worst sort of stigma and would in every way upset the slave-master relationship. For if a man could read words, then he could know Milton, and justice could not permit any man who could quote *Paradise Lost* to be whipped, called a boy, or sold to another man. Despite his wife's ideas, literacy must be taken off the table.

Jane was prepared to fight Henry on this, and in the days that followed, she continued to press the question. Her husband must be won over to the idea of helping and educating the boy, but there was no social precedent to urge better treatment for such a child. In Beaufort, such less-than-white children had traditionally been worked and whipped with equal severity to the other slaves. There could be no argument based purely on blood.

Jane realized that her Henry, though he was a good Episcopalian, would never be swayed by the demands of charity and kindness. After all, this was a slave they were talking about, and harsh treatment was part and parcel of their proscribed position in the world. There would have to be some other line of reasoning.

Sometime during the days that followed, it occurred to her that the entire question might be better portrayed in terms of logic and sound business practice. Any argument about the obligations of blood would require Henry to admit the guilt of his miscegenation, but business was another matter. If by happenstance a certain slave had been favored with the superior qualities of the white race, it would make sense to exploit this blessing to the owner's advantage.

The point was beyond argument. A slave with white blood could be utilized in roles of leadership and in more advanced service on the plantation. Henry would have to agree that the innate endowments of white blood must be cultivated and exploited, like a rich plot of land or a pedigreed bull. To neglect Robert's lineage would not just be an act of unkindness, it would be contrary to the better purposes of enterprise.

So on a Friday morning in 1842, Jane again cornered her husband for another perfunctory discussion, this time of the front porch of the house. In a short discourse of no more than a few sentences, it was decided that young Robert would receive what could generally be described as 'special advantages and training.' Though literacy was conspicuously not mentioned, its prospect lingered, with a hundred other dreams, in the secret corners of Jane's mind. If the stars aspired to chart the course of Robert Smalls' journey, they would have to wait in line behind the notions of Jane Bold McKee.

Chapter 3
Of Better Blood

She got an early start the next morning. After breakfast, Jane half-filled a big burlap sack with a selection of old clothes, with the idea of giving these to Robert's mother. These had formerly belonging to her nephews Allan and Gabriel, who had been their wards in past years. Jane laid out the small pants and shirts on her bed and folded them carefully. Though they had clothed both the boys in their early years, they showed very little wear. It seemed to her like yesterday that they had roamed the McKee house in the bright colors of these garments. The brown pants had seen most of the action, and the knees of them showed the most patches and mend-spots. The blue jacket and white shirts were in the best condition, seeing that they were reserved for Sundays and other special occasions. Young Allan had worn the jacket with a bow tie when he had recited the 23rd Psalm before the congregation at his first communion, and she remembered how splendidly it had looked on him.

Jane had no drawings or paintings of her sister's boys to remind her of their youth, so these clothes were the closest things to pictures she had. Like most families, the McKee's adopted the practice of passing good clothing down from older children to the younger ones. Over time, the practice became more than an exercise in frugality. It existed as an ongoing bond of family, as an almost spiritual connection, brother to brother, blood to blood.

It was because of this that Jane felt uneasy at the thought that an African child would now don her nephews' garments. In truth, she had previously donated worn clothing to the poor of the town, and had even arranged for the most damaged items to be given to their own slaves. But the present situation seemed altogether different. Was it because these little shirts and pants were far from worn out? Was it because she would soon see these actual garments on the dark body of a slave she knew? Or perhaps she was haunted by the thought that, within the body of that little colored boy, flowed the self-same blood that ran through the veins of her husband and her own daughter Elizabeth.

As she walked the foot-worn path that ran between the slave quarters and the big house, Jane felt strangely afraid. The steady rhythm of her heartbeats rang in her head, like the roll of drumbeats she had heard at militia parades. 'Lydia will be very grateful for these,' she silently told herself. But the whole time she had the feeling of one bringing a guilt-offering rather than a gift.

After eight years as mistress of the household, Jane had now become comfortable and adept in directing the affairs of her slaves. She found Lydia to be quiet, hard-working and above all, obedient. Jane had rarely had cause to raise her voice to her, and never her hand. The truth be told, Lydia was so familiar with her routines of caring for children that she hardly needed to be spoken to at all.

Like most slaves, Lydia existed as a dark and almost invisible shadow, moving below and behind the lives of her masters. Always unobtrusive, she performed her duties quickly and quietly so as not to disturb. This was her God-given role, and she did it well. Jane had become accustomed to the routine of commands that daily flowed from her to Lydia. Like the over-worn ruts in New Street that ran from her home to the waterfront, the courses of their conversations were always the same: "Wake the children, Lydia. Bring the tea, Lydia. You may go, Lydia."

So repetitive were their words that it could be expected that Lydia would do most of her duties without being asked. That is why it seemed so strange now for Jane to actually have something of substance, something new, to discuss with her. Jane was obliged to pursue a conversation about questions she had never asked or mentioned before today – questions she would never have to touch upon again.

She found Lydia sitting quietly in a rocking chair in front of her quarters, holding little Robert on her lap as she looked up to see her mistress, in halting steps, walking towards her across the yard. As Jane drew near, it was the mistress and not the maidservant who was filled with trepidation.

Jane remembered that a breeze was blowing in from the sea and it brushed her light brown locks away from her face. It was as if heaven itself wanted to watch her expression as she moved ever closer to the black woman who sat as still as a judge on the other side of the yard. Though they were alone, Jane sensed that the eyes of the whole world and all the angels were falling upon her at this moment.

She thought she could hear whispering in the wind and in the faint rattling of the sweetgrass in the swamp beyond the fence. 'There is no need to feel uneasy,' Jane told herself. She was the mistress of this house. She owned this woman and had talked to her many times. But in truth, her talks with Lydia had never really taken the form of true conversation. There had been thousands of requests and orders, and even occasional questions along the way, but never anything like this. The situation was awkward and ridiculous.

Henry may have been right to suggest that their special relationship with Robert should not be announced in any way. Jane entertained the notion that she might turn around and go back to her house. After all, there was no reason they should be obliged to inform, or God forbid, to get permission, from Lydia for them to train young Robert. It was the McKee's prerogative to do whatever they wished with the boy. Robert was theirs, after all. But here was the very crux of the matter, for he was in truth *theirs*. Henry's to be exact. Everyone in the household knew with certainty what those in the town could only suspect, that young Robert was not just a possession; he was a *son*. Everyone would have to resign themselves to an ongoing conspiracy of silence concerning the child's origins. Robert's special training would proceed upon an unspoken premise – that the part of him that was white was the part that made him worth something in this world.

Neither woman uttered a word at first, as Jane opened the bags and, one by one, showed the folded garments to Lydia. Robert's mother, of course, had seen these clothes before. For years, her task had been to clean, mend and fold them for the McKee children and the nephews. Jane began to regret that she had not just sent the bags to Lydia by way of the other servants. Jane chided herself, reasoning that she should have foreseen the strong feelings that a moment like this would bring. A mother's heart is always touched on the day their children's garments are first received, and then again when they are given away.

With a brief discourse of well-chosen words, Jane told Lydia of their decision to give Robert 'certain help and advantages' in life. There were no specifics given. It was only made clear that the McKees wanted young Robert to be amply provided for in this world. There were vague allusions to the child's potential and extraordinary endowments, though Mrs. McKee was reticent to say what these qualities were or where they came from. During, the whole conversation, Lydia's head was constantly nodding in agreement, but no words came from her lips. None at all.

Jane prayed that Lydia would say something, perhaps at least, "Yes Ma'am," or "Thank You," so they could be done with it. Jane was not at all relieved when her maidservant finally spoke.

"You have told me what my son Robert is to do," she said slowly, "But who should I tell him he is to be?"

"I don't understand your question," Jane replied.

For a long moment, Lydia had kept her eyes averted, but now she suddenly raised them up to meet squarely with those of her mistress. "All these advantages you speak of, does this mean Robert is to still be a slave? Will he be my son, or the son of your husband?"

This was a full frontal assault, and strong slap in the face could not have injured Jane more than Lydia's question. Taken aback by the directness of her colored girl's words, she could think of no immediate, or proper, reply. Jane could only gaze painfully and silently into the dark wells that were Lydia's eyes.

Jane was in writhing in anguish. She chose not to comment on Lydia's words, which were a direct indictment of her husband's honor. Stunned, Jane wondered whether she was in the presence of an enemy or a friend. All she could manage to offer was an answer fraught with vagueness and delay, the type of evasion that so often characterized the discourse between white masters and black slaves.

"Let me clarify it for you," she said coldly and clearly, trying to appear sensible rather than disquieted. "Robert will still be your son and will still be deemed a slave, just something more."

Lydia could scarcely hide her puzzlement. She couldn't fathom the meaning of Jane's clarification any more than Jane could. She watched Missy's lips to see if any other more information would come, but there was only an uncomfortable silence.

"Well enough," Lydia finally said, understanding that Jane's promise might at least represent the chance for something better for her son. This would have to suffice for now.

For the moment, Robert's mother felt she held an odd measure of power over her mistress, but Lydia did not altogether fancy this feeling. Jane Bold McKee now stood before her, nervous and seemingly on the verge of tears, but Lydia knew better than to try to exploit this advantage. She had learned through the years that the only thing more dangerous than a white person intoxicated with confidence was one who was drowning in insecurity. Lydia kept her thoughts to herself.

"That'll be fine, Ma'am," she whispered. "Thank you kindly."

"Yes, then," Jane concluded. "I am much encouraged by your willingness. We will send for Robert from time to time, and he will be offered such teaching and training as we see fit."

Robert's mother offered only a cold and simple nod of her head. Having been offered no choice, she thought it best to choose the only real path presented to her and her son. She reasoned that time and the Good Lord would reveal the true impact of the McKee's plan.

For her part, Jane did her best to maintain the appearance of composure as she walked back toward her house, but behind the serene smoothness of her pale brow, her thoughts were running every which way. She had just gained a curious sort of respect for this little brown woman who for so many years had served them. But Jane was also struck, and perhaps angered, by Lydia's brazenness in asserting that little Robert was Henry's son. Though true, it was clearly not Lydia's place to say such things.

But all the way back to her house, Jane wondered exactly whose place it was to say it. Putting aside her negative thoughts about Lydia, she began to burn with renewed anger toward her husband. She had thought that his disgustful dalliance with a slave woman had been the worst thing he had ever done, but Jane now concluded that his worse offence was forcing her to endure this soul-wrenching conversation with her slave girl. And as troubling as this moment was, Jane was now coming to realize that the suffering and ambiguity of this arrangement was just beginning. Robert Smalls would continue to be an embarrassment, a puzzle, and a part of their family story from this point forward.

As Lydia watched Mrs. McKee make her way across the yard to the big house, her heart began to relax with each step the mistress took. She thought of Robert's future, trying to imagine what special blessings might await him. She also wondered if those special privileges might take him increasingly farther from his slave origins... and from her. As Lydia rocked in her chair, her thoughts were interrupted by a familiar voice from behind her. It was her friend Leena, who had been listening from the other side of a big camellia bush.

"Now ain't that a fine kettle?" Leena sneered. "You'd think it was *her* baby!"

Lydia said nothing in response, and her face showed neither sadness nor joy as they heard Mrs. McKee shut the house door behind her.

After a long moment, Lydia whispered, "It is.

"It is what?" asked Leena.

"It's her baby," replied Lydia, adding, "I'm hers, this little shack is hers, and now my child is hers. *You* know."

"You're right, I 'spect," said Leena. Stunned by the frank and unassailable truth of Lydia's words, Leena did what any good friend would do, she changed the subject. "So what you gonna call him?" she asked.

"His name is Robert. Robert Smalls."

"Robert," Leena mused. "I like it. Where'd you come up with Smalls?"

"Don't rightly know," Lydia said. "A boy with just his mama's last name would walk through this world as a bastard. I figured I had every last name on earth to pick from. Every name except Henry McKee's." Leena chuckled at that.

"But why Smalls?" she asked.

"Oh, I don't know," Lydia said. "I once knew a nice man at church by the name of Smalls. His daddy was a nice man too, but mostly I picked the name because I just *chose* to. They don't let us have much say-so about other things. The only thing they leave us is to name our young'uns."

"Well, then. Robert Smalls he is and shall be," Leena said. "It's a rare that we get to choose much of anything around here. Most times, the only thing they let us pick is cotton. Your Missy's a huffy one to come and tell you she got all these big plans for your baby."

"It did rile me some," said Lydia. "But if she wants to help my child I can't say it's a bad thing. Means he won't be sent out to the fields. He'll stay with me to work the house. Robert can listen there, and he can learn things, maybe even to read. Half-white blood don't mean nothing really, but folks seem to think so. Might open a few doors along the way. If they're inclined to expect something special *from* him, maybe it will pull some better things *out* of him."

"And he's a sweet one, he is," said Leena as she looked down at Robert. "Take good care of that little patch of moonlight!"

As Lydia held the little boy lying across her lap, she began to wonder at what Robert's future might hold. "May God give him a righteous path and a long, glad story," she prayed as she began to think about the course of her own life. It had not been an easy one.

Lydia Polite had been born on Ladies' Island in 1796 to parents who had been brought as slaves from the Guinea Coast in West Africa. Her people, called Swonga, enjoyed a reputation for exemplary character, intelligence and industry. Swonga people were designated as house servants and were thus spared the dreadful life of the field workers. But they were slaves nonetheless, and slaves were born for hard work.

At thirteen, plantation owner John McKee brought Lydia to his Beaufort home to care for his children. The McKees were one of the oldest families in Beaufort and owned Ashdale, a flourishing plantation located just across the Beaufort River from town. In their big house on Prince Street, Lydia fed, bathed and dressed the little ones, Henry McKee included. Henry and his sisters were sweet as infants, but became less lovable as the passing years transformed them from innocents to masters. Robert's mother was there for them through the good and the bad.

By the time Robert arrived, Lydia retained only fading memories of her own parents, her siblings, and her African culture. She vaguely recalled her mother's sad eyes, but could no longer envision the rest of her face. Lydia never forgot the names of her brothers and sisters and in her mind she still retained a few vivid images from her girlhood. She recalled the steam rising from the stew-pot outside her family's shack on Ladies' Island, the grass mat upon which she and her sisters slept, and she could clearly remember the bright view of the ocean where the squatting silhouettes of the old folks gazed off toward their African homeland.

Her new life in town brought Lydia a better level of comfort, but also increased isolation. As a house servant to the McKees, she had never been permitted to marry and she only rarely had occasion to interact with the slaves who lived beyond the east end of Prince Street. But working in the comfort of the big house came with other horrible and unspoken evils. The intimate favors of a female slave were available to any white male in the household who was of age. Such wickedness was prone to occur with greater frequency when the white mistress of a house was preoccupied with the months before instances of childbearing. Even at 42 years of age, Lydia was not immune.

Her violation had taken place in July of 1838 or so it was surmised from the fact that baby Robert arrived nine months hence, in the waning darkness of April 5, 1839. The calculations of such dates and times held little interest in the world of slaves. The brief and brutal life of a slave seemed to them like hell itself, where the everlasting sameness of their daily torment made it worse than useless to mark the days.

While none of the other slaves had witnessed her rape, Lydia knew well that the baby's father was Henry McKee, the wealthy owner of the fine white house at 511 Prince Street. He was well-known by everyone in Beaufort and was called master by all the 72 dark skinned people who worked his fields. Most of his slaves were regularly whipped by hired men on the plantation. Lydia's abuse was briefer, but of a more personal nature.

It began on a Sunday afternoon in an upstairs bedroom of the McKee house while his wife was away for the afternoon. Since Lydia was a slave, society would never have referred to such a violation as *rape*. White folks, if they mentioned it at all, would be inclined to call it a visitation or a *dalliance,* but of course it was unlikely that any proper person would speak of such things at all. Henry, like most white masters, did his best to pretend that the lapse had never occurred.

Lydia likewise did her best to put all memories of the event out of her mind, but a violated woman doesn't easily erase such a memory, not even a single detail. She never forgot the way he took off and carefully folded his church clothes, laying them across the little book table where he had placed his freshly-read Bible. Henry had made her undress before him, yet he mostly looked out the front window as she disrobed, afraid to permit his eyes the intimacy of meeting hers. She remembered that his damp hair smelled of strongly of sweat and more subtly of candle-wax, from that morning's services at Saint Helena's Church. It had been Deacon McKee's turn to light the main candles at the altar.

Though Jane McKee was scheduled to be gone until sunset, Henry made haste in completing his disgusting business. "You must be gone from this room quickly, girl," he said, and you must maintain discretion upon pain of death. It wouldn't do to say anything so as to upset Mrs. McKee."

Lydia marveled that he took such pains to sound considerate of his wife, having so recently violated every divine oath he had sworn to her. "As you say," Lydia said softly as she dressed herself. "It will be as if nothing happened."

She knew, of course, that her feelings for Henry McKee would never be the same again. To be raped was a horror, but to be raped by a child you had raised, this was an unspeakable evil. Lydia had changed his first soiled diaper, now she wished she had rubbed it in his little pink face.

"And for God's sake, put fresh linens on this bed," he said as he turned the pimpled paleness of his backside to her and snatched up his garments. His sense of propriety took him all the way down the hall to dress.

It was only after he left the room that Lydia permitted her face to fall into a trembling frown. Bowing her head, she wept the measured, tearless cry of a slave woman. It would do no good to show either sadness or hate.

Lydia could always recall the disgust, fear and anger that filled her heart as she made her way back to her quarters. Her heart longed to scream, to sob, or at least to tell someone, but in her mind she resolved to tell no one. Traumatized and bloody from this, her first sexual experience, she would need the better part of the afternoon to compose herself. She changed into a fresh set of clothes, but had trouble imagining that she would ever feel clean again.

She had wished for death that day, longing to somehow escape to some other place and time. Perhaps back to the cane fields on Ladies' Island to labor as a field hand or maybe to Charleston where she could lose herself in the big city. Anything other than to face an interminable future at the McKee house. But she had no choice but to stay. From that point on, this place would become a sort of hell to her, and like God's hell, she reasoned that her torment would be everlasting.

Chapter 4
Beloved

Lydia was already 43 years old when Robert was born, but she had always been of energetic and robust constitution. Her ebony arms were slender, but as stout as leather straps, and her tiny hands had a grip you would remember, stronger than a field hand's.

Her son had more than a few times felt the righteous power of those hands – snatching him by the neck when he lingered too long in a daydream, yanking him from his bed on Sundays for church, and breaking off a fresh willow switch when a whipping was called for. Those little hands proffered tenderness in his times of illness, but when needed, could serve as the chastening rod of God. And if the scriptures were correct in saying, "He that spareth the rod hateth his child," Robert Smalls was surely one of the least hated boys in South Carolina. A most beloved son.

A particular incident etched itself in his memory. He was ten, and though he could not recall the particular offense he had committed, he never forgot the conversation that ensued. His mother had, as was her custom, called him to present himself for punishment.

"You'll thank me later," she had said. "Bare me your backside and I will make you a better man." This is what she always said when she was about to put a willow whip to his hindquarters.

"I'd prefer to thank you now rather than later," he replied, "if you'd just for once set that willow whip aside. You'd think I was your slave, all the thrashings I get!"

"That so?" she said with fire in her dark eyes. "Just you reach over there and hand me the Good Book."

'No, Lord, not the Book!' Robert thought to himself, as he reluctantly fetched Lydia's big leather Testament. The Holy Scriptures were greatly revered in their home, providing as they did, both the words of life and the warnings of divine justice. Robert knew well that his mother couldn't read a lick, certainly nothing more than her own name, but he knew better than to say anything.

Inspired or not, her words were the voice of God. Whenever Lydia quoted any inspired verse, she had to do it from memory, and was only pretending to read the words from the pages of that Bible. She could, to be sure, quote many texts word for word, having heard it preached every Sunday for most of her 54 years. But she was just as likely to *concoct* an appropriate-sounding phrase on the spot, if such fit the occasion. "Thou shalt shut thy mouth and obey thy mother," and "Clean ears are pleasing to God," were recurring favorites. Robert learned that whenever his mother grabbed for her Good Book, it was never good, at least not for his nether-parts.

"And let me make clear," she said in response to his words, "You ain't getting a slave whupping but a son whupping. The Lord sayeth, 'Don't be despising the chastening of the Lord, for them what God loves, he chasteneth, and he whups up on every son he receives.' These whippings ain't punishments," she said. "They're reminders. Better you should learn from a willow whip than from the constables in a jail cell downtown."

Though Lydia's words were not a perfect rendition of holy writ, Robert knew better than to say anything. She loved him, and she was usually in the right. He might very well end up in jail and he *did* need reminding from time to time. For his first twelve years, he had received licks from willow whips, switches he often had to cut for himself from local saplings. Later in his life, Robert marveled that there remained any living willow trees in all of Beaufort County.

Throughout his growing years, the demons of Robert's lower nature learned to expect a battle whenever they took the notion to emerge. Blow by blow and verse by verse, Lydia made sure his ignoble urges were taught to stay in their place, and in time, wisdom came and Christian character was built.

And for a slave boy, there was much to learn, especially for a house servant like Robert. Chores had to be done right, right on time, and with the right attitude. Fetched water had to be clean, not spilled, and brought in the proper container. Each morning, the fires had to be started in the kitchen, but also in various rooms of the house during the colder months. Pine fatwood was used as tinder because its resinous knots could be lit quickly. Hardwood logs had to be cut to length, split, stacked and carried into the house. Such things had to be done silently and with careful grace. Good servants strove to look presentable, but remain unobtrusive at the same time.

Robert learned that things went better for good servants, for though house slaves were usually treated well, it was understood that unsatisfactory work brought unpleasant consequences. Of the possible punishments, scolding was the most tolerable, being only words. It was worse to have meals taken away, to be given extra work, or to be assigned to unpleasant tasks like cleaning out the chamber pots. Whippings and beatings were rare, but when administered, they provided enduring instruction concerning which behaviors were expected and which were not tolerated.

For especially heinous offenses, a slave could be sold off, or banished to work in the cane or cotton fields. While the law did not permit a master to kill a slave, the fields would quite often accomplish the same thing. Plantation labor was the nearest thing to death sentence, and was profitable for the master until health failed and death came. It was even more painful of course, for those who had previously tasted the softer life of the big house. Lydia prayed every night that her son would never lose his privileged position as a house Negro.

Robert was born with a pleasant temperament but was, at times, prone to outbursts of passion. It was fortunate that Jane McKee took such delight in him, for Robert was thus able to escape the more serious punishments that his emotional upflairings deserved. Where Lydia was stern and rule-bound, Jane was usually the one more inclined to be forgiving and patient. He sometimes thought of them as his two mothers.

Robert knew who his real mother was, of course, but he always had a fond place in his heart for Missy Jane. From his earliest years, she was his great advocate and encourager. He liked the way she spoke to children – firmly, but with optimism and affection. Where Lydia was skilled in pointing out his trespasses; Jane was more prone to point out his possibilities. Though she never convinced Henry that Robert should read, Jane continually did her best to offer him opportunities to expand his mind.

On Sunday afternoons, and on occasional weekdays, Robert was permitted to sit with the McKee family for what they called story time. These were occasions where family members were permitted to read passages aloud in the presence of the whole group. These might be book chapters, famous poems, or extended passages of scripture. Young Robert took great delight in these experiences, savoring the beauty of the words and scanning the rapt expressions of each member of the circle of listeners. A good story time could almost make him forget he was a slave.

Robert knew the routine by heart. It was usually Miss Jane who would come to the door of the cottage to ask if Robert wished to come to the reading, but sometimes they would send young Elizabeth.

"Can I go, Mother?" he would ask. Lydia never once failed to nod in agreement.

"Listen well," she would say, "and hold that tongue of yours. Sharp ears will get you to heaven; sharp words will get you a whupping."

It was only in later years that Robert remembered the sad look that she had in her eyes whenever she sent him off to story time. He would, on his return, always tell her about what he had heard that day, but Lydia never got more than a summary. He wished his mother could also have been invited to hear these beautiful words, but he knew better than to ask. He felt fortunate that at least one of them was permitted to be there.

Because he was forbidden to read, Robert learned to give special attention to listening. Over time, he committed to memory sizeable sections of literature. He developed a good ear for the English language, learning new words and acquiring the ability to speak in the manner of a gentleman. These afternoons and evenings in the McKee's parlor were glorious to him, but as the years went by, the joy of the occasions began to wane. It all took a sharp tumble downhill in spring of 1850.

During his early years, only Henry and Miss Jane were permitted to read aloud, but it was not long before little Elizabeth was old enough to be asked to read, to be followed in future years by the other children in their turn. Robert remembered the particular Sunday afternoon when Liddie, as they called her, was first allowed to open a book and read to the family. They stood her up in front of everyone with a large black Bible, so big it wavered in her tiny arms as she read. He remembered how prim and straight she stood as she found her place on the page.

As her blue eyes glanced down, she opened her mouth and began to slowly spin the story of Adam and Eve. "And the Lord God formed man of the dust of the ground, and breathed into his nostrils the breath of life; and man became a living soul." The reading of the words was more than interesting, it was unadulterated magic.

Wasn't Liddie the same age as he? Hadn't they swung together, just that morning, from the rope swing in the yard? Robert had always been the one who goaded Liddie when she'd been afraid to climb a tree or walk alone to town. But here she was, like some code-breaker, deciphering the sacred text. Reading was magic, but was apparently a birthright limited to white children like Liddie. Robert hated the rule that permitted only blue eyes to translate the ink symbols on a page, slowly transforming them into a story. In his anger, Robert couldn't help himself. He looked up at Miss Jane to ask, "When can *I* learn to read?"

At these words, the room suddenly became as quiet as an Episcopal funeral. Miss Jane opened her mouth, but then closed it again, as if she'd been inwardly restrained. She turned and looked directly at Mister Henry, silently passing the question to him. But Master had abruptly turned his head and was looking out the window. The parlor got so quiet they could hear old George, the footman, chopping some wood at the far end of the yard.

Henry gave no answer, no nod of approval or shaking of his head. In truth, though he was careful not to move his head at all, everyone in the room knew the answer was no. After an awkward silence, Master Henry looked back to Liddie, and with the slightest twitching of his eyebrow, told her it was time to continue reading. They intended to go on as if Robert hadn't said anything.

He knew enough to hold his tongue at that point, but inside he burned with pain and rage. Closing his eyes, he sought somehow to escape the agony of the moment by retreating into daydreams, but all his mind could conjure up were images of the fences, a world of lines that could not be passed. He worked to imagine a bright fleet of clipper ships, but even in his imagination the harbor was empty. Through the slits of his eyes he became aware that the stool he sat on had been placed at a certain distance from the padded chairs of the family members. Nobody had said anything, but the message was clear.

He didn't belong in this parlor. An unspoken boundary had always kept his mother from the blessings of story time. Now, though he was permitted to listen, Robert had to confront a different sort of slap in the face. What the McKees called advantages were really just an insidious form of torture. He would be forced to watch white children cross the invisible fence of literacy. It was a line neither he nor his mother would ever be permitted to cross. His anger was boiling over by the time he got back to the cottage and told his mother what had happened.

"I may not be a slave," he said, "but I'm damn sure less than a son." The whole business made him furious – so mad he wanted to steal all their books and burn them in a fire. He dreamed of running away somewhere. In the unguarded corners of his heart, he wanted to kill Henry McKee before he left. "I said they should teach me to read," he said.

"What'd they say to that?" his mother asked. "Must've stopped them dead in their tracks."

"Master got himself in a pissy-huff. He frowned and folded his arms," Robert said. "For a second there, I thought Missy was about to give him what-for, but that little boo-hen just kept her little pinchy mouth shut. I thought she was fixing to cry, but she wiped it away fast enough."

Robert never forgot the wide-eyed look of fear on his mother's face. "Lord, Lord," she said, "You've likely roused trouble now!" Lydia turned her back to him and bowed her head down, but she wasn't praying. "You may have put us in a bad fix."

"Oh, I doubt they'll speak their mind," Robert said. "Whites never do." After saying this, he promised never again to bring up the question. He'd thought it would feel good to take a stand, but in his heart there was only regret and fear. He always remembered what Liddie McKee said to him privately the next day.

"My folks are idiots," she said. "I hate 'em." They keep going on about the slaves being ignorant, but they won't let you learn. Mama won't get away with this. I won't let her."

"Thanks, Liddie," said Robert. "But it ain't your mama we need to worry about. Your papa's the man, and he's made his position pretty clear. Clear as a pointed shotgun."

"I'll put my foot down. I'll make them listen," she said.

"No you won't. They've already heard the question, but they're dead set. If you ask nice, they're gonna say no," he said, "and if you push 'em, they're gonna say *never*. If you keep up a fuss, you'll just bring holy hell down on both of us. You'll fix it so I won't hear any more stories as long as I live. I know your daddy's ways. Then the only story I'll get will be words on my gravestone."

Liddie just stared back at him with stubborn frown. "I'm gonna kill him," she said. "Both of 'em if I have to." Her azure eyes blazed like a glassblower's fire as she spat defiantly on the ground. "I'll just have to sneak around and teach you to read myself."

"You're kind," Robert said, "but it won't do. When they find out you taught me to read, and you know they will find out, you'll get whipped. And if I'm caught with a book, they'll likely send me out to chop cane, and there ain't no reading books out in them fields."

"Very well then," she said. "I'll drop it for now, but I'm going to figure out some way to help. I'm not letting this go."

"Knowing you, I doubt you will," Robert said. "I reckon in time I'll get myself to some place where I can learn to read, but for now I'll just have to make the best."

The McKees assigned Robert to empty the chamber pots for the time being. There was no more talk of literacy, and there were no more story times for three months. Not for anybody. It got progressively harder for him to keep his mouth from careless words and his heart from wrath. But he reasoned that holding his tongue presented an easier challenge than being worked to death on Ladies' Island. He just put his head down every day and got his work done. Time didn't fly, but it kept plodding toward whatever future lay in store.

Chapter 5
Notches

For slaves, working at the McKee house was not paradise, but it was, for the most part, a bearable purgatory. Servants performed their labors in predictable harmony and safety. Food may have been simple fare, but it was never lacking. Each slave had to adjust himself to his ordained position in God's creation, and unlike Eden, here in Beaufort there was no Tree of Choice. Colored servants were obliged to obey as their ancestors had, and this promised to be the only way of life any of them would ever know.

If there would be anything in this tedious paradise that might be called The Fall, hints of it began sometime after Robert's eleventh birthday. Lydia had just finished carving an eleventh notch on the doorpost of the small cottage where she and young Robert lived. These notches were annual acknowledgments of her son's birth and they sufficed as her only record of his childhood.

"Come here and look," she said, pointing to the notches. "These are your years, the story of your life, and each one's a blessing."

Robert came over and ran his brown fingers over each one in turn, from top to bottom. The first ten were already gray and weathered, but this eleventh one was yellow and fresh from Lydia's kitchen knife. His finger stopped on this new one.

"Ain't nothing," he said. "They're all just the same. Might just as well cut the whole passel of 'em all at once."

"Life ain't like that," Lydia said. "Good Lord don't give us a whole life all at once. He's a Father. Feeds us like babies, one little bit at a time. Lord's got him a storehouse, filled with a whole big pile of hours and days and years. Knows we can't take everything all at once. Spoons out blessed days and years, and makes us take 'em as they come." Lydia smiled the gentle smile of a story-teller, but was unaware of the anger that was rising in her young son's heart.

Robert's eleven-year-old mouth had no polite or sentimental response to her words. "Bull!" he said. This was the worst word he thought he might get away with saying. Then he just put his finger on the fresh notch and huffed out an audible breath. "Nothin' but pure bull," he said, louder this time. "Them notches are all just the same."

"Hush your foul talk," she said. "I've a mind to slap you good!" Moving closer to him, Lydia gently took his finger in her hand and moved it lower on the post, down to the smooth place where his twelfth birthday notch would go. "Not all the same!" she said emphatically. "Feel this next smooth place right here," she said. "There's number twelve. After that, you go from boy to man. They ain't all the same. Each one's important in its own way."

Up to then, Robert had pretty much gone along with everything his mother said, but this time he didn't agree. There was no fit place left for him to stow his anger and she knew it. He was s stewpot fixing to boil over. All she could think to say was, "What?"

He was sure to get it now. He sensed that she was staring at his lips, ready to pounce upon whatever insolence might emerge, but Robert didn't want to play into her hand. He just pursed his lips in silence. Though she anticipated a subtle nod of his head, he was stubbornly careful to hold it completely still.

She knew he was doing this on purpose, of course. He was full of defiance and he wanted her to feel it. "What?" she asked again. "You seem possessed of some evil notion. You don't fancy the idea of going boy to man?"

"Ain't that," he said. "It's just that what you say, it just ain't so," he said, shaking his head at her now. "That boy to man nonsense, well... it's nothin'. You say the notches are special, but they're all the same, the ones before and the ones after." Robert watched as his mother's face went from soft to stiff.

It was the first time she could remember him standing up to her and it made her uneasy. He could hear it in her voice. "But it *is* so," she implored. "You'll see when you're older."

"No!" he said, "Older or later, won't it just be the same bull?" he said, careful to defend his ground with another *almost cuss word*. "You say God spoons out our years, but in truth, ain't they all the same? Times don't change, Mama, and ain't nobody does nothing to make 'em change." Robert raised his eyes to hers, and just glared directly at her. It was no longer the look of a little boy, but that of an angry young man. The tension of the moment took his breath away. Hers, too.

She didn't realize her son was old enough to make such a face.

Before, he had always spoken to her with his eyes lowered. This was the first time he had ever looked at her and talked out loud at the same time. It felt every bit like disrespect, and that's exactly how Robert wanted her to feel. He was shaking an invisible fist at her, cursing her with his eyes. She sensed, of course, that a shot had just been fired across her bow. All Robert could sense was his heart pounding like a war drum in his ears. He was already preparing a volley of harsh words to fire back at her.

To his surprise, Lydia did not lash back. In fact, she didn't immediately speak. He was prepared for her to take him by the shoulders and shake him the way she usually did, but she didn't come at him. Instead, her look suddenly softened and she sat down beside him in silence, crossing her legs like a friend does.

"So tell me," she said softly. "I'm listening." In that moment, Robert was taken aback. After a long silence, his wrath turned to something more like sadness as he fought to find words.

"I hate birthdays," he finally whispered. "I hate notches. I want to grow up, sure, but it's killing me that they're all the same... and that they come so slow." Lydia could see the tears welling up in the corners of her son's dark eyes. "You say I'm fixing to move up from boy to man," he said, "but you're wrong. Next year I'll still be a boy and they'll still call me one. I'll be a boy this year, next year, and every year, forever. You ever seen it? Ever seen one black man who ever made it to that next damn notch? Went boy to man?"

Lydia was now the one struggling for words. Quiet tears began to roll down her cheeks. "Well, well," she finally breathed. "Ain't you a piece of work? Looks like my little Robert's been doing some growing up. You made you quite a speech, mister." She put her arms around him and held him as close as a newborn.

"Don't care about making no speeches, Mama," he said. "But there's a weight on my heart, all day, every day. And It's about to kill me for sure."

"Maybe you're feeling that weight because you've already started movin' up from boy to man," she said.

"No, Mama, you've missed the point," he said. "I ain't never gonna be a man at all. Not ever. Not so long as I'm somebody's slave. Them notches will keep right on coming, one after the other forever. Being black's just one long stint in the jailhouse. Sentenced to be a boy, and it figures to be a life sentence."

"They call you that," she said, "but them's just words. What you call *yourself* is what matters. Names don't make you what you are."

"But that's just it," he said. "Slave ain't just a name, I really am a slave. You too. Don't matter what I think inside when I'm somebody's boy on the outside."

Lydia was suddenly lost for words, but finally conceded. "You're right, I suppose," she said. "But you still gotta think right on the inside before you commence to fix what's outside. Manhood will come, maybe freedom too one day. All your life these little notches may seem like nothing – seem all the same. But you live for that one day. It may start only as a little somethin' you tell yourself, and Lord knows that day may never come for me. And maybe not even for you in your lifetime, but in God's name it will come."

She took his finger and again pressed it to the blank place just below the eleventh notch. "Maybe you're right that these cuts up above don't matter, but put your finger down here below – on the smooth place on the wood. That next place below the others, that's the important one."

"But there's nothing, Mama. Ain't nothing there at all," he said.

"Don't you say it's nothing," she said. "It is something. That's where the next notch is gonna be cut. That smooth space there under your finger is the *future* and you best not try to take that away from me. That smooth space is hope. How it's cut, well that's between you and the Lord. Hope's the only little piece of this world that God has put in anyone's hands. It may not look like nothin' now, but that uncut spot on the wood, that's the Promised Land."

"But what am I gonna do, Mama? How I ever gonna get free?"

"None of us knows," she said. "Lord knows. But I believe you'll get your chance one day. You'll throw your best card down and play the high-stakes game. You won't just be a man on that day, you'll be a man all day every day. Long as there's some little bit of hope in your heart. It ain't height or age, it's hope that makes a boy a man."

Though there would be times that the weight of life took Robert to other points of despair, he never forgot his eleventh birthday or his mother's words. And every time he saw some little smooth place on a timber, he remembered the decision he made on his eleventh birthday. He would find some way to make his mark. One day he would get free.

As the now-risen sun warmed their newly-notched doorpost, Robert and his mother made their way together toward the big house and the daily chores that were waiting for them. Somehow, the same old yard with its worn slave path didn't look the same as before. The azaleas glowed with deeper pinks and reds, the spring grass was a brighter green, and the songs of the birds were strangely tuneful. Today's work list no longer loomed as something monotonous and endless. Each mundane task now appeared as a step, and each one and each hour took them closer to the day of liberation.

Chapter 6
Pretty Much Free

There were days a house boy like Robert had to work from sunrise to bedtime, but there were also more relaxed times, when the masters went into town, or after his list of chores was done. In these off times, young Robert was at liberty to roam the McKee property, both inside and outside the house. He was, in official terms, on call, of course, but it was rare that his services were required. The McKees needed the skills of a cook or launderer more often than those of a young boy whose salient talent was the making of mischief.

On these slack days, and such days were frequent, Robert liked to sit on the low swing on the McKee's front porch. Here he made snacks of whatever food might have been left there, unfinished bowls of stale peanuts or perhaps a bruised peach deemed undesirable by the whites. From the swing, Robert could see everything in the front yard and much of what was happening on Prince Street.

From this sitting place, Robert's eyes often came to rest on Henry McKee, the 37 year old master of the house. On most afternoons, Master Henry liked to station himself at the front gate, standing in what could best be described as his pose. He said he stood there so as to see the folks who passed by, but there was no doubt in Robert's mind that Henry really did this to be seen by them, for it was only in their presence of witnesses that he assumed his pose.

The stance was in no way spontaneous. Robert had actually seen the master rehearsing it in the big mirror in the foyer. Some folks said Henry stood like an ancient warrior or an Egyptian king. Lydia said he was mimicking the big painting of his late father, John K. McKee, which hung in the parlor. Similar-looking statues adorned the bigger monuments in Saint Helena's churchyard. Robert's mother had once smacked him for suggesting that the master stood like one of those brass jockeys rich men tied their horses to.

Robert was an observant boy. He took note that almost all white gentlemen did their best to stand as Master Henry did. The whole charade made absolutely no sense to a young boy, but there were hundreds of odd customs that ruled the lives of white men. Their stance was just one of the strangest, but it was, as you would expect, not something to be snickered at.

This posing was especially noticeable when they were in the presence of others, because every Beaufort gentleman lived the life of the actor, playing to the audience that was Southern society. The most important audience was, of course, the congregation of his fellow males, appearance being the ultimate measure of one's position in the world. To both the aristocrats and the hoi polloi of Beaufort, a proper appearance was deemed better than sainthood. And every full-dress gathering, whether church supper, lodge meeting, or holiday parade, was judgment day.

As Robert grew in years, his innocent curiosity about Henry McKee matured into a more systematic analysis. There seemed to be something in the way Master Henry dealt with him that differed from his relationship to the other servants.

"I believe Master Henry fancies me," he said to Lydia as they pulled husks off some ears of corn on the wood table in the backyard.

"Why you think that?" she asked. "Did he say something?"

"Didn't say nothing," Robert replied. "It's just the way he stares at me sometimes."

"Master stares at his horses, too," she said. "Don't mean nothing. It's just somethin' he does."

"I still think he fancies me," Robert said.

Lydia was at a loss as the pain of old wounds swelled in her heart, but she could think of no words that might settle Robert's mind and put an end to their conversation. Her eyes flashed nervously, afraid someone might be listening.

"What is it, Mama?" he said. "Ain't nobody coming. Tell me."

"Ain't telling nothing," she said. "We should finish shucking these ears."

"Is Henry my father?" he asked. Lydia's silence and lowered eyes told him she had been shocked by his question. Only something big would make her stop husking.

"Why in God's name would you say such a thing?" she asked.

"I heared folks whisper," he said. "Always reckoned they were joking. But you've got to tell me God's truth. Are they right? Is Master my father?"

"You're a slave child," she said. "Don't make no difference who your papa is. You'd best leave well enough alone." She could see by the look in his eyes that he wasn't eager to drop the matter. He was asking the question she had always dreaded.

"If I tell you," she said, "You must promise never to say nothin' to nobody."

"Promise," said Robert.

"Then yes," was her simple reply.

"Yes, what?" Robert asked.

"Yes, he is."

Robert was taken aback by her answer, even though it was what he had suspected. "But I'm Negro," he argued, "and a slave. If he's my daddy, then that makes me his son. It don't make no sense." Robert's dark eyes widened as he stared across the table at her, he was asking questions that no master, scholar, or mother could easily and painlessly answer.

"It'll all be fine," she said. "Good Lord's over all things. In time, he'll make everything clear. For now, let's just say you're part white but still a slave. Ain't nothin' gonna change. And you keep quiet about this, even to Master Henry."

"Why?" Robert asked. "Don't he know?"

"Oh he knows all right. Knows it well," she said. "But Master won't welcome folks speaking of it. You best make like I ain't never told you."

"For how long?" Robert asked. "How long must I keep quiet?"

"Forever, I suppose," she said. "And don't forget you promised."

"All right," he said. "But who else knows?"

Lydia had to restrain herself from chuckling out loud. "Child, this secret ain't no secret at all," she said. "Henry knows it for sure, and Missy Jane too. From what I can tell, everybody else in this house knows… and all the slaves down Prince Street. Just about everybody else around town, but you still can't say nothing."

"That's madness, Mama," he said. "Every soul in South Carolina knows, but I'm sworn to silence."

"Sworn for sure," she said. "You're obliged to keep shut-mouthed. Just think of it this way," she began. "It's like Master Henry's being a short man. Everybody sees it, but ain't nobody's safe to speak of it. It's just like that."

"Oh," Robert said, finally appearing to understand. "It's like slaves loving their masters. Everyone, white and black, knows it's bull, but everyone goes along. White folks to save their pride, and us to save our skin."

Lydia got a bemused smile across her face. "That's pretty much it," she said. "And you gotta swear to dance along. Swear to dance this foolish dance all your life. And God will hold you to your oath, little man."

Robert crossed his heart and nodded nervously, then took his mother's hand in his. "Can you answer me just one more question?" he said softly, his face now showing a trace of fear.

"I'll try," she said, noticing that Robert was beginning to tear up.

After a long minute of silence, he spoke, this time in only a whisper. "If Master's my father... are you still my mother?"

Suddenly, she too began to cry as she embraced him as only a mother could. "Forever and forever, child," she said, weeping openly now. "It's God's truth and you must never doubt it.

"I love you too, Mama," he said. "It's good that I know the whole truth." His mother rocked him tightly to her bosom as if a big storm was passing over. Robert's young mind began to race as he wondered what difference this information might make.

"I can see you're spinning up there," she said, pointing to his head. "I fear you'd have been happier if I hadn't told you." Lydia moved over closer to him and looked him eye to eye. "Tellin' you who your daddy is don't fix nothing, and it's likely to bring you constant trouble."

"For good or ill," he said. "I reckon it's something a boy needs to know. I'll fare better to know whose son I am."

"A son to Henry McKee?" she scoffed. "Don't commence to dream. You'll never be no kind of kin to him; and not a regular slave boy neither, just a puzzle. You're a torment to his soul and a stain on his whiteness. Just walking around here, you remind him of his guilt." Lydia's features now stiffened. "Since you came, his own wife hates him, and Missy's heart's gone cold toward me too."

"But he knows I'm his," Robert said. "I can tell he seeks my best. That's why he corrects me as he does. I'm his half-son, a dark son, but his son nonetheless."

"Oh he knows who you are for sure, and he resents your very presence, Lydia said. "I expect he would kill you if he could, but Missy and the law won't allow it."

"But if I was to get in trouble, I think he'd take up for me," Robert said. "He has to have some kind of feelings for his own son."

"I wouldn't take it for love," she said. "Henry wouldn't fight for no slave, and probably not for his son neither, only for pride. You're his property and nothin' more, a talking critter at best. His pride couldn't permit another man to beat an animal that belonged to him."

"But it's different," Robert insisted. "Master knows I carry his blood."

"Drops of white blood? That don't mean nothing," she said. "You're McKee's beast, and his alone to whip. And believe me when I say he will whip you any time and any way that suits him. He's been like that since he got out of diapers."

"Master has never hurt me none," Robert said.

"Maybe not so much, and maybe not just yet, but he will soon enough," she said. "He'll hit you whenever he wants, or he might send you off to Ashdale... or to the graveyard if he's a mind to. Hell, he might even sell you off. The time will come, and when it does, you're gonna know you're a slave and not a son."

"Ain't so," insisted Robert. "I know about the fields, and that ain't the life I live. We got our own quarters, we dress proper, and we eat good food," he added. "Working here in the house, we're pretty much free."

"Pretty much free?" she chuckled. "Pretty much? What does pretty much free mean? I suppose I was pretty much free when he took a mind to have his way with me." Robert quickly averted his eyes from his mother's. He turned his back to her but kept speaking and gesturing as if she was still there in front of him.

"Ain't right to condemn a man forever," Robert said. "Not for something that happened just one time. If you look at the whole of it, Mama, Master Henry's been quite good to us for a lot of years. We're pretty much free," he insisted.

"Pretty much free ain't free at all," she said. "Only free 'til Massa takes a notion to have his way. And your Master Henry can have his way with anyone in this place – with Missy Jane, with me, or with you baby. Any time and in any way he cares to. And just to make things plain, he didn't get the notion to rape me just one time. But I swear to you by God, that if it had been just that one time, one time would be enough to tell me I'm just a slave."

Robert knew better than to battle words with his mother, but this time he couldn't let the issue go. "Well, you can just talk on and on if you want, Mama," Robert contended, "but things won't be that way with Master and me. He treats me fair... very fine in fact. I get a little bit more free every day."

Lydia just smiled and slapped her thighs. "You think you're running around free?" she warned as she gripped his arm so strongly that it hurt. "That free feelin' you feel is just a little bit of slack rope. Massa might let you run a bit, but soon enough you gonna reach the rail fence. And they'll shoot you if you try to cross. You're gonna find out you ain't nothing but a slave boy. Naw, you ain't free. You're just a dumb beast that ain't reached the end of its chain."

Robert hated his mother's for these words and he opened his mouth to reply, but in his heart he knew she was right. "I've gotta get me out of here," was all he could say. "I need time down on the waterfront."

"I suspect you're right," she said. "It might do both of us some good to get out."

Later that day, while Lydia and Miss Jane shopped the markets, Robert was free to walk the streets downtown for an hour or so. He carried a storm of questions in his heart, despondent until he finally made his way down to the water. Here he spent perhaps a half an hour standing in silence.

He reasoned that a good Christian would have prayed, but Robert was too tormented to pray. God may have been waiting for him there, but he didn't bow his head, nor did any words come from his lips. Though he waited for the familiar feelings to come, there was no sound, no breeze, and all the boats were snugly moored to their posts. He longed to rise above all this pain, to once again touch the invisible hand of God like he had done as a child, but even the usually swirling sky was empty of clouds. Seeing a few distant clusters at the far edge of the Atlantic horizon, Robert reasoned that maybe God was riding these last few clouds as far out of Beaufort as the angels could carry him.

"I ain't nobody," he whispered, "and I ain't never gonna go nowhere."

Though it was just the same old harbor, it was not like before. With his eyes pinched shut, his soul longed to connect with the infinite refreshment that was the sea. The breath of the surf had always smelled fresh to him, laden with the crisp scent of salt and fish, but now he only felt trapped and alone. "This place stinks," he said.

"Dreamin' again?" asked his mother as she came up quietly behind him.

"No," he said. "I'm all dreamed-out. I reckon the last of my dreams just flew off with those little clouds." Robert was pointing out to the Atlantic horizon. "My high hopes are out to sea by now."

"I doubt they're gone for good," she said. "Dreams are like clouds; they'll always come back."

"I doubt your lame words are gonna bring dreams back," he said.

"Maybe not today," she said. "But would a fresh peach do?" Without further conversation, Lydia handed him a fresh one from her basket, and put her arm around Robert's shoulder. As he bit into the warm sweetness of the fruit, a smile silently drove the sorrow from his face. He just nodded as their steps turned towards home. When a boy feels forsaken, a mother can provide assurance that hope has not departed from the world, but would soon return for another go of it

Chapter 7
The Temptation

The next morning, as Robert and his mother drew near to the back steps of the big house, they saw Henry McKee on the back porch, standing in his usual pose. He was looking across the flower garden the back yard, and he had a sublime look on his face. "Glorious, simply glorious," he said, stroking his beard. "I can't believe Eden looked any more beautiful than this garden on this day. What a world! What a life!" Robert and Lydia had no choice but to nod in silent agreement as they walked past him, into the kitchen and their slave duties that waited for them inside.

"A perfect Paradise," Robert muttered under his breath. "I'll head upstairs to empty Adam and Eve's chamber pots." His mother did her best to shush him, but to no avail.

Even if this place had been Eden, then Robert could never have embraced the notion that Henry McKee was its Lord God. He was more likely its devil. Henry strutted around this place as both father and slave master, occasionally revered but mostly hated.

Robert wanted nothing more than to escape to the farthest reaches of the earth. There were even times he would have made sure to curse Henry McKee before he left. Maybe even kill him. Robert fought the temptation to hate, and over time, he got used to it. After all, life had to go on somehow. There were even some pleasant times. Like when Master set out towards town to blow off steam.

When Henry McKee grew weary of home life, it was not to solitude or church that he ran. Like most other gentlemen, he was drawn to Green Street and Main, Beaufort's dark and delightful district of sin. The unrelenting boredom of the house made Robert want to accompany Master, even to the bad side of town. For good or ill, a boy of eleven needs time with a grown man, and to a budding adolescent, almost any place seems more exciting than home.

Henry usually initiated such adventures by starting some loud argument between him and Missy Jane. His wife would start to weep and Henry would make his way toward the front door, always preaching sermons as he stormed out. Every good speech needed a noble cause. His departure always had to be attributed to some undeniable principle, some philosophical or biblical mandate. Armed with logic and divine truth, a man like Henry was prepared to fight for every inch of his home turf, but mostly he just wanted to get out of the house.

Marital admonitions from the Apostle Paul provided familiar themes for these diatribes, constituting as they did, the trump cards in these marital games. "Wives should be subject to their husbands," was often quoted. Henry McKee had rehearsed these litanies growing up in a house with four older sisters, a mother and two aunts. He would eloquently sermonize that the man of the house had to be respected, and such respect was most clearly evidenced when others did exactly what he said.

The females of the house rarely gave in, of course, but it didn't matter. The point was not to convince the women, but to escape them. And there were countless inviolable principles, biblical and constitutional, that might send a Beaufort husband off to his pubs and his card games. He just had to get his wife angry enough to let him storm off in peace.

It became customary for Robert to accompany Master Henry on these sojourns, as Jane was wont to call them. Robert learned to be quiet while his master marched and blustered, "Strong men require the company of other strong men," quoting the Holy Proverb that "iron sharpeneth iron." But in truth, even an uninspired adage could serve as an excuse to go downtown to sin.

On this particular Friday night, Henry was blustering that men like himself needed to "stop and savor the roses." It was an all-purpose principle, and one that Master had used before. Robert long ago discovered that the "roses" Mister Henry liked to sniff were usually stuffed into in the perfumed cleavage of some bad woman in a pub. In his later years, Robert couldn't remember every principle his master spoke about. He did recall that the speeches Henry made departing the house made more sense than the slurred ones he blathered after midnight as Robert helped him home.

These evenings were routine exercises in debauchery, for Henry at least. Robert's main task was to be a good listener on the way to Green Street, and a sober guide on the way home. He was now large enough to lift his master when alcohol hindered his ability to stay upright. On such occasions, Robert was called upon to play both nanny and slave. He was required to shun all carousing and conversation. Any slip up would call forth the severest of retributions from the constables, from his master, and most certainly from his own mother. Punishment from any one of these individuals could be the end of him.

His only memorable misstep occurred just after his twelfth birthday. It was not the particular misstep, or even its punishment, that made it memorable to Robert. It was a strange interaction that transpired between him and Master. Henry had gone into Painter's Tavern to enjoy spirits with his friends, leaving young Robert to mark time outside.

"Wait here," Master said. "I'll only be a moment," but Robert immediately recognized this to be a polite lie. It would always be some time before Henry would return. Israel's years in the wilderness had been completed with more brevity than such a *moment*. Master's evenings in the arms of sin could extend well into the early hours of the next day.

For a minute or two, Robert waited, watching things through the front window. Seeing Mister walk over to the proprietor at the bar, Robert hoped Henry might only be stopping by to communicate some brief message, but when he saw him sit down at a table with some other men, Robert realized this would not be a short visit. Once women, drinks, and playing-cards arrived, Robert knew he should settle down for a long night.

He decided to amble his way down the row of establishments that lined both sides of this avenue of iniquity. The aroma of stale alcohol filled the street as it wafted from every open door between Blake and Bay Street. Empty bottles lay everywhere and spirits could be smelled on the breath of almost every passer-by, whether young man, old man, pagan, or Baptist. There were, of course, no children there, and the only women to be seen were those who plied the evil trades. As on most evenings downtown, only barkeeps, slaves, and angry housewives remained reliably sober.

As his master reveled, Robert felt free to move about a bit, slowly walking past each place of business, killing time. Through the open doors of the pubs he could hear the loud banter of the white men, each boasting greater wisdom and prosperity than they actually had, and pretending to be happier than they actually were. Sneaking past the less seemly venues, Robert averted his eyes, avoiding the possibility of looking upon the bare legs of some wicked woman. Though these ladies were ruined women, it would be dangerous for a black boy to see any pale extremity of a white female. Such forbidden evils were reserved for the eyes of white Christians.

Robert felt a bit more at ease once he got past the big taverns and the consort bars where the upstairs brothel was the main attraction. He kept his eyes glued to the cobblestones straight ahead of him, doing his best to keep clear of anything that might bring down the wrath of either his mother or Almighty God.

Once he neared the corner of Bay Street, he could smell the salt water. This helped him relax a bit, and Robert began looking in the front windows of the grocery and dry goods shops. Here were displayed various useful items for sale to the general public – tools, dishes, and sundry articles of clothing. Robert couldn't read the small signs and price tags attached to these items, but it didn't matter. He could clearly see each item, and a slave couldn't afford to buy anything at any price. That being said, it was still fun to look.

Events soon took a wayward turn as Robert approached the garment shops along Clay Street. Here he came upon Europa's Salon where a gray-haired male clerk was changing the gown on a headless dress form in the front window. Robert stopped cold in his tracks to watch the slow disrobing of this female torso. He knew in his heart that it was wrong to look. Glancing both ways, and then down, Robert tried to distract himself by humming a catchy tune, even though he had never before been given to singing.

As the old clerk's wrinkled fingers removed the outer layers of clothing, Robert could feel his heart speeding up with the exhilarating mixture of thrill and guilt that a twelve year old boy is prone to feel in such circumstances. He told himself to look away and he tried to keep walking, but Robert couldn't help himself. He stood and stared, grimly transfixed, a mindless moth before an irresistible flame.

Though the dress form was not much shapelier than a canvas stove pipe, it was a disrobing stovepipe. As the forbidden lace of each undergarment was exposed, Robert's heart no longer raced, but had actually started skipping beats.

'I'm going to die right here and go straight to hell,' he thought. Trying to take control of his eyes and mind, he searched desperately for some more alluring distraction, but adolescence has no greater magnet than curiosity entwined with the first flickerings of carnal lust. His quiet humming soon turned to the familiar lyrics to a piano song they had been played in the drinking halls. "Look away, look away, look away, Dixieland!" Robert began to sing it to himself.

Look away, is what he kept telling himself to do, but even though he kept singing, he did not look away. His gaze was so locked upon the mannequin, that he was afraid to take his eyes off it for even a moment.

As the old clerk removed the final undergarments from the dress form, Robert held his breath as his lustful eyes widened. The anticipated moment arrived to reveal nothing, of course. No female charms were seen, only smudged, beige cloth stretched tightly over a cylindrical dress form. After so much anxious waiting, Robert could finally exhale five minute's worth of breath.

Almost immediately, he shook his head and chuckled to himself that his imagination had been so enticed by what looked like a cloth-covered stovepipe. 'What did I expect?' he asked himself. Before he could resume his walk, Robert heard voices from behind him. Someone was approaching, and soon he heard the hoarse sound of one big voice.

"I see you, boy!" said the voice. As Robert turned, he could see a half-dozen unfamiliar white men coming towards him. A freckled red-headed man was the one who had spoken. By their staggering and their demeanor it was clear that these were not gentlemen. Neither were they sober. "I see what you're looking at!" the man said. "It's what all black boys be wanting."

Robert took pains to bow his head and look away, but he could feel his heart going fast again. 'Drunks,' he thought to himself. 'I'm in trouble now.'

Robert stood still, wishing he could be invisible in the shadows of the street. For a moment, he wondered if the men might just keep moving on past him, but they didn't. They were coming nearer, and soon formed a circle of idiots around him. He tried to sneak between two of them, but the redheaded man grabbed Robert's arm and spun him down so hard you could hear his head hit the boardwalk. Another one of the thugs grabbed Robert's foot and dragged him out to the middle of the street.

"Sit tight, little darkie!" one man said. "Don't you be lightin' off so sprightly. We saw what you was doing."

This one turned to another young man and asked, "Was this boy fixin' to pitch woo to that white lady in the window?"

"I suspect he was cravin' more than just a peep at her," the ruddy boy said.

Before any of them could speak again, there was a rattle heard through the window as the old clerk yanked the curtain across the store window. Robert's widened eyes implored the shopkeeper for help, but the old man just shook his head and pulled the curtain shut. This prompted the circle of rowdies to laugh aloud.

"Should we call the constable about this little buck?" the redhead asked, "or should we deal with him ourselves?"

Robert never in his life expected he would long for a lawman to come. Wiggling desperately to get free, he could see the shopkeeper peering at them through a crack in the curtain – a spectator to whatever violence was about to ensue. The big hands of the redhead gripped Robert's shoulders so tightly he could not move.

"I've gotta go," Robert implored the men. "My master and all his men are likely to be looking for me."

"Your master and what men?" the redhead laughed. "By from the fine shade of your skin, we were thinking that you might *be* the master, or maybe some kin to him. Are you kin to some white man?" he asked. At this, the other men began to come closer to join the taunting.

"Weak-brain half-breed!" one said. Another called him *your royal paleness*. Finally, their ruddy leader said, "You were eyeing that lady in the window like that black daddy of yours got him some white girl. Now I guess you think you're gonna pass? Are you white coffee now?"

Robert knew there was no proper answer for fools. Even God's truth won't settle anything once white boys get keyed up and drunk. "I best go now," he said, but before he could turn, he suddenly he felt the sharp pain of boot heels striking his back. Another one of the men knelt down behind Robert while the others pushed him from the side. The next thing he knew, his face was pressed flat against the crushed oyster shells that paved the streets of town. With absolute terror in his heart, he wondered if they intended to kill him. Robert was powerless to fight them off, and began to crawl slowly on his hands and knees, hoping to slither through the circle of men.

As he felt the warmth of his breath against the gravel of the dark street, the men now appeared only as pairs of dusty boots. The circle began to tighten, as all of them tried to get near enough to take a heel-shot at Robert's head and back. All of them began shouting at once. In tears, he tried to wrap his small arms around the ankles of one man, begging him to let him go. But he wasn't going to get away that easily.

He felt one of them take hold of his left heel. The gravel scratched his face as he was dragged facedown into the center of the circle. They all took turns spitting on him, laughing at him the whole time. "Shut your mouth, mulatto!" one said.

Their ruckus so filled Clay Street that a small crowd of onlookers began to gather. Robert closed his eyes as the rowdies began to pummel him with fists and feet. He could smell the whiskey from their spittle as he closed his eyes and prepared himself for whatever came next. Death wasn't the worst prospect he could think of. But as boot after boot smacked his back and ribs, Robert suddenly heard a familiar voice. A man was shouting from the end of the street.

"Stop those men!" the voice shouted. "Call the constables."

But the curses and fists didn't stop as Robert twisted and tried to get away. On his back now, he suddenly felt the heavy body of a man position itself on top of him. As the barrage of words and blows continued, Robert became aware that this man lying across him was absorbing the greater part of the punishment. The familiar voice spoke again, with a commanding tone this time.

"Step back!" he said. It was his master, Henry McKee.

Opening his eyes, Robert heard the sound of police whistles. As the circle of shoes stepped back, Robert's pulse was pounding loudly in his ears. His breath was hoarse and audible – like the panting some cornered creature. As the onlookers muttered amongst themselves, he felt the weight of his master's body upon him, strange and warm.

It suddenly occurred to Robert that this was the first time he and Master had touched each other physically. He felt repulsed at first, but then a sense of comfort came upon him. As Robert's heart tried to beat its way out of his chest, he became aware of another something. Something more felt than heard.

As his hand was pressed between himself and the large torso above him, he could perceive another, fainter pounding. It was the warm rhythms of his father's heart, beating with a slower confidence than his own. It was a strange and singular moment that Robert would never forget.

"Give 'em room," another voice boomed. "Let these men up." It was Chief Constable Rayburn Ewell. He was wearing a silver badge and toted a black-club with which he was putting the drunk boys to silence. As Henry rose to his feet, he tried to brush his hair and his clothes back into the semblance of a proper gentleman. Robert just sat in the middle of the street, staring at the constable and the others who still stood all around.

"What's the trouble here?" Ewell asked, as he drove Robert's assailants back with artistic strokes of his nightstick.

"It's me, Rayburn," Master said.

"Hello, Mister McKee," the constable said. "Are you injured?"

"No, I don't think so," Henry replied. "It's those roughs there you should see to. They're ill-mannered and obviously intoxicated. I expect they have fathers around here somewhere, if they have any fathers to speak of."

With just a slight nod of his chin whiskers, Rayburn Ewell commanded two deputies to take charge of the redhead boy and his friends. They went quietly, sensing that the fun was at an end.

"And who's this one?" Ewell asked as he looked Robert over. "He seems to be the center of this storm."

"This is my Robert," Henry said. "He's my... well he belongs to me." Robert stood up and dusted himself off. A trickle of blood was dripping from the corner of his mouth.

"I'll need the facts of what happened?" said Ewell as he took out his report log book. The constable was surprised when it was Robert and not Henry who ventured to reply.

"Those boys were just having their fun with me," said Robert.

"Looked more like attempted murder to me," Ewell said. "What did you do to set them off?"

Robert had to think for a moment. His mama and God's church had taught him to tell the truth, but there was no way he was going to detail how he had fantasized about a headless torso in a shop window. "I didn't do nothing, sir," Robert began. "They just came up on me as I was walking. I figured they mistook me for someone else. Ain't no cause for the law to punish 'em," Robert said, knowing it would be unwise to make enemies of any white boys.

"Ain't your call to make," said Ewell. "But I suppose we should lock 'em up in someplace where they can sleep it off. McKee, I suggest you keep an eye on this boy. He seems to have a level head on him, but it's likely to get busted if he makes a practice of walking the streets past curfew. You'd better keep him near you after dark."

"Understood," said Henry as he tipped his hat to Rayburn Ewell. "you stay with me, son."

As Henry led Robert towards home, he took note of the fact that young Robert was growing up. The boy's shoulders were broadening and his chin was adorned with the sparse whiskers of an adolescent. This was likely to bring new developments, and not all welcome ones. But, whether blessing or trouble, change was coming. Henry resolved to heed the constable's advice. He would keep his eyes open.

For his part, Robert was not thinking about growing up. He was sorting out the details of his brush with danger, and how Henry McKee had rescued him. All the way home, various notions kept rolling over in

Robert's brain. It wasn't the hateful attack or that his master had intervened to save him, it was something Henry had said. Perhaps it was inadvertent, and maybe it meant nothing special, but Master had uttered a word Robert had not heard him use before. Henry called him *son*.

Chapter 8
The Danger of the Thing

Whether a slave or a son, summer ended peaceably, and autumn came. As always, it was a special time of year for Robert. No longer laden with the humidity of summer, the November air felt refreshingly crisp as the skies became a clear and deep blue. It was harvest time on the island plantations and inland farms, when Beaufort's streets, markets, and wharves were filled with goods, people, and the frenetic energy of commerce. It was also the season for picking the ripe pecans that hung heavy on every branch of the big tree behind the McKee mansion.

Now a budding adolescent, Robert was just the right age and size to shinny up the trunk of that tree to gather the nuts. Older family members and children tied picking forks to the ends of long cane poles. With these they could pick or knock off the lower hanging fruit, but this was only for sport. It took a brave boy to climb up to the higher branches where the best nuts were, and Robert was willing and ready to take his chances.

All year long, his mother and other adults spurned his requests to climb the tree, but at this one time every year, all rules were suspended. Robert knew it was a risky thing for anyone to try to work at such a height, nearly 40 feet above the ground, but the normally cautious adults supposed that the value of the pecans made it worth the danger. To eleven year old Robert, the opportunity for heroism alone was worth the risk. The colored boy who would have normally been called reckless, was suddenly everyone's best friend, provider, and champion.

"Come watch Robert!" Liddie McKee shouted to everyone in the house and the slave quarters. "He's fixing to make his climb!"

"Our hero!" said Missy Jane. "A brave acrobat!"

"A brave fool," said Lydia. "Brave with no brains."

In a matter of minutes, a small crowd of spectators had gathered in the McKee's back yard. As Robert gripped, climbed and swung from the highest branches, he played, and savored, the part of the circus performer. At times there seemed to be more climbing than picking, more theatrics than harvest. He imagined he was a sailor mounting the mainmast of a big clipper.

From below, a dozen voices offered advice. "There are a cluster of nuts off to your left." or "Watch your foothold," some shouted. "Just knock them down, we'll gather them." Every minute or so, some concerned adult felt obligated to say, "Oh my, you shouldn't be doing this!" or "You'll hurt yourself!" But Robert knew nobody really wanted him to stop.

Master Henry always cracked open the first pecans. "Testing this year's crop," he would say. This only served to increase everyone's appetite and diminish their concern for young Robert's safety. This was fine with him. Afterwards, when they were bagging the piles of nuts, Robert knew he would get scolded a bit, and be told he should have been more careful up there, but every year they enthusiastically sent him up again to risk life and limb.

Climbing and picking didn't seem like any kind of work for Robert. It pleased him to make other people smile and he liked the satisfaction he felt afterwards when he could look at the thick layer of fresh nuts that covered the lawn. When his task was finished, he liked to count and carry the full bags of nuts. In the weeks to come, he would feel a measure of delight whenever any of them had occasion to snack on a pecan he had picked or to pitch into one of Lydia's pecan desserts. He was a provider, a host, and in some small sense, a man. The spoils of his victory would sometimes last well past February.

It was not just the satisfaction that pleased Robert, of course. He also relished the very danger of the thing. For most of the year, the daily routine around the McKee house was predictable and painfully ordinary. The inside work was never too hard or tiring and he had a warm, dry place to sleep. There was always ample food, and the house was generally peaceful in the daytime. Every night the doors were locked up safely. Robert despised safety. To him, 511 Prince Street seemed a place of continual and unbearable blandness. Though secure, it lacked the excitement and adventure every young man craves.

There was entertainment in town of course, and family members could walk there just about any time they wanted to. But it was different for the slaves, who were generally home-bound. If one of them needed to go into the city, it was under close supervision, with a tight timetable, and certainly not for fun. Servants might be sent to town during daylight hours with a written pass from their master, but all Negroes had to be home by the four o'clock bell that signified the beginning of slave curfew. It was deemed a serious thing for unauthorized blacks to be out after dark.

Robert's bleak routine held few joys and no surprises. Pecan season offered him a once-a-year chance to feel the satisfaction of success and to taste the exhilaration of danger, the glory of risk. The big tree was a mountain to ascend, an enemy to subdue, a giant to kill. His memories of his derring-do pleased him more than the pecans and lasted even longer.

The topmost branches of the pecan tree were his favorite. Though there weren't as many nuts up there, it didn't matter. To him it was one rung short of heaven. Tenuously balanced on this lofty perch, Robert could see the expanse of God's creation. To the west, he could see the blurry place where the green lawns of town met the grayer sweetgrass of the marshes. Beyond that, he could see the tidal pools and channels which emptied into the distant sea.

To the east, Robert could see the sails of perhaps a dozen boats in the river, most of them making their way seaward with the outgoing tide. With following breezes, ships would be past the turn of the river by nightfall, well on their way to the European and Caribbean ports. From the treetop, the whole picture was enough to leave him breathless. Souls like Robert live for breathlessness.

Though he had lived on Prince Street all of his life, Robert was too rarely permitted to walk alone to the waterfront on Bay Street, and he almost always had to have supervision. Only twice had he actually been allowed to set foot on a boat that traveled the seven miles to where the Beaufort River flowed past Hilton Head where one could see the open ocean. But he could see it all from the big tree.

The islands, the plantations, and the distant waters were a subtle and awesome masterpiece – like the framed watercolors that hung in the foyer of the big house. The beauty of this coast was sufficient to steal the breath of a young boy, mesmerizing him as he mindlessly dropped ripe pecans to the mortals below. He wanted to stay up here.

It was only after the slaves and family had finished filling all the available bags and boxes that Robert's mother began to scold him to come down. He was saddened by the very notion of descending, but knew every good dream must end. With each branch and footfall of his descent, Robert lost sight of his watercolor panorama. He dreaded his return to the insipid drudgery of his life below, where lawns, paths, and fences proscribed the too familiar confines of the McKee property. Tame and plain-looking people waddled back to their assigned roles and chores, never straying from the paths, never crossing the boundaries that for generations had been so clearly marked out for them.

Slave life was, for the most part, bereft of dreams. Whenever the pinnacle of the treetop provided Robert with a view of the bigger world, the descent to the McKee house brought his earthly reality into clearer focus. Even a small whiff of freedom makes vivid the ugliness of slave life. This hideous arrangement between coloreds and their masters was a puzzle, and a hellish one at that. The puzzle was more complicated for those of mixed race. Possessing the blood of two peoples, he was perhaps made more sensitive to the characteristics of each, though he did not fully understand either.

Robert was often told that his dual heritage would be a source of continual advantage for him in life. Whites, they said, would respect the part of his blood that belonged to them. They would assume him to be of higher intelligence and moral character. This seemed to be the case, for unlike other slaves, whites would often take time to engage Robert in conversation. He noticed how some of them expected him to have familiarity with the history of both Europe and America, of literature, and the like. They assumed he loved their books, their customs, and their bland music. The paler shade of his skin required him to accede to the demands of polite society, while enjoying none of its privileges. He was, after all, still a slave.

Though his hair and features did not generally distinguish his appearance from other Negroes, there seemed to be something about the shape of his eyes that unnerved the whites. Over time, Robert noticed that they were reluctant to look him square in the face, and especially to let their eyes meet his. He could notice no special beauty or homeliness in how his eyes appeared. His mother had said he had handsome eyes. Robert thought that they looked more like those of a white man, and he concluded that whites were made nervous because they felt they were looking into the eyes of one of their own.

At first, Robert felt self-conscious about this, and he tended to lower his gaze in the presence of whites. But in time Robert cultivated the opposite habit, opting to look his masters square in the face. He discovered that allowing his eyes to meet theirs, gave him a feeling of confidence, and he soon learned that it was they and not he, who felt uncomfortable. Making them uncomfortable pleased him, and through life, his piercing eyes granted him a measure of equality, sometimes even power.

From his own people, Robert received a mixture of envy, scorn, and occasional deference. Whenever he was sent somewhere by his masters, he received a greater measure of respect than other slaves. His words held increased weight because of his lighter hue. He came to understand that Negroes' deference to him did not arise from their belief that he was superior, but from the assumption that a paler house slave was likely sent on the orders of some master. In that sense, his lighter skin gave him a leg up.

Robert was careful not to let his guard down in situations where race entered a conversation. Talking with whites, he had to walk a narrow rail. They would occasionally bait him with references to his skin tone, hinting that he might somehow be a cut above the other slaves – smarter, or perhaps more self-controlled. This is where he had to mind his words. It would be a dangerous thing to agree with them, since such might easily appear as insolence. It was of course equally risky for him to reject the notion that his white blood made any difference. This they would read as disdain for the white race and might appear to endorse the nefarious notion of equality.

Robert had to make certain rules for himself. Whenever race came up, he found it best to respond first with utter silence. Then he would follow the conversation with tentative agreement, nodding along with whatever the white person seemed to prefer. This obsequious dance seemed humiliating and pointless to Robert, but was easier to endure when he realized that the whites continually played such games with their own kind. It was an important means of survival in Southern society.

Robert had long ago concluded that no creature on earth was as adaptive, imitative, and insincere as white people. The men, especially the rich ones, were the worst. Though they had no real duties to perform, they were in their own way, diligent workers. From their earliest years they labored to appear different from their true selves – smiling when they burned with inner resentment, expressing a gentle "bless his heart" when they wished destruction on others, and always striving to seem happier, nicer, and richer that they actually were.

Their passion was to fit in to their society, to assume some acceptable niche as a gentleman or lady. Ironically, their unrelenting affectation for pretense only served to make them strange. For all of their childhood years, they were awkward understudies. Upon reaching adulthood, they assumed their various roles as lead actors, but none of them were altogether convincing in their part.

Pretense was the unconfessed yet absolute duty of every white man. To Robert, their social gatherings were very much like high theater. Their conversations were plays, and their children, a cast of minor characters.

The God-assigned duty of every Southern man was to seem. To seem intelligent, to seem noble, to seem righteous. Outward appearance was the thing, the only thing.

When at church, they took pains to exude pious humility, while inwardly longing for the best pews, or the bosom of their neighbor's wife or daughter. In their speech they sought words that were both proper and stylish. Their profoundest phrases were reserved for discussions about scriptures and politics. Their wittiest venom oozed out in their whisperings about each other. Feigning reluctance, they slid their tongues into savory morsels of gossip. About the rector, the neighbors, or even their own kin.

Their women likewise strove for the manner of royalty, yet with stylings peculiar to their gender. Hair was coiffed – stacked as high as the laws of propriety and gravity would allow, stiffly arranged and frozen by French emoluments, applied and dried. Cheeks were painted with creams, powders, then pinched and rouged. Voices were carefully inflected with overlong vowels, dropped their final *r's* in the manner of Londoners. Any natural aromas of humankind were carefully masked by newly-arrived perfumes from the Continent.

While Robert did not admire the affectation of white people, he did not resent them for it. Their pretense seemed to be its own pernicious form of slavery. Though they were masters, it was their obligation to be bound by the chains of public perception. Their reputations were their shackles – gossip and exclusion were their punishments. They could no more ignore public opinion as a slave could disregard the master's fences. Southern society existed as its own hideous sort of plantation, and the price of membership was high. Whiteness was not the type of freedom Robert craved, for their wealth and prestige had been bought at the price of their own souls.

Despite his resentment of their lifestyle, Robert had from an early age tried to learn what he could from them, imitating their imitation, so to speak. If he hoped to escape them, he must learn to beat them at their own game. As a lad, he often entertained his fellow-servants with a strutting impersonation of his masters. By the time Robert was seven, he could mimic the walk of every member of the McKee household – Master Henry, Miss Jane, the children, and even old George, their carriage driver. When once or twice Robert's theatrics had been noticed by his owners, none of the whites ever realized that Robert's posings were intended to be a likeness of themselves. "Rowdy foolishness," they called it.

Robert thought them quite blind, but continued to impersonate them nonetheless, and more and more as the years unfolded. By age nine he could portray even the smallest physical mannerism of any person, black or white. At ten he could imitate words and inflections. Even Robert's mother was amazed at his ability to switch in a blink from the Gullah banter of a field slaves to the high English of their owners.

"You best mind your manners," his mother would say. "The masters have no fondness for such mimicry. They're likely to put the whip to your back."

"Nobody's watching, Mama," Robert said, "and if they were, they'd have no idea what I was up to. Mister Henry couldn't recognize his own face in a mirror!"

"You'd better hope they can't," Lydia said. "To them, mocking's just like killing. There'll be hell to pay for any man who makes sport of them."

"Don't worry, Mama," he said. "I'll be careful."

"Or dead," she muttered. Lydia always warned him about what she called "his mocking game," but she nonetheless marveled at his devilish gift. Robert knew play-acting was much more than a game to the whites. Their game of pretense was a match to the death.

They even rehearsed their little ones for interaction with society, training them the way they introduced them to music, riding, and cursive penmanship. In this case, the goal was not to be good, but to *seem* so. The McKees taught their children to be gracious to the mean, respectful to the inept, and to feign laughter at the jokes of the dull. All the children, save one, caught on to the game and followed its rules in short order. Of them, Elizabeth McKee was the worst at pretense, and Robert always loved her for it.

For the first twelve years of his life, Liddie was Robert's best and only friend. Called Liddie by everyone but the Episcopal Rector, she was the same age as Robert and just as adventurous. A small-boned red-haired girl with delicate features, Liddie was both sweet and brave. Her blue eyes could blaze brazenly when she got angry, but could well up with sympathetic tears whenever she sensed others felt sadness or fear. Robert would one day name his firstborn child after her.

When Robert sought to bedazzle Liddie with his impersonations of white people, his act was soon deflated. "You may sound white and walk white, but you'll always be who you are, Robert." said Liddie, "and that's fine with me. Mockery never gets a person anywhere but in trouble."

"In trouble you say?" Robert asked. "You may be right, but I kind of *enjoy* trouble."

"And why do you want to be like them anyway?" she asked.

"I don't mimic so I can be like them," he said. "I do it so I can one day escape them. If a man learns to act free, he'll know how to act cleverly when the time comes for him to *get* free."

"Or get *dead*," she added. "White men like Papa are fond of guns and duels of honor. If they shoot other white men who disrespect them, what are they going to do when they're mocked by some half-black boy?"

"Folks say imitation's the sincerest form of flattery," Robert said. "They should feel flattered."

"But play acting isn't being free," she said.

"The way things are going, acting free may be the only freedom I ever taste," said Robert.

Liddie suddenly got quiet and leaned over to Robert. "Don't tell my folks, but I hope one day you will be able to get free. You and all of the slaves."

"Don't tell me the McKee family's got a closet abolitionist!" he said. "You best keep such views under your hat. Someday they'll kill me for running, but I believe they might hang *you* first if you try to help me."

"No, really. I promised God I'll help you when the time comes," she vowed, taking out a small pocket-knife. "Blood oath!"

"Blood oath," whispered Robert, as they both made small cuts on their thumbs and pushed their wounds together. "I'll remember this someday... on my honor."

"On mine, too," she said. Then she suddenly grinned. "Now that I've got a drop of colored blood, I guess I'm an official Negro," she laughed. As their young eyes met, Robert sensed that Elizabeth Jane McKee might be the only white person whose honor could be counted on in a pinch.

They parted then, each of them returning to their respective world. In the coming years, their friendship became for both of them an ongoing source of inspiration and encouragement. From now on, they were forever bound by a mutual covenant of blood and the savory sweetness of conspiracy.

Chapter 9
The Fences

By the time he turned twelve, Beaufort's split rail fences had become a hateful thing in Robert's eyes. None was higher than a goat's back, in places so low a new calf could traverse them with ease, but every slave in the Low Country recognized them as the dividing line between life and death.

Just four rails tall, it was not their height that intimidated. One could observe white children and even hens hop over them almost every day. But it was well-known that a black man could be punished for even standing too near one of the fences. Old Uncle Judah now labored lame because he once chanced to rest himself by sitting on a top rail at a property line. Five strong blows from a rifle butt served notice to him, and everyone else, that boundary violations were not trifling offenses.

It vexed Robert that he could be imprisoned by something he could have crossed without either foot leaving the ground. The most disheartening thing was not that the fences were so low, but that they were everywhere. They lined roads, divided fields, and proscribed boundaries that separated slaves like him from the realm of free men. Robert despised every fence and the whole idea of fences.

From the time a slave rose until his last waking moments, his whereabouts were everywhere governed by such hedges, fences and walls. Negro lives were also limited by even more sinister boundaries – the invisible lines of laws, rules, and custom. As their words and deeds were monitored by overseers and fences, so also their thoughts had to be *minded* at all times. Obedient slaves might be whipped if even their demeanor appeared sad, or perhaps amused, at the wrong time. In this way, even their notions and sentiments were fenced-in.

Servants knew their place, or rather their places, for there were benches and areas where they were forbidden to sit, and times they couldn't be out in public. In Beaufort, unescorted blacks had to wear engraved necklaces as symbolic authorization from their owners. By law, no more than three black men could gather for any purpose without white supervision. An hour before every sundown, Beaufort's town bell was rung to warn of the arrival of slave curfew. To be caught on the streets after dark was a serious offense.

Servants were even forbidden to linger too long in certain parts of their master's house, unless it was to sweep up or empty the chamber pots. Slaves cooked food for the masters, but had to take their own meals outside or in assigned places. Chewing any morsel of food or swallowing drink in the big house was forbidden. Food trays were designed to require two hands to prevent slaves from stealing food with a free hand, and they often had heavy metal or glass covers for the same purpose.

On the plantations, slave punishments were considerably worse, of course. Field slaves could be shot for approaching a fence line and were often punished for just asking to do so. Lydia had trained her son to cheerfully obey the masters' rules at all times. This, he was told, would please heaven and would serve to keep Robert out of trouble. And though he did not hunger for punishment, Robert's urge to cross fences was increasing rather than diminishing through the years.

The idea of slavery was everywhere endorsed and could never in any way be challenged. The Yankee term *emancipation* was the filthiest of all forbidden words. Like *abolition,* it's utterance was avoided like the Holy name of Jehovah himself, except that, upon occasion, one might be forgiven for using God's name in vain.

The whites could talk for hours of events happening a thousand miles away in Washington – of secession and impending war, but they could never utter a word to explain why they should buy and sell other men. Even the slaves played along, if such could be called playing. They found it possible to pour tea, tend children, and scrub a thousand plates without once asking why. The question was too dangerous to utter and too painful to hold in one's mind.

Robert was different though. How could a black man bow obediently to a white one without inwardly screaming, "Why?" All his life, he had craved some plausible explanation, but even God himself seemed unwilling to answer. Robert's unbowed spirit became a growing problem in his last few years in Beaufort. He learned to shun human conversation as much as possible, fearing that something might set him off.

Though Robert loved the company of others, he now found himself continually seeking times of solitude, but not the way he did as a child. No longer driven by any passion for divine connection, he simply wanted to be out from under the eyes of those whose human rank exceeded his. A man by himself is, in some sense, a master. The head rooster in that particular barnyard. Alone, a man is free to be himself, without concern for the whims or rules of others.

For most of his early years, Robert had done his best to obey those rules. He was honest, diligent, and had never once missed church. Even at twelve, the grownups had all said the Robert was wise beyond his years. A level-headed boy. But the days came when certain demons began to enter his heart.

More and more, he found himself at odds with the masters, and even with his own mother. When she offered advice, he was increasingly inclined to talk back. He honed his formerly civil tongue to a snide edge and he became quick with a come-back. Robert became plodding in his obedience and often wore a sour look on his now whiskered face. His once-rare mistakes became more frequent and more intentional. All this led up to a particular instance when he first ventured to deliberately flout a rule.

It was a warm day in early June of 1851. Robert had been sent to town with some servants from the Fripp's house to pick up some goods for supper. Just after noon, the time approached for the group to make their way home, but young Robert was not to be found. Leena did her best to look for him, but no one had a notion as to where he might be, so they were forced to leave him in town.

Robert had vivid memories of the first part of that afternoon. While the women bought provisions, he wandered off. In truth, he did not think of it as wandering at all, because he had deliberately decided he would go off on his own even before they had left home.

He recalled the sense of freedom he felt as he walked alone down New Street toward the waterfront. He picked up a stone and threw it against a street sign. He whistled a bawdy tune he had heard outside one of the pubs. Robert put his hands in his pockets as he walked, strutting the way he had seen rich white men walk through town. He felt the emptiness of his pockets and wished he had a cluster of coins to jingle for this was something the white gentlemen liked to do. But before long, he heard a man's voice from behind him.

"You got a voucher in one of those deep pockets of yours?" said the man, an older white fellow with a big cloud of chin whiskers. Unaccompanied blacks were sometimes asked to show a voucher token from their master, indicating that their trip was legitimate.

"No sir," Robert said. "I'm here with a group from Prince Street.

The Fripp's girl Leena has got our pass."

"If it's a voucher for a group, you've gotta stay with the group," the man said gruffly. "Where are the others?"

"Up that way, sir," Robert said, pointing up New Street, "buyin' goods." Robert felt surprisingly calm. He even entertained the notion of pushing the old man down and running away, but he quickly dismissed the idea, deciding rather to tell a lie. This seemed a safer form of wickedness, given the situation. "I'll run right back and find the others, sir," he said. "Then we'll get on home."

"Yes, you better do that, boy," the man said as he turned to walk down Bay Street. "We got lawmen who'll find you. And they ain't a old fellers like me; them boys will put the hurt to you."

Robert made sure to walk toward the market area as he had promised, but once the old man was out of sight, he quickly ducked into an alley. 'To hell with him,' he thought, and Robert soon found himself walking right back down New Street toward the water. In his heart, he was pretty much daring anyone to get in his way.

As he passed a white couple who were strolling by the sea wall, Robert actually hoped they would ask him for his voucher, for he had by now prepared some snide words. It irked him a bit that no one was saying anything. By the time he reached the piers, his heart was full of rage and his head full of what he later called "his adolescent madness." For the first time in his life, he cared nothing at all for what anyone else might say or do to him.

Robert swaggered around the waterfront for the rest of the afternoon, searching his heart for the magic feeling he used to get when as a boy he had watched the boats come and go. But now there were no dreams and no sense of awe – only a cold, numb sort of anger. The sailors were still sailing the open water, but he was stuck here on land. Those men might be free, but Robert felt trapped. It now seemed certain that he would never be one of them.

He wondered how long he would be allowed to sit where he was. A number of whites came and went, but no one ventured to say anything. There were still no constables in sight. In his troubled heart he longed to jump on one of those boats and sail off somewhere. There was part of him that thought it better if he were dead and gone, free from the unendurable agony of this life. Alone and restless, he wished that something – anything – would happen. Trouble, or even death, would be welcome if it could rescue him from all this.

After four o'clock he pretty much got his wish. In the distance, a loud bell signaled slave curfew. For just a brief moment, it occurred to him that it might be time for church, but of course it wasn't Sunday. The bell just rang once, and Robert knew what that meant. Slave curfew. At sundown, any unaccompanied Negro that walked the streets of Beaufort was in violation of the law and was in trouble of the deepest kind.

Robert suspected he could sneak home undetected by way of back paths and wooded yards. Since it was rare for law officers to patrol the streets, he might even have made it home safely if he moved quickly on the main thoroughfares. But he was not in a compliant mood – resolving to enjoy what remained of this sunny afternoon. Come what may, he would take his own sweet time, walking in the middle of the street all the way home. "Bring on trouble," Robert said to himself, and as always, trouble was quick to heed the call.

Within minutes, a town deputy had spotted him walking where no black boy belonged. On the street after dark. "Stop where you are!" the man shouted. "I got you for dang sure."

"I'm sorry sir. I was left behind by my overseer," Robert said, intentionally staring the man straight in the eyes. "I should be home soon."

"I don't care none about your excuses and fancy words," the deputy said, "and I ain't impressed that you don't talk like no slave."

"And I'm not offended that you *do* talk like a slave," Robert snapped back. "And your grammar's quite poor."

The constable had heard enough. Within an hour, the stern-faced deputy was knocking on the front door of the McKee house to inform Henry that one of his slaves had been locked up for the night. He was told he could post bond and take custody of Robert Smalls the next day. By the time Master Henry made his appearance at the bailiff's desk, the Clerk of the Court was there to have words with him.

"You should keep a closer eye on your darkies, McKee," said the Clerk. "This one we picked up, he just seems to be itching for trouble." Two deputies, Robbins and Withrow, were escorting Robert from his cell with his hands tied behind him.

"He's a good boy," said Henry. "They tell me he got lost somewhere in town. I imagine he was on his way home."

"No sir," said Robbins. "When Withrow came upon him, the boy just stood his ground real snooty-like and gave us what-for."

"I see," said McKee. "I certainly apologize for your inconvenience."

"We've seen his kind of boy before," Withrow said. "If you'd like, we can rough him up for you. We had a mind to do it last night, but we need a master's signature for a proper beating."

"No sir," Henry answered. "That's all right. This boy will most definitely get what's coming to him when we get him back home."

As they made the long walk home up New Street, Robert wondered what Henry McKee would say to him, or if he'd say anything at all. There was no question that his master was steaming mad. Henry had had to pay a civil fine for Robert's offense. Even worse was the embarrassment of a public display of defiance on the part of his house slave. In this small town, the word would get out. Such would constitute a stain on his honor as a gentleman and his reputation as a Christian. Neither Henry nor Robert said a word until they reached the front gate of the big house.

"I just want to say that I'm sorry, sir," Robert said. "I can't really explain what got into me."

Henry did not speak, but motioned for Robert to follow him behind the house. Robert supposed that some major punishment was on the way, but to his astonishment, McKee led both of them to the oak swing that hung from a tree branch behind the kitchen. It was here that the McKee children used to play in their younger years.

"Sit with me," Henry said. "We need to talk."

Robert's twelve-year-old mind began to run in every direction. Was he going to be beaten or whipped? Who would do it and how many lashes? Cane rod or leather strips? He could think of no appropriate words to offer that might mitigate his punishment. He simply bowed his young head and waited for the verdict.

"You have to understand something," Henry began. "This type of thing can never, ever happen again."

"It won't sir," Robert said. "You're absolutely right in what you say." Robert just kept nodding his head over and over.

"And you must also understand," his father continued, "that circumstances are such that I'll be required to take, well... some sort of action."

Action, Robert didn't like the sound of that. There were a number of possibilities available to Henry, and all of them were painful. "I understand, sir," said Robert. "I'm prepared for whatever your wisdom tells you to do." Robert was anxious to find out what his punishment would be, and he very much looked forward to getting this thing over with. In this regard, Robert would be dismayed at what Henry said next.

"For now," he continued. "I think it best to just keep an eye on things. I'll speak to Jane and with your mother and we'll seek some suitable solution.

Robert did his best not to appear alarmed or confused at Henry's words. 'What on earth does this mean?' he asked himself. Robert almost wished he had received a simple beating or whipping. As painful as these may have been, at least they would have been clear, and quickly finished. But Henry said he sought "some suitable solution." More white nonsense. The last time Robert had heard this phrase, the family was deciding to shoot a renegade dog that had been stealing hens. His master was doing his best to seem magnanimous and patient, but the waiting would be more tortuous than any possible beating. For the next weeks he sensed that an executioner's axe was hanging above his head.

When he got back to his cottage, his mother was quite a bit more disturbed than McKee had been. Robert had never known a moment when he didn't trust his mother's love, but after his return from the jail, she didn't utter a single word to him. Not for three days straight. At certain points she would walk up to him, her lips poised to speak, but then would just wag her index finger in the air and walk back to her chair. Robert felt like a disabled sailboat being circled by a 40-gun frigate. His mother was just looking for the most glorious way to finish him off.

Even in his own mind, Robert could think of no lasting solution to his situation. He found himself drowning in a swamp of adolescent emotions, and he saw no hope of escape. The law decreed that he was forever destined to live as a slave. His Christian faith ruled out suicide as an option, but he couldn't imagine any circumstance wherein his restless heart could forestall further sufferings or defiance.

By the end of that week, his mother was ready to offer a plan that she hoped might save his life. She had been inside the big house for an hour, and Robert could tell by the way she strutted across the yard that she had made some sort of devil's agreement with Master Henry, a painful agreement it turned out.

"I did my best to save your life, your soul, and your hind parts as well," she began. "I persuaded Master Henry not to have you flogged like the common jail trash that you are. I had to pretty much swear you'd be good forever, but it bought me a year to put you into proper shape."

"Thank you, I guess," he said. "I know you always do your best, even if it seems like you're signing my death warrant."

"Oh, you ain't begun to see my best," she said. "And you may very well yearn for death when I get done with you. You've set your feet on the highway to hell, and it's my fault. I let you get soft and uppity. I let

Missy Jane talk me into all her silly advantages, but everything they did just made you think you're some big somebody. Gave you big ideas and a big mouth. Well no more. They been trying to make you something you ain't never gonna be. I been lettin' you grow up spoilt."

"But they've been good to me," said Robert. "They've been good to *us*."

"Them being good didn't make you good," she said. "Folks been coddling you like some cream-colored prince, but I'm fixing to put you in touch with real life. Slave life. You don't know what all I had to go through, but by God you're gonna learn. Mama's gonna be your schoolmaster. I intend to show you some things."

And show him she did.

Chapter 10
Ladies' Island

Lydia prayed long and hard about the best way to put Robert in touch with the horrors of slavery. She knew better than to simply start an argument, for her son didn't like to be told how to think or what to do. He did better when he could see a thing with his own eyes. She unfolded her plan on a hot Saturday when they had just finished storing some items in the McKee's attic, which the afternoon sun had turned into something like an oven. She and Robert, drenched with perspiration, were refreshed to finally come down to the breezes of the garden.

"Come sit with me," she said, patting the seat of the small swing that hung from the huge branch of a live oak. At this point, he still expected some kind of a lecture from her, but as they sat, she said nothing. Their faces slowly cooled off as they rocked in the swing, gently at first, and then higher. Soon high enough that they both began to smile. For a brief instant, Robert had the feeling they were more like childhood playmates than mother and son.

Her shiny brown face now took on a more youthful glow as her mind went back to her childhood at Ashdale Plantation. "This is just like when I was a girl," she said, "comin' in from the fields to dry off in the sea wind."

"Tell me about the island" he said. "I guess I'm about the same age you were when they brought you here."

"Well, it's been quite a while," she said. "At thirteen, I figured I'd work the fields all my life. I'd seen old Master John McKee prowlin' around Ashdale. Never thought he'd just up and snatch me off like he did."

"It was hard," Robert said.

Was the only life I'd known," she recalled. "It surely broke my heart to leave my people. My family all smiled and celebrated though, talkin' like the big house was heaven or something. So I stopped my cryin' and just smiled along with 'em. I was too green to know I'd been living in hell."

"But the island must've been a pretty sight," he said, "seeing the water every day."

"Well," Lydia said, "I hardly recollect seein' the sea at all. Not after I was old enough to pick and chop. It was lucky if we got 'nuff water to drink. Slavin' from sunup to dark, and at picking time, we'd even work by the moonlight."

"But you rested sometimes," he said. "Right?"

"Oh there was some rest, but I saw folks worked till they dropped dead," she said. "Both young and old. A body can only take so much heat, you know. It was worse at harvest time, of course. Master figured being quick to market was worth a few lives here and there. And we did lose a few. I was blessed to get out."

"But why *you?*" Robert asked. "Weren't there lots of other slave girls?"

"Oh, there was 'nuff of us to choose from," she said. "It's somethin' I've asked myself lots of times. Mama said it was owing to the fact that I was bright, and was the right age to tend young'uns. But there were other girls they could've taken. Lord had some plan for me I suppose, and now for you."

"Don't God care about the ones that didn't get picked?"

"Oh, he cares, I think," she said. "Sometimes he takes one and leaves the other. Not even King Solomon could tell you why."

"Ashdale must've been bad," Robert said.

"Was hell for sure, but it was home," she said. "A girl can abide hell if she's got family. My mam always said we gotta make soup with what's left in the pantry." Lydia and Robert looked across the garden as they swung together. A cluster of young redbirds we're just now pecking up their lunch from some freshly turned mulch in the flower bed.

"Master Henry will be heading over to the plantation tomorrow," she said. "I reckon time's come for you to take a look for yourself."

Robert had seen this plan coming, but he nodded, supposing it was time he took his medicine. "I'll do what you say, Mama," he said quietly.

It had been a while since Lydia had been back to visit her kinfolk on Ladies' Island. Henry McKee had agreed with her suggestion that it would benefit Robert to see life outside the comforts of the big house. Her son could be better kept in line if he could witness the plight of the field slaves, and Ashdale could serve to put the fear of God in him.

At first, the trip across the Beaufort River seemed to him like a reward rather than an ordeal. Though the day was hot, the sea air felt good as they stepped on to the foredeck of the ferry. A one-eyed mulatto man with a bandana was manning the helm, and Robert watched him carefully as the boat slowly traversed the two miles between town and their destination. The old man looked every bit the pirate as he moaned some sailor song Robert couldn't understand. He was filled with anticipation as the distant shore of Ladies' Island came into focus, but Robert would soon discover that these green fields were no Paradise.

The slaves near the dock stopped their work as he stepped off the boat, all of them staring at this brown boy and his black mother. The ink-black laborers only dropped their pointing fingers when they saw Master Henry McKee watching them.

"Who dah be?" the younger ones whispered. Their words sounded strange to Robert's city ears.

"Hushy!" said one mother, wagging her finger across her full lips to dozens of them who had gathered to stare at Robert. "Be massah's chile," she said. "Dah be *moonlah-bai*."

Lydia wasn't watching these women and their children; she was watching her son. Robert looked ill at ease as his eyes flashed back and forth between the black-skinned field slaves. "You hear 'em?" she asked Robert. "They're talking about you."

"Sounds like gibberish," Robert said. "Is something wrong?"

"No, baby," Lydia said. "They're just pointing out the master's boy. They're calling you the *moonlight boy*. And it ain't gibberish, it's pure Gullah. I spoke like this when I was your age."

"I didn't come all this way to be made fun of," he said.

"It'll be all right," Lydia said. "You look funny to them because you're part *buckrah*."

"I might take a guess whether that's white or black," he replied with a smile, "but I suppose it doesn't matter since I'm half of each."

"It means white," she said. "And no, it won't matter much to them. They'll get used to you quick enough."

As they rode along through the fields, it was hot as blazes and Robert was soon soaked with sweat, which helped him relax a bit. He noticed that the field workers seemed to relax around him too, once they sensed he was at ease with them. He did notice that they seemed to work harder whenever Henry McKee was watching. From the oldest to the youngest, they lowered their eyes as the master's carriage drew near.

All across the acres of cane fields, the slaves went about their work of chopping and bundling the stalks. In the distance, Robert could see scores of others picking cotton. The workers close to them were almost close enough to touch, and Robert could see the insects buzzing and landing on their shimmering bodies. Almost all had welts from insect bites and a great number of them had other scars. From work and whippings, he supposed. Those who labored on the far side of the cane field were concealed by green stalks and could only be detected by the occasional movement of the cane tops. From clusters of choppers and the pickers in the far fields, he could hear a dozen different songs, all sung simultaneously. The resulting symphony was both cacophonous and beautiful.

"What are they singing about?" Robert asked.

"Oh, lots of things," Lydia said. "I still know most of these songs. Most of are about shade, cool water... or heaven. And lots of these old songs have African words that are a mystery, even to the ones singing. Been passed down from old times." Lydia's eyes were squinting in the sunlight as she surveyed the scene. Robert figured she was remembering something.

As they made their way toward the supervisor's shack, Robert could hear the ocean winds rustle through the swaying cane. The textured chorus of voices faded behind them, but the music had touched something in Robert's young soul. He had the feeling that all of heaven's angels, and all the slaves around the world, might be joining in.

"It's somethin,' ain't it?" he said, whispering so as not to interrupt the music. His mother, cocking her head back and forth to the rhythms, said nothing at all. Her eyes were wide as she looked straight into Robert's. She smiled the cryptic smile of a nursing child – a smile of connection.

After they passed a big open warehouse, they came to the slave quarters. A small woman in a brown dress came racing up the road toward them, shouting something. Her skin was black as polished iron, but her face shown with the joy of family love. "Lid! Lid!" she cried as she ran up and hugged his mother's neck. Robert soon discovered that this was Lydia's older sister Elora, who Robert had heard so many stories about.

The old women laughed and cried and chattered to one another in the pure, familiar tones of the Gullah language. This musical dialog, a mystery to Robert, flowed between his mother and her sister like life-blood from a shared heart. Lydia was home again, and Robert envied her tears. He slept fitfully that night, lying awake in an unfamiliar world.

The next day, dawn arrived clear and bright, but already as hot as afternoon. If today's tour of the fields was intended to shock Robert, their plan was successful. The violence of plantation labor was horrifying, and throughout the day, he was often tempted to look away. Scores of black men, women and even children were unrelentingly driven in their field work. And driven is the word for it. Few discernible orders were ever given. When it was time for the workers to move from row to row, there were only inarticulate barks from the white foremen followed by the loud cracking of whips.

Cane slaves and cotton pickers were worked like animals. This was not the kind of life Robert was used to at the McKee's. In the big house, slaves did their duties in accordance with a clear and reasonable routine. Assignments were clear, questions were answered, and *please* and *thank yous* were exchanged between slave and master. Servants were called by name and most tasks were performed methodically in the comfortable confines of the house. In the fields, it was different. The fields were hell.

What Robert witnessed that day left an indelible impression on his mind. It was not completely accurate to say that field slaves were treated like animals, for domestic beasts are not regarded as expendable commodities. These slaves were not treated like service horses, but as despised vermin. At times, Robert wondered if the slave drivers cared as much about production as they did about cruelty.

Their delight seemed to be in inflicting humiliation and punishment. Bosses seemed only to drive and punish, giving few directions and no explanations. Robert heard them shout obscure orders, and if a slave could not understand, the whip would be called for. Usually, the worker would slump down into a kneeling position with both hands covering his or her head. At that point, it was the job of the whip man to bludgeon the confused worker unmercifully. There was no clear point to any of it, and no possibility of escape. If a slave curled himself up into a ball, he was whipped, if he stood up, he was whipped, and if he spoke, he was whipped for that as well. Robert struggled to hold back tears and to hold his tongue. He spent much of the day infuriated by what he saw.

"How can they live like this?" Robert asked his mother. "Why do they just curl up and take it? Why don't they run, lash out, or just kill themselves?

"I was one of them," she said, "and when men are screaming and whuppin' you, you don't have time to ask why. You don't ask nothin. You got no notions of freedom or vengeance. You just ball up, take your licks, and pray for your next breath, waiting."

"Waiting for what?" Robert asked.

"Just waitin' for the whuppin' to stop," she replied.

Later that day, Robert was able to meet a number of Lydia's relatives and friends. Many of them were skilled laborers, permitted to do most of their work without a lot of supervision. Robert supposed that four generations of field work had taught them how best to avoid the whip. Certain ones of them had acquitted themselves so as to be assigned to less strenuous duties inside the barns or the overseer's cabin. Others worked here because they had gone lame or lost limbs.

At their meals, Lydia's people had a thousand questions, mostly about life at the big house. One of her male cousins, Mayes Polite was particularly curious. And envious.

"It's all gravy for you folks up there!" he said, pointing across the wide river toward Beaufort. "You and your mama are the next thing to free. You're livin' the life!"

Robert couldn't help but like Mayes, but he couldn't hold back words. "Don't get me wrong, Uncle," replied Robert. "It's a sight better in the big house, but a slave's a slave nonetheless."

With a blast from his lungs, Mayes just scoffed. "Nonsense!" he said. "You don't know what you got. Out here? Boys like you work for damn sure. Harder work than you ever knowed. Most don't live long. Almost none to full years. Ask your mama, she knows."

Lydia just nodded and stared straight at Robert. "He's right," she said. "You and me are blest. It's a frightful thing to work these fields. Wears a soul down to the nub. A slave lives out all his days... never gettin' even one little sniff of the free life we have across the river." His mother talked of the McKee house as if she were speaking of heaven.

"Maybe so," Robert said. "But I'm not sure which is worse..."

Before Robert could finish, Mayes held up his right hand up to stop him mid-sentence. "Woah, now! Put a cork in that mouth of yours!" his uncle said, slamming his hands down on the table loudly. "Ain't no slave on this island that don't work ten times as hard as them in the house. And we don't eat the half as much."

"... And don't live half as long," Lydia added. "As a girl I lived thirteen years out here. Was too small to chop cane, but I picked cotton all day long. Got me some thick and bloody fingers. Never once dreamed of the life I got now. Never heard there *was* such a life as you and I've got."

"I know, Mama, I saw it. It's the devil's hell," Robert said. "But I ain't sure which hell is the worst kind." The table was absolutely silent and everyone stopped their talking and even ceased chewing.

"That's enough!" said Mayes. "You just a soft little boy. You best not speak of things you don't know nothin' about."

To everyone's surprise, Robert didn't back down. "But what's hell anyway?" he asked. The table went silent as he went on. "Maybe hell's *this* place where nobody even dreams of freedom. But maybe hell's that nice white house across the water – a place where day after day you have to stand by and watch the freedom of others. Field slaves starve out here where there's no food, but house slaves sniff a banquet every day, but never get a bite for themselves. Maybe that's the purest hell."

The table remained dead quiet until Uncle Mayes smiled and slapped young Robert on the back. "Lid, you've got you quite a boy here!" he laughed. "A smart... and a smart-mouth boy."

"Yes indeed," she smiled. "He's both of those!"

"I'm sorry if I spoke out of line, Uncle Mayes" Robert said, lowering his head. "Ain't my place to preach to nobody, much less blood family."

"It's all right, son," said Mayes. "I spoke my piece, and you spoke yours. Your good mama did, too. Fair's fair. Don't reckon it matters who wins when you're squabbling over which hell is the hottest." They all nodded and laughed.

"Well," Robert concluded, "Cotton field or big house, it's pure slop to be a slave," concluded Robert, only he used another word instead of slop.

"Lid, you need give that boy a honey biscuit when you get home," said Uncle Mayes, "and then put some lye soap in his foul mouth for me."

"I reckon he needs a good helpin' of both," said Lydia. Then they all laughed again.

On the ferry home, Robert's head was spinning, but he didn't feel like saying much. The one-eyed mulatto didn't look much like a story-pirate any more, just a tired old slave. Lydia was silently praying that seeing Ashdale had helped her son to appreciate his lot in life.

"So do you still think the hardest thing in life is getting home by curfew?" she asked.

"You don't have to say no more," he said. "I'll keep a clean nose from here on out."

"So when you see all this out here, does it make you want to change?" she asked.

"Well, Mama," he said. "I'm not real sure how to answer. Part of me wants to promise I'll stop acting up and talking back, but there's a part of me that wants to bring a gun over here and shoot every white cracker in the place. Makes me want to take all these folks to freedom somehow."

As Robert stood at the bow of the ferry on their way home, he watched the last amber rays of sunset disappear behind the distant wall of purple clouds. As seagulls darted to and fro, he could feel the salty breath of evening against his back. Behind them, a big moon was rising over Ladies' Island, as the waves scattered its reflection like a thousand spilled diamonds.

"I think I understand what you're saying," she said. "You know I'm just wanting you not to be snooty or mouthy. And I don't want you to be too white."

"I don't want to be white, Mama," he said as he scanned the horizon. "I just want to be free."

Chapter 11
The Auction Block

Plans for Robert's second lesson were set into motion on the following Tuesday. Desperate squawks echoed across the McKee's backyard as a half-dozen chickens felt the wrath of old George's axe blade. The headless birds continued to twitch and bleed-out as they were tossed, one by one, into the wicker basket at Lydia's feet. She was humming as she vigorously plucked the still-moving hens, but her eyes were not on her work. Miss Jane Bold McKee was making her way from the big house down the servant's path toward Lydia's cottage. Missy took a deep breath as she stood quietly in front of her maidservant.

"Oh my," Jane said, watching the bloody basket of quivering chickens. "I can't bear to look. It's sheer butchery."

"No ma'am..." Lydia responded. "It's supper."

"Yes, of course," Jane said. "I suppose I'm more comfortable with the finished product."

Lydia called to her son, who was cleaning the axe blade on the other side of the yard. "Robert, I need you to hustle this basket around to the other side of the house till these hens quiet down. Then wash up and fire the kitchen stove for me."

"Yes, ma'am," he said as he left. He knew the women were about to talk about matters that were not intended for his ears.

"Henry said you and Robert were with him for his rounds at Ashdale," Jane said. "I hope you had a pleasant visit."

"Not so pleasant as all that," Lydia said, "but I reckon it was good for us to go." I saw my people there, but I mostly went for Robert's sake. Master Henry and I thought it might help to put the fear of God into him."

"Well," said Jane, "I sincerely hope he wasn't too horrified by what he saw. He's a bright and a good boy."

"Ma'am," said Lydia, "I suspect if he'd been a good boy, he'd not need this kind of trip. It's a helpful thing for a young man to see and fear hell's torment, and I reckon Ladies' Island is the closest thing to hell we got here in South Carolina."

"Well, I would suppose that is so," said Jane. "I wanted to ask you if you think the visit had the desired effect. Do you think Robert's learned his lesson?"

"Oh, I suppose he's always learning something," she said. "He's just at that age when knowing what's right don't always lead to doing what's right. He's a headstrong little so and so, and I doubt we're out of the woods yet."

"Mercy," Jane said. "I hope that whatever comes next doesn't have to be so appalling."

Robert's mother just looked up at Jane sternly and with just a trace of sarcasm in her eyes. "Well, since we're all pretty sure your story time ain't got the job done, he might still need a few more jolts of appalling. It won't kill him, and it just might save his soul."

"Yes, hopefully," Jane replied. "I want us to be praying for him. We'll need God's help."

Lydia did not answer with words, but just bowed her head and held out her open hands to her mistress, inviting her to pray. Nervous, and not knowing what else to do, Jane took Lydia's dark hands into her own and worded a prayer for them. "Dearest Heavenly Father, we beseech Thee for Thy help on behalf of young Robert. May you guide, guard, and direct his heart to more closely walk in Thy paths, that he, along with all of us, might one day be with Thee in the perfect bliss of heaven. Amen." As they both lifted up their heads, she noticed that Lydia had tears in her eyes.

"That was so pretty," Robert's mother said. "It stands to reason that the Good Lord would gladly hear and answer such pretty words!"

"Thank, you, Lydia," Jane said. "May God bless you and your son." As Jane slowly made her way back to the house, she heard the sound of another chicken being slaughtered behind the house next door. Pausing, she did not turn her head, but only glanced down at her own pale hands which bore drops of blood from holding Lydia's. "And may God help us all," she whispered.

It was just the next day when Lydia sought Miss Jane to inform her that she and Robert would be spending most of Tuesday in town. Dismissing the children to the backyard, Jane said, "But Tuesday we will be having story time, and we would so much like Robert to join us."

"I'm sorry, Miss Jane," she said. "But Master Henry said it would be all right to do it. Tuesday is the best day for us to continue Robert's training."

"And this is because…." Jane asked.

"Because every Tuesday is the public whippings and the slave auctions," Lydia said. "It's something I've hid from Robert all his life, but it's something else that should help him wise up. I told Robert it was auctions, but he doesn't know what kind yet."

"Oh, merciful Lord!" Jane said. "Are you sure this is what's best? Was this Henry's idea?"

"No ma'am, it was mine," she said, "but Master Henry was fine with it, too."

"Well then, I wish Robert well in this," Jane said. "I will continue to be in prayer for him."

"And you best be praying for me too, Miss Jane. This will be a hard thing for me to see also. They're likely to be selling a lot of boys about Robert's age."

"I can only imagine," Jane said.

"No ma'am, I don't think you could," Lydia said, but even Lydia would be shocked at what they would witness on Tuesday at Beaufort's slave block.

On their way into town, Robert's mother did her best to keep the conversation pleasant. She had told him they were going to a market, but not what kind. She spoke so much of the beautiful morning and the flowers that by the time they reached Tandy Street, Robert was already terrified. He sensed his mother was setting him up for something. Even before they turned the corner to the arsenal, Robert could hear the shouts from the hawkers and the customers at the auction place. The tone of the conversations up ahead were not friendly ones. What took place on Tuesdays was a nasty business.

"Draw near! Draw near!" the auctioneer shouted in a thick Irish accent. "Come close and look this one over carefully," he said. "The keen eye will notice that he's healthy and sharp-minded. A young buck, just twelve, but already firm of limb and quick of foot. They call him Frederick, but you can tag him with any name you fancy if the bid is right."

It was then that the serious shouting began as plantation owners and slave brokers started the bidding. An adolescent boy in suitable condition would fetch around 500 dollars. Younger children could be purchased for less, and older folks for even less than that. The most desirable slaves were males between 19 and 30, who might bring as much as 900. Some slaves were purchased individually, while others were dealt in groups, sometimes groups of ten or more. Most slaves sold at the Beaufort auction came from the inland plantations, but occasionally, local Negroes became available when an owner died or moved away. Frugal buyers were always seeking a low price, but quality was the most important thing. Wise buyers looked for workers with clear eyes, good teeth, and who bore no marks of being punished for disobedience.

Robert got a good look at the black boy who was up for sale. Frightened and shaking like a leaf, the lad was no bigger than Robert and he had shackles on his hands and feet. The hawker kept turning the boy around and around so buyers could inspect the goods from every angle. Bids were made with nods, gestures, but mostly with words. At first, offers came one by one, but soon there was an inarticulate storm of shouting. To Robert they sounded just like a pack of hounds. Above these barkings, he could hear the shrill voice of a small black woman, who was crying uncontrollably.

"Who's that?" Robert asked. "And why's she throwin' such a fit?"

"That's his Mama, baby," Lydia said. "Frederick is her son."

Robert was stunned and stone-faced. "She's sure got herself all worked up," he said. "Are they gonna sell her too?"

"No son," Lydia said. "She's just come here to see him this one last time to say goodbye." As dozens of white men began to bark out their bids, Robert's eyes kept staring at the face of the boy Frederick."

"Could be you," his mother whispered. "Yesterday that boy was with his family. Tomorrow, maybe Ladies' Island."

"Or maybe he'll just be a house slave," Robert offered. "Maybe they'll work him inside."

"Maybe," Lydia replied. "Maybe you're right, but how'd you like your whole life to hang on a maybe? Some white slave driver's whim? Those men are going to call him by whatever name they like and send him God knows where."

"I can't watch," said Robert. "We gotta leave."

"No, you're gonna watch," Lydia replied. "It's better you see it from here than from up on that block. And if Master Henry hadn't bailed you out, that would be you up there. Might still be you someday."

For the next two hours, Robert and his mother saw 54 people – men, women, and children, sold off to the highest bidder. "If there's a hell this side of Ashdale, this is it," Robert whispered.

"Don't speak so soon," Lydia said. "The day ain't finished."

The crowd began to disperse around noon. Brokers who had purchased slaves *in bulk* were now busy distributing them to individual, prearranged buyers. There was middleman money to be made from group purchases. At nearby tables, white families were enjoying boxed lunches of chicken or sandwiches, joined by their husbands and fathers who had worked today's auctions.

Robert and Lydia did not bring food and did not feel like eating anyway. They used the lunch interval as an opportunity to stroll, as far as they could, away from the horror that was the auction.

"So what do you make of all that?" his mother asked.

"Oh, I already knew about the auctions. Everybody does," he said.

"No doubt," Lydia said. "But what's it like to see it for the first time? Learn anything."

"I don't think *learn* is the word for it," he said. "It all just hurts my heart. And makes me mad as hell."

"How 'bout afraid?" she asked. "Don't it make you afraid of what might happen if you don't shape up?"

"I guess that's a good question, Mama. But I'm torn."

"Tell me," she said. "Torn?"

"Well, I suppose it's like this," he began. "You always taught me to do right and to be God's man. A good and an obedient man. But when I see all this," he said, pointing back to the slave block, "I start to think about what it really means to be God's man. Don't God want a man *not* to obey sometime? To stand up to risk his very life to make things right?"

"But you know too well what would happen," she warned. "I don't never want to see you up there on that block."

"But that's just it, Mama. If nobody ever stands up, my children and my grandchildren will still be standing up there fifty years from now! Isn't bravery something noble and pleasing to God?"

"But don't you see? They've got the power and we got the chains," she said. "Those men will hurt you, sell you, and most likely kill you if you keep making waves."

"But they can't keep killing us forever," Robert said. "Not *all* of us! The Lord Jesus promised that the gates of Hades shall not prevail."

"Well," his mother said, shaking her head. "Hell's gates seem to be holding up fine so far."

Just as she spoke these words, a bell rang to signify the beginning of the events of the afternoon. Robert looked on as a white man walked up to the blocks. It was deputy Withrow and he held a long whip in his hand. A line of six shirtless black men were lined up behind him. They wore small loin cloths around them and were here to be punished. Perhaps twenty more slaves, males and females, were just now making their way up to the auction dais. These were various rule-breakers. Some were sentenced by law officials to receive public punishment, others were here as private offenders, sent by their angry owners to be, for a small fee, whipped in public.

"Scourging begins with James Meeks, for multiple theft of edible livestock," the deputy shouted. "Ladies and children might wish to visit the promenade," he added. A bald-headed white man, short and stocky of build, came forward to carry out the whipping. The offender was bent over with both hands bound to a large post.

"How many blows?" the bald man asked, loud enough for all to hear.

"Twenty and five," the deputy shouted back. From where Robert and his mother stood, the specific blows to the man's back could not be clearly seen. They could however, hear the deep groans of this James Meeks as he was whipped. As blows fell, each one in measured rhythm, the crowd in unison murmured the running count, "one, two, three…" By the time they reached eighteen, Meeks was unconscious and Robert found himself whispering the numbers, right along with the crowd.

"Hush your mouth," Lydia said. "Last week, that could've been you."

"It pains my heart to hear his cries," Robert said.

"Yes," she said, "and it hurts to hear the crowd counting out the blows and to see the faces of the folks watching."

"Are you going to make me watch them all?" Robert asked.

"I'll decide when it's time for us to leave," she said.

As the beatings continued, some for theft, some for violence, and at least two for curfew violations, Robert chose not to watch. He remained at his mother's side, but positioned himself a bit to the front of her. Standing here, he could close his eyes and take his thoughts elsewhere. In his mind, the rhythmic blows of the whip now melted into the sounds of the waves slapping the sea wall. He suddenly imagined himself there, gazing out at the tall ships as they left the harbor for the freedom of the Atlantic, and of distant ports. A man on the bow of the boat was counting the knots on the rope that measured the depth of the channel, "twenty-three, twenty-four, twenty-five."

"Now the next…" shouted the deputy up at the whipping post, as he introduced another unfortunate offender to the audience. Robert's daydream was gone, as it all began again. After an hour of this, Robert could no longer take his mind back to the waterfront. Even with closed eyes, the sounds and the images from the auction block were too much to ignore.

"Oh my God, she has grown so much," Lydia said. She was looking at a young woman who was just now approaching the front of the line for punishment. "It's Susannah. You used to see her at church."

"I remember," said Robert. "She sings well. What did she do?"

In a few minutes, it was Susannah's turn to be whipped. "The girl Susannah Lowe," the man shouted, "for refusing a master's prerogative. Twenty lashes."

"Twenty? She's just a girl!" Robert said, almost loud enough for nearby whites to hear. "What did she do?"

"Nothing," said his mother. "It's for what she *wouldn't* do. She's some master's personal girl now. A pretty thing."

"My God!" said Robert as the whip came down upon the dark smoothness of Susannah's bare back. "She's fourteen."

"No look, just look!" his mother whispered. "You know how I said earlier that that could have been you?"

Robert nodded his head. "Yes, Mama."

"Well, that one up there… that could've been me." The scene was becoming too brutal to watch. Lydia turned and walked away, with Robert close behind. Even after she was two blocks away, she could still hear the cracking of the whip and the cries of the young girl on the slave platform. Her son said nothing at all as they made their way home.

The well-scrubbed facades of the homes and the bloom-filled window boxes seemed hideous and incongruous now – like paper flowers in a graveyard. Robert's brain was an angry whirlwind of thoughts. He'd had enough of these lessons and enough of slavery, but he could envision no possible path of escape.

Chapter 12
The Guest Room

His mother's face had a steady but determined look when she woke him the next day. All through that morning, she barely spoke at all as she kept eyeing him with a wary look. As the minutes passed like years, Robert was terrified by the thought that his moral lessons were not yet complete.

"I need you to come with me," she said later as she led him across the back yard and up the path toward the big house. She spoke and walked with slow but deliberate steps. In the manner of an executioner. The McKee's carriage was gone from its place and Robert silently thanked God that everybody had apparently gone into town.

"Looks like we missed them," he said. "I wasn't hankering for any more of your lessons anyway."

"Ain't my lessons but yours," she muttered. "And we ain't headed for town. There's well enough truth to face right here at home."

"Wonderful," Robert whispered sarcastically, bracing himself for whatever was to come. Lydia took him into the dead quiet house and led him slowly upstairs. Though no one was around, she seemed jittery– as if they had been sneaking into some forbidden area.

"Our business is upstairs," she whispered softly as she led them up to the guest room at the far end of the upper hall. Robert was a bit surprised when his mother opened the door and entered. She had always made him, or someone else, do the cleaning in that room. He had never asked her why she avoided it, but he couldn't recall ever seeing her go into it.

"Should I bring some clean linens?" he asked.

Lydia just shook her head. "We won't be needin' such today," she said, her eyes glowering as she silently and methodically surveyed the room. Robert's nerves were on edge now, for he had learned to be afraid whenever his mother got this quiet. She'd been acting oddly all morning and her normally strong face now looked strangely gaunt. For once, afraid. With pupils as dark as midnight, she drew a shaking hand from her apron and pointed across the room.

"What?" Robert asked. "What do you want me to do?"

"Nothing, don't do nothing," she replied. "Just look."

"At what?" he asked. The room looks just like it always does." His eyes flashed around in turn to every object in the room. From the silver candlesticks to the dusty pictures on the walls.

"You see anything? It may be nothing to you, but shut your eyes." she said.

"Don't see nothing," he said.

"Shut your eyes," she whispered. "Can you feel what's here? Memories are floating here. Nightmares and pain. The air is thick with 'em."

Robert usually liked games, but not this kind. "Don't be playing, Mama. I don't like guessin' games." He opened his eyes and just stared at her in frustration.

"Ain't no game," she said, "but venture a guess anyhow." As her eyes glanced down to the flowered bedspread, she crossed herself the way Episcopalians like to do when they're frightened or guilty. Whatever she was seeing here was invisible to him.

"Did somebody die here?" he asked.

"I 'spose that's one way to put it," she said.

"Old Miss Margaret?" he asked, referring to Henry's mother. "Is this where she passed?"

Nothing in Lydia's face offered any sign that he was getting warm. "Not that," she said. "Granny McKee gave up the ghost downstairs." His mother then raised up her hand, motioning across the room with her dark trembling fingers. She seemed to be pointing toward the bed – a large, four-posted affair with a fringed canopy. The bright lilies on the spread looked like the ones that grew in the cemetery beside Saint Helena's.

"You gotta talk to me," he said. "What happened here?"

Robert just stood for a long moment, preparing his heart for whatever words would come next. Beams of sunlight from the east window revealed that her face was lined with tears. Robert noticed that she had begun to stroke her hands over the embroidered silk flowers on the bedspread.

"I promised myself I would never speak of it and you'll never hear me speak of it again," she whispered. "Just stand where you are and I'll do my best to get it out."

Robert stood frozen in his steps, and Lydia turned away so he would not be able to see her eyes and her tears. Staring the back of her head, he listened for words that took forever to pierce the silence. He remembered that her hands moved first. With trembling gestures, she began to open her heart to the opposite wall of the room. Her anonymous audience. Her fingers moved nervously, as if they had been kneading some invisible handful of clay or dough. Even then, there were no words.

She was really scaring him now. Were these fidgeting hands the hands of a sculptor or a preacher? Perhaps a madwoman. He longed to hear her familiar voice, some cluster of wise words. But in this moment there was only awkward silence, so quiet he could hear her breathing.

"Tell me, Mama. What happened here?" he asked again, softer this time.

"You," she said, in a voice so low Robert could scarcely hear. "You happened here."

At that, she turned around to face him, her eyes swollen and now dripping with tears. She moved closer to him now, so close their faces almost touched. He could smell the saltiness of her tears.

"Henry had just got back from church," she said. "I didn't know what he was up to at first, but I can still recall the look on his face, that dizzy look he wears when he's had a few drinks. He grunted something 'bout the "master's prerogative." I had no idea what he meant, but I found out soon enough."

"God!" Robert said. "It happened here."

His mother just nodded in stunned silence. "At first I had the notion to fight back, and to this day I wish I had."

"He'd have killed you," was all that Robert could say.

Lydia nodded. "There are days I wish I'd have told Missy, or maybe George or Leena," she said. "But life had to go on somehow. It was hard to live with, and even harder to speak of. Henry McKee pretty much killed me in this room. Stole the very soul from me, I think. For twelve years these lilies on this bedspread have been my grave flowers."

Robert's own heart was now filling with a mixture of sadness and rage. "Damn his soul," he whispered. "Damn this wicked place."

"I done my best," she said, "but every time you said we were "pretty much free," it stuck like a dagger in my heart. That man raped me here. Did it right here on this pretty quilt. After that, he took me whenever he liked." His mother kept wiping her tears away, but there were always new ones flowing. "I remember it all," she said. "Every detail of every time. Every morning I wake to bright dreams of where you might go and every night I sweat in nightmares of where you came from."

Lydia took labored breaths as she searched her heart for more words, but it took her almost a minute to speak again. "A mother should never, have to tell her child of such a thing," she said. "Many times I've longed to put a torch to this room."

As his mother began to sob again, Robert slowly paced around the room, stepping carefully between the furniture, as if the headboard and chairs had been tombstones. Gazing down at the bed, he whispered softly. "Here." The images that flashed through his mind were ones no son should be forced to imagine. "A horror," he said. "A damnable horror." Unable to lift his eyes to look into those of his mother, he closed them and drew her frail body close to his.

"I died in this place," she said. Putting her finger to the sparse whiskers of his young chin, she raised his face to hers. As their eyes met, she said, "But from that death came my greatest joy. I lost every living piece of my soul that day – all my pride, all my tears, but then I got you. You're my soul now – the only little piece of pride that's left to me."

"You were wise to stay out this room," he said. "Things so painful; should be left behind."

"You know," she said. "I've done pretty good at blocking them from my mind, but I'm kept sad by the one thing I'm forced to see every day."

"Him?" Robert asked.

"Not him" she said. "You. It ain't your fault, but just looking at you brings sadness to my heart." Lydia then held up her black forearm and pressed it next to his. "Every mama dreams her little boy's skin will look just like hers. But God help me, when I see your skin, I don't see me, I see him. His skin, his eyes."

When I first held you in my arms, I thought, "The McKee's robbed me of my freedom and my family. Now they've even stole the blackness of my child.'"

Still seeing the sorrow in his mother's eyes, Robert said, "Pretty much free. I wish I'd just shut my stupid mouth. Let's get out of here. This may be where I started out, but God help me, if it's where I end up."

"Well," she said. "If there's anything I've learned, it's that life has to keep going on. The good and the bad. The Book says 'God works out everything for the good.'"

"I doubt that rape can ever be any kind of a good thing," he said.

"Good Book don't call any sin good," she said. "But God works out all things to some good purpose. Even evil. The Lord's an artist. He takes our darkest days and mixes them into his paint, and when he gets done, it all makes sense somehow. He uses our dark shadows to bring out the beauty of the colors."

"Well," said Robert, "right now I ain't seeing no pretty colors. Just darkness. Just pain."

Lydia could see large tears rolling down both of her son's cheeks. "You've got nice eyes," she said. "Life's too short to fill 'em up with tears. It's in those eyes of yours I remember that you're half white, and maybe that's a good thing."

"White blood, black blood. Blood don't make me any better or worse, Mama," he said.

"Maybe not," she said, "but maybe so. White blood don't give you a better soul or a mind, but what it might give you is a better chance. White blood may never make you the master's son, but it might open up some wee little crack in some closed door – a crack you might just slip through some day. Might give you some little chance at freedom, and in Beaufort South Carolina, having any kind of chance is a rare and precious thing. For a black man; any chance is gold."

"Pray I get such a chance," he said, "and that I'll have the sense to see it when it comes. Pray God gives me the courage to jump on it."

"I do pray... and I will pray," she whispered with a mother's smile. "I swear I'll pray for you every day until the day I die." In her dark smile that day, he saw love. And in her eyes he always remembered hope. Life went on.

Chapter 13
Last Straws

It rained the next Monday, so outside chores and trips to town had to be cancelled. All the McKee servants were kept busy with various inside tasks and a number of repairs that had been postponed. The kitchen floor needed to be scraped and re-waxed, and two upstairs doors needed hinges. While the slaves worked, the family decided it was a perfect day for story time to come early. To his delight, Robert was invited to forego his chores and sit in on the readings.

As part of her training, young Liddie was now being asked to do most of the reading at story time. With Henry, Miss Jane, Robert, and younger children circling her, Liddie continued her selections from the Book of Genesis.

Having already covered the chapters about the patriarchs, she picked up where she had left off – in the story of Joseph. This was one of Robert's favorite sections of the Bible. After recounting Joseph's early successes in Egypt, Liddie blushed visibly as she read the verses in Chapter 39, recounting how Potiphar's seductive wife cast her eyes on the muscular Joseph and said, "Lie with me."

William and Henry II, being younger children, didn't make much of these words, but Liddie and Robert were both visibly unnerved by the sexual reference. The adults were likewise made uncomfortable that such words had been spoken aloud in the presence of youngsters. 'Missus Potiphar was a hussy,' Robert thought to himself. She was ripping off Joseph's clothes.

The story wasn't new. of course, but to a boy entering the uncharted frontiers of puberty, any references to nakedness, seduction, or sin were of particular interest. Such prurient subjects, even in the scriptures, could never contain enough detail for him. Robert noted how Liddie's voice trembled a bit as she went on to describe how the false accusations of the temptress sent Joseph to prison. To Robert, the greatest surprise of the story was not that Joseph shunned the advances of Potiphar's wife. It was that such a thing could be included in the Holy Book of God.

With divine protection and a heavy dose of self-control, the reading was completed and all snickering restrained. In his heart, Robert felt an odd mixture of titillation and guilt. He silently prayed that Henry would not open the floor for any discussion of the tawdry text, as he sometimes did with other readings. Master might dabble in wickedness in town, but it was unlikely he would permit such things to be discussed in his own parlor.

But before Henry could say anything, a loud knock came at the front door. Robert felt great relief that an awkward discussion had been averted, but as it turned out, his relief was premature.

"What on earth?" asked Jane. "Who's walking about town in all this weather?" It didn't take long for the answer to come.

Two rain-soaked deputies had come to collect Robert. "We got a report that six panes of glass were knocked out of Grayson's Store yesterday. Some bread and peaches went missing and we've got one man that says your Robert did the deed. Other folks spotted your boy in town after curfew."

Henry, stunned, said nothing at first, and just turned toward Robert. Understanding that his master's silent stare was a question, Robert blurted out, "It wasn't me! I don't know what they're talking about!"

"We should be able to clear this up," Henry said. "The boy was here with me and my wife all morning until noon."

"The crime happened around three or four," deputy Robbins said. "Where was your boy?"

"I don't know," said Henry. "My wife and I were at our friend's until after dark." Both Henry and Jane looked at Robert, who now had a terrified look on his face. He had not been involved in the break-in, but he had been in town well past curfew.

Deputies Robbins and Withrow whispered to each other for a moment, then turned back to Robert. "Boy," they said, "What were your whereabouts yesterday afternoon? This ain't looking to go your way." Robert held his tongue, hoping for some kind of divine intervention.

"Robert? You've got to tell the truth." urged Henry. "You promised there would be no more of this."

Eventually, it was Liddie who broke the silence. "He was with me all afternoon," she said loudly. "The other children were playing upstairs. Robert and I were on the back porch and then in the yard. He didn't do anything wrong. He was here."

Robert was pleased that his friend would take up for him, but Liddie's gift for honesty got the best of her this time. She was a terrible liar. Her father recognized that this was pure fabrication, but he tried not to act shocked. "Liddie, are you quite sure? You don't need to protect Robert. We just want the truth."

"He was here," she insisted. "It had to be somebody else."

"Hmmm," said Withrow, "I'm still inclined to take him in for this. The boy's been nothin' but trouble." The deputy's eyes scanned every face in the family, and he seemed not to know what to do next. "It might suffice if you'd swear to keep him from leaving your place at any time," he finally said. "If you'll sign a paper to that effect, we might be willing to let him off the hook."

"And if not?" asked Henry. "Can there be some other solution?"

"No sir," said Withrow. "I think not."

"Then tell Ewell I'll come by tomorrow to sign," said Henry. "We have to put an end to this one way or another."

The deputies were well out of sight before anyone ventured to say a word. "I can't believe you let them do this," said an angry Liddie. "I'm ashamed to be part of this family!"

"Up to your room, young lady," said Jane. "I won't abide your talking to your father this way."

"I wasn't talking just to father," she said angrily. "Somebody had to say something." Liddie wanted to say more, but she knew it wouldn't do any good. Rolling her eyes back in her head, she showed her displeasure by making her way upstairs, walking as slowly as she'd ever walked in her twelve years of life.

Robert was angry and devastated, but understood when he was hopelessly licked. As he headed back to his quarters, his mind jumped uncontrollably from thought to thought. The prospect that he wouldn't see town again was outrageous, but even more unbearable was the thought that he might never again stand at the waterfront to watch the waves and the boats. They might as well banish him to everlasting hell. Robert resolved not to stand for it, but now was not the time for rage or action. But he made himself a solemn promise that that time would come.

The next morning, as usual, Robert and Lydia began working before sunup. Master wanted his breakfast early on Fridays – always busy days for him. As Robert was gathering the eggs, he wondered if he could get away with spitting in Henry's breakfast, or sprinkling in some dead flies he saw on the windowsill. "That man's the devil," he said to his mother. "Henry left me hanging in the wind."

"You best just shut that mouth of yours," Lydia advised. "I know you was in town after curfew again, and I 'spect you did what they said you did."

"No way I broke those windows, and I didn't steal nothing," he said.

"But you *were* in town, and you missed the slave bell again," she said. "Guilty is guilty."

"But I didn't do what they're saying," Robert replied. "They can't lock up people for something they didn't do."

"Oh, they do it all the time," she said. "And you ain't so innocent. God knows where you were after the slave bell, and so does everybody else I think. What you call innocent is just a being nabbed for the wrong crime, that's all."

"I still say Master's a devil," he said, "and so is that prissy Miss Jane. They're always trumpin' up lies against me." Just then, in the dark distance, a rooster crowed from a nearby yard.

"Well," his mother said, "Before you crown yourself a saint, you best shut your mouth and do your work. You have put the both of us in a sticky fix." As they spoke, a small figure emerged from the back door of the big house and quickly came their way. It was Liddie.

"I need words with you Robert," she said. "I rolled in fits all last night thinking about what they did to you." Lydia pretended to busy herself with the preparations for breakfast as Robert and Liddie walked to the other side of the yard to talk.

"You shouldn't be out here," he said. "Your folks are already pissin' red flames."

"But none of them even took up for you!" she said. "Even after I said you were with me all day. They as much as called both of us liars."

"I thank you, Liddie, but you are a liar, a bad one at that," Robert said. "And to be honest, I was lying too. You don't even know where I was or what I did!"

"Oh, I know, but I thought if I stuck up for you, they'd have to let you off," Liddie said. "They just figured I was lying to protect you."

"You were, of course," said Robert, "and I'm glad you tried."

"I'm afraid there's more," Liddie said. "It's what I came out to tell you. I was listening to my folks later on. They're talking about sending you off to Charleston. Papa's having to sell off some of his field slaves down there next month, and he plans to take you too. Robert, I'll likely never see you again."

Robert could scarcely believe what he was hearing. He had recoiled at the notion that he might be whipped and he'd prayed that he'd never have to spend time in the Beaufort jailhouse. Just two days ago, he had been outraged to learn he would no longer be permitted to leave the confines of the McKee property. And now, it appeared that his punishment would exceed all these.

He was about to be sold and sent away. He would no longer be a house servant to the McKees, but would likely be sent to sweat and perish somewhere in the fields. Robert Smalls might never see his home, his mother, or the seashore again, and for what? He had stolen nothing. He had murdered no one, nor had he broken any law of God. His only offense was to walk on a street after four o'clock in the afternoon. One ring from that damnable bell signaled the end of his sorry excuse for a life. Before it rang, he was free to walk, to sing, and to laugh on his way back to a comfortable home. But after it sounded, he was a condemned man, for all intents and purposes, a dead man.

"I'm sorry!" said young Liddie, the wisps of her red curls now dampened by the tears that were rolling down her cheeks. "This is my fault. I should have lied better. I was begging my parents all night, but they won't even listen."

"You did your best," said Robert. "This ain't your doing."

"I can't believe they could do this," she said. "God, I hate white people."

"It won't do to bellyache," he said. "Breaking curfew is a trifle, but if it wasn't that, it would be something else. Something was bound to happen. There are just too many fences. I was hoping I could run past 'em at some point."

"You're brave," she said. "Brave, but a bit untamed."

"I guess they'll do to me what they do with any beast," he said. Deep in thought, he saw the first hints of dawn outlining the wall of clouds in the east. He whispered to Liddie in a soft but solemn tone, "But I reckon a beast can strike back. A beast can get free."

"You should pray... and think, too," she said. "Don't do anything to make things worse. You won't hurt my father, will you?"

"No. You need not worry about that," he said. They hold all the cards in this game. I gotta wait and watch, but by God, I'll find me a way."

"A way to where?" she asked.

"Freedom maybe," he answered. "Somehow... freedom."

From the back door of the big house, the voice of Henry McKee boomed across the yard. "Elizabeth McKee!" he said. "You've defied your parents again!"

"I'm sorry, Robert," she whispered as she quickly got up. "Game's up, and I'm gotta pay the piper."

"But what did you do?" Robert asked.

"Nothing," she said as she left. "They forbade me to warn you. Father's headed your way and it may be bad. Very bad." Liddie ran around to the other side of the house, in full view of her father who was now marching across the yard toward Robert.

"You'd *better* run!" Henry shouted. "I'll deal with you shortly."

Robert braced himself, trying at the same time to appear nonchalant. He was about to say "Good morning, sir," but thought better of it. It was definitely not going to be a good morning, and there had been too much lying already.

"Come, Robert," Master said. "Sit down over there." Henry was pointing to the far end of the yard to the chopping table where hens were slaughtered. Whatever dark stains remained on it were now dry, but it was still a place only suitable for killing. "I must discuss something with you," Henry said.

Though Robert heard the word *discuss*, he immediately knew that his master was about to do most of the talking. He made Robert sit behind the bloody table on a single stool. Henry stood upright, occasionally pacing back and forth as if he had been an attorney arguing a case. Robert simply lowered his eyes and began to nod his head as his master's speech began.

"You've put all of us in a precarious situation," he said. Recognizing an ominous beginning, Robert began nodding his head faster than before. "You have continued to defy authority. To your mother, to us, and even to the laws of the land. More than once you have caused officers of the court to come with accusations, and up to this point, I have interposed myself to shield you from the punishment. Punishments that have rightly fallen upon you." Henry was moving back and forth in front of the table, but kept his face to Robert the whole time.

'I'm a dead man,' Robert thought to himself. 'Like the hens that have lost their heads on this table.'

"We've done our best, offering you every chance to repent," Henry said, "but in the end you've left us with no alternatives."

"In the end." Robert did not much like the sound of that.

"In two weeks you'll be sent to work in Charleston," Henry said. "This will get you away from Beaufort to a place where you can do no further damage to the reputation of this family. Our hope is that you might have a chance to start a new life in a new place. You'll have a clean slate, so to speak."

At first, Robert wasn't sure if he was supposed to answer, but Master Henry just stood there, staring at him in silence. Robert just continued to nod in agreement. It appeared that he was about to be auctioned off in the slave capital of the nation.

"Do you have anything to say for yourself?" Henry asked.

Stunned, Robert worked to measure his words. His blood was boiling at the thought that punishment had come down upon him for simply as flouting a curfew. He'd stepped over some meaningless and symbolic fence, but he knew better than to argue. For a slave, defiant words are serve much the same purpose as a grave-shovel.

"I'm very sorry for what I've done," he said, in his best humble voice. "I will do my best to learn from my mistakes."

"We'll do our best to make arrangement for your next steps." Henry said. "Are there questions?"

"Do you know to whom I will be sold?" he asked. "Will I labor in a house or in the fields?"

Henry seemed surprised at Robert's question. "No, no, neither," he said. "You are not to be sold at all. We've arranged for you to be employed at the Baines Hotel in Charleston. The wages you earn every month will be sent back here to me. You'll be quartered at the residence of Miss Jane's sister, Eliza Ancrum, but you will most certainly still belong to me."

No pardoned criminal has felt greater relief than Robert did at that moment. He would not languish and die in the cotton fields or be danced around on some auction block. Though he was about to leave everything and everyone he had known and loved, he would still belong to the family of his master, his father. He might still be able to see his mother, and his friend Liddie from time to time. It appeared his life was not over at all, in fact, it might just be beginning.

Chapter 14
The Dark Dream

Despite his initial fears, it became clear to Robert that he wasn't being sent to the fields, but to Charleston. By arrangement, he'd be contracted to work a job there with the earnings being sent back to his master Henry McKee.

Though the idea of leaving home terrified Robert, the plan seemed to be a more pleasant option than the punishment he had anticipated. All his life, he'd wrestled with two conflicting passions. He was blessed with an unquenchable thirst for the fresh and the new, but also cursed with a persistent dread of things unknown. Just as the open sea was his dream, it was also featured in his worst nightmares, and in his bed, Robert began to be visited with dreams most every night. At times he envisioned himself in far off places, but at other times he had nightmares of shipwrecks where he was being drowned under huge waves.

In the weeks before leaving Beaufort, Robert slept even more poorly than usual. At first, it was just that his mind wouldn't shut off at bedtime. Though he tried to relax, his thoughts were consumed with every detail of the upcoming transition. There was a growing list of things that needed to be done. What should be taken along, and what should he leave behind? These, and other worries crept in, and eventually filled his brain to the point that he thought his head might explode. Then, of course, there were the memories.

Though he was still very much a child, he had many treasured recollections of Beaufort, his home and his mother. Lydia would have to remain there to serve the McKees, and it pained Robert that she would now be all alone. She would have no one to help her, to hear her stories, and to share evenings with her in the little cottage behind the McKee house.

"You ain't likely to be needing these anymore," his mother said as she sorted through a box of little shirts and pants Robert had worn as a boy. "Missy brought these to me when you were just a tot," she said with a smile.

"Might be a bit tight now," he laughed. "Save 'em for your grandbabies." At this remark, Lydia just closed her mouth and gave him a wistful look.

"I doubt you'll be needing me in any case," she said.

"Don't be playin' on my heart strings," he said. "I'll always need you, Mama. It's gonna just kill me being so far away."

She nodded and smiled at him. "Here are some other things you might want," she said. She pointed over to a walking stick, a little printed American flag, and an out-of-round wood hoop that she had laid out for him. The stick had been given to him by old George, who'd passed it along to Robert after the bottom part of it cracked off. George had glued the old brass tip on the remaining end, making it just the right height for him at five. Though it was too short for him now, he had kept it by the bed for protection.

The little paper flag was one of those that had been handed out by the militiamen at Beaufort's Fourth of July parade back in 1848. Alongside a thousand other people, he had waved it proudly as the gray marching bands of the South Carolina Reserves marched by. The little flag's colors were faded now, but Robert could remember the crowds and the music as if it were yesterday.

The hoop was the only actual toy he had ever owned, a treasured gift received from Liddie McKee on his seventh birthday. As a child, he had been thrilled at the idea of rolling it on and on, but through the years, he had lost interest. Though he never figured on playing with it again, it always served to remind him of Liddie.

"I'm afraid I ain't sendin' you off with much," his mother said.

"Mama, you know I don't need a lot," he said. "And I suspect I will be back home soon enough."

"No," she said quietly. "If things go like usual, I may never see you again in this life." Lydia turned her face away from him, unable to look him in the eye. "There's always a sight more folks lightin' off from Beaufort than comin' back, you know."

Robert's eyes welled with tears as she said these words. "Don't even think that," he said, and though he shook his head in denial, he knew she might very well be true. "I'll do my best to get home, Mama. and if I don't come, it'll be because I got free. In any case, I'm gonna do you proud."

"It's a pretty big notion that you can do all that," she said. "Just do what you got to... and be God's man. That's enough." Reaching into her closet, she took out one of the two brooms she owned. "Keep this under your bed each night," she said. "The old folks say it'll keep the Boo Hag away. You'll sleep better, in any case." Robert just shook his head in doubt, but he took it anyway. He was more afraid of riling his mother than he was of any Boo Hag.

"And here," she said, "I'm wantin' this to be yours too." With tiny hands she was holding out her old King James Bible to him. Robert was stunned at first, but he took it, smiling and stroking the worn black leather of the old book.

"Mama, you can't give me this," he said, "Besides, neither one of us can read a lick anyhows."

"Uh, huh," she nodded. "But you know I've got a good bit of it committed to memory. You best keep it under your pillow so you can remember God... and me. I won't be in Charleston to watch over you. and I'll sleep better knowing the Lord is with you. His word will guard you." She moved closer to him and put her hands tightly on top of his. "Promise me you'll learn to read it for yourself before you die."

Robert could only bow his head, opening the Bible and burying his nose in the cleft of the old book's pages. Its dusty leather smelled of dust and time. "You're fixin' to break my heart, old woman," he said as a tear dropped onto the page, blurring the cheap ink where it made a spot in the text. "I suspect my Charleston work may keep me too busy to learn to read these scriptures," he said.

"Well," she said. "Do your best. Just make sure you don't find the time in some big town prison cell."

"Amen, Mama! I promise," he vowed. Years later, he always liked to open his Bible to page 377 where his tear left its blurry mark on the words of Psalm 25. "I think I'll leave the little cane and the play-hoop with you here," he said, drying his eyes. "I'll take the Bible and the flag. They'll help me trust the Lord and be strong."

"I'm glad you've carrying your chin up high again," she said. "I'm feel in my heart that somehow everything's gonna end up all right." Robert nodded his best manly nod, but there was deep sadness in his heart. With everything he set his eyes upon, it occurred to him that he might be seeing it for the last time.

Through his remaining days at the McKee's, he did his best to walk with a strong and resolute gait. He didn't want the home folks to worry. But though he stroked his newly-sprouting chin-whiskers and tried to speak in the deepest ranges of his now-changed voice, inside, he was filled with a storm of emotions. Out of that storm, the nightmares came.

His dreams were no longer the flights of whimsy that children have.

Bright images of thrill, discovery and adventure. Now his visions were more ominous and haunting dramas. And there was a particularly terrifying dream that began to return almost every night.

The dream was always the same. He was in the McKee's backyard, playing with the other slave children. There was laughter, running, and energetic games. Liddie and her brothers were there too, standing to the side with Missy Jane. Everyone was saying Robert's name over and over. "Come and play, Robert!" they shouted. "Robert, come here!"

His mother was at the other side of the yard, stooping over a steaming kettle of stew. In a song, she too kept repeating Robert's name, "Robert, Robert! Come and eat!"

As the chorus filled the air, Robert's eyes flashed all around. Everywhere around him he saw other faces – of old George, of Deputy Robbins, and of everyone he had ever known. In the distance, Henry McKee stood on the front gate in his familiar pose. His arm was pointing off down the road towards Charleston, and Henry, like the others, kept repeating Robert's name. Then the sound of thunder came, and along with it, fear.

Amidst all the echoing voices, there came whispers, quieter voices that could somehow be heard above all the shouts. It was Chief Ewell, a police bat in hand, saying "Bring him here." Deputy Withrow was next to him, holding chains shackles prepared for Robert's wrists. "Bring him here," they kept repeating.

Robert felt trapped like an animal headed for slaughter. He opened his mouth to scream, but no sound came. He could hear nothing except the shouts of all the people. From deep inside, he could feel the pounding thunder that was his own heart, and he remembered running. Running as fast as he could from his father, from deputies, and the others.

The road glowed hazy with a swirling fog as Robert put some distance between him and the others. The dark silhouette loomed in the blurry distance, just in front of the split rail fence that marked the edge of the property. It was an old black man, and he had his shirtless back to Robert. Robert was frightened, but found himself strangely drawn to the stocky figure up ahead. The man's wooly head and beard was stroked with streaks of gray. Every muscle on his dark and weathered body bore the deep scars of a slave. The man was looking off somewhere far beyond the fence.

As all the voices continued to roar in Robert's head, the black man raised his foot up to cross the rail fence. Turning his face, the old man motioned for Robert to follow. As Robert began, there was a loud clap of thunder and once again he heard the voices shouting, "Robert, Robert! Come and play!" The young ones were calling him back to join them in their games. Lydia was urging him to come home to eat whatever she had been cooking. Henry McKee, glaring at him with condemning eyes and a whip in his right hand, was coming after him. Miss Jane, far behind, was weeping and screaming, "No, no!" Robert wanted to go back.

It was the same dream every night, over and over, and sometimes in the dream he could see other people as well – the slave-sellers from the armory, the redheaded man from Clay Street. Once, Robert even saw the face of the Lord Jesus himself. Robert always reached a point where the voices became a rainstorm of shouts, but in the end, there was always one sound that rose to drown out the other voices that called for him. It was his own heart, booming in his head like cannon shots, thunder, or a big drum.

At the end of the vision, the scarred man always stepped over the fence and walked off into the darkness, with Robert right behind. Robert always lost his breath then, and awakened in a sweat, never sure whether he and the black man departed to glory or to destruction. As the dream fled, he was always left puzzling over the same question. Had Robert been right to follow the old man, or should he have run back to the McKees and play with the children? Drenched in perspiration, Robert felt spent, yet relieved whenever he awoke from the dream. But there was never any doubt that it would keep coming back again and again.

As his departure drew near, Robert's sleep was rarely long and never deep. At first he was only troubled by worried thoughts, but as time passed, it was more and more about the dream. Robert came to know every frightening detail of it, but the only person he ever told was his mother. It made him toss and turn and in time, its images even came to haunt his daytime thoughts. He had hoped his mother might give him comfort and perhaps even some interpretation of the vision.

"I just can't seem to shake this thing," he said.

Lydia feigned motherly calmness, but in her eyes he could see alarm. "Don't mean nothing," she said, but she could not bring herself to look him eye to eye. She seemed uncomfortable. Staring out the window of their little shack, she said, "It's just a dream, that's all. Let it go."

"But Mama," Robert said, "It won't let *me* go. It's like a storm inside my head. Comes to me over and over so it's got to mean something."

"It ain't nothing," she said. "Slave folks, young folks... all folks, they've been having dreams since way back when. It's just pictures in your mind, some from heaven, or sometimes hell. They don't hurt you none, they don't mean nothing, and you can't do nothing about them. Dreams just come sometime."

"Well I wish they'd just *go*," chuckled young Robert, comforted a bit by his mother's willingness to listen. He put his arms around her as they both shed a little tear the other didn't see.

"Don't fret over your fears," she said. "Mind your *words* and your *deeds*. Those are the only things you have any say-so about."

The next Wednesday, the third of September, was day for food shopping in town. Robert's mother was having trouble getting Robert to come with her until she promised to take him to the waterfront one last time. He wanted to go by himself, but he feared the constables might be eyeing him closely. Lydia walked with him most of the way, but then stood at a distance, allowing him to be alone with his thoughts.

Though the familiar scene of the boats and the water were perhaps more beautiful than ever, it did not bring him much joy today. He felt like a condemned man eating his last meal. Everything touched his young heart with sadness. As the wind filled the sails of one of the big clipper ships, he could hear the sad creak of her rigging as the masts strained forward. He could hear the fleeting sound of the sailors' singing as they departed for God knows where. Robert waved them farewell, though he knew no one saw him, and in the cries of the white gulls, he thought he heard "Goodbye."

By the time they left for Charleston the next morning, Robert was wondering if he would cry, but he didn't. He now felt only a cold, numb feeling in his heart, and he resolved to shed no more tears as long as he lived. Though he politely kissed his mother, he shunned her attempts to embrace him too closely. When she brought her lips near to his, he turned his now-whiskered cheek towards her, figuring it was time to grow up. At that moment, Lydia shed enough tears for both of them.

Robert and George helped load the carriage with the bags and supplies for Master Henry and their neighbor, Mister Brayton Fripp, who was also traveling with them. Behind their wagon walked a group of 25 field slaves Henry was taking to auction off in Charleston.

Beaufort's downtown businesses were just now coming to life but a number of busy town folk took time to stop and wave. Robert kept his eyes down, feeling no urge to say goodbye to this hell hole. If there were any pangs of sentimentality, they came when, instead of stopping on

Main Street, their entourage kept going to where the gravel road of town turned to dust to make its northern turn toward Charleston. Beaufort, and his childhood, would soon be far behind him. Only God knew what lay ahead.

Chapter 15
On the Turnpike

There were 76 blistering miles of red clay and gravel between them and their destination. As the McKee carriage made its way down the Charleston Turnpike, Robert was so free of duties that he permitted his mind to wander. Walled on either side by the picket-fence forests of scrub pines, he tried to fix his eyes on the road ahead, far out to where the ruler-straight road shrank to a pinpoint on the horizon. The land was uniformly flat and each mile of trees looked exactly like the one before.

There were, of course, sections where the trunks of the larger trees had been slashed. Below each bark-cut, the locals collected pine sap to make their turpentine and creosote. Robert figured there were dwellings at the end of the paths that branched off of the highway, but there were no living souls to be seen.

This miserable road seemed to have neither beginning nor end. Once out of Beaufort County, there were no more houses or barns to be seen. Unmarked by fences or posts, every identical, shadeless mile between Beaufort and Charleston sweltered under the gigantic sun that beat upon them without mercy. If this was not hell itself, it was at least its sweltering anteroom, and, like Hades, it went on everlastingly.

Possessed of the notion that the Baines Hotel would want Robert to have new shoes, Master Henry had bought him a new pair, his first that were not hand-me-downs. But by mid-morning, Robert's feet had already begun to throb. As noon approached, he could feel blisters forming where the stiff leather rubbed the more tender parts of his feet. It was only a matter of time before these swellings would burst, but there was nothing one could do. There would be no real rest for anyone until they reached Charleston, which had begun to linger in Robert's minds-eye like some sort of Promised Land. By afternoon, he wasn't craving milk and honey, he just wanted to find some shade and sip some water.

All through that first day's travel, Robert's fatigue and pain were only surpassed by his boredom. The masters riding inside the coach occupied themselves with idle discourse. Robert could overhear them chatting about politics, the stagnating economy, and speculating about all that must be done once they reached their destination.

The field slaves who walked behind them talked amongst themselves in their customary way, their Gullah language flowing between them like soft but unintelligible music. Robert liked to listen to it, but only occasionally did their words have any meaning to him. 'How wonderful it must be!' he thought. He deemed it a precious thing to be able to communicate in this way. So shrouded, unguarded, and mysterious to the masters! Their words of course, were mysterious to Robert as well.

His mother had done all she could to cultivate Robert's pride in his position as a house servant. To him she was always careful to speak only in proper English. She trained him in the manners that would endear him to the whites. This would win him better treatment. Unlike field workers and housemaids, he was taught to stand upright and to answer clearly. Lydia taught him to exude the proper balance of confidence and deference. He must look the masters in the eyes, alert enough to appear competent, but humble enough to stay out of trouble.

As a half-black, Robert was trained to walk the thin rail that lay between slaves and free men. And the space between the two was by no means wide. At times there seemed to be no space at all. Acting too smart could earn you a beating, but empty-mindedness might be just as likely to get you put out to chop cotton with the black blacks. "Black blacks." Even Robert's mother had at times used that odd and offensive designation. So what did that make Robert?

He certainly was not white, but at most times he was made aware that he wasn't all black either. As a mulatto, he was a mixture of two races but a full member of neither. Folks, mostly white folks, had coined a number of bizarre terms to designate race according to the percentage of African blood one possessed. One might be called a *quarteroon, octoroon,* or *quintroon.* Of course to his masters, Robert was simply classified to be a Negro and a slave. Whatever percentage of black blood he possessed was sufficient for this, for only one drop was enough to guarantee an insurmountable chasm would always exist between Robert and the world of free men.

Upon entering manhood, Robert's relationships with whites became increasingly tense. Some didn't like that his manner was so direct and his words weren't the simpler slang of a field slave. They also didn't like his eyes. To them, Robert's eyes seemed unusual and at times, sinister. Perhaps it was because he didn't cast them down when he was spoken to, and he also had the unnerving habit of looking a white man eye to eye. As for himself, Robert very much liked his eyes. His mother always said they were handsome. He noticed that some whites were made uncomfortable by the fact that his eyes bore a haunting resemblance to their own.

In the eyes of the blacks, Robert was viewed in a more complicated way. On the surface, the darker slaves might tell him he was lucky. House slaves, often being of lighter complexion, were generally given the better tasks. They worked in shade and pursued more interesting duties. They were even called *servants* rather than slaves. Unlike the darker Africans who were treated like expendable beasts, house-slaves dressed better, lived longer, and were addressed in polite words rather than with the crack of a whip. Field slaves would have envied him for the most part, but they could never relate to the particular challenges faced by the servants of higher rank.

House slaves may have avoided the back-breaking life of those in the fields, but they lived the life of Tantalus. Every day in the big house, they were cursed to sniff the sweetness of white people's freedom. Their domestic duties presented them with the continual enticement of things they could not have, or touch or taste. They could cook and bring the masters' bountiful dinners but could never savor more than a fingertip's taste. They made clean beds with turned-down sheets, but they themselves went home to a straw-stuffed tick that sometime crawled with lice. Slaves might feed table scraps to the masters' dogs on the back porch, but were forbidden to take even a napkinfull home to their own children.

Robert was reminded of all this on the turnpike, as he watched Master Henry recline in his comfortable carriage. Henry and Mister Fripp's political debate went long and became heated at times. Their discourse seemed to have ended at the point where Brayton Fripp fell sound asleep on his seat. Even this did not stop Henry from sneaking in a few last words.

A bit after that, Master Henry had tried to engage old George in some sort of conversation, but George rarely had much to say. Gray-headed now, George had been the McKee's driver for over 40 years, and a slave doesn't survive as a carriage driver by being mouthy. The carriage, and those that walked around it, soon found themselves traveling along in silence.

As he trudged through the rust-colored dust of the Turnpike, a clever notion began to enter Robert's mind. Without speaking a word, he made a point of walking closer to Henry McKee's window, feigning an ever-increasing limp in his right foot. This was not at all a difficult part to play, for Robert's blisters had been swelling all day.

"Are you all right, Robert?" Henry finally asked. "You seem to be favoring your right foot."

"Just blisters sir," he replied in his best martyr's voice. "Don't worry. They should burst soon enough." Robert's stoical grimace was worthy of high drama.

"I won't hear of it," Henry said. "George, stop the carriage and let Robert come up with me." George was not oblivious to Robert's game, but just rolled his eyes and stopped the horses long enough for Robert to step into the passenger compartment.

Robert had wanted to join Mister Fripp in napping, but his plans soon were thwarted as Henry initiated a conversation. Master had been looking for an opportunity to prepare Robert for his new life in Charleston.

"We know you'll do your best for Mister Reynolds," Henry said. "He'll make sure you're apprised of your schedule at the hotel and all your duties. He'll be sending your wages along to us at the end of each month. You needn't feel nervous at all, as we've told him what a good worker you are. Jane and I have no doubt that Reynolds will get his money's worth."

"I'll try to work hard, sir," Robert said, "and I'll be sure to give them no trouble."

"I hope you'll keep your eye on that aspect," Henry said. "You'll come to find that Charleston isn't Beaufort. There are a thousand more opportunities there, both for good, and for evil."

"I hope to make a good start," said Robert. "You said I'd have a clean slate, and I very much plan to keep it that way."

By now, Henry McKee was beginning to look as drowsy as Brayton Fripp, who was now snoring loudly on the other seat. "I think I'll catch some rest with my friend here," he said. "You might want to climb up and sit with George for a bit. He has family in Charleston and might provide some helpful knowledge to you." Robert liked the idea, and after a bit of climbing, perched himself on the seat next to George.

"So you've been to Charleston?" Robert asked.

"Quite a lot," George nodded. "Got a son who's lived there for 'bout twenty years now."

Robert waited for George to say something more, but no words came. For many minutes they just rode along past a few thousand more pine trees. Eventually, the silence became unbearable. "Master says you can tell me what to expect," Robert said. "Is Charleston much like home?"

George again, was slow to reply. "Like Beaufort, yes," he eventually said, "only worse...and better too, in some ways."

"Worse? Worse how?" Robert asked.

"Well, it's a big town, and the bigger the town, the badder the town," offered George. "Every man's a sinner, of course, but with more people comes more sin. They got plenty of thieves, got plenty of guns... and got bad women. Lots of 'em. Charleston's got more loose women than they've got thieves and guns. All of 'em fine-looking, and all of 'em bad as a devil's mistress."

"Do slaves have the curfew like back home?" Robert asked.

"Oh, yes," George said, "but ain't watched so careful as in Beaufort. Too many of us to watch. They got black folks walking all over everywhere. Not many deputies neither."

"So," Robert asked. "Tell me what's *better* than Beaufort?

"Money. Charleston's got money," George said. "Greenback dollars being tossed every which way. Folks carrying so much they're prone to spill it."

"Folks got money back home too," he said.

"No, ain't the same in Charleston," George said. "In Beaufort, rich folks got the money, and most been rich for so long they don't even crave to spend it. Up in Charleston all kinds of folks got money. Folks in the big houses have it, but so does most everybody else. Hell, even slaves got money in Charleston." George, usually frugal with words, gushed on and on, as he explained things to Robert.

It seemed that in Charleston, quite a few slaves also worked regular jobs on the side. Like Master had said, these slaves sent their wages home to their owners. But they could also pick up odd jobs after work, and keep any money they got. In this way, a slave was really just a slave during work hours. After that, he was free to earn his own dollars. Dollars that could be kept or spent.

It might be just a few coins at first, jingling money for his pockets. But in time, Robert would be able to save up coins and those coins would turn into dollars. So just as he belonged to Henry McKee, those saved up dollars would belong to Robert. It might be just pennies at first, but they would be his and his alone. That money could be spent well, or wasted foolishly, but whatever things Robert bought would belong to him. Such dollars might even be saved up and might someday grow into a sizeable sum. A slave could save, and if a slave could save, then he could buy.

George went on to tell of things even more shocking. In Charleston, lived a special class of black men who had even used money to purchase their wives, their children, or even themselves from their owners. Robert had heard about the free black men who lived up North, but he always assumed that black in the South always meant slave. But on the streets of Charleston there were thousands of Negro men and women who walked free – free to own homes and businesses, free to ride their own horses, and free to buy their own food. Some of these freedmen even owned their own slaves. It was almost too amazing to be believed.

"You ain't pulling my leg, are you, George?"

"No, sir," he said. "You'll see a whole lotta new things once you get set up in the big town."

"I'm going to find me some extra work, I will," Robert said. "The very first day!"

"Fine enough," said George. "But I'll tell you one thing. You best not be jingling your pocket money all over town. Charleston's got some hard-working thieves too. They'll slit your throat just like that, they will." George ran his finger across his neck like it was a blade. "Then they'll leave you in a puddle of blood on the street. Then they'll walk off with your jingle in their pocket."

Robert's young eyes were wide now. "Like you said, like Beaufort," said Robert, "but better... and worse."

By now, Robert began to feel excited and was impatient to get started in his new life. For good or ill, he was tickled with what he was hearing of this new place. As George urged the horses toward the big city, Robert slipped his hands into his empty pockets, imagining the feel of all the coins that would soon be there. He dreamed lavishly of Charleston until Henry and Fripp awakened from whatever dreams white masters dream.

Upon opening their eyes, the masters began to busy themselves with a small map they had brought with them. "We should be approaching Lanesboro," Henry began saying, but after two more hours they still saw nothing but scrub pine and dust. As they traversed the long stretches of straight road, night was coming and everyone was becoming urgent to rest. Lanesboro had to be somewhere just up ahead. Soon enough, they spied a few shacks and then a barn where some old folks told them the town was nearby.

"I've had about enough of this turnpike," Henry said. "I'm past ready for this day to be over." But their opportunity to rest would have to wait. At first they were just two dark specks on the horizon, but as they came closer, Robert could see it was two intimidating white men riding the biggest horses he had ever seen – black stallions 18 hands high with monstrous hooves. Robert reasoned that these were important men by the deferential way Masters Henry and Fripp spoke to them.

"Good evening gentlemen," Henry said. "We've been on the road since dawn; we're much relieved to see you both. I'm Henry McKee and this is Mister Brayton Fripp of Beaufort."

"We ain't your damned welcoming committee," said a giant man with a dark waxed mustache. He didn't even bother to identify himself. There was no badge on his blue shirt, but he brandished a long shotgun with a polished oak stock. "Who's in charge of this here party?" he asked.

"You're speaking to him," said Henry, feigning confidence, but Robert could see that Master was jittery.

"A simple *I am* would've sufficed," the big man said. "No need to get all fart-fancy with me." Henry said nothing to this, but watched carefully as the other marshal, a thin balding man, was looking their group over suspiciously. He was less formidable of stature, but wore twin pistols on his hips.

"Who's darkies are these?" the thin man asked. "We've had somebody poaching slaves of late. They up and stole twelve of mine last month."

"These are mine," replied Henry. "Those there," he said, pointing to Robert and George, "and the 25 others over yonder," he said, indicating the field workers, who had by this time begun to cluster themselves in fear.

"How many we got here?" asked the big mustached man.

"Like I said, there are twenty-seven in all," said Henry.

"Not you!" barked the big man. "I want my man count them." Henry just nodded and cast his eyes to the ground.

"It's twenty-seven, all right," said the deputy.

The big man now addressed Henry. "Is that field *and* house, or just field?" he asked.

"Twenty-five field slaves and two house slaves," Henry answered.

"You got paper on 'em?" asked the big mustached man. "I'll need to see documents before you can pass to town. Need proper paper, with the number and the *names*."

"Certainly," Henry said as he nervously fumbled through the small box stowed under the seat of his carriage. "Here." As Henry handed the documents to the big lawman, Robert was anxious to understand how white men could tell a stolen slave from an owned one.

"Round 'em up over here," commanded the big man. "Bunch 'em together so I can count 'em off."

Henry, weary of this uncomfortable interaction, almost asked to see the lawmen's badges, but thought better of it. Under the circumstances, he supposed that big black horses and guns would serve as good as a badge. "Do what the officers say," Henry McKee said.

Henry began waving his arms, attempting to herd the field slaves to his right, but his every move appeared tentative and awkward. "Please assemble to my right," he said. His soft words and gestures only seemed to puzzle the slaves, who staggered in confusion. They were used to whips, not words.

It occurred to Robert that Henry had never personally had any dealings with these field workers. Master tried some other commands, but the slaves didn't understand. Then he began to clap his hands at them, as if they had been a group of pet goats, but the slaves just huddled together where they were, all in one trembling bunch.

Seeing that Henry was without a foreman, the two officers jumped in to help. "Yaah!" they bellowed in the universal language of slave drivers. The small man picked up a stick, and with a stern face, struck one of the male slaves across the back. The he pointed to a spot beside the road. The whole group of 25 slaves immediately moved there and stood. As the two lawmen began to confer with one another, Henry walked over towards them to offer help.

"These two over here," he said, pointing to George and Robert, "They're my house servants." Pointing to his right, he added, "And those there, they're from the plantation." As Henry spoke, the field slaves began to pace back and forth a bit.

"Make 'em all sit down and quit their moving," the captain said. "Sit 'em all in one group. All together, for God's sake." Then, looking over at George and Robert, the big man motioned to them. "You house boys! Git yourselves over here with the rest," he barked.

As Robert and George made their way over to where the field slaves were, it surprised Robert that these lawmen made no distinction between him and the field workers. 'We're all the same in the eyes of these crackers. Despised black animals,' he thought to himself.

"Twenty-seven, all here," said the thin man.

"It's as I told you," said Henry. "So are we free to move along now?"

The big man just shook his head disapprovingly. "Names," he snarled. "I need the damn names." Calling Henry to his side, he looked down at the piece of paper. "I'm looking at this here list, and I want you to walk 'em up here, one by one. Say each name out loud, and I'm going to check them off. All twenty-seven, or we'll have us a problem."

As the house servants rose and slowly walked to pass before him, Henry calling each one by name. "George, he's our coachman, and this is Robert Smalls. He's a smart boy who serves in the house," he began, looking into each dark face as their eyes met. Robert couldn't remember seeing his master so shaken.

"Faster," the big man said. "Ain't needing no darky's life story." Henry nodded and continued calling the names. "George, check. Robert... check,"

As Henry spoke, the deputy made marks next to each name. "Who's next?" the thin man asked, but at this point there was a problem.

A sudden and uncomfortable silence came as the first of the darker and less familiar field slaves approached the Henry McKee. The first one, a small older woman with a yellow bandana approached and stood before her master, but he spoke no words. Stunned, and almost paralyzed by the sad gaze of her brown eyes, Henry turned his eyes away, and then down. "I'm sorry," he muttered, almost to himself. "These are my slaves, and I am familiar with most of the names on the list, but I confess I don't know which one is which. I'm sorry."

The big captain was in no mood for apologies. "Sorry won't do," he snarled. "They gotta match. The names and the faces."

The slaves, of course, said nothing. They did not even whisper among themselves, but huddled together in a sad, shabby huddle as the bickering white men began to point their fingers and argue. The two lawmen shook their heads, and conferred briefly with one another. Henry McKee paced nervously as the marshals walked back towards him, waving the piece of paper.

"We can't check them boxes unless we match names with Negroes," the big man said. "Just the number ain't enough. We need some clear checkmarks and we need 'em done proper."

Henry, now visibly bothered, turned to George for assistance. "You must help us with this, George," he said. "Stand next to me and tell me who each one of them is."

"I'm sorry sir, but I don't know 'em," said George. "Ain't set foot at Ashdale for long about thirty years. Don't know any of them. And Mister Henry, it's likely most of these slaves don't know the names writ down on that list. They mostly go by their Gullah names."

"Good Lord," Henry whispered, looking up to heaven, and then over to where the marshals were standing with folded arms. "This is a disaster!"

Seeing that his master was melting down and that the lawmen weren't going to let them go easily, Robert took the bull by the horns. Thinking fast, he said, "Sir, I know these folks from my time on Ladies' Island. Just hand me that list and I can match names to faces for you."

"Thank God," Henry said.

George closed his eyes and prayed as Robert took the paper and ran his finger down the page, pretending to read it. After looking over the group of slaves, he said, "It appears to me that they're all accounted for." Robert handed the list to the bald man and said, "Read me the first name, and I'll point them out."

"Lark Bilay," the man said. "Which one's Lark Bilay?"

"That one there's Lark," said Robert, pointing to a young woman. He motioned for her to pass by the man with the list. "Check her off!" he said. The bald man hesitated, just looking over for the big man's approval.

"Do what the boy says," the captain barked. "Make the mark."

After the woman passed by, Robert shouted, "Who's next?" As the names were called out one at a time, the parade of frightened black faces slowly streamed by. Robert stopped each one and looked them in the eye, even touch a few of them to turn their faces to the side. In short order, there were marks next to each name. It was an uneasy ten minutes, but once all the slaves were accounted for, Robert could finally breathe naturally again.

"I suppose everything here looks to be in order," the mustached man said, finally lowering his shotgun. "You can move along, but keep your slaves close. And keep your eyes open," he advised. "A man's property ain't safe in these parts."

"Most certainly, Sir," Henry said. "We'll bed in town tonight and be gone by morning."

The two men mounted their horses and rode off loudly toward Lanesboro. The big hooves slapped like cannon shots on the road as they left. It was never ascertained whether these two had been deputies, marshals, or what, but everyone felt a measure of relief as they and the black silhouettes of their stallions galloped out of sight. "The dark angels of death have passed us over," Robert said.

"You were our salvation tonight, Robert," said a relieved Henry McKee. "I'm amazed you could remember all those names. We owe you a debt of thanks."

"No problem, sir," Robert said. "I was glad to help."

As George and Robert mounted the carriage and urged the carriage towards town, Henry and Fripp went back into the coach for the remainder of today's journey. The sunset was quickly turning the western clouds a deep orange color as the road stretched out before them. A bit later, as darkness fell, old George finally leaned over and whispered a question to Robert.

"That was all pure bull," George said. "You can't read nothing and you didn't know a single one of them slaves by name, did you?"

"Well," Robert replied with a smile, "It ain't always about what you know. It's knowin' what the masters don't know. Ain't nobody ever gonna know the names of those slaves anyway," he said.

"You're a fox, you are. A wily black fox!" said George with a smile. "I 'spect you'll find yourself right at home on the evil streets of Charleston." They both let out a relieved chuckle as they went. "Watch out, big town."

If Robert felt any joy or satisfaction, it didn't linger. He couldn't put out of his mind the whole ritual of counting the slaves. Images of the incident began to turn over and over in his mind like some unresolved dream. He could still see the frightened faces of the slaves as the marshals shouted. Robert couldn't forget their sad and confused eyes when it became clear that their master had known none of them by name. Robert also kept seeing the names written on the paper and feeling a cold chill as the first marks were scratched next to his name and George's, forever defining them as a possession of Henry McKee. Just two of twenty-seven – slaves all.

For the rest of his life, Robert retained that image of himself – a twelve-year-old house boy with a white shirt and black trousers, herded into the same circle as 25 plantation workers. They may have spent their years separated by their duties, yet today they were united as slaves, counted as a single herd of beasts. Though Robert now knew that he would always be just one of them – a possession to be inventoried. The phrase "pretty much free," would never again pass his lips.

By the time he laid down to sleep that night, he was too tired to be angry anymore, and he decided to put all memories of the slave-counting behind him. For good or ill, he would arrive in his new hometown by sunset the next day. The Lord had brought him this far, and Robert woke the next morning with faith in his heart. His bright future was about to arrive.

Chapter 16

Charleston

Despite his optimism, Robert was nervous as the carriage drew near to Charleston. All through the three-day trip from Beaufort, he had wrestled with fears. The only mental image he had of the city was from an ink drawing of its slave auction which hung next to the window in John McKee's reading room.

As a child, he had first seen this portrayal of arguing slave brokers. They were pointing at a row of chained black slaves as a crowd of buyers looked on. For the past few weeks, Robert's mind had cultivated an increasingly ominous vision of the city – a crowded place where no one knew his origins, and where a boy like him might end up like one of those chained slaves in the picture – preyed upon, whipped, or altogether forgotten.

Back home, he had basked in the modest advantages of a half-white son; in Charleston it seemed possible that he might be assigned to suffer as just another field slave. Yes, he belonged to Henry McKee, but now, so far from Beaufort, he reasoned he could be snatched up and sold to just about anybody. This strange place held out the promise of a fresh start, of money, and the possibility of freedom one day. But it was also a place where the comfortable routines of the life he knew might be ripped from his hands. The very thought of Charleston made his heart race with both faith and fear.

Having traversed the sweltering miles from Beaufort, everyone in their party felt dirty and exhausted as they made their way down Meeting Street, where Henry was eager to check into the Mills House Hotel. This was known to be the finest hotel in town, many prominent people having slept there. Robert and old George had begun to take the McKee's luggage up to their quarters, but the uniformed servants at the hotel beat them to the task, quickly taking charge of the valises. Robert decided to walk up to the room anyway, wanting to appear helpful, but mostly desiring to take a look around.

Henry's stateroom was among the most beautiful rooms Robert had ever seen. The furniture appeared to have been brought over from the Old Country, with lots of well-varnished mahogany and shiny tabletops, every one unmarked by any gray rings left by cold tea glasses. This was quite a step above Beaufort. The canopied bed had a maroon silk spread, which almost glowed in the rays of the sun. An eight-foot wardrobe stood like an ornate monument on the far wall, flanked by still-life renditions of flowers.

Both opposite walls were not walls at all, but were dominated by big glass windows that presented breathtaking views on two sides of the suite. To his left, Robert could see all the way down Meeting Street, which teemed with people, horses, and wagons. The other window faced to the east, and from there, the whole seaward side of the Mills House had an impressive view of the Promenade and the Battery area. Robert could see a grove of huge old water oaks, perhaps 60 feet high, and beyond them, the blue waters of Charleston Harbor. Robert could not imagine himself being able to sleep at all in such a resplendent place.

Master Henry would be staying at the Mills House for a week. During his stay he would sell his slaves, secure Robert in his new job, and would pay his respects to Jane's sister, Eliza Ancrum, who stayed on East Bay Street. Miss Eliza was plainer looking than her sister, and was married to an unpleasant but rich man named James Hasell Ancrum. Robert would be sleeping in a small room above the family's stable.

Robert and George would have charge of the field slaves while they waited for Tuesday's auction. Some of them had been sold ahead of time and only needed to be delivered to their new owners. Master Henry would need most of a week to complete the paperwork on the sales and the auctions and to finalize the arrangements concerning Robert's employment at the Baines Hotel. Henry had been told he could secure temporary quarters for his slaves while they waited to be sold. His plan was for Robert to sleep there the first night or so, until his new quarters at the Ancrum's could be prepared.

Henry walked with Robert and George the two blocks from the Mills House to the slave quarters. There he paid for their lodging and signed a pass plaque so that Robert could roam the streets without him. "We won't be able to do much until Monday," Henry said. "I'll likely be occupied with business between now and then. I trust you and George can handle things."

"We'll know where to find you, sir," Robert said, "and you us." What folks called the City Slave Quarters was actually more like a large warehouse. Something near to a hundred slaves were lodged there, comfortable but chained. Most of Henry McKee's field slaves used the occasion to lie down and rest from their journey.

"It saddens my heart," Robert said, "But they don't act like condemned men. They seem at peace."

"They don't know where they are," George replied. "And they've got no notion of what's fixing to happen."

"Well, maybe it's for the best," Robert said. "Tuesday won't be a pleasant surprise, but it might be better to be surprised than to live in dread."

"I think I may join them for a nap for now," said George. "You can stroll the city a bit, if you like. It looks like a nice afternoon."

"I might just do that," Robert said, "and I'll be careful to stay out of trouble."

"Fine and dandy," said George, who smiled as he pulled his straw hat over his face to sleep.

Back out on the street, Robert marveled at the rows of large buildings and the myriad of people who flowed like colliding rivers through the canyons of the city. Workers scurried about, carrying boxes and packages, always chattering, and always seeming to be in a rush. A thousand boot heels clicked along the cobblestones, as cart wheels grinded and horse hooves clip-clopped.

Everywhere was heard a chorus of conversation, arguments, and even whistling. The boisterous music of town seemed to surround him and drowned out everything else. Though Robert could occasionally catch a glimpse of the waterfront out of the corner of his eye, the distant harbor and waves were rendered strangely silent. More than once, passersby nudged and brushed Robert as he stopped, stared, and took it all in. He was mesmerized.

"Hey boy, you best move your lazy black butt," said a stern voice that came from behind him. "Don't just stand there like a damn fool!"

Instinctively, Robert lowered his eyes and humbly blurted out what every black man in South Carolina was trained to say. "Sir! Yes, Sir!" Though he fully expected to hear further angry reprimands, the sound that came was something else. Laughter.

It began softly then grew into a loud guffaw. Robert turned to see a strange new face grinning at him, a black face as it turned out. Here was a smile was full of whimsy and welcome.

"For the life of me!" the young man said. "I do believe I was your master for a moment!" The lanky stranger then roared a laugh that was as big as the city and deep as any ocean. The man clapped his hands and then waved them in theatrical gestures toward Robert's face, as if he were putting a magician's spell on him.

"Since you're mine..." he said, pausing dramatically for effect, "I think I'll... set you free!" Then the young man twirled his long black fingers in Robert's direction. "Poof," he exclaimed, wizard-like. The strange fellow brought his face up so close that Robert could smell the boy's breath. "You're freee!" he squealed, then backed away, again laughing that hearty laugh.

Robert was stunned. He tried to think of some clever retort, but could only smile and try to catch his breath. As they looked into each other's eyes, they both began to grin, and then laughed uncontrollably. Robert, for good or ill, had found him a friend.

"The name's Risus Jefferson," the young man said elegantly, but don't call me that. "Master took to calling me Spider, and now everyone else does too. I've been watching you for a spell, and you appear to be green as a newborn pup, and just about as lost." Spider put his slender arm around Robert's shoulders as they turned to walk off together towards the waterfront.

"The Lord sent me down to be your guardian angel, my boy... sent here to save you from this most wicked city!" Spider chuckled. "Just keep close to me. As the Lord says, "I will never leave you nor forsake you" ... and this you will eventually and most certainly come to regret."

Robert had never in his life heard such a slathering fountain of words, but seeing that this Spider was a jovial soul, Robert ventured a little fun of his own. "I suspect from what I've seen so far, that you might not be an angel at all," he said.

"Oh, I'm an angel all right," Spider replied. "But there are many kinds of angels, you know."

"I'm Robert Smalls," he said, reaching out his hand.

"Nice to meet you, Mister Robert Smalls. Welcome to Charleston, young sir," Spider said, vigorously gripping and shaking Robert's hand. This charmer was talking a mile a minute. Robert had never seen anything like it, but he was delighted.

"But I must inform you that your greeting falls abysmally short of that required of a gentleman's slave in these parts," Spider said. "Look here. Your stance is wrong. Put your lazy feet together! Your eyes are wrong. Cast them down real humble-like... like a servant, not eye to eye like a master. And your words... dear God! Your words! They're all wrong too. The Robert Smalls part is fine, but you should always add, "If you please, sir," at the end. Then you have to say who you belong to, like "Robert Smalls, if you please, sir, a slave of ... a slave of ..." Spider again pushed his face up against Robert's. "A slave of...?"

"A slave of Henry McKee of Beaufort," Robert finally said. Never had he felt so plain and slow of speech.

Spider laughed and clapped his hands together in approval of Robert's brilliance. "Yes! The boy's got the hang of it now!" Spider said, adding, "I really like how you put in the "of Beaufort" part at the end. I do believe you've passed the test and qualified yourself."

"Qualified myself? For what?" Robert said.

"Oh my noble child!" Spider said. "You've now elevated yourself to the highest office in this fair city. You're now an authorized, certified, qualified Negro slave. A whipping boy of the finest sort! If you'll bend yourself over, I would be happy to give you your first whipping." They both laughed so much they could hardly stand up.

"Well," said Robert, almost breathless, "It's likely that I will need me a guardian angel or two... just to save me from *you*."

Spider began to rub his own sparse chin-whiskers, so few they could have been counted. "Now let's take us a long look at this," he pondered aloud. "If I'm an angel, which one of your shoulders shall I sit upon? If it be the right, then I will be your guide to the Promised Land. But maybe I'll sit myself down on the other shoulder. In this world every young man needs an angel with pretty white wings... but in Charleston, every young man needs him a dark angel too. A naughty one to sit up there on his left side!"

"And which one are you?" asked Robert, "...as if I need to ask."

After contemplating the question for a moment, Spider replied, "I suppose that depends on your mood, my boy. The Good Book says God lays out both life and death, right there before us. It's up to every young man to choose which angel's gonna roost on which shoulder at any given time."

"I think you're welcome to choose either shoulder for now," said Robert, looking deeply into Spider's dark eyes. "I'm going to need a friend. For good or ill, you'll be my guide and guardian."

"And may God have mercy on your soul!" Spider said. Taken aback by Robert's sincerity, Spider was now the one who was at a loss for words. After a moment of reflection, he could only add, "There's also a good possibility that God sent you to save me, but you'll likely need a miracle in that enterprise." Then together they commenced to stroll through the streets and alleys around Charleston's Battery and along the Promenade until the time Robert had to make his way back to his quarters.

"If you like," Spider said, "I'll come by here tomorrow morning at two bells to fetch you. If you wear a decent shirt, I'll show you how we can make us some spending money."

"Two bells?" he asked.

"Two bells is navy talk," Spider said. "Nine in the morning for sailors on the forenoon watch."

"But tomorrow's Sunday," Robert said. "There won't be any place to get work on the Sabbath."

"You must learn to trust me, my friend," Spider answered. "You're not in Beaufort anymore. Here in Deviltown, there ain't no regular clock time and there ain't no day of rest. Just dress up clean, and I'll explain things when I fetch you."

"I'll be ready," said Robert. As Spider turned his back and departed, there was a mixture of excitement and fear in Robert's heart. He was happy to find himself a friend so quickly, but he was a tad uneasy about what might be waiting on the other side of this newly-opened door. As it turned out, even after the subsequent years of friendship, Robert still had not begun to solve the puzzle that was Risus Jefferson.

His first master, Doyle Carson, had given him the name Risus after the ancient god of laughter. In 1849, Carson sold him to Roswell S. Ripley, who was then the General of the South Carolina Militia and later the port architect and commander of the Confederacy's second military district in Charleston. Spider served in General Ripley's house across from berth six on the South Wharf. A Swonga slave with shiny, blue-black skin, Spider was tall, lean, and an overflowing waterfall of energy and words. Quick-witted, he was fascinated with just about everything he saw, and he asked questions incessantly.

An afternoon with Spider could test your patience and make your ears tired, but despite the gushing of his unrelenting nonsense, Robert came to love Spider as his dearest friend and closest confidant. Spider was a devil, a confessor, and a circus clown all rolled into one. In Spider, Robert found the brother he had never had, a less reverent version of himself, and he sought out Spider whenever any off hours presented themselves or when any wayward impulses came upon him.

Bright and early that next morning, Spider found Robert standing in front of the Mills House Hotel, holding the voucher Henry McKee had given him so he could move freely around the city.

"You look as fine as a footman," said Spider. "Just right for church."

"Church? I thought you said we were going to earn money," said Robert.

"That I did," said Spider, "and I doubt anyone will ask you for that silly pass of yours. I've got us lined up to escort some white ladies to the First Presbyterian Church. Out of towners are always in need of a slave's services at the services. The two of them are waiting for us over at the King Street Hotel, each of them with a coin in hand."

"So they hired us to serve them for the day?" asked Robert.

"Well," said Spider. "We don't really have to do much serving. Mostly we're there to accompany them. In other words, to make them look like rich slave owners. Their job is to look snooty. We just have to walk them to church, wait outside, and do our best to look black."

"Sounds pretty easy," Robert chuckled. "What do they need us for?"

"For a lady to show up at the best church without a slave gives her the appearance of poverty, and that wouldn't do," he said. "These are Presbyterian ladies, come up from Savannah, they need to look like God's chosen ones. Blessed."

"Doesn't sound like very hard work to me," said Robert.

"Oh it's grueling enough," Spider replied. "Just wait 'till you hear the choir!"

"So do I appear all right for the job?" asked Robert, adjusting his white shirt.

"Perfect," said Spider. "And you've got that paler complexion the Calvinists seem to like. Classic upper class!"

"I'm only half black, you know," said Robert.

"That's good," smiled Spider. "I'm half black too, but I'm pretty sure the *other* half's black as well." They both did their best to stifle laughter as they walked up to the main lobby of the hotel.

As it turns out, the ladies were a mother and daughter, both small of frame and dressed for a fine occasion. "We have an entire hour to make our way to the church," the older one said. "Perhaps you boys could walk us through some interesting section of the city on our way."

"Yes, ma'am," said Spider. "Is there anything in particular you would like to see?"

"I've heard there are some wonderful clothing shops nearby," the daughter said. "There might be some dresses in the windows."

"Very well," Spider answered. "The garment district is close by and is fairly much on our way to First Church."

Neither Robert nor Spider uttered a word as they walked down

Market Street toward the center of town. The ladies commented about the beauty of the blooms in the window boxes of the bigger homes they passed. The mother endeavored to identify the various flowers by name. The daughter just listened at first, but then began to mention the names of a number of various young men she knew in Charleston, trying to ascertain whether any of them might be Presbyterian.

As they turned left on Wayne Street to walk past the shop windows, it was not clothing that caught their attention. The pavement stank of stale beer, urine, and last night's vomit. There were sleeping bodies – of mostly men and a few women – lying in the sidewalks outside these *establishments*. These folks were obviously the casualties of last night's revelries. Robert guided the ladies to step around one unconscious man who slumbered face down on the cobblestones. The man's dark trousers were pulled down in back, exposing his pale buttocks to greet the rays of the Sabbath dawn.

"Oh, dear God," the older woman said. "We seem to have made a poor choice to come this way. Mind your eyes, daughter."

"You did this on purpose," Robert whispered softly to Spider.

"I'm sorry, ladies," said Spider, feigning both shock and politeness. "I had no idea." Spider's sly smile let Robert know this seemingly inadvertent outrage had been entirely orchestrated. "Everyone in Charleston is not as pious as you fine ladies," he said. "These drunks here are all Catholics, I suspect."

The remaining two blocks of shop windows were mostly ignored as they sped on their way to worship. "Wait out here for us," said the mother as the women entered the sanctuary. "If you stand close to the door, you might be able to hear the service."

"That would be a great blessing," said Spider. "We'll await your return when the service is done."

Unlike the Baptist and Methodist churches, Presbyterians did not permit slaves a place to sit in the rear balconies of their sanctuaries. They did however, have the sincere hope that the truths of their religion might be overheard by any foreordained Africans who be blessed enough to be standing on the front steps. In just a few minutes, a single low blast from the church organ called the congregation to worship. Two hundred white souls were about to knock upon heaven's great front door.

Chapter 17
Stained Glass Words

Robert was well-acquainted with white worship services. During his last few years in Beaufort, Robert had become accustomed to sitting outside Saint Helena's Episcopal sanctuary, as the McKee's worshipped inside, and this Sunday's experience was no different. The side windows and the big front doors were left open to allow fresh breezes to refresh those inside. Standing with Spider, Robert was close enough hear the songs, sermons, and prayers of the Presbyterians, and this was not altogether a good thing.

Their services represented to him the purest distillation of Southern pretense. Freshly cleansed from their Saturday baths, Charleston's most prominent citizens gathered to present themselves to God and to each other, fashionably clad in pastel dresses, starched collars, and the best pious face each one could muster.

Protestant sermons were as dismal as they were meticulous. Surmounting the common vernacular, each stained-glass word was delivered in an affected British accent. Sitting through these homilies was intended to purge listeners of their sins and to refresh them spiritually. Robert considered them uplifting only in the sense that everyone seemed pleased when they were over.

Interspersed within this labyrinth of words was their bland music. Episcopal and Presbyterian hymns were generally classical in style – most often directed to the Majestic Jehovah rather than his more amiable human Son, who seemed to be the centerpiece of the less affluent churches of the Methodists and Baptists.

The liturgy was orchestrated to inspire congregants toward greater faith and piety, but rarely produced much of either. The only thing they excelled in was their length. Robert had been told that as a rule, white church services went on longer than slave church, but he reasoned that they just *seemed* longer. This morning's service was no different.

Listening to the choir's extended presentation of one grandiose hymn, Spider leaned over to ask, "Where did they get this poison?"

"From some dead German," Robert ventured. "All the long, depressing hymns are German."

Spider just nodded. "Well, they inspire me to live a better life," he said.

Robert was a bit taken aback. "How on earth can these dirges possibly inspire anyone to live better?"

"Well," Spider said, "Because this must certainly be what the choir of hell sounds like. If I mend my ways, maybe I won't be sent down there to hear it!"

Robert clenched his teeth to forestall laughter. "Eternal punishment," he whispered. They both grinned and did their best to gasp for air.

Of course the blacks also had their own churches, and these seemed more enjoyable than anything the whites had to offer. Slave gatherings in no way resembled the scripted tedium of the Protestant services. Here the Africans could, for perhaps the only time in their week, be themselves.

Unencumbered by hymnbooks or Bibles, they were free to clap their hands, or to wave them about in praise. There was dancing, shouting, and even crying as they blessed God from the deepest depth of their souls. If there were words, they were simple and heartfelt. They sang of the love of Jesus, the sufferings of life, and almost always about a wonderful Promised Land beyond this world.

More often than not, there were interludes of inarticulate humming – an almost visceral moaning. Bereft of words or rhetoric, the blending of their voices rose as a singular, palpable chorus – sometimes quiet, but sometimes loud. From afar, their singing was fascinating, but also frightening to the whites. In tuneless and oddly beautiful strains, it whispered of their African roots, their present trials, and their future glory. For most of them, there would almost certainly be no glory here.

Robert had become increasingly nervous at Slave Church. In the cracks between the words and stanzas of old hymns, one could hear the undeniable and rising lament of the oppressed. Their cry was for justice and for freedom, and the message was unmistakable. Robert feared that the masters might suddenly understand what they were hearing.

These sermons, moans, and prayers proclaimed a clear message of hope and freedom, but most dangerous of all, they proclaimed discontent. Was it possible that the whites could miss this bubbling cauldron of unrest? Were the slaves' urgency for Freedom Land so hard to see? Generations of masters had lived in Paradise, but only as blind men. Robert reasoned, and often hoped, that something like a day of reckoning was approaching, as Sunday after Sunday they sang "How Long, How Long?"

Robert had often asked himself the same question about freedom, but right now he was more irked by the length of the church service. He was eventually bored and restless enough to speak. "Spider, you promised me this would be easy money," he whispered.

"If you remember," said Spider. "I just said money. No sane man ever said sitting through a Presbyterian service was easy. If you want a better time, let's escort Baptist ladies next time. Baptists don't pay as well, but they've got a piano with a pretty good twinkle to it. Got hand-clapping too."

"So we either get money, or rhythm, but we can't have both," Robert said.

"Life's full of hard choices," Spider said. "Welcome to Charleston!"

Despite their complaining, Robert and Spider continued to earn extra money escorting out of towners to church almost every week. Mostly this was the *First Prezby* downtown, because it was big, and was the shortest walk from the hotels. Sometimes it was Saint Michael's Episcopal. White church may have been depressing, but the money was good, and no one's going to pay you to have a good time.

It helped Robert to think of white churches as his universities. The sermons might not tell him much about God, but they taught him various things he was pleased to know. At least he could learn new words every Sunday or catch a cat nap if he could find a sitting place somewhere.

Spider, on the other hand, couldn't stomach the idea of formal education. He did his best to think of white churches as a source of amusement. This didn't sit well with Robert. He could have understood if Spider was simply a hell-bound atheist, for there were plenty of people who denied God's existence. But for Spider, religion was sport. He didn't dare to deny God, for true sacrilege requires God. What joy could there be in ridiculing the emperor's new clothes if there was no emperor? Spider Jefferson didn't hate going to church, he loved it.

He laughed aloud at every odd hat, every strange face, and every plump parishioner that came into view. To him, these services were not a sacred worship. Instead, it was a circus – a big-top spectacle where the preacher was the ringmaster, the choir was the calliope, and the communicants were trained animals, all bowing and kneeling simultaneously on command. It was an object of derision.

If Spider did occasionally listen to the homilies, it was only to find humor or fault. He made obscene jokes about God and Bible characters. He ridiculed ideas that aspired in any way to be noble or sublime. Spider pounced readily upon any story that seemed to him fantastic or contradictory in any way.

Whenever Robert made the mistake of standing too close to Spider on the church steps, there would be an under-the-breath dialog going on all during the preaching. Back in slave church, Robert used to say "Hallelujah," but standing with Spider outside white church he mostly just said "Hush." The reverend might say, "God was in the beginning," and Spider would mutter something like, "How does the preacher know? Was *he* there?" If the minister would say "We know God was in the beginning because it's written in the Bible," Spider would whisper to Robert, "Where did they get the paper to write it on?" To Robert, all such speculations were an affront to religion. For Spider, speculations were his religion.

Talking in church was bad enough, but Spider would often chatter all the way home, asking obtuse questions, but mostly blaspheming religion and things spiritual. Robert knew better than to venture an answer. Answering Spider was like pouring oil on a fire. Besides, Robert knew it was the questions that Spider enjoyed, not the answers.

"I'm hard pressed to believe in something I ain't seen," said Spider.

Robert just shook his head and smiled. "Brother," he said, "That's the whole point of religion. You've gotta have faith."

"Well, right there I think you put your finger on the biggest error of all religions," Spider said.

"And that is..." asked Robert.

"The problem with most religions," said Spider, "is that there is no God." He smiled like a boy who had just won a game of checkers.

"You ain't gonna shake my faith," Robert said, "so you best not try. I don't have to see God to know he's always right there beside me. Always been there. Scripture says he doesn't call me a servant but calls me his friend."

"Friend?" asked Rom. White preachers told you that. But if a man treated his friends like God treats us, he probably wouldn't *have* no friends. God lets us go hungry, lets us get sick, and lets us strut around here for a few years 'till he takes a notion to kill us like a dinner-hen. If a man did such things, he wouldn't have him no friends at all. Of course some men might flock to him if he was famous, rich, which I guess is how it is with God. But them folks still wouldn't like him much."

Robert had figured out a long time ago that it was useless to argue with his dark angel. Spider simply enjoyed it too much. But he couldn't allow Spider to win this one. "No, God guides my life every day." said Robert.

"Guided you all the way to a slave life!" Spider said. "Got you sent off from your home and mama."

"Well, I still believe he's got some plan to work everything out," Robert replied. "The Lord never closes one door without opening another."

"Or slamming it on your hand," Spider laughed, just waiting to throw cold water on the next spark of faith. Robert was angry now, but decided to just keep his mouth shut and pray for Spider. Any reasons he gave would be pearls before swine.

Robert was not at all shaken by Spider's nonsense. He was comfortable letting mysteries be mysteries. A man could read every book in the world and seek wisdom from dawn to dusk, but no man could ever plumb the ways of the Almighty. And even if you could discern God's plan, it was likely the Lord would see you coming. Then he'd change his plan just to surprise you. Just so you would have to live by faith. His mama had always said that good Christians have to "wait upon the Lord." Good Christians wait a lot, and this was the hardest part for Robert.

Robert was a doer. His religion was less about theory and more about action. If Spider asked why God made hell, Robert would be more interested in how to avoid it. Spider wondered why God let whites rule the world, Robert was more concerned with finding the quickest path to get free of them. In the end, where Spider was enamored with talking, Robert worshipped at the altar of action.

Winning over Spider Jefferson's soul became one of Robert's greatest hopes, but he often feared that Spider had the same goal in mind for him. Robert figured the game might continue for some years, but the Good Lord was sitting on his throne... holding all the aces. This was just the beginning of a long fight and a deep friendship.

A week after arriving in Charleston came a day for sad goodbyes. Having auctioned off the last of the field slaves, Henry McKee wanted to see Robert one more time before they left town. Before he headed home to Beaufort, Master took it upon himself to do what he so often did. He made a speech. This time his topic was diligence and young

Robert was the sole member of his audience. His boy was about to begin his employment at Charleston's Baines Hotel, and he needed one last talking-to. Even at twelve, Robert had learned how to feign attention while thinking about other things. But on this occasion, there were no other things Robert cared about more than doing well at this new job. For once in his adolescent life, he actually listened.

"You only get one chance to make a good first impression," Henry said. "At the hotel there will be many employees buzzing like busy bees, and you must aspire to rise above them all. If you watch the staff carefully, and if you imitate them, you'll do well. If you can look the part, you'll passably act the part," he said. Henry was pleased with the way Robert's new white shirt fitted him and how grown up he looked in his red bow tie.

"You present yourself well, son," he said. "You must always do your best to make us proud."

"Thank, you, sir," Robert said, sensing that their time together was ending. "I doubt very much if we will see much of each other in the years to come. Give my best to Miss Jane, to Liddie, and to the others."

"We'll miss you, Robert," Henry said. "You've always given us good service."

"I was pleased to do it," he said.

Taking a small wrapped package from the carriage, Henry handed it to Robert. "Here's something from Elizabeth." It was a volume of poems from Shelley and Keats. Robert had always enjoyed it when sections of this particular book were read at story time. "She asked me to encourage you to learn to read it as your new life unfolds."

"It will be a formidable challenge, but I reckon it gives me a star to strive for," Robert said. "Please thank her for me."

"I think we may all have some sizeable challenges ahead," Henry said. "But I'm confident we will see each other again in better times."

"And such days will come, sir," Robert replied. "Much better days, I think."

Robert was excited about the opportunity to succeed in the world of working men, but at Henry's words, he now felt afraid. 'Buzzing like bees?' he thought. Hotel work would be no party; it was a contest. The Baines would be no Paradise, but rather Judgment Day. Upon their arrival in Charleston, Robert had witnessed the buzzing of such bees. The uniformed bellmen at the Mills House Hotel had swarmed around the McKee luggage. In a flash, they had taken it upstairs, before either he or George could even step down from the carriage.

'I'm just a greenhorn,' Robert thought to himself. 'I'll have to work like a madman just to be noticed.

"If you watch the other workers carefully and imitate them, you'll do well," Henry had said. Robert resolved to throw himself headlong into his new tasks with unflagging energy and a thirst for excellence. If there were to be tests, they would likely come the next morning.

As the McKee's carriage rolled out of sight, Robert had the clear sense that better days had already arrived. With a good God above him, and his friend Spider beside him, he would soon feel the rattle of coins in his pocket. Robert was ready to take on whatever challenges the glorious city of Charleston might provide. Tomorrow would bring his first day at his first job, and the sky was the limit.

Robert had asked Missy Ancrum to make sure he woke up on time. His quarters above the horse stable had no east-facing windows, and Robert would not be awakened by the first beams of sunrise.

"Trust me, young man," she had said. "You will need no assistance from me."

If these assurances were intended to provide comfort and confidence, they failed. He was puzzled. Robert spent all of Sunday night drowning in a fitful storm of frayed nerves and worried thoughts. He hardly slept at all. 'I mustn't be late,' he kept telling himself. Through his open window, he could hear the chimes of the carillon at First Church, as hourly it measured his sleeplessness. Even after he managed to fall asleep, Robert flashed back to the same horrifying dream that had tormented him in Beaufort, the vision of the old black man. It was three in the morning before he got any rest to speak of, being finally overcome by fatigue.

The sky was still ink black at five when he got his wakeup call. Two calls to be exact. The long building next door to the Ancrum's turned out to be the barracks of the North Charleston contingent of South Carolina's Home Guard. This particular squad of militia was blessed with a number of trained musicians, a number of whom were skilled trumpeters. Loud trumpeters. Rather than rotate their duty assignments, these men liked to play reveille in unison, sometimes three horn harmony. At their first flourish, Robert almost hit his head on the low rafters of the stable loft.

His eyes thus being opened, Robert propped himself up in the darkness to listen to the completion of the buglers fanfare. He was talking a deep breath to wake himself when suddenly, from just behind his head, there came another blast. It was Cornwallis, the Ancrum's monstrous Virginia rooster, who had roosted in the stable loft for the past year or so. As it turned out, the big bird's perch was located just behind Robert's headboard. Folks in the big house were pleased that Cornwallis' daily crowing could be clearly heard from where they slept, a hundred feet away. The cock's song was less soothing at point blank range, where Robert slept. It seems he had traveled to Charleston to take up residence in what was something like a bell tower, and his head seemed to be positioned inside the bell.

It was time to start his workday, but what Robert felt was nothing like the energy of a 'buzzing bee.' He nonetheless resolved to push through his fatigue and work hard that day. All the way to work, he prayed that God might give him a diligent heart and a lively body. His first day at the Baines needed to be a victorious one.

Mister Warren Reynolds had told him to arrive by seven, but Robert made sure he arrived a few minutes early. He wanted to impress them with both his eagerness and his punctuality, but when he got there, no one was there to notice either one. The entrance was locked and there were no employees or supervisors to be seen anywhere. Through the plate glass of the front window, he could see most of the lobby, which remained in darkness. Robert could see an open-mouthed night watchman lying back in his chair, sleeping like a baby. Another man, a bespectacled clerk at the desk was also asleep, his cheek resting upon the guestbook.

Robert was learning the first of many lessons he would pick up while working at the Planter Hotel. One didn't need to fret about getting to work before everyone else – that race was an easy one to win. And as the activities of the work day unfolded, Robert discovered that the buzzing bees at the Baines were neither as fast nor as busy as those at the Mills House. But he resolved not to let this slow him in the least.

He pounced upon his duties at once – sweeping floors, cleaning windows, and straightening the furniture. 'This is easy,' he thought, but it wasn't long before he began to get his first criticism.

"Slow down," the front bellman said. "Ain't no masters to whip you here. Leave a bit of work for the rest of us."

"I aim to keep this job," said Robert politely.

"Well, son," the bellman said, "They're only paying you fifteen dollars a month, try to act like it. Hold back a little."

Up to then, Robert had no idea what salary he made. Since all of it went to the McKees, the amount really didn't matter to him. He just wanted Master Henry to get his share so Robert would be clear to add more from elsewhere. It wouldn't be long before he found such opportunities.

Chapter 18
The Queen

Mister Warren Reynolds was the daytime king of the front desk of the Baines Hotel on Market Street, and his son Joshua similarly ruled the evening hours. Every management question had to go through whichever one was on duty. Both father and son were slight of build and were similarly ugly men with conspicuous noses. For this reason, each was easily mistaken for the other, and most people didn't attempt to differentiate between the two. Everyone simply referred to both father and son as 'Reynolds.'

Jacob Broller, the hotel's owner made weekly rounds to check on things, but mostly to gather his profits. The various stewards, coachmen, and maids were always feigning urgency, shouting as they hustled to and fro, but generally slack in discharging their appointed duties. Young Robert soon came to ignore the impatient buzz of this hive, but he soon realized that there was one voice that ruled over all the others in the day-to-day workings of the Baines. Her name was Hannah Jones. Behind her back, folks called her Queen Hannah because she always carried herself with the assurance of a monarch.

When all was well, she was the picture of pleasantness, but when any detail fell short of perfection, Hannah had strong words to say, and things were quickly set to right. Her services were much-prized by management and much-feared by hotel personnel. Even the guests were careful to address her respectfully.

It was said that in her youth, Hannah had worked alongside her family in the rice fields of Summerville. Her owner, Samuel Kingman, taking note of her industry and strong-mindedness, had lent her services to the Baines Hotel in her eleventh year. For the next eighteen years she earned wages as a maid, and this was the title she still held when Robert met her. But after so many years at the hotel, Miss Hannah Jones had seized powers which exceeded those of any maid he had ever seen – or any that had ever lived. She fine-tuned the work of every cleaning girl, porter, and sweep in the hotel to a point where even white staff members deferred to her highness.

Since his first day at the hotel, Robert had never once seen Hannah soil her own hands with any menial labors, but she made sure things were done with excellence. Unlike most slaves, she could read and write. She watched, listened, and always spoke with appropriate and concise wisdom, with rarely an unneeded word and *never* an apology. Hotel guests and residents, wanting to communicate special requests to the staff, always went through Hannah. Even day manager Warren Reynolds, was reluctant to assign a particular room to new arrivals without first consulting her. If there was any unanswered question, one only needed to ask Miss Hannah, and the answer was always the correct one. She was, all in all, a formidable woman.

Though she was now neither young nor remarkably beautiful, Hannah, in her own way, glowed. With the manner and mind of one in charge, she seemed unstoppable, and this attracted Robert to her immediately. From the first weeks at the Baines, Robert found every possible opportunity to put himself near Hannah. Avoiding conversation, he would glance at her out of the corner of his eye so as not to be noticed, watching how she worked, and listeing whenever she spoke. He was delighted that she read the *Charleston Mercury* each morning, having received instruction at the secret Episcopal slave school before it was shut down in 1850. Hannah was *somebody,* and Robert reasoned he could learn a lot from her.

A dark-skinned woman, she had round cheeks under piercing brown eyes. She was sturdy of build, and her face could be fearsome at times. But it could also be warmly disarming when she chose to flash an occasional smile. You had to do something really special to get one of those smiles. Hannah could speak with the precise command of a mother, but she could occasionally brighten a room with her quick wit. When delighted, her laughter was musical, like that of a young girl.

Despite Hannah's constant and firm correction, Robert could detect a growing kindness in her manner toward him, even though she was stingy with words of praise. From his first days at the hotel, Hannah made a point not to speak to him directly, always instructing others to "Tell Robert this," or "Have Robert do that." As a novice, he made many mistakes, and Hannah seemed to delight herself in pointing out every one.

On his fifth day there, Mister Reynolds had met Robert coming up the path outside the stables and had asked him to water the horses before he began his work inside. By the time Robert reported for duty inside, he was ten minutes late. Though he owned no timepiece, he could clearly tell he had arrived late by the widened pupils of Miss Hannah's eyes. This time she would speak to him directly.

"You best move your slothful backside, moonlight boy!" she said. "You think you're somebody around here? I've a mind to send you back to chop cane on Hilton Head!" For an instant, Robert considered offering an explanation, but he thought it best to remain quiet, hoping Reynolds might explain what had happened. It was possible Miss Hannah might soften towards him once she was told the truth about why he was late, but no truth or mercy ever came.

He saw her write something down in the little leather book she carried, and that same day, she appointed Robert to empty and clean all the hotel's chamber pots and cuspidors. Though disgusted and humiliated, Robert pounced upon his assignment eagerly, intending to seek some future opportunity to get on Miss Hannah's good side.

For the next months, Robert's respect for Hannah continued to increase as he saw the way she reveled in her leadership role at the hotel. He had often seen white men throw their weight around in the bluster of anger, but he marveled at how Hannah exercised power with such elegant and measured grace. Right words and good plans flowed from her naturally, as if they were something she was born to supply to God's world. Robert had never seen such assuredness in a woman and certainly not in a slave woman. Hannah Jones carried herself like no man's slave.

Their first opportunity for a deeper connection came a few years later, in the autumn of 1855. Robert was walking past an open door on the hotel's second floor when he heard the faint sounds of a woman crying. Room 201 was dark, save for a thin crack of sunlight that slid in through the drawn curtains. It ran in a bright splinter across the room and up a woman's back and onto the letter she was holding on her lap. It was Hannah.

As she turned to face him, her eyes did not pierce him with their usual strength, but had a wet-eyed sadness that could not be hidden. "I didn't call for you, Robert," she said. "Get the hell out of here and be about your chores."

"Are you all right?" he asked softly. "Ain't like you to weep so." Robert gently put his hand on her arm, which was shivering in sadness. It was the first time he had touched her and he always remembered this moment. "Tell me what's wrong," he whispered. "I ain't leaving."

With his emotions aroused, and her demeanor relaxed, he for the first time sensed a connection between the two of them. In the brief silence that followed, she and Robert now approached each other, if not as friends, at least as something closer to equals. She had a torn envelope in one hand, and she held up a small piece of note paper she had in the other. He feared she might ask him to read what was written on the paper, so he quickly threw the question back to her. "What is it?" he asked.

Hannah's brow wrinkled and for a long moment her lips uttered nothing, but only shivered nervously. "This letter here says my mama's dead," she finally said. "Been gone since Christmas."

"I'm sorry," he said. He tried to look her in the eyes, but Hannah intentionally focused on something out the front window.

"She'd been asking for me to come home, but I've been too busy here to go down to Savannah. Mama's up and gone. Died all alone." Robert drew near to comfort her, but could find no words, and Hannah didn't want or need any words right now anyway. Heads pressed together, their tears ran down their faces and mingled as they soaked into each other's white collars.

"Bless her poor soul… bless her poor soul," Robert began to repeat, moaning as if he was speaking the words of some sad slave song or church hymn. "She's in a better place, bless her soul."

After a few more whispers of comfort from Robert, Hannah suddenly pushed him away. "Just shut your damn mouth!" she said. "Bless her soul, what's that mean?" Hannah screamed. "What soul? What blessing?" The masters took her soul, just like they took her life. Used her up and tossed her out like garbage – all before I got time to see her one last time."

"Let her go, Hannah," Robert said, "her soul's up in heaven now."

"Heaven, you say? In heaven?" Hanna shouted. "I figure the masters sent her wherever the hell they decided! To her grave! To chop wood! Sent back to the fields!" Her dark eyes grew wider in her rage. "Maybe they sold her soul to Charleston like your white daddy sold you?" she yelled. "Her soul? What soul?"

Robert wanted to say something, but his words would only be fuel for this fire. He just nodded slowly but deliberately. Hannah's broken heart was poisoning her words. Though her words were uttered in pure emotion – almost crazy, in his heart he knew they were true. "I know," he said softly. "God help me, I know."

"I know," she said, "and I know you know. Sorrow's something all slaves know." She held his hands with both of hers, and pressed her crying face into them. He could feel the warm wetness of her tears in his palms. He pulled himself as close to her as he could, but his thoughts were flying all around.

'When would it stop?' he asked himself. Would it ever stop at all? They had tried to follow all the rules so as to somehow endure slave life. They clung to the hope of freedom, telling themselves they would get free from their chains, or at least free in some fanciful inner world of the heart. But in the end, it was all just words.

A slave might strive for peace or contentment, but any notion that he was a free man was an exercise in self-deception. This was the white man's South, and though a black man might sing of Freedom's Land on Sundays, there was no imaginable mind game by which a slave could transcend South Carolina. Here there could be no peace until there really was freedom – not the secret liberty of the mind, not financial independence, and not the spiritual freedom of God's heaven. No slave could pretend his soul was free while his body was not his own. Such a man was just acting a part; just saying his lines to himself.

Robert held his arms around Hannah as tightly as if this moment was his only remaining possession in the world. He had no idea where to go from here or what the future held, but he was sure of two things – and only two. First, he swore to himself that one day, with the help of God or the devil, he would get free. In addition to this, Robert was now absolutely convinced that Hannah Jones would one day be his wife. The notion seemed insane, but of course, so was the idea of getting free.

Though she was 15 years his senior and lacked the delicate prettiness of other girls, Hannah possessed every noble quality he had ever longed for in a woman. At this moment, he wanted her more than any earthly prize – maybe even more than his freedom. She was born to be the mistress of a house, not a slave girl, and he wanted to be the man who put her on that throne. She was clever, tough-minded, and like him, she had her face resolutely set toward freedom. It was not just something she longed for, it was a prize she would die for.

That being decided, Robert thought it best to put off for now any romantic ideas about him and Hannah. He would have to figure out the arrangements that might be required for two slaves to marry, and there was also the small matter of getting Hannah to say yes. He would need some time for prayer about the matter, and to come by some money. Life had taught him that he would likely need a goodly supply of both.

Hannah, for her part, was irritated, and fascinated, by this upstart boy. Sixteen now, Robert had literally grown up before her eyes. Early on, he had shown himself to be strong in mind, but now he was powerful in body too, with well-muscled arms and darkly compelling eyes. She had often felt those eyes staring at her, but today was the first time she had ventured to let him come close. Close enough to touch. Close enough to hold her tears in his hands. Usually when she felt sadness, she just wanted to be left alone, never sharing her tears with anyone, much less a man. But now, for good or ill, was this boy.

After Robert left the room, Hannah just stood there for a while, reflecting upon what had just happened between her and him and gazing out the upper window at nothing in particular. Hannah pinched the soft fold of flesh that was beginning to sag ever-so-little from beneath her chin, and she remembered the tight smoothness she used to feel there. She had spent her life being strong, but she now remembered the old days when she'd been more fragile and innocent. And happy.

She recalled the soft touch of her first man, Moses Jones, who had fathered her Charlotte and Clara. "I'll give a penny for your thoughts," he would say, always trying to probe her inner world. And he had liked to stand behind her when she spoke of her dreams, wrapping his arms around her and caressing the tender skin of her throat. She often wondered what might have happened if they had not been so hasty to make their union official. But she loved Moses with all her heart, and there was no reason she could see to wait for something better. He called her his "Flower Patch."

They had sneaked out one Sunday night to find a preacher that would marry them and had given the man some apples for payment. This reverend promised to do the deed and not tell a soul, but word got out anyway. No sooner had they spoken the *I dos'* but Moses' master, in anger, had sold him off to work at a rice farm down Savannah way. Moses had vowed to return one day, and to write to her in the meantime, but soon enough the bad news came. Moses was dead, she never learned how, and was buried without even a prayer service, leaving her nothing but his last name.

In time, such things came to be expected, woven together like dark threads in the story of her life. Having dreams pulled up by the roots had become a habit with her and she had resolved never again to hitch her heart to any man or any dream.

With her eyes wept dry of tears, she had to pick up the pieces and start things all over in 1841. Though her heart wanted to scream out that her life was over, there was still work waiting for her at the Baines Hotel the next morning. Her spirit might be dead, but her body still had a long list of rooms to clean. And there were also the girls to think about.

Having said goodbye to girlhood, Hannah found satisfaction in making Charlotte and Clara happy. While they were little, their enthusiasm and innocence kept her soul afloat. They played games together, talked and sang the little songs mothers and daughters are wont to sing. But through the years, the songs turned to complaints and the smiling girls into hard-faced young women.

At twelve and fourteen respectively, the girls very much deemed themselves to be women now. Hannah had tried hard to give them the best start she could, but they both had inherited their mother's strong spirit. And even Hannah was not queen enough to raise this pair of princesses. Mama might be able to run a big downtown hotel, but the task of corralling two pubescent girls pushed her to, and beyond, her limits.

Any time she thought too long about her story, she wanted to cry, but after being beaten down by so many years of suffering, fresh tears were hard to come by. There were many times she just closed her eyes and prayed, contenting herself to take life day by day, and sometimes, just one breath at a time.

By sunup the next morning, Queen Hannah had her crown back in place again. There was a tall stack of work to do, so she did her best to light a fire under the hotel staff. She reasoned that a busy day would help her forget the painful and vulnerable moments of the previous day. By four that afternoon, she was counting the linens and feeling like herself again. It was then that she heard a polite cough from behind her. Robert had found her.

"You best stay away if you ain't done with your chores," she commanded.

"I had to find you," he said. "I was worried about you." All morning he'd been thinking Miss Hannah might need someone to lean on, a male someone. As he walked around to stand in front of her, there were no tears in her eyes like before. He could see she was once again wearing her hotel face. Yesterday, her tears had aroused his masculine strength, but right now all he felt was weak in the knees.

He tried to bolster his composure by looking out the front window, but instead, he only found his own reflection there. There was a tired and frightened look in his eyes. 'My God, I look like hell,' he thought. Robert wanted to say something bold or clever, so as to somehow recapture the tender connection they'd had the day before. But now all he could do was look down at his young hands in silence. They were trembling. She was his supervisor again, and he was a child before her.

They chatted for a minute about what work had been done that morning and what remained to be done, speaking about the hotel and even touching on the weather once or twice. Their eyes glanced all around the room but never engaged the eyes of the other. Yesterday she had shown him her tears and he had offered her solace, but right now, neither one of them was comfortable.

Once Hannah finally turned away, Robert breathed deeply and was able to relax a bit. As she stepped toward the linen closet, he began to imagine what she might look like underneath that stiff hotel uniform of hers. His eyes were drawn to the tight knot of her apron that pulled her loose cotton garment into the shape of a woman. Her face was turned from him, but he sensed that she was smiling. At least he hoped she was. As she slowly stepped toward the other side of the room, she swayed herself gently, and intentionally. The way women move when men are watching.

'This is this how women move when they're in love,' he thought. He pinched his eyes closed and imagined himself moving towards her, embracing her. Then, terrified at the notion of touching her, he was suddenly possessed with a different desire. Suddenly, he wanted to run out of the room altogether, out of the hotel and maybe all the way out of Charleston. He wanted to run so fast and so far that he could escape this world entirely.

As he stacked the folded sheets into their bins, his heart was racing. These were new feelings for Robert as a battle raged inside him. His manly passion was warring with his reason, and his fears were doing the same. His heart told him to go to her, but his head told him this was not the right time. Holding himself back, he wondered if there ever would be a right time.

Hannah was equally puzzled. Robert was sixteen and she, thirty-one. She had spent the last four years scolding him like his boss. Like a mother, like a queen. Here alone with him, it was different. She suddenly felt like a damsel in distress, an object of love. She was altogether sure she didn't like the feeling. It was unprofessional. Uncomfortable. In one singular, vulnerable moment, Hannah trembled with the fears of a schoolgirl, yet also exulted that she might be a woman in Robert's eyes.

As she turned and walked toward the hall, Hannah took graceful and intentional steps, like a fine lady in some oil painting. Though he was halfway across the room, Robert wondered if she could hear his deep breaths and the thumping of his heart. When she finally raised her dark eyes to meet his, her beauty shined. 'Oh my God,' he thought. Her face, so often held with the stiffness of authority, now glowed with an adolescent softness. Her hands, which she usually put angrily on her hips when giving orders, were now gently crossed in front of her. To Robert, she looked every bit like someone's daughter at a ball, waiting for her first dance.

For a brief moment, his heart was bold. He envisioned himself walking up to her. Then he pictured her, holding out her hands to him. He even imagined that he heard her voice. "Come over here," she said.

When Hannah finally did smile at him, he suddenly knew within himself that he wanted to hold her, to kiss her, to run off and marry her. He would fight any man that might come between them. Struck by waves of desire, and then chills of embarrassment, he couldn't bring himself to draw near to her. Both youth and reason were kicking in now. 'I'm only a boy to her,' he thought. This might be his golden opportunity, but he quickly decided it was also the perfect time to say nothing.

She could actually hear him exhale as he turned away. Though he was already looking out the door to the hall, she raised her hand up between them as if to push him back – back from a move he had been too young, and too timid, to make. 'Am I pushing him away or trying to hold myself back?' she asked herself. For heaven's sake, she was thirty-one years old and the mother of two half-grown girls. She had bossed this upstart boy since before he had whiskers.

Both of them were, for that moment, frozen where they stood. Like so many other slaves, and so many other lovers, the answer was a decisive, "Wait," and resolute, "Later." For both of them, there were things that needed to get done before it would be time for dreams to come true.

Robert and Hannah continued to care for each other and to speak kindly, but it would be over a year before either of them would even consider speaking any words of love.

Chapter 19
The Jingle

Lying in his bed above the Ancrum's stable, Robert had been a bit homesick during his first weeks in Charleston. Slaves back in Beaufort lived out their days in sad but predictable peace. It had been a culture wherein every person knew his place, and, like it or not, stayed there. What the whites called stability might have more accurately been called stagnation. Robert soon discovered that in Charleston, this was not at all the case. An almost electric transformation was in the air.

For both whites and blacks, the world was changing, or it was at least trying to change. The isolated plantations and farms of the low country were becoming part of a widening world economy as railroad and sea travel opened up new markets for commerce. Immigrants from Europe were swelling Charleston's population as they came seeking freedom and opportunity. New business enterprises sprang up almost every week and the expanding urban economy put more and more money into more and more pockets. Even slave pockets were getting *the jingle.*

Black slaves had first been brought from Africa and the Caribbean to the Carolinas in the early part of the 1600s. Since the beginning of the 19th Century, a growing community of free Negroes had been gaining employment in skilled professions. By 1820, Charleston had hundreds of black tailors, seamstresses, shoemakers, and carpenters. One freedman even owned a hotel. By 1849, they were employed in over 50 different trades, and by 1860, these professions numbered at least 65. The burgeoning of enterprise among slaves and former slaves was alarming to many white owners.

Charleston's City Council tried to limit the wages of free Negroes to $1 per day or 12 cents an hour. It was thought unseemly for coloreds to make more than their white counterparts. Efforts were made to give legal clarification as to which jobs were *Negro jobs* and which were for whites only. Bitter feelings of competition developed, and by 1848, a law was passed requiring free blacks to wear a tag to identify which jobs they were eligible for and limited to.

Those of lighter complexion were more likely to enjoy greater opportunities and wages, and though mixed race individuals made up only 5% of South Carolina's colored population, by 1860 they made up three-quarters of the state's 9,914 free Negroes. While the racist categories of the whites did not sit well with Robert, he, like so many blacks, resolved to play along. An open door was an open door.

He always remembered the special feeling he had on that first Sunday in Charleston. As he and Spider Jefferson had walked home from escorting the ladies to church, there were, for the first time, coins in his pocket. Not coins Henry McKee had given him to buy provisions in town – this money belonged to Robert. For the first time in his life, he owned something, and he was not the only slave in Charleston who did.

The town that greeted Robert in 1851 was more than just the slave market he had seen on the McKee's wall. He had first seen the move to Charleston as a type of punishment for his adolescent misbehaviors – banishment. Robert was surprised and elated to discover that slave life in Charleston was a varied menu of new and curious freedoms. Most blacks were still enslaved of course, but a fresh breeze was blowing in. That breeze was money.

If making money was a game, then it was a game Robert very much wanted to win, because he came to see that money could buy freedom, and freedom was all that Robert cared anything about. Up to now, the economy of Robert's life was gruesomely simple – his person, his time, his labor, even his future children, all belonged to his master, Henry McKee. Robert was owned, but could not himself own anything. The things he created and any wealth he generated belong to the McKees. In Charleston, it was different.

Yes, he was still Henry McKee's property, but with a small but important difference. His employment at the Baines Hotel would bring him wages, and according to the hotel's contract with McKee, fifteen dollars of his monthly pay had to be sent to his master. But any income above that would belong to Robert. If he took on additional hours at the hotel, the proceeds were his to keep. If he did odd jobs on the weekends, the profits were similarly his. Henry McKee had owned him – body and soul – for his first twelve years. But now, for the first time in his life, there was something that Robert owned: his little slivers of free time, and free time was money.

He had heard the old expressions that 'money can't buy happiness' or 'money isn't everything' but he began to believe that in the end, money *was* everything. At times it very well could buy happiness. If money wasn't everything, it was certainly something very close to it.

In his off time, a little bit of work might bring him coins, sometimes just a nickel here and there. But in just a short time, Robert's coins became dollars, his dollars, and dollars were the thing that made a man somebody in Charleston. Dollars were what separated poor white trash from their betters. Dollars could raise a man to political office, to a prettier wife, or a better seat in the church. Dollars could make vulgar folks into proper ladies and gentlemen. Money could make an unkind man more loveable and a short man seem taller. In certain situations, it could almost make a black man white.

And, as Robert would soon discover, dollars could also make more dollars. He could buy an entire box of twenty peaches for less than a quarter, and could then sell those same peaches two for a nickel along the Promenade. Suddenly, that 20 cent box of peaches had brought him another whole dollar. In the same way, Robert could take on a two-man job for a dollar, paying his helper 25 cents. This brought him 75 cents for himself. Some men used their money to buy businesses which in time, brought them many hundreds of dollars. Robert, of course, didn't covet the dollars themselves. But dollars bought freedom, and freedom was everything.

Robert came to see that all this *keepin' money,* as it was called, was more golden than gold. If men's time could be bought with dollars, then in a sense, dollars were life. Paying a man in exchange for an hour of work was buying a little piece of his lifetime. Slaves like Robert might still owe their daytime hours to their owner, but their off times were theirs to sell. Once any slave was granted any time off, even a little slice of an evening, then he was no longer owned altogether. He was now a little bit free, and a little bit owned.

Charleston had opened his eyes to a whole new way of thinking. Whereas a slave might be locked up for stealing a hat, but the whole hat situation changed when that slave had a dollar in his hand. Any man with a dollar – be he black, or poor, or ugly, or Irish – could step into a Charleston store and then freely walk out with that hat. That cracker who owned the store might hate you, or call you a vile name, or even own you, but he would usually trade you his hat for your greenback dollar – that dollar you had bought with your little slice of time. When you walked home, that dollar was that cracker's dollar, but now that hat wa*s your* hat.

Robert soon found that the things people wouldn't do for brotherhood, or for God, they would eagerly do for a dollar. With that dollar you were somebody, and when it was gone, you were back to being nobody again.

Robert remembered the feeling he felt the first time he plunked one of those dollars on a store table and walked away with his hat. In Robert's case it was a wide-brimmed gray one, and he thanked heaven for the dollar that bought it. The very next week he went back to that same store and came home with four shiny brass rings, all of which he wore on his right hand. He called that his *fightin' hand*.

Robert came to see that money was like the very power of God, who long ago said "Let there be light, and there was light." From the dark void of nothing, a dollar could speak powerfully in this world. And in the universe that was Charleston, South Carolina, those dollars spoke everywhere with persuasive eloquence.

At that time, almost 40,000 people lived in Charleston proper, and most of them were black. Unlike places like Beaufort, many of Charleston's Negroes, both free and slave, worked in skilled occupations like needle working, bricklaying, shoemaking, and carpentry. Being a port city, there were a growing number of jobs on the waterfront and on the ships. Immigrants from Europe were flowing in during this period, swelling the town's population and creating demand for more goods and services at a time when a greater number of blacks were in a position to earn income by meeting that demand. These new opportunities for personal enterprise were more than a blessing for people of color – they made waves in the very fabric of southern society.

Robert soon discovered that some whites were uneasy with the new arrangements. Even though the city's Negroes looked just as they had looked before, and most continued to do the same tasks they had always done, the whole situation felt different. Everywhere in Charleston, slaves had the jingle in their pockets.

Some feared that the blacks might be made lazy by their newfound wealth and freedom, but in fact, the effect was the opposite. These so-called *employed Negroes* carried out their normal tasks with even more enthusiasm than before. They were more punctual and more energetic in discharging their duties, for they were eager to move on to their own free time. Early mornings, before their work, and the evenings after, these became their highest aspiration and their greatest reward. It was then that their time was their own to sell, even if it was just a few minutes a day or only a few odd jobs. Those treasured minutes of *free time* soon added up to hours and days, and those chronological cracks before, between, and after slave time became their life – their own life. Though still oppressed, their freedoms were expanding, and try though they might, the masters could do little to stop it.

When Robert started his work at the Baines Hotel, he was paid fifteen dollars a month, but in truth, he didn't care spit about what salary he made there. All of his hotel pay went to Henry McKee anyway, so the amount really didn't matter. He knew Master would get his share, but once that obligation was checked off, Robert could figure out ways to make his own money. And it wasn't long before he found such opportunities.

Since Robert's hotel day ended at sundown, he began to investigate any kind of employment that began after that time. 'Who goes to work at sunset?' he asked himself. Folks who worked the night shifts came to work at that time, but these shifts, like his hotel work, lasted ten hours or more. Even a hard-working man couldn't do without sleep altogether. But Robert kept his eyes open, and he prayed the right position would open up somewhere. The Lord answered quickly, for by that evening Robert had found a job that was delightfully suited to his schedule and abilities.

He had just left to go home. Turning down Center Street, he noticed one of Charleston's many lamplighters at work. Here at five o'clock, the man was just now beginning his day's work.

"Excuse me, sir," Robert said, "How long does it take you to do that work?"

"Depends," he said, "...on how fast I go... and on how much I might have had to drink. A man can't light as many lamps if he's *lit*.

"So," Robert chuckled, "Are you paid by the number you light or by the hours?"

"By the street, actually," the man said. "City don't care too much about the time it takes, just so long as they all get lit by dark."

"Perfect," Robert said. "What about Negroes? Do they hire Negroes?"

"Yeah, but they pay Negroes two dollars less than whites," he answered. "I should know. I used to be one."

"A lamplighter?" Robert asked.

"No, a Negro," the man laughed. "The city made me start out at colored wages because my great granny was colored. But once Maw Maw died, I applied for the job all over again with a different name. Just had white family alive then, so they gave me a fresh start as a white man. Got a nice raise in pay, too. But my back still hurts like it did when I was black though," he chuckled.

"Lord above!" Robert smiled. "Charleston is one crazy place." By the end of that week he was hired as a lamplighter and had was assigned a list of streets to work. Robert quickly memorized his route and learned the location of the lamps. The city loaned him a ladder, a cloth, and a trigger-wick. He could use these for a week until he could purchase equipment of his own.

In short order, Robert learned to quickly clean the jets, wipe the globes and spark-start the flames. He decided not to shell out for a ladder, for he was adept at shinnying up the lampposts, when required to do so. For a boy of twelve, the iron posts might as well have been tree trunks. When globe-cleaning was not needed, Robert could light and extinguish the wicks with his taper-pole. If he moved rapidly, he could finish his route in a fraction of the time it took the others. To Robert, time was money, and his aim was to maximize both.

His best times off usually came on the weekends. Charleston's lamps had to be lit every night, but Saturday and Sunday's daylight hours sometimes offered opportunities for rest. As it had been in his Beaufort days, Robert was drawn to the waterfront, and Charleston's Boardwalk provided a marvelous place to relax and watch the passers-by, but this of course, was not what attracted Robert's attention. His eyes were on the wharves, the ships, and the water.

Along the Battery, Robert found his holy sanctuary, his place of communion with the God of free men. Here, if only in stolen moments, he could transcend time, feeling as old as the grizzled sailors who now slept on the benches, and as young as the boy he had been on the seawall back in Beaufort. In the azure expanse of the harbor, there were no rows of sugar cane or cotton, no marked avenues, and no mansions. A million shining whitecaps stretched before him, none of them formed by any mortal hand. Here there were no fences, for this boundless property belonged to no man and to every man.

As the days and weeks passed, Robert learned to complete tasks in the shortest possible time. His salary at the Baines was raised, and the number of lamps on his route was increased. Fifteen dollars was still sent off each month to Henry McKee, but anything above that came to Robert and was stored in a secret place behind some wood slats behind a chimney at the Ancrum's. Things seemed to be moving in a good direction but Robert felt little satisfaction. This was not his dream.

One of those Saturdays, Robert found himself at the Boardwalk, in his usual place at the seawall. At that very moment, a three-masted schooner was leaving the dock area, headed out to sea.

"Just look at her!" said a stubble-faced gentleman who was standing near him. "She's a beauty!"

"Without doubt," said Robert. "How in heaven does a man get a berth on one of those?" he asked, not really sure if he was speaking to the old man, to himself, or to God.

"Son," the gray-haired man replied. "That's a privilege indeed, and one not easily come by."

"It's no stretch for me to say I'd die for it," Robert sighed, "Or kill for it."

"Well," the old man chuckled, "There's lots of men who've done one or the other. I'll tell you my story if it helps any." Then he commenced to tell Robert of his family farm, his harsh childhood, and recounted a list of forgettable jobs he had had in Charleston. Robert's interest was only enticed when the old man mentioned how he got his first chance to set foot on a boat.

"The sailors are quite protective of their turf, if the sea can be called turf," he said. "If I had tried to set foot on a ship, I'd have been a dead man, but they were quite willing to let me break my back for them on the docks."

"So you were a stevedore?" Robert asked.

"Yup. I was just watching one day, very much as we are watching right here," he said. "I was hoping for some opportunity, and by God's providence, a fist fight broke out right over there on the Atlantic Wharf. Two young loaders had bloodied one another up pretty good, but then they both made the mistake of cussing the boss. Well, that boss man had had enough of them and he called out to all the men on shore. Picked two new stevedores right then and there, and I was blessed to be one of 'em."

"Must have been something," Robert said. "To get on a boat, I mean."

"Oh," the man said, "it was quite a while more before they let me on a boat. You see, there are dock stevedores – these men are called *mules,* and then there are men on the boat that take the loads to their place in the ship's hold. These are *stackers.* Stackers are the first class loaders. Mules ain't allowed on the boat at all. It's easier to slip past Saint Peter's pearly gate than for a mule to get up that plank to the deck. I tried it once when I was still green and that story had a very sad ending. Very sad."

"But you got through after a while," Robert said.

"Yes," the man said. "Seemed like a long hard road at the time, but lookin' back, it seemed like just a minute. Once you're a real sailor gone out to sea, you don't remember things that came before. First time you hit the open sea, you're born again."

"Born again. It sounds like getting baptized or something," Robert said.

"Naw," the man said. "Folks get baptized to wash their sins away. The day you become a sailor your life of sin is mostly just beginning!" The old man laughed, putting out his hand to Robert. "Clarence is my name," he said, "and I truly do hope you get your wish one day."

"Nice to meet you, sir. I'm Robert Smalls," he said, shaking the man's weathered hand. "You've helped me greatly."

No one was ever sure of how it happened, but by the end of that month, Robert was doing mule duty on the Atlantic Wharf. This paid more than enough for him to quit his job at the Baines Hotel. Henry McKee still got his money each month and Robert got closer to his life-long dream. It was only a matter of time before he got his foot on board as a cargo-stacker, and after another year, he found his first chance to join a crew as a full-fledged sailor.

Chapter 20
Taking the Helm

It was at that time that Captain John Simmons first took note of Robert's eagerness and skill. Charleston Harbor had always been well-supplied with strong backs, but not all of these sailors were born with brains to match. Robert had ample muscle but was quick-witted as well. Bull Simmons noticed that Robert could see a thing done once, and after that, could do it by himself. He could also be relied upon to carry out every command on time and to the letter. Many a gifted seaman has been held back by slow ears and a stubborn heart.

Robert had no lack of cleverness, but early on he understood the importance of simple obedience. He was convinced that just as the church only needed one Lord and Savior, a ship needed only one commander. The important thing at sea was to understand that both officers and crew were important, and that the survival of all depended on wise orders, well executed. Thus seen, it was an honor both to give and to execute commands. For Robert, any life lived on open water was a blessed thing.

As a sailor on the *Lone Kestrel* he came to see that a Negro was more of a man when he was on a ship. Southern sailors like Captain Simmons had traveled to foreign ports and were accustomed to the look and manner of non-Europeans. They had encountered dark-skinned seamen and helmsmen, even officers and owners. As a class of men, blue water Southerners were more inclined to see a black sailor as an equal – as nothing less than a man. It didn't matter that rednecks on shore chose to see him as something less. Black sailors stood a head taller than the slaves on land.

Simmons was almost never called by his given name but had been *Bull* for as long as anyone could remember. Like Robert, he was burly of build and was known as a hard driver of men. Though brusque in manner, everyone considered Bull Simmons to be a fair man, and any sailor with a willing heart could rise in rank quickly under his command. Robert was eager to do this very thing.

And for Robert there was much to learn. Greenhorns began as objects of ridicule and suffered abuse as they learned the ropes. Early on, they were assigned to difficult, and sometimes even impossible, tasks. They climbed bare masts, loaded four-man pallets, and learned to tie every knot in the manual, and there were hundreds. These challenges seemed small to Robert. Such sacrifices were trivial when balanced against the unbridled privilege of being at sea. Robert was soon to discover that not all of sea life was unbridled.

Charleston Harbor, like the plantations, was not an altogether free expanse, but was everywhere fenced and regulated. A manual of countless rules governed the wharves and channels. Blue markers stipulated a boat's direction, and red buoys told ships which side of each channel belonged to them. Harbor-masters had bells, horns, and whistles that they would sound whenever they saw a boat break a rule. Violations could bring great shame on a captain, his helmsman, and the whole crew.

The harbor's rules took Robert's mind back to the constraints he had grown up with in Beaufort. He loved Charleston Harbor, but it soon began to seem like just another fence-lined plantation. Like every true sailor, Robert hated the confines of the wharf area and always longed for the unlimited freedom of blue water. To him, the boats at full sail reminded him of wild stallions. Those tied up at their docks seemed like barned-up cart horses.

Their trips out of port provided excitement, but also opportunities to think and reflect. In these peaceful moments, Robert often took time to count the blessings of his life. God had always helped him to avoid the grueling work in the plantation fields. He held three jobs of his own choice and carried more money in his pockets than many white men. Though he had not found a sure way to escape slavery, the events of his life led him to believe that even this might one day be in his grasp.

Later in life, when he was called upon to name his life's greatest moment, Robert could answer with singular confidence and clarity. It was a summer morning in June of 1854 when the *Kestrel* was making her downhill run off the Danker Shoals. Old John Mack Lyle, a ruddy Irish sailor, had been manning the helm but wanted to go below to refill his flask with some hot coffee. "Assume the helm, Smalls," he commanded, "and hold our her course." Lyle's words were as welcome as a message from heaven.

Robert had already enjoyed many wonderful moments at sea, more happiness than most slaves were privileged to taste in a lifetime. Though he had always preferred to pass up jobs until he was fully trained, there was no way under God's heaven Robert was going to tell Mack Lyle that he had never manned a helm before.

"Aye, Sir." He answered quickly as he grasped the spoked wheel, making double-sure he made no twitch that might change their direction. "Holding steady, Sir," he said, the whole time hoping no one could see how much his hands were shaking

As Lyle headed below, Robert was so taken aback that he almost lost his breath. It didn't matter whether Mack Lyle was gone for a minute, or for an hour, for Robert had the wheel in his hands. Though he might presently rank as nothing more than a scrubby, for that moment he was the pilot of the ship – a bona fide helmsman. And though Robert did no more than hold their course, he reveled in the thought that with the slightest twitch of his hand he might have changed the direction of the *Kestrel,* and if the direction, then their port of call. His heart leaped within him and he could feel its pulse down through the tips of every finger and toe.

Gripping that wheel with a warm breeze on his cheek, Robert could happily have died then and there. "Thank you, Lord," he whispered. For the first time in his life he saw before him an undivided expanse of blue water with himself the wheelman. That first taste of piloting became the inspiration and goal for every remaining action of his life. He had been born for this.

When Lyle too soon returned with his coffee, Robert went back to his usual chores. Years would pass before he was again offered a ship's wheel, but he longed for and prayed for that day, just as he had prayed for this one. His wish was that every child of God might, sometime in this life, savor such a feeling.

Even after sending Henry McKee his fifteen dollars every month, sailor's wages provided Robert with enough to spend on his own needs and wants, but mostly he saved. By the end of the year, the roll of currency stored in his wall had grown plump. What he would spend it on would be decided during a particular voyage in the spring of the next year.

It was 1855, and there was already a lot of talk about secession. As South Carolina's senators and congressmen made speeches, it became apparent that the opponents of slavery were gradually winning the day in Washington. Everywhere in the South, folks were hopping mad. Regardless of whether war came or not, they wanted to maintain control of their freedoms and, of course, their Africans. More and more, vessels like the *Lone Kestrel* were employed to carry armaments and supplies to the fortifications that protected Charleston Harbor and the Carolina coast. Another turning point in young Robert's life came when orders arrived in February.

The crew was to spend the next two days clearing the *Kestrel's* decks and most of the hold, making room for what they called *special military cargo*. The crew was told nothing else, and even when they cast off from the Atlantic Wharf on Saturday morning, they still had no clear notion as to where they were going. This, of course, was in no way unusual. Black crew members had long known that it was best to feign ignorance and blindness in these situations. These secessionists liked to guard their military secrets closely, as modestly as their private parts.

Robert guessed that their orders would take them to at least two of the forts in the harbor – one to pick up the cargo, usually armaments, and the other the point of delivery. Usually there would be cannon, boxes of artillery supplies, and big barrels of black powder. The loading and unloading would be the hardest part, of course, but not too hard. The boys didn't really mind moving gunpowder, since the round casks could be rolled rather than carried. Supply boxes were a more cumbersome challenge. The iron balls and grapeshot were heavy and could roll around inside, shifting the weight whenever the box was held at any angle off of dead level. Loading these crates required a cool head and an adept combination of urgency and patience.

Though their explosive cargo was combustible, Robert knew there was really no reason for fear. Black powder could only be ignited by a flame or the sizeable spark triggered by pulling of a cannon's lanyard, and this took a prodigious yank by a strong man, sometimes two. Though Robert had occasionally seen a stevedore lose control of a cask of powder, and had seen one or two break open, there was never anything but loose powder to clean up, creating no particular cause for terror. Of course, there would always be punishment for the clumsy worker who damaged any cargo, black powder included, but such could be survived.

Perhaps the oddest thing to Robert was that Negro workers were under no circumstances allowed to touch the barrel of any artillery piece. This privilege was reserved for whites only. Robert was amused at their fear that a five foot five inch colored boy like himself might snatch and run off with a two thousand pound gun. Did they fear he might point it at them pistol-like, like some highway bandit or perhaps hide the barrel down his breeches for some future revolution?

In any case, Robert learned to stand aside whenever the big guns were loaded or unloaded by the white men. His exclusion was altogether fine with him. He had no hankering for such heavy lifting, and he had seen mishandled artillery crush a man's hand or break a limb. He would no sooner touch a white man's cannon as his manhood, and the masters always guarded both with uneasy suspicion.

The *Lone Kestrel* made plodding progress as it negotiated the shoals and mines of the harbor. Standing quietly at the helm, Robert sought ways of keeping his mind occupied. He meticulously counted the red buoys and the less colorful tops of the explosive torpedo-mines. He could also make out the darker forms of the submerged bombs that lurked shark-like below the surface of the water. Brushing any one of them could send a ship, be it friend or foe, to Davy Jones' Locker.

After dozens of trips like this, these images were no longer a cause for alarm. In his boredom, he often sang songs to himself, and to the Lord above. *Now Let Me Fly,* was one of his favorites, and he sang with joy in his heart,

> *Way down yonder in the middle of the field,*
> *Angel is working at de chariot wheel.*
> *I'm not partic'lar 'bout working at da wheel,*
> *I just wanna see how de chariot feel.*

Robert waved cheerfully as he passed a number of smaller boats along their way. A full helmsman now, he felt perfectly at ease at the ship's wheel by now. Charleston Harbor had become as familiar as the McKee's backyard to him, and he supposed he could navigate all the way from the South Wharf to Fort Sumter and back with his eyes closed. The only real danger presented itself whenever they approached one of the five checkpoints at the forts.

Upon approach, every friendly vessel was required to sound its whistle with the proper signal. These consisted of various short and long blasts, accompanied by occasional soundings of the ship's bell. The code for these signals was changed every Monday and was written into each captain's log book. Bull Simmons, like most captains, kept his log stored in a locked drawer beneath the *Kestrel's* bridge, but he sometimes carried it on his person.

A captain's log might as well have been the Holy Bible of God, for its contents held the power of life and death. Lacking the authorized signal, the forts were under orders to challenge the approaching boat once more. If a ship again failed to sound the proper code, the fort was to fire upon it. The whole harbor would then sound the general alarm for battle, but it was likely that the offending boat would be destroyed by the first cannonade. To traverse the harbor without the captain's code wasn't a risky thing, it was suicide.

"On our approach now, Captain!" shouted Robert, aiming his words downstairs from the bridge. "On approach!" he repeated as the dark parapets of Fort Johnson could just now be made out in the distance. Captain Simmons made his way up to the bridge with rapid but meticulous steps. Robert's eyes met his and there was an awkward, but customary moment of silent acknowledgment between the men.

"Stand aside, helmsman," the old man said. Robert nodded and stepped back from the helm. He had learned to be careful at this moment, recalling that one time, and just one time, the captain had inadvertently given him a salute at this point in their routine. The gesture had almost stopped his young heart. Unsure of proper protocol, Robert had returned the captain's salute, but immediately sensed that he had made the wrong choice. Bull Simmons' eyes widened and they followed Robert's right hand as it was lowered down to his side. The captain stared at it for a second as if it had been a pistol being returned to its holster.

"You will never do that again, do you hear?" John Simmons had said. "You will never salute me. Never! You're a hired conscript, not an enlisted man, and you'll remember that!"

And Robert always did remember. Though it had been Bull Simmons who had initiated the salute, Robert knew enough to keep his mouth shut. After holding his head still for a long moment, Robert had simply twitched a nod of agreement, saying nothing. Such a quick nod had sufficed between them ever since.

As Captain worked to locate the drawer key on the huge ring of keys that was attached to his belt, Robert grasped the cord of the whistle into his right hand, simultaneously taking the one for the bell in his left. Taking the ship's wheel in one hand, the captain opened his small leather log book in the other and barked out this week's code. His voice was as deep as a pastor's as he spoke each word, enunciated as if it had been an inspired text. "Short, short. Bell, Bell. One long," he said.

"Short, short. Bell, bell. One long," replied Robert.

"Code Confirmed," said the captain.

As he surveyed the long seaward side of Fort Johnson in the dim haze of dawn, Robert sounded the signal – two short whistle blasts, two rings of the bell, followed by one final long whistle blast. After a few seconds the reply came back with the same series of blasts and bells. They had successfully cleared checkpoint number one.

When they had drawn close enough to see the silhouettes of the fort's sentries, a shout came from atop the wall. "What ship is that?"

"*Lone Kestrel* requests to pass," shouted Robert, knowing the routine by heart.

"Request to pass the *Lone Kestrel!*" the distant voice shouted. A second voice responded, "Aye, pass the boat!" as Robert guided the ship through the narrow channel that guided them directly under Fort Johnson's biggest guns.

Once again taking the helm, Robert permitted himself to relax a bit and breathed deeply again. At their nearest point to the fort, Robert could make out the faces of three young men atop Fort Johnson's east tower.

"Where are y'all bound?" a voice shouted from the wall.

Robert had no answer to offer, but only looked over to Captain Simmons for approval. "Sir?" he asked.

"Tell him Stono River ramparts," the captain answered.

"Stono River Ramparts," shouted Robert to those at the checkpoint.

"Aye, aye," the voice replied. "Heard you folks might be coming through. You all best keep your eyes peeled for torpedoes and other sea monsters," he added.

"Duly noted," shouted Robert, exchanging a smile with the captain.

"Proceed carefully, maintain speed," commanded Simmons as he began to descend the stairs. "You got the code now, Robert?"

"Aye, Captain," he answered, pointing a finger to the side of his head. "Got it right here."

"Very well. Very well," Captain muttered as he left. "Wake me when we near the ramparts at the Stono."

"Aye, Sir," said Robert, who only fully relaxed when Captain Simmons was finally out of sight below decks.

As the now-risen sun began beat down upon the harbor and the Sea Islands, the wheel felt familiar and warm in his hands. After a score of such trips, its spokes had almost become a part of him. There would be more checkpoints to pass, but it had all become pretty routine business, like breathing in and out. With Bull Simmons and John Mack Lyle below decks, and the ship on a clear course, Robert's thoughts were free to venture elsewhere.

Chapter 21
Better Than Burning

The first rays of sunlight made the rippling waters of Charleston harbor glisten like a thousand diamonds before them. Robert counted himself fortunate to taste the glory of such freedom. At that very moment, there were slaves sweating to feed the boilers below decks, and thousands of others sweltering in the cane and rice fields that lined the shores. But up here on the *Kestrel's* bridge, a man, even a black man, was as free as the fellow who owned the boat. Almost as free as God. Robert was living a sweet dream. After five years, it was becoming increasingly harder to remember what it had been like to be Henry McKee's slave.

But Robert did remember. The only thing worse than the repugnant work was the unbearable sameness of it. From sunup to evening, there had always been a tedious and repetitive list of orders, and to disobey even one of them was unthinkable. It was something beyond evil, it was madness. And if the unpleasant duties were repulsive, the punishments were more so.

Robert had seen many whippings, in Beaufort, and here in Charleston, too. He concluded that the sting of the lash was not the only pain of it. The sharper agony was in the *humiliation*. A slave was not scourged like a vanquished enemy, for to be an enemy was to be a soldier, a human. Neither were they flogged like criminals, for a sinful man was still a man. No, a slave was beaten like some wayward beast or recalcitrant tool. Like an object.

He had often watched the faces of the men who did the deed. Rarely was there any type of malice behind the beating, for malice would connote some type of personal feeling or hatred. Slave punishment was administered without emotion – as if one were rounding off the sharp edge of an ill-fitted plank or hammering a popped nail back into its rightful place. Like a peg that happened to pop out of a floor, a slave did not need to be cursed or despised, only fixed. That was all there was to it.

The details of the punishments Robert had experienced or

witnessed in his life had been mostly forgotten now. When he recalled the beatings, the single memory that lingered was one that burned hot and bright. As the lash struck his back, or more often the back of a friend, Robert only rarely had thoughts of retaliation. Oh, there was anger and hatred all right, but mostly he had longed for control rather than retribution. A whip welt might sting for a day or so, but the pain of a subjugated will goes on and on. Robert's only real relief would come with control, but he, for the most part, had no control. None except the for the ship's wheel. Any dreams Robert had of vengeance were gradually overshadowed by the sweeter notion of taking the helm.

This was what drove him toward the boats, for the sea was a place without fences or property lines, a place beyond black or white, north or south. At first he just dreamed of the coolness, the quietness, and the welcome escape from the sweltering life of town. But it was on the boat that he first came to understand the role he dreamed of – to be the helmsman. It was a place where a man had his druthers. The helmsman did not have to be taller than other men, not richer or even smarter. His strength did not surpass the strength of other men, yet at the helm he held a miracle in his hands, the wheel. The hands that gripped that circle of wood had the power to guide the largest of ships. Whether to traverse the harbor's channels, or perhaps out to sea, the boat's course was his to set. This man might have been a nobody in the city, on the plantation, or in the church, but grasping the wheel of that boat he was the nearest thing to being God Almighty.

Robert even remembered once saying this very thing to his friend Alfred Gradine when they were together on the *Kestrel's* bridge. Gradine, who everyone called Deke, had once preached as a deacon in the Negro church.

"Right here at this wheel," Robert said, "I sometimes feel just like God!"

Deke, taking umbrage at Robert's remark, said, "Well I pray to God every night, young man. And the last time I checked, you ain't him." Deke squinted as he pointed all around at the harbor and the ships. "The Lord's the only pilot of heaven and earth. Rich white men think they own these boats," he said, "but everything and everyone belongs to God. A helmsman ain't no be-all and end-all." Then Deke pointed out to the a big purple cloud bank that was presently moving in from the Atlantic. "When the Lord blows a storm, this here boat's gonna go right where the he tells it to."

"Yes, I know," Robert said, nodding. "I ain't about to argue that the

Lord ain't over all things. He's certainly blown *me* here and there through the years."

"Amen to that," Deke said, and for the next few minutes, both men stood quietly there on the bridge. But Deke still sensed that Robert had more to say. "I know you're thinking something, little brother," he said. "You can say what's in your heart. You needn't worry about what some preached-out old deacon says."

"Well," said Robert. "With all respect, I know there's powerful forces behind the world we see, and no man's gonna stop the plans of God." Then Robert got quiet again as he gazed out to the darkening horizon.

"But Deke," he said, almost is a whisper now, "Don't you think that every now and then, maybe just every once in a while, the Lord decides to hold off on the wind? Maybe in those special times, God steps himself back from his big captain's wheel in heaven. And sometimes, maybe just every so often, he puts the wheel in a *man's* hands. And just for that moment, God lets that *man* decide his own course – a gift of sorts. God gives a man a choice, and with just one twitch of that wheel, that man is free to chart his course, and maybe in some way, the course of this whole world. And on that day, that man knows he's God's man. Made in God's own image. Free."

Deacon Gradine could only nod in silent agreement with the words of this young boy, feeling in his heart that he'd just heard the very whisper of God. "Amen," he said softly, as a tear flowed down his old dry cheek. "That'll preach."

The sun was high in the sky now and had warmed the decks, fore and aft. The journey to the mouth of the Stono River was a longish trip, but the blue water was the easy part. The mouth of the Stono, located just down the coast from Charleston, was less of a river than a tidal channel. It took tricky turns as it wove its way northeast between the mainland, Wadmalaw Island, and Johns Island, all the way up to the back door of Charleston. Slaves from West Africa had started a rebellion there back in 1739, the largest slave uprising in the colonies before the American Revolution. Robert loved this trip down the coast of the Low Country, but was not looking forward to the treacherous channels of the river.

Robert didn't own a watch, but he could tell the approximate time by the smell of the boat as the heat dried its decks rigging through the course of a day. By the time they reached the mouth of the Stono, everything was well-dried and the sun had become a scorching ball in the afternoon sky. Far ahead on their starboard side, he could just now make out a group of dark figures on the distant shore of Folly Island.

It was customary for slave women to wash and beat laundry there, but Robert soon discovered that this wasn't laundry day. The monotony of the journey had gotten the best of him, so taking the captain's spyglass down from its hanger, Robert tried to make out what was going on in the distance.

Through the fine French scope, he could clearly see what he was accustomed to seeing here – the details of the sand, the breakers and the dark seaweed that was clumped along the beach. He gasped however, at the sight of something he had not seen before. Here were perhaps twenty women and children, all as naked as the day they were born, swimming and bathing in the salt surf.

Robert immediately lowered the scope from his eye, as if he had been King David gazing upon the forbidden Bathsheba. "This can lead to nothing good," he whispered to himself.

It didn't take long for his curiosity to get the best of him. He slowly raised the captain's glass to his eye, carefully adjusting the focus this time, to get a clearer look at the women. He especially lingered on the forbidden regions of their nether parts. In his heart, he knew he was leaving footprints on the devil's path, but this savory opportunity would be fleeting. He could repent later on.

Though Robert generally knew what women looked like without their garments, he was not accustomed to this kind of firsthand experience. From his youth he had seen the imitation Rubens paintings that hung at the Fripp's home next door, and at Grayson's restaurant on Bay Street. There had also been some nude images in a stained glass window of Saint Helena's Church. But these had all been works of art. Biblical women. But now, right before his seventeen-year-old eyes, were real females. Women with playful arms, laughter, and hazy darkness in their secret places. He was both curious and terrified. He was also on fire.

As he steered the boat as near as possible to the shore, Robert felt a powerful urge to turn his head away. He wondered if the Holy Ghost was vying for control in order to save his poor soul. 'This ain't right,' he told himself, but at just that moment he heard voices shouting in the distance.

"Ho there, sailor!" came a shrill squeal from a girl on the approaching beach. "Yoo-hoo, black sailor man!" she cried as Robert tried to hold his course. But the siren's song was too great. He turned his head to look and made no effort to look away. The girls were all in the water and moving away from shore. Brazen. Beautiful.

His conscience told him to spin the wheel hard to port, but his wicked heart said otherwise. The helm didn't twitch at all. Though Robert knew he was running straight down hell's gangplank, he couldn't restrain his eyes. His mouth fell open as looking became staring, and staring became lust.

Seeing him gawking and altogether frozen in place, the girls began to laugh, squeal and dance. "Sailor! Sailor!" they repeated, musically. Mercilessly. As their sultry sing-song rang out louder in his head, Robert could remember every wise warning he had heard from every Sunday sermon. Armageddon raged in his heart, a battle from which there seemed to be no escape. The more he tried to ignore the women, the more they sang. Robert felt his soul sliding into the quicksand of concupiscence. His better angels had been tossed overboard to fend for themselves in the *Kestrel's* frothy wake.

Then suddenly, there came another, louder sound. A grinding roar was rising from below decks as the ship began to run aground. The noise soon filled the whole ship. Robert could hear the crunching sound as their hull scraped against the edge of the shoal. He felt the shuddering vibrations of the deck beneath his feet and a sort of buzzing hum along the rails.

With a rapid spin of the wheel to port, he jerked the *Lone Kestrel* off the sandbar and back toward the deeper water of the channel. The grinding of the hull gradually diminished, and then ceased. Needless to say, Robert was greatly relieved that disaster had been averted. They were back on course now, and the females on the beach could no longer be seen or heard.

Robert silently prayed that the moral stain of his straying eyes might similarly be washed away by the forgiving Blood of Jesus. "Please have mercy, Lord," he whispered. "Forgive me." This brought his heart a measure of peace, but not lasting relief. In a matter of moments, he heard the snap of quick footsteps coming up the stairs to the bridge.

"What in God's name was that?" the captain shouted. "Have we hit something?"

"No sir," Robert replied, quickly fabricating a sailor's lie. "Just an unexpected sand bar. The tides must've played havoc with the channels after last week's storm."

"Are we back to right now?' the captain asked. Robert just nodded and kept his eyes on the channel. He was afraid to look the old man in the eye.

"Good work, Smalls." Simmons said. "We'll have to make a note so they can correct the harbor maps. How would you word it?"

Robert had to think for a moment. "Why don't we just tell them to keep clear of Folly?" he said. "There are hidden dangers." Even in deceit, Robert had managed to speak at least a tidbit of truth. He had just survived some very unsafe waters. John Simmons scribbled in his little log book as Robert made a similar note to himself: 'Keep clear of Folly.' Good advice for any boy or sailor.

Once the captain was below decks, Robert was again left to his own thoughts at the helm. On the voyage home from the Stono, he prayed fervently, perhaps more intensely than he had in years, repenting of his wicked ways. He resolved to find himself a good wife, a godly woman to keep his heart and body from the snares of Satan. As Saint Paul had said in the Good Book, "It's better to marry than to burn." Today, Robert had come so near the fire that he feared he might smell of smoke. He made a solemn vow to God that he would set things right as soon as the opportunity might present itself.

Chapter 22
The Lord Provides

It was later that week that heaven provided such an open door. On Thursday morning, Pralene Maple, one of the downstairs maids at the Baines Hotel, was arrested for stealing money from a guest's room. Robert arrived at the hotel just in time to see the Charleston deputies taking her into custody. The constables seemed to be taking their own sweet time with Pralene, a comely, big-chested girl who had already been deemed of questionable character. Robert was curious. He knew enough to be hustling about with his hotel duties, but he kept an eye on the situation.

Once the deputies had sufficiently frisked Pralene and taken her away, the hotel workers felt relaxed enough to talk. And talk they did, venturing various opinions about Pralene's fate, her morals, and recounting sordid tales of her work history.

"Pralene's been though all this before." Hannah said. "Been let go from some of the best hotels in Charleston."

"For stealing?" asked Robert.

"For stealing and worse," said Hannah. "Her services seem to be popular with certain male guests, porters, and more than a few night watchmen." At these remarks, a number of the maids jumped in with stories about Pralene — so many stories that Hannah had to make everybody get back to work.

"It's sad in any case," said Hannah. "A comely young girl may be held in the jail for some time to come... and maybe more than *held*, if you follow my meaning." They all shook their heads as they went back to their work, shocked and also a bit titillated by the gossip.

As Robert left to go up to the second floor, he passed Hannah at the foot of the stairs. When their eyes met, Robert did something he had never done before. He winked at her. Surprised at himself, he had no idea why he would risk doing such a thing. What shocked him more was that Hannah had said nothing. He couldn't stop thinking about it as he made his way down the long hall. 'She saw me wink,' he thought. But curiously, she had said nothing.

Later that afternoon, Robert found himself folding towels and washcloths in the supply room upstairs when Hannah happened to come in. As usual, he kept his eyes down and worked quickly. She was always monitoring the quality and diligence of his work.

"Well, they locked up your sultry sweetheart," Hannah said. "Dream girl's gonna do some jail time downtown."

"What are you talking about?" Robert said. "Pralene ain't my girl."

"I heard tell you were scouting out a wife for yourself," she said. "That nasty boy, Spider, he's been yacking quite a bit to the hotel staff."

"Spider's a fish-mouthed fool," Robert said. He went back to his work, hoping Hannah would drop the subject, but she just stood there staring at him in silence.

"But you *are* looking for yourself a girl, ain't you?" asked Hannah.

Robert just kept working, faster now, but Hannah just stood her ground. Her dark, muscular arms were folded in front of her and she had that *look*. He hated it when she folded those arms. Realizing she wasn't about to let it go, he decided he would have to he would have to say something.

"Not a girl," he replied, "a woman."

"Well, well!" she said loudly. "Pralene, she's a whole *lot* of woman, or at least the menfolk think so."

"So exactly which menfolk is that?" he asked, moving over toward the windows and beginning to wipe the sills.

"All of 'em, I suppose," she said. "Maybe just about every man on earth."

"Well ain't no concern of mine," Robert said.

Hannah was not about to let him escape so easily. She walked over to where he was working, her arms still folded as she came near. "Pralene's a thief though," she added, laughing, "and a bad one at that. She goes and gets herself caught every time."

Robert racked his brain trying to think of some way to evade Hannah's interrogation. "Oh, Pralene, she *looks* like something," he said. "She's something special. A real looker."

"Oh, she's special, all right," said Hannah, "sizeable up on the top, as the men say. She be *quite* so. Big where men like big. Blessed, as they say, but still a stinkin' thief."

"All right. You can stop with all your boom-boom talk," Robert said. "So she's big where most men like a woman big. Don't mean nothin' if she's not big in the right place. Way up on top she ain't big. Up here," he said, pointing to his head. "She's pitiful small up there, and empty. Girl's slow of mind. Stupid as a stump."

"Boom-boom but no brains," Hannah laughed. "I'd think most men fancied that particular combination." Hannah came and stood between Robert and his work. "So you ain't looking for a slow-witted thief to be your wife?" she asked.

"Oh, I could be happy to marry a thief," he said. "But I just don't fancy no thief that gets herself caught right off like that," Robert said. "A crafty woman, now that's what I like. Pralene's too dull to find her way home at night."

Hannah just chuckled. "What do you think?" she asked. "Maybe Pralene's brain blood all flowed down there to her bosoms. I would think that's just what a young boy like you was wanting."

Robert went back to folding the sheets and tried to look nonchalant, but his heart was pounding nervously now. Hannah was following him around the room. "Bosoms encourage a man for a night," Robert said, "but a stupid mind just goes on and on."

"... And she's a thief," Hannah added.

"Oh I can put up with the stealing," he said, smiling now. "Just not the stupid."

Both of them were smiling now as their back-and-forth continued. "So let me get this straight," Hannah said, "you crave a smart and sly girl... but one that don't get caught." Hannah raised her dark eyes up to meet Robert's.

For some reason, he suddenly felt braver than he'd ever felt in his life. Here was Hannah Jones, High Queen of the Baines Hotel, trying to stare him down somehow. She re-folded her arms again and stood eye to eye in front of him. With every strong muscle he could flex, he folded his own arms like hers and stared right back at her, almost nose to nose now.

"Yes, a smart and sly girl," he said, now lowering his voice to a whisper. "A thief like you, Hannah Jones," he said. "Just like you."

His words almost stopped her heart and his own heart as well. Hannah could only stare back at him in disbelief. For the first time Robert could remember, Hannah was lost for words. And then she did something else he had never seen her do. She blinked.

"Like *me*?" she whispered, looking right at him. He was now close enough to hear the sound of her breathing in and out. "I never stole nothin' in all my life," she said.

Robert locked his dark eyes with hers for a long moment, and in them she could see the piercing look of a young man in love. He struggled to catch his breath. "Miss Hannah," he said in a coarse whisper, "Don't you know by now that you've stolen my heart? Plumb stole it away."

At that point, Hannah almost lost her own breath. All she could do was to squint at him, eye to eye, with just a hint of a smile at the corners of her lips. Her brows pinched together as if she wanted to ask a question, but it was a question that was slow to come.

"Really?" she asked, unfolding her defiant arms now. She took his strong young hands in hers and could feel the moisture of his nervous palms. "But you said you don't fancy no stupid girl," she said. "...no thief that gets herself caught."

Robert teased right back, "Well maybe I'm just one of them greenhorn colored boys who don't know he's just been robbed. A simple, foolish boy who don't even mind that he's been taken in by some conniving, small-chested black woman with a sharp mind." He pulled Hannah near to him and kissed her mouth strongly. "Or maybe I'm the one that's doing the stealing," he said.

"It's a smart thief that can thief a thief," she said, kissing him back now. "I was afraid to even hope for this. I hope you know what you're doing, baby child. I've got two half-grown daughters, you know."

"Yes," he nodded, "and now I have their mother... if she'll have me." He wrapped both arms strongly around her now and pressed his cheek to hers. "And before God," he said, "I'll never let you go."

Hannah drew him so tight to her, she sensed that their very souls were touching. "The Lord provides," she whispered. "This is *his* work."

The moment was interrupted as they heard footsteps coming down the creaking floorboards of the hall. They both straightened their clothing and resumed their chores, but the whole rest of that day they each labored with energetic hands and heads full of dreams. She felt like a girl again, and he for the first time in his life, a man.

Chapter 23
A Handshake with the Devil

Having studied Charleston for five years, Robert had become convinced that, while money couldn't buy everything, it could leverage almost anything he longed for in this life. Not that he needed much. Robert was content to have friends to laugh with, a dry bed to sleep in, and a bit of food on his table.

And his hat, of course. It was a smart-looking gray number he had bought back in 1851 with the first dollar he earned in Charleston. He was pleased with how he looked in that hat, which in a way, had represented his first act of manhood. Even with such blessings, he reasoned that if he somehow lost it all, he could stand the loss, and start over if he had to.

But now, having lost his heart to a good woman, things were different. Yes, he loved, and felt more loved, than he had ever known. But he also, for the first time, had something to lose. The thought that Hannah Jones was owned by another man just about killed him. It bothered him so much he hardly slept that first night after they had kissed. As a slave, she could be kept from him, whipped, or even sent away, never to be seen again. These thoughts were unbearable. He had to be with her somehow.

When what could be called their courtship began, Robert could only see Hannah during their working hours at the hotel. In the other times, her master, Samuel Kingman always had a list of things for her to do. When Hannah first mentioned her interest in Robert, Kingman was surprisingly positive, but as it turned out, the old man was only interested in money. He arranged for Robert to pay him 25 cents for every hour of courting time. Robert had always heard that you can't buy love, but he deemed Hannah's affections to be worth the price. She would later remark that Robert treated her better in those days because he was paying for the privilege. By the fall of 1856, he had had enough of renting a sweetheart. Robert decided to approach Hannah's owner about a more permanent arrangement.

Samuel Kingman was nobody's fool. He was a jovial soul, but in matters of business he was famously frugal. Robert would be at a disadvantage in any negotiation about buying a wife. Kingman knew Robert wanted Hannah desperately, and the old miser held all the aces.

"I've heard you've got your eye on my Hannah," Kingman said.

"Yes, and I've *heard* that you heard so," said Robert. "I fear this puts me over a barrel."

"Of course it does," smirked Kingman. "But the door to commerce is never slammed, is it?"

"I suppose not," Robert said, encouraged that Kingman might be willing to explore some kind of deal. "But I fear I may not possess enough oil to loosen the hinges of that door."

Kingman chuckled and put his forefinger to his plump cheek. He concluded that Robert was short on funds, but he had also heard about Robert's penchant for enterprise. "Perhaps if I only asked a modest sum from you? Say five hundred? It's the bottom rate for a slave these days."

"That's not the bottom rate," Robert said. "That's the price of a male slave."

"Well," said old Samuel. "I expect you already know Hannah can work circles around most men."

Kingman recognized that Robert wouldn't be an easy mark, and he also knew that almost any price would be unreachable in Robert's present situation. Samuel leaned back in his big leather chair and pretended to stare up at the ceiling, but Robert guessed that the old man's mind was buzzing with numbers.

"Even if you lowered that price, sir, I can't do it," Robert said. "I just don't have all the money yet."

"Yet?" Kingman asked. "Or ever?"

"Yet," replied Robert, a bit irked by Kingman's games. "I save my money every week."

"So how much do you have on hand?" Kingman asked. "Can you do three hundred?" He knew well there was no way Robert could meet even this lowered price.

"I'd prefer not to talk about a lump sum right now," Robert said.

"I don't doubt it," Kingman said. "The way you darkies squander, I'd doubt there's any lump to talk about."

Robert held his tongue, angry now, but knowing Kingman was toying with him. "I was hoping for some kind of arrangement," Robert said. "I could pay something each month until you get your asking price.

Hannah could live with me until then."

"A bird in the hand, so to speak," Kingman said, "But wisdom tells us that such a bird is worth two in the bush. What you're proposing turns things around and puts *me* over the barrel. You get everything here and now, and I'm tossed a few coins and a promise."

"My promise is good, sir," implored Robert. "With me and Hannah working together, we should be able to pay you off right quick."

"Well, if I'm kept waiting for the whole amount, then you'll have to sweeten the pot somehow," Kingman said. The old man was good at this.

"Just how sweet are we talking?" Robert asked.

"Now honey-sweet," answered Kingman. "I was thinking seven hundred."

"But you just said three," Robert said. "That's more than twice!"

"So it is," said Kingman, "But all dollars are dollars only when we're dealing in the present. Future dollars, that's another thing. That's dream money. Dream dollars ain't worth half as much as dollars in hand. If you want Hannah, it's gonna cost you five a month until you reach seven hundred. And if I don't have it all by the proper time, I'll get Hannah back and I keep whatever you've already paid me." Kingman stroked the arms of his chair with both hands, then reached out his right one toward Robert.

After a brief moment of fear and worry, an overmatched Robert clasped Kingman's hand. "Done, I suppose," he said, fully convinced that he was shaking hands with the devil himself. But Robert reasoned that Hannah's soul was worth it.

"I came prepared," said Kingman, trying not to smile too much. "I took the liberty of drawing up the details before you arrived," he said, pulling out a written contract. "Put your mark on the line at the bottom."

Robert felt like an accused criminal whose grave had been dug last week. "Fine," was all he could think to say as he made his mark.

Kingman held out his hand again, but as Robert reached out to take it, Kingman pulled his hand away. "Oh no, no, he smiled, "We've already shaken on the deal. I'm holing out this empty hand for the first payment, that is, if you want to take immediate possession of... the *goods*." Robert took five dollar bills from his small roll and stacked them one-at-a-time on Kingman's now upturned palm.

As he left Kingman's office, Robert felt a bit poorer and a lot wiser. He was a bit afraid of what he had set into motion, but was happy to have himself a new wife, or at least five dollars' worth of one. A chunk of his monthly money would now be going into Kingman's hands, their future would have to be in God's.

With regard to the wedding, everything came together in a beautiful way. Bull Simmons arranged free passage for Robert, Hannah and Hannah's girls to go down to Beaufort on the *Lone Kestrel.* God blessed them with a whole week of sunshine and mild weather – at least by December standards. The heavens were painted in strokes of red and lavender as the boat turned the corner at Hilton Head to sail up the mouth of the river toward Beaufort. At the helm, Robert spent most of the last hour of the voyage squinting into the brightness of the sunset, straining to catch his first glimpses of his old hometown.

Beaufort's waterfront looked the same as before, but perhaps a bit smaller than he remembered. Robert invited Hannah and the girls to join him up on the bridge as he pointed to every sight on the shore.

"See those boys standing by the big trees," he said to Clara. "That's where I used to do my dreaming when I was your age."

"Dreaming what?" she asked.

"Oh, I mostly dreamed of being a sailor," he said, "and sometimes about your mama and you two."

"You didn't even know us!" Charlotte said with a smirk.

"Mama says you're full of silver-tongued nonsense," added Clara.

"Well," said Robert. "Maybe I didn't know your names, but I prayed for God to give me a good life," he said. "I left it to him to fill in the details. And now, he's led me to a real good wife... and a real good life." Hannah pulled them all together as Robert put his arms around all three of them.

"Maybe I wasn't never dreaming of you," Hannah said, "and I suspect you weren't dreaming of us, but I do believe the Lord had plans." As the *Kestrel* tied up at the wharf, Hannah turned Robert's face to hers and kissed him on the lips. "And if it is just a dream," she said, "then you girls don't need to wake me up." Then she kissed him again, longer this time.

"Eeeew!" they squealed, but Robert could see that Charlotte and Clara were both smiling. Whether his dream, Hannah's dream, or God's, Robert was happy it was coming true.

Jane and Henry McKee were delighted to hear that Robert had found himself a bride, volunteering their backyard as the place for the wedding. Hannah had many family members in Beaufort and some of

Lydia's kinfolk were even permitted to come over from Ashdale Plantation. Jane and the McKee children helped decorate the backyard garden where the winter camellias were still in bloom. Lydia, as usual, did most of the cooking.

Christmas Eve 1856 was wedding day. Clara and Charlotte served as flower girls and Old George dressed up to give away the bride. Robert joked that it was rare that anybody ever gave away a Negro in South Carolina. With so many wonderful friends and beautiful flowers, it was the closest thing to a storybook experience that two slaves might enjoy.

"Congratulations, Mrs. Smalls," Robert said to his new bride as they walked through the crowd of onlookers. "I hope you heard the part about "love, honor and *obey.*"

Hannah just winked and gave him a stern look. "Just remember," she said, "all that head-of-the-household stuff gets switched around once we set foot in the Baines Hotel where we both know who is boss."

"Yes, your majesty," he said as he smiled and bowed to her. "I just hope I can steal a kiss from time to time." Hannah just nodded as they stopped to embrace.

Looking past Hannah, Robert could see his mother coming towards them. "Excuse me," he said to Hannah as he took Lydia's hand and walked out to the old swing that hung in the yard. They sat down together, gently rocking in silence the way they had so often done in his childhood.

"I sometimes doubted I would live to see this day," his mother said. "I wish the best blessings for you and Hannah."

"She's solid gold, she is," Robert said. "I'm a lucky man."

"She's a whole lot of woman, seems to me... with a strong head on her shoulders," Lydia said. "I expect she'll be good for you."

"Better than you know," he said. "She's a hotel manager and she can even read some."

"Glory to God," she said. "She can teach your children. One day, maybe they'll be free." As Robert smiled and listened, familiar bird songs drifted from the shade trees of the garden. After a minute or two, he pointed out toward some afternoon clouds that were just now gathering over the distant Atlantic.

"Look there, Mama," he whispered. "There's some fresh rain clouds fixing to come. Just feel sweetness of the breeze. I'm not sure what my future holds, but I get the feelin' some big things are on the way. Changes. Maybe even freedom for all of us. I've heard talk, and where there's talk, they'll be more talk. And if there's enough talk, maybe then there will be action."

"What you mean, action?" she asked.

"I don't rightly know," he said. "The world is changing in Charleston and soon enough, it'll change here too. Now I don't dream of just the children gettin' free. I still got that dream for Hannah and for me and for you too."

"Well and good," she said, trying not to show worry on her face. Hearing Robert's words reminded her of the way he talked right before he started defying curfew. Bold ideas could often mean nothing but trouble. Just then Hannah came up behind them.

"Mr. Robert Bridegroom, It's your wedding day!" she said. "What've you been sayin' to your poor mama to put such a frightful look on her face?"

"Just small talk," he said. "We were just sayin' what a lucky man I was and that I should go pay my respects to some folks right now."

"He *is* lucky," his mother said as she and Hannah watched Robert walk away. Lydia put her arm around her new daughter-in-law, whispering, "He's blessed to get himself such a fine woman and we're blessed to have you as part of our family." Lydia wiped a tear from Hannah's face and adjusted her veil, which had been blown askew by the growing wind. "I was already too old to be a mother when Robert came into this world I expect you'll discover I've left some things out in raisin' him."

"Well," said Hannah, "I'm too old a bitty-hen to be marrying such a wild rooster, but between you, me, and the Good Lord, I believe there's still reason to hope for improvement. You should know that he talks about you 'most every day. Prays for you, too."

"Daughter," Lydia said, "I wish you the best. I doubt I'll be seeing either of you in the few years left of my life, but I on this day I believe the dearest dream of my life has come true. Just look at him," Lydia said. "Makes me want to cry." Across the lawn she watched as loved ones offered congratulations and encouragement to Robert on his big day.

The McKee family seemed pleased that Robert was finding his way in the world, and that he had found love. For their part, Henry and Jane seemed for once to be happy together, certainly much happier than Robert remembered. With him gone, perhaps the fences between them had been lowered a little. As expected, in the five years since he'd left, the McKee children had grown up quite a bit too.

Liddie McKee was busied by the cluster of young men who swarmed like insects around her sweetness. Her bright laughter could be heard above the conversations of their many friends and family members that strolled the yard. Later on, she looked all over for Robert, only to find him found him outside the little slave shack where he had grown up. He was rubbing his fingers over the twelve notches in the doorpost.

"It's been amazing to see you again," Liddie said with a grin. "I can't believe you're an old married man at seventeen." No longer an awkward girl, Liddie was a comely young woman now, but still with that dramatic red hair. Though she carried herself like a proper lady, Robert could still see that same naughty girlishness in her blue eyes.

"I hope you've been staying out of trouble since I left," he said, "and watching that sassy mouth of yours."

"Oh, you know better than that," she smiled. "I suppose I just picked up where you left off, Robert – making waves here and there."

"Not in the jailhouse, I hope."

"Oh, not that bad yet," she chuckled, "and no public whippings so far. Papa has threatened to send me off to school somewhere if I don't repent. But I won't, of course."

Robert just smiled at her the way he had when they were children. "You seem hell-bent on straying from the straight and narrow," he said. "Troublemakers pay a high price in this world, you know."

"You're one to talk!" She replied. "As I remember, you earned yourself plenty of warnings. Besides, I *want* to get away. Misbehavior is part of my plan." With that, she gave him a coy wink. "We slaves are always dreaming of getting free, you know."

"Ha ha. I've missed you, sister," he smiled. "I do pray for God to guide you... and protect you."

"Thanks," she said. "You should also pray God will protect my parents."

"Is there some new peril I should know about?"

"My, yes!" Liddie said. "I'm likely to murder them any day now," she joked, "or they me." At this, they both chuckled.

Robert would have liked to chat longer, but he noticed that his new bride was watching them from across the yard, less than pleased that her husband was not at her side. "It appears I'm a wanted man," he said. "For the first time in my life I'm actually pleased to belong to somebody. A slave of love."

"I wish you and Hannah well in your marriage," Liddie said. "But remember, we've still got a blood oath to help each other." With this, she pressed her pale thumb against his. "Remember?"

"Blood oath," he whispered with a smile. "I haven't forgotten, and I might just hold you to it one day."

Before Robert and his new family departed for Charleston, Jane McKee had occasion to take him aside. "We do congratulate you, Robert," she said, and then lowered her voice to a whisper. "And I have something for you." She pressed into his hand a leather envelope. "There's money and some valuables. These might help you purchase freedom for you and Hannah."

Robert was utterly shocked by her gesture and was so moved be didn't know exactly what to say. "You didn't have to do this, Missy," he said. "If Mister Henry finds out, it might bring trouble down upon you."

"It's all right, Robert," she said. "Henry knows about this. It was his idea actually, but as usual you mustn't say anything. He knows, but doesn't want you to know he knows."

"Well, if I'm sworn not to say anything, you must tell him I was greatly encouraged," Robert said, wiping a tear away. "As you know, there have been times I hated him, but I have also loved him dearly. You mustn't tell him either thing, of course. It would likely just prompt him to make one of his big speeches," Robert said.

"... and then probably head into town for drinks," she joked. It gladdened Robert that Missy could smile so.

"Quite likely so," Robert laughed. "But please let Mister Henry know my heart is greatly lifted. There is goodness in him, but I suspect it keeps him uncomfortable."

Miss Jane just nodded. "We're proud of you, you know," she said. "Both of us."

By the time the family made it back to Charleston, they were all extremely tired and hungry. "It feels odd to have us all in the same house now," Hannah said, as she looked around their quarters over the Ancrum's stables. "I'll have to get used to this arrangement."

"...And the smell," Clara said, holding her nose.

"I suspect we'll discover certain improvements over livin' alone," he said to his new wife with a grin. It ain't a fancy place, but I know you'll brighten it up with the woman's touch. I may even do a bit of touchin' of my own," he whispered with a wink.

After a supper of beans and greens, the bride and groom held one another close as the girls went down to sleep in their own little side room. Robert heard the city bell ring out midnight as they lay back exhausted. They would all need their rest. A full day's work awaited them tomorrow.

Robert awoke at five the next morning to the sounds of trumpets, rooster-crowing, and the loud screams of Hannah and the girls. "What in God's name is all that?" Hannah shreiked.

Robert introduced her to Cornwallis and explained the routine of the militia next door, but his best answers didn't seem to satisfy his new bride. "We'll just see about that," she scowled. "Just leave this to me."

By the next afternoon, Hannah had made some sweet cornbread for the buglers next door. The militia welcomed the snacks in exchange for a week of silent mornings, an arrangement that continued for the next six years. Seeing no way to negotiate an amicable agreement with the rooster, Hannah made a deal with the Ancrums to purchase the bird. By suppertime that evening, the family was sitting down to a fried chicken dinner. Everyone was full and satisfied that they would all be able to sleep a bit later the next morning. Robert had discovered two more precious things a dollar could buy: supper and silence. The woman's touch, indeed.

Chapter 24
Thunder in the Harbor

The world changed at 4:30 a.m. on April 8th 1861, when the rhythmic buzzing of dishes and window glass awakened every resident of Charleston. At first, some of them thought it might be a spring thunderstorm somewhere afar off, but the distant thuds and flashes in the sky made it clear that these were not the sounds of weather. Fort Sumter was being shelled from Fort Moultrie, Fort Johnson, and the big howitzers on Cummings Point. War had arrived.

As glowing ribbons of light arched across the dark harbor, husbands and wives, grandfolks and children, some still in the nightclothes, made their way up to the rooftops of the big houses along East Bay Street and the Battery. The little ones jumped and clapped as the sparks and explosions illuminated the sky above the distant rectangle of Fort Sumter. Many older folks just sat stone-faced, remembering their own parents' description of the British fleet's attack of 1777. Sweethearts, some betrothed and others long-married, kissed and embraced in silent sadness, knowing that war would likely bring enlistment, separation, and perhaps even death.

Every male was busy providing analysis and explanation – a chief duty of Southern men. As they watched the far-off flashes, each of them made clear that he was not surprised, and each took his turn to expound on their various theories concerning the war.

Some supposed that this bloodless barrage was merely symbolic, a warning shot across the bow of Washington. Other men took opportunity to curse the Yankees for their blindness to the clear promises of the Declaration, the Constitution, and the better light of reason. Clergymen quoted scripture, tracing the divine mandate for slavery all the way back to the curse of Ham in Genesis. All agreed that the Unionists would be fools to think they could drag South Carolina back into the old nation by force.

Brave and eloquent males were too impassioned to notice the tears that dampened every female eye. Their women mostly nodded in demure silence, knowing full well that the menfolk up north, like their own husbands, brothers, and sons, would not back down until one of the sides was out of bile, ammunition, or blood.

Back in December of 1860, Charleston's Mercury had announced that the Union was dissolved and stated so in a banner headline. By the time Sumter was fired upon, the editors lamented that their largest typeface was not enough to announce the news. The April 9th edition included lengthy articles by every politician and military authority within a hundred miles. To a man, they affirmed the justice of their cause and their willingness to fight every step of the way, either to victory or death, in any war that might come. Everyone from senators to priests endorsed in great detail the legality and nobility of their principles.

In the weeks after secession, citizens had smiled and clinked glasses of sweet tea and spirits on every front porch along the waterfront. Everyone was careful to exude optimism. The questions, if there were any, concerned whether the North would allow them to depart in peace or whether generous concessions might be offered to entice them to return to the Union. If anyone harbored fears, such notions were quickly dismissed, or at least internalized, lest any disparaging words should be uttered.

Charlestonians had, of course, kept up with the murmurings in the Yankee papers too. Firebrands up North had talked of making war if secession came. While most South Carolinians scoffed at the idea that the Northern states would actually shed blood to reestablish ties with their hated rivals, a few people thought that armed conflict was at least a possibility. But educated voices had long-ago concluded that the North's sabre rattling was pure affectation. War, if it came at all, would likely be trifling and brief. Bloodless symbolism.

Despite these assurances, most young men were eager to hone their military skills. Those who could teach horsemanship, shooting, or swordplay were much sought after. Ladies organized societies for the sewing of flags and uniforms. Some female members of the Episcopal choir composed a booklet of battle songs for the boys, modifying old Christian hymns from pious to patriotic, all in four-part harmony. Church attendance increased as South Carolina's mothers became increasingly diligent in their regimens of prayer.

As the ranks of the militia swelled, there was frequent marching and drilling in the public areas around the Battery and downtown's armory. The few men who had any real military experience were given special respect, not to mention high rank. Those with old war wounds were especially revered.

Early on, it became clear that the prosaic design of the old militia uniforms lacked the desired *elan*. Any books with pictures of European soldiers were studied like Bibles. As a result, epaulets and gold braid were added wherever possible, with various pins, medals, insignias, and other bits of color. Officers, mostly wealthy men, dusted off English military manuals that had been brought over from the Old Country. They practiced barking out commands in their best Shakespearean voices. Some of them, who had previously spoken in a nasal Southern drawl, now addressed their volunteers in a tone that would have made King Lear proud.

Proper soldiers all, their ranks had swelled with each passing day. Their marches were not so much drills as high drama. Brimming with dash and fervor, they only stopped their maneuvers to collect cookies and kisses from the ladies. Up till now it had all been something like a church picnic with snare drums.

But with tonight's bombardment of the fort, Robert got the haunting sense that the picnic was about to come to an end. He could see it on the faces of everyone he passed in the dark streets. Everyone looked afraid and urgent to find a place to watch what remained of the bombardment. Robert wanted to get over to the hotel as quickly as he could, as it was likely they'd be paying overtime to any servants that could serve refreshments to those who gathered on the Baines' observation deck. As expected, the rooftop was crowded and the drinks were flowing as prominent men made toast after toast to Southern victory. Robert sensed at once that there was an uneasy atmosphere in their gathering.

These gentlemen blustered with confident talk of course, but he knew the masters always made their boldest speeches when they felt fear. As he brought beverage trays up from the kitchen to the rooftop of the hotel, Robert tried to avoid eye contact with anyone, white or colored. Already on edge, the whites were likely to react to any unusual expression in their slaves' demeanor. In truth, he himself didn't know what to make of this whole affair. After distributing the drinks, Robert took his empty tray to the far corner of the rooftop, looking away from the nervous crowd, and away from the war.

In the darkness, he stared down to the narrow streets of town. Among those who scurried to and fro, he made out a lanky but familiar figure looking up at him. It was Spider, all alone and walking slowly. He seemed to be headed toward the hen cages behind the shops on Market

Street. Robert knew what this meant, for he and Spider would almost always go for eggs when they wanted to talk with each other about current happenings. Robert hastened down to the back door and escaped silently down the lane toward the coops.

Spider was smiling, but Robert noticed that his dark hands were trembling and fidgety. Spider always did this when he was afraid. "What do you make of all this?" he asked.

Robert did his best to look calm, but could feel his heart bumping strongly from his chest to his forehead. "There's no question that we've got a full out war on our hands," he said. "Their highbrows won't want to believe it, but it's done come anyway." Lightning from the distant explosions flashed across both men's faces, followed a few seconds later by loud thuds, and then echoes.

"You really think the game is on?" Spider said, trying his best to smile. "A real killin' war?"

"Those ain't bass drums you hear," answered Robert, as cadent discharges of cannons resonated off the nearby buildings and across the harbor. "Southern men won't content themselves to strut and cluck like fighting roosters. Not for long," he added. "It's war all right."

"Holy pissin' angels," muttered Spider as he shook his head in disbelief. "Impossible." Spider kept looking around at the people who continued to rush past them. "No way I see all those boys and all those states agreeing together to risk life and limb. Likely, it will all be nothing but talk. White men love to talk."

But Robert shook his head right back at Spider, and for a moment there was tense silence as both men stared straight into each other's eyes. "No," said Robert, raising his voice just a bit. "Listen. You hear it. That's the thunder of the biggest storm you're ever gonna see. When one of these white boys steps up to a fight, all the others are obliged to join right in. They won't want to seem cowards, and every Southern state will fall in behind every Southern man."

"But don't you reckon their fear might give 'em pause?" Spider offered.

"Sure, they'll be afraid to die, but they're more afraid of something else. They mostly dread what all the others might think of them. There'll be a war all right. Surely war to the death, I fear."

"Holy, Awful God!" whispered Spider.

"Buck up, brother. This could be the hand of the Lord," Robert began. "There might be something tasty in this big stew pot...

something good for *us*. Our masters won't back down, but the Yanks will have something to prove, too."

"You think they be coming down here and set us to free?" Spider asked.

"I doubt they care a pig's pants about freeing black folks, but I think they'll be coming down here nonetheless. Yanks got 'em a navy with lots of gunboats – the big ones." Pointing off to the far horizon beyond Sumter, Robert went on. "Higher-ups along the wharf say there's talk of a blockade, with a long line of warships stretched all across that harbor. No cargoes will go through – none coming in or going out. No cotton, no rice, no goods. And no dock work."

"It would be something if the Yanks bring their army down here to free us."

Quietly amused, Robert just smiled. "To hurt us, free us, maybe to own us. But they'll most surely be coming, I think. It may have come time for us colored men to decide if we're gonna fight and who we're gonna fight. And blood, no question. I 'spect blood'll be flowing like River Jordan in any case."

Another long silence ensued as Robert and Spider continued to stare at the distant spectacle. "It's a time for brave men, I suppose," said Robert. Spider, for once, was speechless, but eventually he found a few words.

"And who you think will be brave enough to win this bloody game?"

"Well," Robert said, "maybe not the brave one. There'll be brave men both North and South, and brave men are usually the first to find their graves. Could be the smart one will take it in the end, the man who keeps his head down," Robert mused. "A scrap like this can make a man brave, but it can also make wise men do stupid things."

"An angry white man's a crazed animal sometimes," Spider offered. "Sometimes you just have to get out of his way. No way you're gonna stop him."

"Oh, we stop animals all the time," said Robert, now pointing to the skinless hindquarters of hogs and sheep that hung up on the front porch of Rayfield's butcher shop. "The ones on these hooks were brave critters, but mostly oak-head stupid. I doubt they ever saw it coming." Robert then looked up at the white men who by now had positioned themselves on every rooftop in Charleston. "These gentlemen may talk like professors tonight," he said, "but soon enough they'll be slaughtered like cattle."

By lunchtime the next day, the Federals had taken down their big striped flag over Fort Sumter and raised a white one. Everyone did their best to go back to normal life, but the dark clouds of war, and the smell of gunpowder, lingered over Charleston. The city that had so recently buzzed with the frenetic energy of commerce was now stirring with different sounds.

The cobblestone streets echoed with the cadenced footfalls of soldiers and the rattle of supply wagons and artillery. It was as if Charleston was bracing itself for a hurricane. Every night, the whole city slept only fitfully – in a persistent and ominous atmosphere of fear. But it was different in the daylight hours – when snare drums and bugles served to awaken the beguiling and intoxicating spirit of war.

Robert and Spider took every opportunity to run errands downtown, and this was especially so on Saturday mornings. It was then that the brigades marched. Thousands of uniformed troops – most of them in step – stretched down the whole length of Meeting Street. There were always drums and fifes, and on most Saturdays, there was even a marching orchestra. Most of their songs were renditions of Baptist hymns, re-written in the more masculine rhythms of war.

"It's something, ain't it?" Robert said to Spider. "What a spectacle!" He just kept looking around at the crowds of white men, women, and children who cheered the gray soldiers as they passed. There were also scores of slaves who stood by, and they clapped, too. It was hard not to be caught up in the whole thing. Robert had never before seen Charleston's upper crust display such fervor for anything. They clapped and danced like Campbellites at Cane Ridge. Here they stood, proper Presbyterians and Episcopalians, shouting in the unfettered frenzy of revival.

"It's a sight," Spider said, his eyes widened by all the music and clamor. "If they keep all this drumming up, they might even give *me* a notion to enlist." He then stood up straight, doing his best imitation of attention, grinning and saluting Robert stiffly. "How do you think I'd look in one of them fancy gray uniforms?"

"Pretty impressive," said Robert, smirking. "Until they see you grinning like that and kill you!"

Spider's face suddenly lost a bit of its giddy grin, but in a moment it brightened again. "Well at least I'd look good at my funeral," he laughed.

"Yeah," said Robert, "Lynched with full military honors."

Spider couldn't help but smile. "You think that big marching band might play one of those tunes? I might dance right out of my casket!" Spider then began to dance along to the music and continued to do so until the tail of the parade marched out of sight.

Robert always remembered those first months of the war as a relatively pleasant time. There was a steady flow of news and conversation in Charleston, but no more explosions. But soon the parade music was replaced by full military mobilization in towns North and South. The time for real war was drawing near.

A gloomy mood fell over Charleston the day their boys made their final parade through the center of the city. As before, the crowds cheered and the bands played, but this time the columns of soldiers did not stop at the green parade grounds at Marion Park. They kept on marching past where Meeting Street made its half-turn to head north on the Columbia Turnpike.

As the last gray row of boys vanished in the distant dust, there came a new and awkward silence – as if the very life-blood had just been drained from the city. White families and their slaves walked back toward their homes, together, but without conversation. The politicians folded the notes for their speeches and stuffed them into their breast pockets as musicians returned trumpets to their velvet-lined cases. The party was, for all intents and purposes, over.

Robert and Spider, their wellspring of humor now run dry, silently made their way back to their places of work. In the dead quiet of the downtown streets, any laughter would have been as conspicuous as a love song in a graveyard.

A few optimists began to offer assurances that the army would make its show of force in Virginia and would soon be back, by midsummer at the latest. Mothers, sweethearts, and sisters endorsed these notions, but as all their heads nodded in agreement, their hearts were presently filling with prayers and fears. The next days were sad ones, but they were but a few.

Charleston was a buoyant place, and it would not permit itself to linger too long on the memories of a sad farewell. Both Robert and Spider were surprised at how soon the town again overflowed with rumors that the war might soon be over. White folks were, after all, people of faith and reason. Their religion filled their hearts with confidence that Almighty God would vindicate the rightness of their cause, and if the angels of vengeance were slow in coming, there were a hundred logical reasons to expect peace. The Yankees were an educated people, and there existed no plausible reason for bloodshed. Any army they mustered would certainly be filled with journalists, bookkeepers, and actors. The preparation and resolve of the brave Confederate army would make any invasion of the South unthinkable. After all the bands and bravado were done with, certainly cooler heads would prevail.

But any such notions soon faded as the casualty trains began to arrive from Virginia at summer's end. Once-strapping young men now returned to Charleston looking gaunt and suddenly aged. Many had to be carried on stretchers and pallets. Most arrived with limps and bloody bandages, with many having lost limbs.

Robert and Spider earned money unloading the thousand or so coffins that were sent home from the first big fight at Manassas Junction. The brave sons of South Carolina were now returning – without the applause, fanfare, and kissing girls that had so recently sent them northward. Robert had never seen the Market Street Station so sullen, now bereft of war drums and ranting politicians.

Even the colored loaders went about their work in near silence. These dead white boys weren't arriving in lacquered coffins, lined with quilting. They came stacked on flatcars like so much harvested fruit, all in identical crates, quickly fabricated from sap pine planks. Packed loose, the bodies rattled around inside as the dear ones were moved from the boxcars to the carriages of their kinfolk.

Soon, the eerie peace of the station was disturbed by shouting and crying as the name on each box was called out and the dead were claimed. Many crates had no names, and some family members had to spend the next two days prying open box after box, trying to identify the ghastly remains of some familiar and beloved face. The whole place stank like a slaughterhouse and Robert would never forget the scene – or the sickening odor.

It is testimony to the resilience of hope that even after witnessing this, and many other similar scenes, citizens of Charleston clung to the hope that the North might relent and call an end to the carnage. It seemed illogical, and unimaginable, to think otherwise, but logic and imagination would be sorely tested in the months to come. After this, there came no more train-borne boxes. The dead would from now on be buried where they fell, and they fell by the tens of thousands.

Chapter 25
On the *Planter*

In the months that followed Fort Sumter, work opportunities around the docks gradually dried up as the Union's blockade choked the life out of Charleston's seaport. An occasional blockade runner got through from but these vessels had to be both fast and lucky. The beaches were littered with the burned and broken hulls of those that failed. Paying jobs were scarce, since most of the ships that came and went now were performing military tasks. Transporting men and weapons around the harbor was now every man's patriotic and unpaid duty.

With the flow of dollars squeezed down to a trickle, a good number of the white dockmen had enlisted in the Confederate Army. Some were stationed locally for harbor defense, but most of these were sent up North to fight in the Virginia campaigns. A few of the men who had worked the wharves before the war chose to serve on the handful of armed boats they generously called the Confederate Navy.

At the outset of hostilities, most of the deep-water sailors and almost all of the U.S. Navy ships had gone to the Union side. Having almost no proper warships, the South scrambled to arm whatever boats they had for the defense of their harbors. Most of these were vessels conscripted from private owners, who were paid a nominal sum for their use. None of these ships would have been any kind of match for the well-equipped warships the Yankees had, but their presence posed at least a symbolic line of resistance within the local waters, and what meager firepower they had was well-supplemented by the heavy cannons of the Southern forts.

Charleston's tiny squadron of Confederate vessels were at their best when they were used as dispatch boats, carrying messages and supplies in the harbor. With shipping all but shut down, it didn't take many men to work these vessels and the wharves that served them. Every day, there were fewer and fewer men on the docks, and even those that remained were unpaid for the most part.

Blacks who had labored on the waterfront began to disappear as well. Some masters, fearing Yankee conquest, had gathered their slaves and retreated to safer plantations inland. A different course was charted by the black sailors, many of whom were not slaves but freedmen. After Sumter, many of them chose to head north with the other two thousand or so free Negroes of Charleston. Other Negroes who had worked the wharves were either hired out, or freely donated to support the Confederate war effort. They were assigned to load wagons or dig entrenchments, and, later in the war, some were even armed for combat.

There were quite a few blacks who took advantage of the wartime chaos to escape between the cracks. Secessionists were often too busy watching for Yankees to watch their slaves very closely. Those who disappeared were not quickly missed on the waterfront, though many runaways were eventually captured. Even some, who had been freedmen before the war, were sold back into slavery. The world was in turmoil and everyone's life or business was feeling the effects of war.

In the summer of 1861, Bull Simmons and the *Lone Kestrel* were impounded by the Confederacy. Being a blue-water vessel, it was a valuable commodity in the South, which had few such boats that could venture out to sea. The *Kestrel* was sent up the coast to serve around Fort Fisher off Wilmington, North Carolina. Robert and the other black crew members were left behind to find other work. With so many of the whites being dragged into military service, a few opportunities began to open up around the harbor, but you had to know somebody. Fortunately, Robert knew just about everybody.

Alfred Gradine had picked up the nickname Deke when he was a preacher in the AME Church. He was de-frocked as a clergyman a few years back when he repeatedly mentioned abolition. Being no longer able to mount the pulpit, Deke found work as an engineer, a boiler man, and over a period of years, he worked on a number of boats. Robert first got to know him on the *Lone Kestrel*. After the war started, Deke got a job on a big side wheeler called the *CSS Planter*. Once Bull Simmons and the *Lone Kestrel* went up to Wilmington, Robert begged Deke to put in a good word for him with the *Planter's* captain, one Charles J. Relyea.

Robert was dying to find some way to get back on the water, but in the meantime, he had to make money doing odd jobs. White folks in Charleston were almost always prepared to pay for help on their bigger projects. These were usually onetime tasks like cleaning out a basement or moving furniture. Robert was not averse to hard work, but he preferred to broker the off-hours labor of others. He would sometimes go down to Market Street and beat a tin pot to *drum up* a group of willing colored workers. At day's end, each of these boys would chip in a few coins of their pay to him – their broker. Robert found that if he could contract enough boys for enough jobs, he could go home with quite a roll of money, and he might not even have to work up a sweat.

Things changed one day in mid-June when Deke invited Robert to drop by the *Planter* at Wharf Six. With all the arms and supplies to be transported around the harbor, word was that they might be taking on some additional crew. Robert made sure to spend extra time in prayer that Saturday morning before he made his way from East Bay Street to the wharf. With God's help and a good first impression, he hoped to once more sign on as a sailor.

As he stepped onto the foredeck of the *Planter*, Robert felt like he had just walked through the pearly gates of heaven. He could once again smell the salt of the damp ropes on the gunnels, and the slow rise and fall of the boat felt delightfully familiar under his feet. This was where he belonged.

"Here's the boy I told you about," Deke said to the Captain. Quite desperate to get hired on, Robert did his best to stand up straight like a strong man, but also to appear relaxed like a sailor. Mostly, he felt nervous. The old man looked him over from top to bottom.

"Got no money to take on any new swabbies or mess monkies," he muttered. "Especially not some soft houseboy." Relyea took a sip from his water flask, which from where Robert stood, didn't smell much like water. Looking out to the clouds in the distance, the captain asked, "What do they call this one?" At this point, the captain deliberately avoided any eye contact with Robert.

"Robert Smalls, sir," he said, adding, "I'm a hard worker." Robert walked around in front of the old seaman, making sure to look him square in the eyes. "I've put in time at the helm, sir. And I know the harbor and its channels."

The captain rubbed his sparse gray whiskers between his thumb and forefinger, trying to appear deep in thought, but it was mostly for effect. "Bull Simmons is a good captain. Turns brick-headed boys into seasoned sailors. I ain't totally disgusted by the way you carry yourself. Come stand over here where I can see you." Robert stood smartly at attention the way he'd seen white sailors do it. The captain frowned and glowered at him. "How come you don't salute?" Relyea asked.

"Well sir," he said, "Cap Simmons told me never to salute him 'till I was a proper sailor." Robert feared he might be sinking his own chances, but he had to tell the truth.

"Commendable, very commendable," Relyea said. "I'm partial to a boy that knows his place, but right now I got no place for you. Bursar's been snapping at me sayin' we're coming up short every month. Gradine, you best send this one back to his master... or his mama. Keep an eye on him though. We may just need us a boy somewhere down the line."

Seeing his opportunity slipping away, Robert ventured to speak again. "Please, sir," he said, "I'll do anything! I've got to get my feet on this boat. It's a splendid boat, sir." The captain stopped for another moment to stroke his beard again. Even if this was for effect, it encouraged Robert greatly.

"There's no call to flatter me by calling this tub splendid," he said. "She's just a side-wheeled horse barn." The Captain then wagged his old head slowly. "But no money's no money," he said. "Sam Smith can handle the helm."

"Lieutenant Smith's over-matched at the wheel," said Deke. "He got us stuck on a grass bank last week, Cap. This boy's tested. Knows every inch and twist of Charleston Harbor."

Against his better judgment, Robert decided to go all in. "I'll prove myself if you let me," he said. "Pay me nothing the first month and let me show you what I can do."

"Whoa now," Relyea said. "Stand down, John Paul Jones. I already told you to let it go."

"Please sir," Robert pleaded. "You said the money was the reason, but I'll work for you for no money. Off the books till I prove myself. You won't be sorry."

"You're persistent for a darkie," Captain replied. "Blast me, I'd say you drove a hard bargain, but I've never had a man bargain me into letting him work for nothing. If this ain't the dangdest thing."

"So you'll take me on? asked Robert.

"Don't you be putting words in my mouth," he growled. "I'm gonna have to sit down and think this over some. Be here at sunrise tomorrow when we cast off. I'll have you an answer by then."

Deke winked over at Robert and asked, "So Cap, can I take the boy around to get the lay of things?" Relyea scowled and shook his gray head at first then nodded as he took another big sip from his flask, waddling down the stairs that led below.

"Cap's a piece of work," Robert said. "Likes to throw his weight around."

"And he's got a bit of heft to throw," laughed Deke, "Mostly around his middle and his backside."

"Plays games with the rank and file," said Robert. "I've known nervous men, but Relyea likes to make other men nervous."

"Oh, you don't know the half," said Deke. "We're used to his mean ways... and it always makes for open berths on the boat. Cap's got a way of running good men off."

"He's not partial to colored men, is he?" asked Robert.

"No," said Deke, "But don't let that irk you. In truth, Cap's not really partial to nobody. I 'spect he'll finish that flask in his cabin and he'll come back warmed up to the idea of taking you on. For now, I'll give you a good show-around fore and aft." Deke motioned for Robert to follow, as they took a brief tour of the *Planter*, and quite a ship she was.

A cotton steamer before the war, she stretched 148 feet in length with a beam of over 50. She was among the fastest ships in Charleston Harbor, and because she required less than four feet of draft, the *Planter* was invaluable in negotiating the shallows and shoals. After secession, she had been converted from a cotton steamer into a warship and was commissioned the *CSS Planter*. South Carolina paid her owner, John Ferguson, $100 a month for the privilege of using her for government service. In the span of two days, she was stripped of her passenger rails and loading cranes. The cotton racks in her hold were cleared out and bolstered for munitions and guns for the rebel forts. By the time two small howitzers were mounted on its fore and aft decks, the *Planter* was designated the flagship of the Confederate fleet in Charleston. She may not have been a fifty-gun frigate, but no first-line frigate in the Yankee's navy could safely navigate the harbor the way the Planter could. Deke always said the Planter could cruise up a wet lawn on the morning dew.

"She ain't got tall masts like the *Kestrel*," Deke said, "but she can fly though this old harbor without so much as a puff of wind," Deke said. "At full steam she can plow straight into the face of a squall. You can't do that on a clipper."

"I thought you said God could blow a boat anywhere he wants," Robert said.

"Oh, I suppose he can," said Deke, "but this side-wheeler can give Mother Nature a run for her money. A wheelman like you can just about fall in love with a headstrong steamboat like her. Sailboats can fluff-out all pretty-like, but most helmsmen crave the power – and this boat's a warhorse."

Robert couldn't help smiling and nodding as they walked along the port gunnels. The captain would just have to say yes. "And now," Deke said, "you best loosen that collar of yours. We're fixing to step down into the devil's house." Robert followed Deke from the sunny foredeck down the narrow stairway to the darkness below. The engine room swirled with steam and wood smoke as the glow from the boiler fires tinged the hold a hellish red.

"It's like walking into a fireplace," said Robert. "How do y'all stand it?"

"Oh you should feel it when we're all ahead full," Deke said. "Me and the boys strip all the way down to naked sometimes. Clothes get too sweat-heavy to wear."

"Well, that's a grim picture," Robert smiled. "Naked black men prancing about like demons in the bowels of hell."

Deke laughed but couldn't disagree. "You pretty much hit the nail on the head," he said. "I venture I'm the only man what once preached against hell on Sunday and now earns wages there all week!"

"Oh, I don't think you're the only one, Deke," Robert replied. "I've seen quite a few preachers strollin' the Street of Sin on Saturday nights!"

"Amen," said Deke. "I just reckon the Lord'll have to let me in heaven since I already done my time in hell."

"Well," said Robert, wiping his brow. "I don't know how you stand it."

"Engineers need know-how, but I reckon their biggest skill is being able to take the heat. It's a lot like when I preached. If you say too much about hell, the church will give you a bit of hell in return. Ministry's not all hallelujahs and chicken dinners."

"I'm happy to let you be the king of Hades," Robert said. "But you better take me topside for some fresh air or I'll die."

Deke led Robert back to daylight and then walked him through the rest of the boat. When a bell rang out, the crew scurried to take their places around the big table that served as their mess. There were some apples in a basket that were cut in half and distributed among the men. And each man got a slice of hardtack smeared with sloosh, an all-purpose concoction sailors made from dried peas mixed with bacon leavings. It was not the freshest sloosh Robert had ever tasted, but he was happy to eat something and was anxious to get acquainted with the men.

Robert asked Deke if he would say grace for the crew, but he shook off the notion, saying he wasn't a legal preacher anymore. "Just bow your own head and say some words if you like," he said. "That's what most of the men do." Deke didn't seem to be unnerved by Robert's request.

"So you just let them shut you up from preaching?" Robert asked.

"Well," said Deke. "I suppose that's one way to put it. I could've stood my ground, but I've seen more than one such preacher buried right under their own pulpit."

"It's a shame though," Robert said. "I'd wager you were a good preacher."

"Oh, I doubt my leaving was any great blow to the Lord's Kingdom," he said. "I reckon I ran out of fine words a few years back. I figure I've pretty much said all God sent me to say. Now I'm content to stoke a boiler every now and then."

"Well," said Robert. "You're a good Christian in any case, and godly men seem to be in short supply these days. There never seems to be any shortage of preachers."

Deke said "Amen," and proceeded to introduce the crew members one by one. "These here are good boys, and good friends," he said. "Men I'd lay my life down for, and they for me." One by one, Deke introduced the crew of eleven men – three white and eight colored, and like every boat in every navy, each one had his assigned title and role. Like Deke Gradine, most had nicknames.

The senior deck hand was Abraham Allston. At 46, Allston was the oldest of the boys, but was still of robust and energetic constitution. Originally from Savannah, he'd been sold off to Charleston right after his second son was born. Abe hadn't seen his wife or children for many years, but he liked to tell pleasant stories about them and their former days in the Low Country. Old Abraham was quite a spinner of yarns, and his words could touch the heart at times, inspiring young men to dream, or bringing a white-haired seaman to tears.

Gabriel Turno was another interesting character. He was 28 but looked to be quite a bit younger than his years. A good swimmer, Gabe came in handy whenever something got dropped overboard or when an anchor got fouled. Sailors called him Fish for as long as anyone could remember and he wore that nickname like a badge of honor. Gabe could stay underwater longer on one breath than any man Robert had known.

J. Samuel Chisholm was a muscular, bearded man of medium brown complexion. Chiz, as they called him, had a rich deep voice and liked to sing while he worked, and work he did. He was the man to call when something big needed to be lifted or moved. Though he always seemed to be of even temperament, Chiz looked like someone you would want alongside you in a street fight.

William Morrison was a most agreeable and energetic young man, who split his service between the *Planter* and the *CSS Etowah*, Ferguson's other steamer which was berthed at the North Wharf. William could read and write a little, and could scratch enough to send letters to his wife and mother back in Montgomery, Alabama. He was presently owned by a man named Emile Poinchignon – a tinsmith and plumber.

At 16, Abe Jackson was the youngest crewmember. He and David Jones were the boat's greenhorns, and were often loaded up with the most unpleasant of duties, mostly swabbing decks, clearing tables, or emptying the chamber pots in the head. Perhaps the most backbreaking job came twice a year when they scraped the decks with blocks of sandstone called holystones. They called them that because they were shaped like a bible and brought proud young sailors to their knees. Whereas the older men liked to spend their off time alone, these restless boys were always looking to tag along with somebody, and after hours, they loved to listen to Abe Allston's tales or even Deke's Old Testament stories.

Probably the quietest man among them was engineer John Smalls, who was no kin to Robert. Sailors on the *Planter* had long referred to him as Dark John. This was because the boat had formerly employed two sailors named John, Smalls, and a mulatto man named John Remo. John Smalls, being of blacker complexion, became Dark John, and Remo was simply called John. After Remo was sent inland, they were down to one John again, but they were reluctant to change things. John Smalls continued to be called Dark John ever since. He was an intelligent and insightful fellow, but was always a man of few words. Robert had noticed that even at slave church, Dark John was shy to speak, to shout praise, or sing out like the others. When the preacher would ask for a Hallelujah, Dark John would always just nod his head in silence. Robert figured the Lord knew what he meant. John's quiet ways served him well down in the engine room, where the hissing steam and clank of the pistons drowned out every word of chit-chat. A closed mouth pleased Dark John almost as much as an open one was a delight to Spider Jefferson. But on the rare occasions when John opened his mouth, the boys were prone to listen.

They all looked up to Deke Gradine, even though he was the newest man on board. It was hard for Robert to imagine Deke had ever been a preacher, for now mostly talked in short sentences. Like Chiz, Deke had a voice as deep as a well, and it always pleased the crew when he was in the mood to sing his old gospel songs. Though Deke spoke with slow deliberation, his words were heavy with wisdom. A humble man, he always had love in his heart, but also carried a measure of pain in his eyes. The scuttlebutt was that he'd been married once, but his wife had been sold off and paired up with some younger buck. Robert had only brought this up with Deke one time.

"Did you fancy the married life?" Robert asked.

"Oh, I liked it well enough," Deke said. "As a Christian man I needed the influence and warmth of a good woman, but our parting was the worst kind of grief. The master just up and sold her away from me."

"It must've been hard to see her go off with another man," Robert said.

"I guess it might have been more bearable if she had shed a tear or two," said Deke, "but in truth, she seemed right happy to go. I suppose I hadn't put a fire in her boiler for some time, if you know what I mean." Robert just nodded.

Deke recounted the details of his next few years, when a number of the eligible sisters at church expressed willingness to fill his wife's shoes, so to speak, but Deke found none of them comely enough to soothe his broken heart. He chose rather to sign on as a sailor, and in time, an engine man. After his wife left, he had felt like a nobody, but becoming a boiler man on a twin-engine boat helped him feel like a man again.

Engineers were responsible for stoking the boilers on the steam boats and the *CSS Planter,* being propelled by two engines, always needed a lot of fuel. Since the *Planter* had no sails, Deke's work was of supreme importance, steam being the ship's only means of locomotion. Most warships in Charleston burned coal, but the *Planter* ran on split hardwood logs, though pine could be used when a hotter fire was desired. Wood-burners like the *Planter* could be fired-up quickly and could generally outrun the coal steamers, but sometimes fuel was hard to come by.

As nightfall approached, Robert made his way back to the foredeck, but Captain Relyea was still nowhere to be seen. Climbing up the spiral stairs to the bridge, Deke silently watched young Robert as he fondled the dark spokes of the ship's wheel.

"She's a fine ship," he said to Deke, as they watched the huge sun set over the church spires of Charleston. "It'll kill me if I can't get me a berth on her. Just one cantankerous pig-head stands in my way."

At that moment, Robert noticed Deke was silently trying to get his attention. Deke was holding his finger to his mouth, trying to shush Robert, but it was too late. Behind him stood the glowering captain, who had been listening to everything they said. The 'pig-head' had his arms folded and still wore that same scowl Robert had seen earlier. Robert knew it wouldn't do any good to apologize for his ill-timed words. He figured he had likely just shipwrecked his chances of getting hired on this, or perhaps any other boat. The captain's next words, however, took Robert by surprise.

"Hell's bells!" the captain bellowed as he looked Robert over one last time. "Oh why not? I suppose I'm allowed to make one more fatal mistake before I die. I'll take you on, Smalls, but you've gotta start tomorrow." Robert was both pleased and shocked and just began to nod eagerly, having miraculously finagled his way back on to a boat.

The next morning, Robert arrived early, as he always did. It was good to see the first glimmers of sunlight run across the big river and hit the distant trees beyond the marshes. Standing on the *Planter's* foredeck, he was finishing a cup of coffee with Deke when, through the mists of dawn, he saw an imposing figure of a man slowly making the long approach down the South Wharf.

"Who is that?" Robert asked. "He marches like an admiral or something."

"That, my friend, is the captain," said Deke.

As it turned out, his friend was not joking. Suddenly resplendent in his dress uniform, a combed and cleaned-up Captain Relyea mounted the gangplank as if he had been Lord Nelson himself. Yesterday in his street clothes, he had seemed to be just another stringy-haired old salt with a pot belly and a whiskey flask. Now, strutting and sober with epaulettes on his shoulders, the Captain looked considerably taller and more imposing.

"Prepare to cast off at six bells," he shouted. At these words, the crew members held themselves in silence, almost bowing as Relyea moved past them to assume his place at his exalted position on the *Planter's* bridge. The old man surveyed the foredeck of this, the Confederate flagship, and gazed out over the whole of Charleston harbor. Dressed in spotless gray, Relyea looked every inch an admiral – the ruler of the boat and master of the fleet. Cap did not speak, nor did he need to, as one by one the various mates made their reports.

"All cargo is stored," reported Abe Allston.

"All crewmen aboard, sir," echoed the first mate.

Dark John's black forearm emerged through the shouting hatch, giving the thumbs up to those on deck.

"We're steamed-up and ready, captain!" Deke shouted.

"Half steam ahead at my order," growled Relyea in an authoritative tone that seemed to echo through the whole ship. "Untie us and prepare to cast off." After Captain inhaled from his huge, longpipe, a cloud of smoke emerged as he spoke to Chisholm who held the whistle cord. "Three long and four short," Captain barked, this week's harbor code, Robert supposed. Down at the end of the pier, the dock master sounded his horn twice in approval. They were cleared to cast off.

Once underway, Robert's heart was free to dream again. He took in the sounds and smells of the waterfront as if it had been his mother's bacon soup. He was finally back aboard ship.

Chapter 26
Free to Speak

As the Captain fired out orders, The *Planter's* crew scurried into action like chickens at sunup. "Half-ahead," he crowed, "Slight rudder to starboard." A volley of "Aye, ayes" came back, shouted above the hiss and grinding of the engines. The stampede of heels pounded across the fore and aft decks as they got underway. Robert had never seen so many men jump to obey orders. He was beginning to like this boat.

"What now?" Robert asked Deke.

"When we turn up the main channel," he replied, "Report to Cap, then just do whatever he says."

Obey orders. It wasn't a new concept to Robert. For all of his twenty-two years, he had become accustomed to showing deference to those of higher rank, and pretty much all whites on earth were of higher rank. He thought things might change when the war arrived, but now the chain of command was, if anything, clearer.

There seemed to be more officers and more orders every day. At least the rank of each man was visible now, being spelled out clearly by the various stripes and insignias of the military. The stripes did not make any man wiser, but made it more dangerous to disobey. Every officer basked in the obsequious salutes of those beneath them, but most all of them had someone above them to whom they bowed. Since the Creation, there had always been pecking orders in God's great world.

For men like Captain Relyea, there were of course fewer superiors to deal with. Even requests from the Confederate headquarters might be scoffed at. Relyea deferred only to the Lord God and General Ripley, but even orders from these were mostly dismissed. In time, God issued no further commands from heaven, and the General only called upon Captain Relyea when he needed a reliable drinking partner. Ripley's house was, after all, located right across from berth six where the *Planter*, and Relyea's stash of whiskey, was moored.

For his part, Captain Charles Relyea embraced the illusion that the Confederate Navy was among the greatest in the world, and if the *CSS*

Planter was its flagship, then that made him the de facto admiral. In truth, the South had no real warships to speak of. After the surrender of Fort Sumter, the various Confederate states had scrambled to convert every boat of size, both commercial craft and private yachts, into a fighting ship. Fishing boats became sentinels or courier vessels. The larger boats confiscated from private owners were fitted with iron rams and small cannons. Even a cargo barge might be fitted out as a mobile fortress. One of them was armed with cannons, clad in iron, and was towed to a strategic location for defense of Charleston Harbor.

Relyea felt it was incumbent on him to play the part of the admiral, doing his best to talk as an Old World commander might have spoken. He tried always to hold his head in an aristocratic way, scanning the far horizon as if he expected some vast foreign fleet to suddenly appear. In reality, his flagship was relegated to assignments of a more modest nature. The *Planter* mostly carried messages, transported personnel, and checked on the proper positioning of harbor mines, which were called torpedoes.

Captain's chief responsibility was to project an image of dignity and self-assurance, and this he did well. Gray-headed and well-uniformed, he resembled the other senators, governors, and high-born white men who ruled the South. Though not an admiral in the titular sense, he had occasionally used the word to refer to himself, since he commanded Charleston's Confederate fleet. There was, of course, no real fleet to speak of, since the warships that comprised his command were only a meager collection of converted tugs and crab boats – a less than formidable armada.

In truth, neither Relyea nor his mates, Samuel Smith and Zerich Pitcher, were actually in the Confederate Navy at all, but were paid conscripts. Nevertheless, not-quite-Captain Relyea made every effort to carry himself like somebody important. His salt-and-pepper locks matched his well-trimmed beard. He even wore an impressive-looking uniform which was custom made for him by a local tailor. A masterpiece of his own design, his outfit was a splendid all-gray affair, complete with a ruffled collar, gold epaulets, and a long-tailed topcoat. Relyea had every visible edge and seam embroidered with gold stitching and braid. Forgoing the tradition bicorne of a British admiral, Relyea always wore a broad-brimmed sweetgrass hat that had been made especially for him by one of his older slave girls. What it lacked in military dignity, it made up in the width of its shade. The captain wore it both day and night, and folks joked that perhaps he even slept in it.

Sentinels at each of the harbor checkpoints could recognize the familiar image of Relyea at his command post on the *Planter's* bridge. His burly figure always stood like a marble statue behind the helm, donning his big hat and smoking the long, curved briar pipe his late wife had brought him from Scotland. Relyea fit his part so perfectly that young Robert could not imagine what Relyea would possibly have done with himself had the war not come.

When he was not posing atop the bridge, Captain Relyea walked with an unmistakable limp. This injury was variously attributed to either a bullet wound from the Mexican War, an arrow from Andrew Jackson's Cherokee campaigns, or a shark bite received while rescuing a maiden. Stories regarding the origin and severity of the wound were expanded with each retelling, and no one ever verified whether Captain had become a captain on the land or the sea. Robert supposed that it didn't matter, since war tales from any branch of the military tended to be tall ones. But all in all, he endeavored to show the Captain proper respect and tried to learn all he could from him.

In his own way, Captain respected Robert too, though he would never say so out loud. After many hours spent together on the *Planter*, he came to trust Robert's integrity and judgment. Though he would never condescend to fraternize with a Negro on the level of friendship, he would often talk with Robert on the ship's bridge and on their after-work walks to Relyea's house on Grayson Street.

When asked, Robert would carry the Captain's bag along with the leather satchel that contained the *Planter's* logbook and other items of paperwork, stowing them into the coat closet just inside the front door of Relyea's home. Robert was paid a few coins for this service, for delivering documents to the harbormaster, and even for taking the Captain's dress grays to be laundered and pressed. Robert reasoned this would be his only chance to get anywhere near the stripes of an officer. Though long acquainted, neither the Captain nor his dark helmsman, knew the other very well – not their history, nor their families, and most certainly not the inner notions of their heart.

Robert once made the mistake of telling Captain he dreamed of getting himself a shiny-billed cap like other helmsmen wore. "Don't be getting ideas, Smalls," Relyea replied. "You are in no wise a proper helmsman, so don't let anyone put such an idea in your head. You take the wheel in your hands because I order you to. You obey me that way.

You're a low-life darkie and don't you ever forget it," he said, adding, "And I don't expect to have to tell you this again."

"No sir," said Robert. "You won't." There was no need to say anything after that. Robert would not be allowed to be called a helmsman and he would not be allowed to wear the hat or any such thing. Thankfully, he would still be permitted to steer the boat. The boat, the rudder, and God in heaven would still know who the helmsman was. And, damn the Captain, Robert would know.

Lieutenant Sam Smith, the captain's first mate, was a fine officer and a fair man. He executed Relyea's orders and oversaw the work of the colored crew members. The other white lieutenant, Zerich Pitcher, served as the *Planter's* chief engineer. His job was to operate the boilers and the engine. Robert and the other colored crew members did the real work of running the boat.

Pitcher and Smith had been friends before the war came. Zerich Pitcher volunteered for naval duty because he had worked the docks and knew all about ship's engines. Sam, on the other hand, had no fondness for sea life. He only signed up for ship duty so as to be with his old friend. The *Planter* was the first and only vessel Sam had ever set foot on. Robert soon boiled it down to its simplest form: Sam was the nice one and Zerich was a spiteful pain.

Sometime during the first months of the war, Zerich Pitcher and Sam had stopped speaking to each other. None of the crew ever found out what had caused this rift, but whatever friendship there had been between them was long gone by the time Robert arrived. Though their mutual loathing was palpable, neither man had requested to be transferred. To spend the war despising one particular idiot seemed preferable to the ghastly carnage of land combat.

Like most engine chiefs, Lieutenant Pitcher's goal was to orchestrate misery to everyone under him. It was rumored that he got his training from Lucifer himself, tormenting crews that sailed the Lake of Fire. It wasn't just that Pitcher pushed his men, for driving others was, after all, his job. It was just that Zerich enjoyed the cruelty a little too much.

Black men were accustomed to being called every wicked name under heaven, but Pitcher was obstinate to the extreme – to every man of every race. If you chanced to say it was a good morning he would affirm the opposite. If you said the wood was all stacked, he would find some reason to make you do it over again, probably with some punitive assignment tacked on. The boilers were either too hot or not hot enough. It has been said that some people brighten a room by entering it. Men like Zerich Pitcher brighten it upon their departure. As one might expect, Pitcher had no friends. He went into the city at every opportunity but only to get drunk by himself or to sample the *horizontal refreshment* of some professional woman on Water Street. And even some of these streetwalkers felt undercompensated in the exchange.

Lieutenant Sam Smith, on the other hand, was not such a bad sort. He permitted Robert to call him by his first name. When so ordered, Sam could drive a crew as hard as anyone, but unlike other officers, Sam was eager to take his ease once the day's tasks were completed. After hours, he liked to converse with the colored boys at the wharf or perhaps go into town with his white drinking buddies. Sam was the first white man Robert could call a friend.

He always remembered a particular time he first had occasion to converse at length with Smith. Captain Relyea had sent them to Market Street together to fetch some boxes of provisions that had been ordered. It was a fine autumn afternoon, cool by Charleston standards. As they left the waterfront, Sam, in a talkative mood, surprised Robert with an uncomfortable question.

"What do you and the boys think of Lieutenant Pitcher?" Sam asked. "I mean, what do you really think?" The question made Robert uneasy, for never before had any white person asked him what he really thought about anything. For a slave, transparency can sometimes bring unfortunate consequences.

"What do you mean?" Robert asked, feigning confusion, but really trying to buy time. He wanted to be sure of where Sam was going with this.

"I mean," said Sam, "Does the crew hate Pitcher as much as I do?"

Now that the question was clear, Robert still reasoned that he should choose his reply carefully. "I'm not one to speak ill of any man," Robert said. "I do my level best to live and think as a Christian." Robert and everybody else knew Pitcher was an unendurable monster, but he thought it best to choose safer words for now.

"But what do you really think of him?" asked Sam. "Is he not the very devil?"

Robert did his best to be diplomatic. "I'm a slave, and a subordinate on the ship, sir," he said. "It wouldn't be good for me to disparage any son of South Carolina."

"Even a son of South Carolina who is also a son of a bitch?" asked Sam, with a smile that gave confidence to Robert's heart.

"Yes, sir," said Robert. "Even if the particular son of South Carolina was, well... the other kind of son."

Sam Smith chuckled. "Well, you're likely a better Christian than I am, Robert. You're not a boy who speaks honest and openly, are you?"

"Well sir, folks know me to be truthful," replied Robert with a sly smile. "But the colored cemeteries are filled with the graves of honest and open slaves."

Sam was obliged to nod in agreement. "Well, I see your point, Robert. I admire your tact in any case. It's just that Zerich Pitcher is such an insufferable idiot. I must confess I used to occasionally entertain the idea of throwing him overboard."

"Only occasionally, sir?" Robert asked. "Me and the crew think about it just about every day."

At that, Sam laughed out loud. He wrapped his arm around Robert as they made their way down Market Street. "You're a good man, Robert," he said, "a very bad, good man."

As Robert watched the lieutenant walk into the storefront, Robert continued to think about this inoffensive young white man. He was a likable fellow and easy to talk to. Robert was greatly comforted by the thought that Sam treated him with affection and respect, almost as an equal, but it also gave Robert an odd feeling. Men like Smith were his enemies, his oppressors. Truth be told, if Robert was ever to escape, a man like Sam would be obligated to sound the alarm, to tie him with ropes, or even put a bullet in his back.

Robert wondered if he himself might be willing to return similar violence to Sam, blow for blow. Could he kill a kind man if freedom required it? It was not an easy notion to contemplate, much less embrace. Robert would be quite willing to slash Zerich Pitcher's throat, of course, but Sam had become a friend. Emboldened, Robert began to speak more freely to Sam on their way back to the boat.

"What do you think about what's happening?" Robert asked. "The war, I mean." Sam seemed a bit taken aback by the question, but after just a moment, his blue eyes met Robert's brown ones.

"It's a kind of suicide, I think. Pure stupidity," Sam said. "I just wish both sides would back off and allow one another to live in peace. All of us were better off before the affair started, don't you think?"

Now it was Robert who was taken aback. His sanest inclinations told him to nod in agreement, or at least to hold back an answer. The lieutenant had asked what seemed to him to be an easy question with an obvious answer, but Sam did not want the real answer. The idea that "we were all better off before the war" was like a sharp stone that stuck in Robert's craw.

In the obvious silence, Sam sensed Robert's reticence to answer. "You can speak freely, Smalls," he said. "We're just two sailors talking here."

"Well," Robert began, "You said all of us were better off before the war, but remember you're talking to a slave here." Robert looked deeply into the lieutenant's eyes. "We get no pay, you whip our backs, you call us boys," he said. "You can't be surprised we're holding out hope for something better?" Robert's heart was filled with fear the moment these words had left his lips. Even white gentlemen pull their pistols at such words from a Negro.

Lieutenant Sam's face did not distort with anger as Robert had feared, but instead softened. "Robert," he said, "You've got a fair point there, I suppose. When I think about it, I would guess this war gives you occasion to hope for better things. I can't rightly blame you for resenting the hell out of us."

"Well, Lieutenant," Robert began.

"*Sam*, remember?" the Lieutenant said. "Call me Sam."

"All right... Sam," Robert began, the name falling a bit nervously from his tongue. "If you really want to know how we feel, here goes. Think about the way it is when you catch hell from Zerich Pitcher, or from Cap when he's chugged his whiskey, when they get in the mood to cuss your soul without mercy. Well that's pretty much how slaves feel all the time, every day and every night. Feel spat on, feel pissed on, feel despised like rats."

Sam's eyes did not widen with anger, neither did they look away. "I see," he said softly. "It's a hard life for you boys."

"Men, Sam," Robert clarified, "We ain't boys, we're men." Just then, Robert could see something like a light flicker on in Sam's mind.

"Heaven help me," Sam said with a smile of recognition. "I venture most days you fellas feel like throwing all of us into the sea, don't you?"

"Well, I can't say I've never thought about it," Robert chuckled, "but most of the time it ain't like that, Sam. It ain't about hating nobody. Mostly, we just want to get free."

"But now life's hard for everybody," Sam offered. "Is there really even such a thing as free?" he asked. "We all feel beat down most days."

"We'd surely settle for our share of hardship," Robert said. "It's not some soft life we crave, but we ain't free."

"But it seems to me," Sam offered, "for the most part, you people live pretty much the same life we do. All of us have at least a bit of food and some clothes, and a roof over us. Since Sumter, it's all getting worse for everyone, black and white. Worse in most every way. Don't it seem like things were better before the war?"

"Well, sir," said Robert. "This war's been messing with lots of things for sure. Trade's shut down, folks are going hungry, and the young men have been coming home in pine boxes. Everyone, slave and free, has been praying for the day it's all over with. But as near as I can see it, if the South wins out, you all will go back to free and we'll still be slaves."

"But peaceful... and with full bellies again," countered Sam.

"But still slaves," said Robert. "Still just slaves."

"But," offered Sam. "A safe slave's better than a starving one, right?"

"But that's just it," Robert said. "Are those really my only choices? Can't I be fed *and* free? And if I'm gonna starve, I'd rather it be as a free man."

"Fine words," Sam said. "But as a sailor in this sorry excuse for a navy, I can't see I've got any more freedom than you colored men."

Robert's face stiffened as he said sternly. "Sam, your problem's that you've got your freedom, but don't know how sweet it is. Black men have to watch your freedom day in and day out and it just about kills us."

"I'm ain't all *that* free," Sam said. "Life on this boat's a living hell. A stinking slop jar where we kiss the rear end of men like Relyea and Pitcher all day long. Just like you do."

"But here's the truth, sir," Robert said. "When Pitcher's swill is too much to swallow, you sometimes have to grit your teeth and bear it. But every once in a while, if it gets bad enough, you can take a notion to jump ship and run off to town. You just take a notion and go. Sailors even call it what it is...taking *liberty*. Freedom's like that, sir. To get our own notion to tell Pitcher to go to the devil and then just run off to town. That's all we want. Ain't wanting to kill nobody and we don't dream of doing a bunch of fancy lah-dee-dah. We just want to make a choice. To be free."

"But you boys do get to go into town," said Sam.

"Yes, sir, but no, sir. There's quite a lot of difference. You get a notion to go into town, but we are *sent*. Sent ain't a choice. Sent's not freedom," Robert concluded. "One day, and maybe it will come soon, I dream of going off somewhere when and where I get the notion to go, not just where I've been sent."

Sam nodded, and finally looked at Robert with understanding in his eyes. His next words to Robert took almost a minute to come, and when they finally did, it was just a whisper. "It's a sweet thing for a man to get a notion, ain't it?" he said. "It's a good thing once in a while to have the say-so."

"It's a royal thing," said Robert. "Just a tiny notion can be a glorious thing. When all's boiled down, that's all we long for. All any of us ever really longs for." As his lieutenant nodded in agreement, Robert just looked squarely into the wells of Sam's blue eyes. For the first time in his 23 years, here was a white man who was doing his best to listen and understand.

"Enough talking for now," said Sam, as he saw they were approaching the gate to the South Wharf. "We're almost back to our own little corner of hell. I need you to take these boxes down to Lieutenant Lucifer in the engine room."

"Certainly, sir," answered Robert, grinning broadly. "But only because I choose to and not because I'm sent, thank you."

"And I'll choose to mount the bridge to kiss the captain's tail end again," said Sam, "enjoying the grand privileges of my race." They both smiled and went off to their duties, hoping that the future might somehow bring both of them to a better place in a better world.

Chapter 27
Monsters

Every piece of news from the warfront spoke against any notion that a better world was on its way. It is testimony to the resilience of hope, that, even after a year of death and destruction, citizens of Charleston still clung to the notion that the North might relent and call an end to the carnage. Neither side could claim victory and the only ones celebrating were those who trafficked in bullets or caskets. Robert and Hannah prayed every night that God would bring freedom, peace, or at least one of the two. But it was hard to keep fanning the flickering wick of faith.

Robert's last hopes for an imminent peace ended on a misty August evening when his eyes saw things that came to haunt his dreams. The white officers of the *Planter* had gone off to play cards in town, leaving the colored boys on the boat to finish up for the day. Robert and the crew completed their work quickly, and by dusk they were gabbing and bickering about how they might spend the remaining hours of the evening.

William Morrison suggested they might go visit some Creek Indian sisters who worked two streets down from the North Wharf, but only David Jones had a clean shirt, and none of the boys had any money. These women were not working girls, but they would nonetheless expect the boys to spend some money on them.

"We could play cards," Spider said. "Or maybe roll bones for next month's pay. Who's in?"

"Not for me," said Fish. "You still owe me last month's pay!"

"Count me out, too," said Abe Jackson. "If I lose, I won't trust the dealer and if I win, I won't trust myself to stop." They all nodded in agreement.

Sam Chisholm reached in his inside pocket and pulled out an almost-full bottle of rum. He smiled broadly and passed it around the circle. "How 'bout you, Robert?" he asked. "What do you fancy?"

As a helmsman, Robert was looked to as their leader. "A game of chance suits me, but McKee and Hannah have already writ their names on next month's money. You know how it goes." They all nodded again. "But I feel like if I just sit here one more night, I'll surely turn into a statue," Robert said. "I'm afraid the gulls will perch on my head if I don't venture out."

All eight of them continued to sit quietly along the *Planter's* starboard rail, allowing their legs to dangle out over the dark water. The lantern on the foredeck was beginning to glow brighter as darkness crept over the harbor. In the dead silence of the evening, they could even hear the flies that were buzzing around what were the fragrant heads and tails of today's catch. After a few minutes, it was Allston whose deep voice finally broke the monotony.

"If y'all will be still for a just an eye-wink," he whispered, "I'll tell you a tale. A thing you won't believe."

Spider lit the wick of a small lantern he had set down in the center of their circle. The boys inched closer, squeezing so close they could see Abe's wrinkles and the little scar that was under his lower lip as he spoke.

"You say you crave excitement," he began, "Well I'm fixing to tell you of fearful things. Monstrous things." Allston stuck his chin way out and made his best deadpan face. "Any dainty girls among you best be going home before I go on. This story's for grown men with stout hearts."

The boys were quiet as they hung on Abe's words. He looked around the circle, waiting a long moment before he spoke again. Abe always liked to spice up the suspense of his tales, and he was about to spin a yarn he hoped would make them shiver all night.

"We've heard 'em all before," scoffed Fish. "You sound like my old granny who talked of spooks whenever our candles burned out."

The others just smiled in agreement, but each man could feel his heart speed up a little as Allston continued. His story began the way his best ones always did, with a long minute of dead silence. Abe's widened eyes looked all around, as if he expected someone, or something, was nearby. By now all traces of dusk had fled and a rare bank of fog was presently moving into the harbor – a perfect stage upon which to spin a ghost story.

"The old folk say..." he began. "Not the old folks like your sweet mother back home, but the old, old folks, way far back. The ones long dead and gone, pitch black folks from the islands and from the deepest forests of Africa. These folks are sleeping down in their graves tonight but when they still had breath they passed along tales of somber terror.

Told of things they saw with their own eyes and touched with their own hands."

The eyes of each man in the circle widened as Spider leaned over to turn up the wick in his little lantern, and it was around that flame that Abe Allston spun a tale that was as chilling as a nightmare, and as ancient as the slave bones in the Pitt Street graveyard. His big lips shaped each word as if it were a spirit emerging from his mouth. His rocky voice was as deep and low as a dead man's moan.

"In the secret places of the darkest night, way out in the loneliest woods, there lives a creature," he began. "A creature such as few men have seen, and even fewer lived to tell about. This thing don't really have no name, but the gray-heads came to call her the Boo Hag."

"Nonsense," Robert whispered, trying to deflect his fears. "How many sips have you had, Abe?"

"Don't stop him," said William. "Go on, Abe."

All the others nodded and leaned closer to listen, reasoning that even fear is better than boredom. "Shhhh," they whispered to each other as they watched Allston's lips. Another long minute of silence set their hearts to thumping, then suddenly, they all jumped back as Abe slapped both his hands down loudly on the deck. "Hush!" he barked. Boo Hag don't like folks to even say her name. They say she comes for the one who's the first to say it out loud."

William immediately put his hands together over his mouth. "Oh, my Lord!" he said as his pupils widened in the dim lamplight. "I done said it." Some of the others looked at Will with sympathy, some pointed at him, and others inched back in fear. Even Deke's face didn't glow with confident faith like it usually did.

"It's all right," Abe said, pretending to offer comfort, "You got no cause to fear, William. We're all here and you're still awake, so she ain't gonna touch you."

"Good," young William answered. "I ain't never gonna say that name no more anyhow."

"That's likely a good idea," said Abe. "But you best try to stay awake for now. The Hag, she likes to do her wickedness at night while folks sleep. She slips in through cracks and holes in the house. Goes right into the place where her poor victim sleeps and she hides down under the bedding."

"This Hag," Fish asked. "What do she look like?"

Allston paused again for effect, then replied, "Well, it's best I don't tell you much about that. If I say what she looks like you might not be able to sleep tonight."

"If you don't tell me, I may never *get* to sleep,' said Fish.

"And maybe that ain't such a bad thing," smirked Robert. As everyone settled back down, they allowed Abe to continue.

"Boo Hag's a woman... more or less," he said.

"Well, she's *got* to be a woman," Spider said, as a halo of firelight silhouetted the head of each man in the circle. "Women are among God's most frightening creatures."

"She's an old woman usually," said Abe. "Though some say she can show herself young and pretty if it suits her. Hags don't walk up straight like most folks do. She mostly slinks along, bent over and all. She creeps low like a hunchback or a devil.

The lamp's wick began to flicker a little as the first breaths of night breeze were coming in from the east. Soon, the fog was thick enough to swirl, and the he boys began to huddle closer as the tale was spun.

"This Boo Hag is the ugliest and scariest thing you ever did see," Abe said. "Folks have been known to drop dead just from the sight of her."

"Abe," said David Jones. "This Hag, is she white or a Negro?"

"Ain't either one," Abe answered. "Boo Hag ain't got no skin to speak of, just red raw meat and muscle and such, like a fresh-skinned buck. She likes to steal the skin off of some livin' person whilst they sleep. But mostly she just comes to ride 'em."

"To ride 'em?" asked David.

"Yep," said Abe. "While her victim's sleeping and dreaming all peaceful, she gets up on top and straddles them in their bed. Rides 'em just like man rides a horse, only they're sound asleep. She rides 'em all night long like that and she don't stop 'til they wake up in the morning, all sweaty and spent and wore out. Sometimes their family just finds 'em stone dead in their bed at daybreak – fearful sight!"

"You ever seen any of this?" asked Will Morrison.

"No," he answered. "and I'm glad I ain't. I doubt anybody's seen a Boo Hag up clear and close. Hags always finish their business before light of day. Can't stand neither light nor fire. And she don't like the smell of gunpowder neither."

"Then how do they know all this if nobody's ever seen her?" Spider asked.

Abe thought to himself for a moment, then said, "So, you ain't never been tossed and troubled in your bed some night? Eever felt any kind of heavy feeling in your chest? Never tossed and turned and woke up all wrung out?" The boys all looked nervously down, then all around at each other.

"Lord, Lord," said William. "We shoulda stuck to card games tonight. I might have lost all my pay, but at least I'd sleep in peace."

"I'm not sure I'll ever sleep again," said Fish. "I hope she gets Abe first."

"No way she's likely to skin me," said Abe, smiling confidently. "I always put a pinch of black powder on the bedpost and keep a broom under my bed. They say sulfur smell keeps her at bay, and if she gets under the bed, she can't help counting the straws in the broom. Keeps her busy 'til sunup, so I'm told." The boys nodded in assent, but they still looked a bit fidgety.

None of this spook-talk frightened Robert. From his childhood, he'd heard the fascinating tales of the hags and haints of Carolina's Low Country. He remembered how he used to count all the blue shutters and doors along the shadowy streets of Beaufort. Every house was different, but for most of them, the color of the doors and shutters was always the same bright, powder blue. Though it always looked pretty to him, Robert found out that the color was not chosen for its beauty. This was *haints blue*, chosen for its particular ability to repulse the presence of haunting spirits. He often saw the very same color all over Charleston for the same reason.

The first slaves coming from the African and Caribbean voodoo and hoodoo traditions had a strong faith in the existence and activity of such beings. Their old people told terrifying stories about spirits, demons, and other horrors. The most pervasive were probably the tales of the Boo Hag. Robert's mama had often spun these yarns to him as a child, mostly to keep him in line, he supposed.

Both whites and blacks in the Low Country knew these ghost stories. There were various opinions as to where the term *haints* came from. Some thought it was connected to the English word haunt, since these beings devoted themselves to the business of haunting – haunting homes, graveyards, and maybe even a person's body. Other folks said the word came from *saints*, because of the rhyme, and because such departed spirits were said to flit about at Halloween, which was celebrated around All Saints and All Souls Day in the Christian calendar.

Robert had never been convinced that such things existed, but he nonetheless honored his mother's request that he keep a straw broom under his bed. Though these legends had seemed ridiculous to most people in Beaufort, they still painted their shutters blue. Robert's own Mama did it, and so did the rector of Saint Helena's Episcopal Church. It all seemed to be done with a wink and a chuckle, but almost everybody played along, just to be on the safe side.

"Abe," asked Chiz, "Where did you get all this?"

"Mostly sitting down behind an old daddy cow," Abe said with a deadpan face, turning up the wick of the lantern. As the men one by one got back to their feet, young David looked over at Spider, hoping for some interpretation of what Allston had just said.

"Old daddy cow?" he asked.

"It's Bull dung" said Spider. "Of the purest kind."

Robert just smiled as he looked around at the boys. "Mama used to warn me about the Boo Hag, but she would've done better to warn me about *Abe.*" They all laughed again, anxious to see what other excitement the evening might offer.

From the nearer parts of town, they could hear indistinct sounds of music and laughter. Captain Relyea and the lieutenants would not be back until morning. What a shame to have a free evening dropped into their laps with nothing to do. They again sat in their circle, this time with no lamplight or ghost story. A few minutes later, it was Spider who spoke up.

"Enough of this hag nonsense," he said. "I've seen some other monsters that are much bigger and a whole lot badder than Abe's. Real-life monsters."

"OK, brother," said Robert, "It's your turn to spin a yarn."

"I'll do you one better," Spider said, taking a big swig from his bottle. "I ain't gonna tell you. I'm gonna show you." He wobbled a bit as he stood up, now feeling the effects of the alcohol. "Walk with me, boys," Spider said, "But remember, we're past curfew."

Spider led them down the foggy boardwalk that led from the South Wharf to East Bay Street. In the deserted streets along the waterfront, no one took notice of this unsupervised group of black men as they made their way over to the North Wharf. None of the boys said a word until they reached the gate to the Caldred Pier.

"We ain't supposed to go past here," said Robert. "Not even white men are allowed to walk down this pier."

"You were the one saying he craved to venture a risk" Spider said.

"Well I'm not sure I was talking about risking my life," he said.

"We can go back and sit like half-wits," Spider said, "or you can let me show you something nobody in all the world's ever seen."

"Fine enough," said Robert, "but everyone needs to tote something. We gotta look like we're carrying something somewhere for somebody. And if we come upon anyone, let me do the talking." They all nodded soberly.

It was a dead calm night, with no crickets and breeze, and hardly any sound of waves smacking the pilings of the piers. They were undetected, but everyone had wide eyes and a wary heart. The creak of each loose plank rang out like a three-bell alarm. Robert noticed that William and David were hunched over as they walked, so he motioned to them, saying, "You ain't invisible! Stand up and stop slinkin' around like chicken thieves."

As usual, Spider found it hard to restrain his words. "Yeah, get up," he said. "We want them to think we're just a bunch of rich black gentlemen going sailing at night." He expected them to laugh, but nobody did.

"Gonna feed you to those monster of yours," said Robert, as the boys quickened up their steps.

"Or maybe to the Boo Hag," added Fish.

"...or your mama," said Spider.

The mist had continued to roll in as it sometimes did on cool August nights, thick as chowder now. Two lanterns glowed where the wharf made its split. The boys took a quick glance both ways. Whatever guards there might have been were either off duty, asleep, or drunk in town. Each boy in his heart said a silent prayer of thanks.

"Come on," said Spider, "The first of 'em is down this way." Together they walked, much slower now. Their eyes flashed about nervously, as if they were walking into a trap or some haunted place.

Spider, always the joker, began to purse his lips and made a sound like the swelling winds of a thunderstorm. "Ooooohh, wooohh."

"Shut up, fool," said Robert, with stern eyes. "Or some ugly monster's gonna get you."

"I thought you left Hannah at home," Spider said. He listened for Robert's comeback, but couldn't get a rise from him.

"This better not be no nest of Boo Hags," William whispered.

"I hear they always grab the fat one first," Spider said, smiling over at heavy-set William, adding, "You've got the most flesh."

By now they were all too nervous to talk. Finally, Spider spoke up. "Down here," he said. "Past the tug." He was pointing to something low and dark in the water two berths down. It appeared to be some kind of boat.

"What in God's name?" whispered Deke, not using his usual preaching voice. "Have mercy!"

Twenty paces later they found themselves at Slip Four, which was lit by a single oil lamp hanging from a small wooden crane. They formed themselves into a rough circle, as every man fixed his eyes upon the first monster, which was barely visible through the low-hanging wisps of fog.

"They call it a David," Spider said. "What do you make of it?" But none of them ventured to speak. The wharf area was so quiet you could hear the music coming from town. "Well?" said Spider softly.

"What a thing," Robert said. "Ugly for sure."

To Robert, it looked for all the world like a steam boiler of some kind, floating in the misty water. On top of it was a smokestack and small helm tower which had a ship wheel on it. A long spar pole was mounted on the front of the vessel, and it stood straight upright, with some kind of torpedo attached to the top end. Ropes ran down from the spar to the where the wheel hatch was.

"It's a monster, for sure," said Abe. "A death machine."

"A David," Chiz whispered.

"It's built to ride low in the water so it can't be seen," said Spider. "They take it out into the harbor on moonless nights so as to sneak up on the Federal ships. That's the spar sticking up on the front. That business on top of the pole, that's the explosive charge. It's like the ones the Rebs float in the harbor channels. They sneak up and ram that long pole right into the side of a, enemy ship and, *boom.* They blow a hole in it."

"Never even see it coming," said Deke, shaking his head. "Blown clear to glory."

"A small boat sent to kill a big one," said Robert. "A David."

"A good idea, but a terrible one," said Abe. Just look at it. It ain't no ship."

"It's a deadly monster," said Fish. "A fright just to look at."

"For sure," said Spider, "but I'll show you more." He motioned for them to follow him further down the wharf. Through the hanging fog, they could make out another something that loomed in the distance.

"This appears to be a bigger one," said Robert.

"Maybe David's daddy," ventured Chiz.

About fifty yards away was another vessel. It was dark and rusty like the David, but many times larger. Some type of warship, no doubt. Completely covered with iron plate, it was shaped like an A-framed rooftop, squatting low in the water like some huge malformed tortoise. There was a large smokestack on top, and portholes with cannons which protruded from both its flanks.

Robert paced off its dimensions, finding it to be over 150 feet in length. The thing was huge, but resembled no warship he had ever seen. Without proper rails, bridge or rigging, it was no sailor's dream – altogether hideous.

"Ironclads, they call them," said Spider, "and there ain't anything noble or beautiful about 'em."

"Terrible... and formidable," Robert muttered, "Grotesque machines designed to kill."

"They ain't sneaking up on anybody with this thing," proclaimed Abe. "If this one ain't David, it must be Goliath."

"The Confederates call this one the *Chicora*, and they're building another just like it called the *Palmetto State*," said Spider. "It may be too big to sneak up on the enemy, but it doesn't have to. That iron armor is four inches thick. I heard Cap say a forty pound shell will bounce off it like a sparrow peck on a tin roof. On her bow she's got a two-ton iron beak mounted down below the water line. Any ship she can't sink with her guns she can ram and send it right to the bottom." The eyes of every man were wide with fright by now.

"Leviathan, the piercing dragon," said Deke, "like in the Bible."

"But this one's a man-made monster," Robert said. "I think we best clear out of here. I doubt the Rebs want any guests taking this tour, even though we're all loyal Confederates." As Robert began to lead the men away, Spider took another swig from his bottle and called them back.

"Wait," he said. "I got one more thing you've gotta see." None of the boys seemed overjoyed by this news, but they stopped walking nonetheless.

"All right," said Robert. "One more, and then we go. And quit sippin' that whiskey. God only knows what you'll be showing us next."

"I thought you ain't afraid of no Boo Hag," Spider joked as they walked back past the stern of the *Chicora*, and turned toward where the wharf made its loop towards shore.

"If it is only a Boo Hag, I think I'll be *relieved,*" laughed Robert.

"Relieved? If this monster's anything like the others, I might relieve *myself*... in my drawers," said Fish. The men chuckled quietly then, the way gravediggers do when plying their trade. As the boys came near to Slip Twelve, everyone was staring at the surface of the black water, bracing themselves for the next horror that would emerge.

"Don't stop walking," said Spider. "This one ain't *in* the water. Just look up over here." He was pointing to a flatcar that was parked on the railroad tracks across from the dock. "They brought it in on Monday, all the way from Alabama."

Coming closer, the men could see something that looked a little bit like the *David* – another long cigar-shaped vessel. It too was made of riveted boiler iron, but this time there was no smokestack, no tower, and no ship's wheel on top. Robert, always the brave one, mounted the flatcar, reaching his hand up to stroked the side of the thing.

"Ain't much," he said. "Looks a bit like a big stovepipe that's been pinched at both ends."

David Jones then jumped up on the car with Robert, and feeling the cold iron with his hand. He rapped his knuckles on the vessel's side, producing a hollow sound like when you hit an empty metal drum. "Don't look like nothing to me," he said.

"She's a puppy next to the other ones," said William.

"No," said Spider, "This one's the worst of all. An man named Hunley came up with the idea. He called it a submarine, but most of the Reb sailors call it the *Fish Boat*. They're still working the kinks out, but I'm told this one can slide all the way under the water and cruise about."

"*Under* the water?" said Chiz. "You're a liar!"

"Ships can't even see it coming," said Spider. "It's got a torpedo on a spar pole just like the *David*, only this one swims down deep like a fish. And they've got men inside cranking the propeller to make it go. See that glass dome up on the top? That's where her pilot looks out."

"But this one's so small and thin-skinned," said Chisholm. "One good shot would sink it like nothing."

"But first they'd have to see it," said Robert. "They can't shoot what they can't see."

"Unbelievable," said Abe. "I couldn't make up a beast like this in my worst dreams."

"An underwater boat," said Deke. "May God forgive us. He made him a whole sea full of pretty fish, and we have to make monsters."

"And the worst kind of creature," said Robert. "A predator." At this, some of them shook their heads in disbelief, as a few others bowed their heads. There was, however, no time for shock or prayer. At the far end of the wharf, Confederate guards could just now be seen returning to their posts.

"Let's move!" Robert urged. "And not a sound!"

As the departing shadows of the *Planter's* crew disappeared into the gray fog bank near shore, there was no more chatting or joking. Having seen three nightmares of iron, none of them ever again entertained any notion that peace might come soon or easily. Upon returning to the Planter, every man was eager for a relaxing game of cards.

Chapter 28
News from Home

Their modest apartment over the Ancrum's barn was not an easy place for Robert, Hannah, Clara, and Charlotte to live. A corner of the barn's downstairs storage room was set up for the girls, now thirteen and fifteen. After baby Elizabeth arrived in February of 1858, and Robert Junior in 1860, it became even more uncomfortable. "This place smells like a stable," Robert would always say, poking fun at the fact that the Ancrum's horses lived just below them. On hot days, the odor of warm manure was almost unbearable, and on winter days, with all the windows closed, it wasn't much better. Robert, always one to make a game of things, liked to tease his daughter Elizabeth by asking her if she had soiled her pants.

If there were to be any breezes of refreshment, they arrived in the late fall of 1861. Robert had just gotten home from his work at the Atlantic Wharf when he was greeted by a smiling Hannah, who seemed to be hiding some kind of a surprise behind her back. "I've got something you've got to see," she teased. "But you'll have to come over to the window bench and put your strong arms around me."

Robert hated her games, but the prospect of wrapping his arm around her did not seem all that unpleasant, so he complied. Elizabeth ran across the room and crawled up between them, squeezing in as close as she could. "Come look at this," Hannah said, bringing out a tattered edition of the *Charleston Mercury* from behind her.

As Robert pulled himself closer to her side, her index finger pointed to some writing on the top part of the paper. This was another game Robert hated, but he resolved to play along if it would preserve peace for the evening. She knew he couldn't read.

"Now you remember why I married you, don't you?" he asked. "I needed a black wench to read me my paper." On the page, Robert could see the woodcut picture of a building, some warships, and soldiers marching down a big street. "It must be good news or you wouldn't be smiling," he said. As his face got more serious, he asked her what the newspaper said. "Don't you toy with me. Just tell me what it says."

"The Union fleet has captured Port Royal," she said, "and the Federals have taken all of Beaufort County."

Robert could only stand there with his mouth open. "Good Lord, Almighty!" he said. "How in God's name did they get past the forts?"

"It don't say nothing about forts that I can see. Says the Union Navy sent all its big ships through," she said. "But it don't mention much else about it."

"The Fort Walker and Fort Beauregard must've got busted up pretty good," Robert said. "The *Mercury* would've said something if the forts had held out. And they were the only things standing between the Yankees and Port Royal."

Looking at a picture of a group of celebrating Negroes, Robert said, "And just take a look at that. Ain't often they show any of our people in the *Mercury* unless they're hanging from some tree."

"It tells the story right here," Hannah said, pointing to the words on the page. "Says the Yankee army has done set the slaves to free. Paper says it's an outrage."

"An outrage for sure," said Robert, "and good news for us. I've gotta find out if my Mama's all right."

"Well, it says they've turned loose all the slaves there," Hannah said. "The Yankees are calling 'em 'contrabands of war,' but they're all set to free in any case, at least the ones the masters left behind."

"It don't say much about who went where," she said. "Says most of the whites have gone inland." Hannah then lowered her voice to a whisper as if she was part of some great conspiracy. "I've got me two sisters down there," she said. Then she put her hands to Robert's face, she drew his eyes to hers, so close that Robert could almost taste her breath. "My sisters are free, and I'd bet money that your Mama is free, too. Glory to God!" Robert saw big tears beginning to run down both of Hannah's cheeks.

"We don't know nothing," Robert said. "The McKees might've took her along, and George, too." With all his doubts, Robert longed to believe Hannah's words. "This ain't some joke, is it?" he asked. "Good God! We've gotta find out what became of Mama."

"Ain't no joke," she said. "It's true. And from what I've seen of your mama, she's a tough old bird. She's bound to turn up just fine."

"Well, I don't need no more chit-chat," Robert said. "I want you to read me the paper, the whole of it, word by word," Robert said.

For the next hour or so, Robert had his wife read him that entire newspaper out loud, line by line, over and over. He wanted to savor the fact that his home town and his mother might very well be free. Hannah also read him the longer articles that were in the front part of the paper. Robert wanted to make sure his wife wasn't holding back anything.

Most of the longer articles described Confederate victories. Editorials expressed support for the nobility of the Southern cause. Only the short article on the back page was about the loss of Beaufort.

"This one's quite a bit shorter," Hannah said. "I wish they'd say more."

"I ain't surprised it's short," Robert said, "seeing that it's about a Northern victory." Robert made Hannah read him the Beaufort article again. It told of the Yankee's brutality toward Beaufort's white citizens, how they ransacked Southern homes, and how they chased helpless women and children out of town. The *Mercury* described the situation as 'unorchestrated chaos' and told of freed Africans running through the streets and homes like uncaged animals. The brief account of the Confederate retreat was generously described as "a temporary setback."

In truth, the Union's capture of Port Royal, Beaufort, and the Sea Islands around Hilton Head was not back page news. Symbolically, it provided the North with good news at a time when their war effort was going badly. It was also significant, in military terms, as a strategic victory. With this major seaport in hand, the U.S. Navy now had the base of operations it had been seeking for its Atlantic fleet. Here, their blockading warships could be safely refueled and refitted for the duration of the war. The blockade having been strengthened, the fledgling Confederacy would continue to feel an ever-tightening noose around its economic neck. The "setback" was neither temporary nor inconsequential.

"It's something, ain't it?" asked Robert, running his fingers over the ink on the page, typed words he couldn't read. "It's the holy judgment of God! A sizeable storm! I surely pray it's headed our way." Holding the newspaper out, he suddenly turned loose with both hands, letting it gently drop to the floor. They both stared down at it, as if it had been a combustible explosive.

"Mama might be free," he said, "I suppose I could just be happy for her, but Lord, how I wish I could be there!" Once he was convinced he could learn no more from the paper, Robert asked Hannah and Elizabeth to bow and pray with him. They petitioned God for the safety and liberation of their loved ones. Little Elizabeth added a sweet "Amen" at the end.

The next morning as he made his way toward the waterfront, Robert couldn't get his mind off the liberation of his Beaufort. He shared the news with every Negro he met that day, and of course, said nothing at all to the whites. He wondered to himself whether something good might actually come from this terrible war? Robert thought it ironic that, after all his hopes in moving to Charleston, it was the folks who stayed behind that reached Freedom Land first.

Robert had little notion of what it might feel like to be free. In the years before secession, both he and Hannah had heard the stories about freedom up North. There were said to be freedmen up there who were owned by no one. They lived and worked as free people, almost as free as the whites. Freedmen owned houses, worked paying jobs, and raised whole families without any fear that their children would be sold off.

Though they had often thought about these stories, Robert and Hannah had pretty much dismissed them as spruced-up tales and isolated cases. Slaves liked to talk about such things in their private moments. As for himself, Robert had always put these notions to the very back shelves of his mind. Like heavenly crowns and streets of gold, the land of freedom seemed a long way off. But now, here and there, there were glimmers of hope that the day of the Lord's favor might be on its way.

Since moving to Charleston, Robert had been troubled whenever he thought of his mother. She was a woman alone, slaving just as she had for the past 66 years of her life. But now the Yankees had taken Beaufort, and she lived in the land of liberty. He was sure she still had to work to earn her bread, but it gave him cheer that she now labored as a free woman. Robert and Hannah talked into the dark hours of evening about how life would change for the newly freed slaves in Beaufort, and what a pleasant talk it was.

Their chat across the kitchen table reminded Robert of the many times he and his mother had conversed by lamplight in their old cottage behind the McKee mansion. It was really just a shack, having but one simple room, where they worked, ate, and slept. Lying in their beds, they had long conversations almost every night at bedtime, speaking of the things only mothers and sons can talk about. They sometimes spoke of their futures, but just as often they reflected on the bitter challenges of the present.

"I'm not like the others," Robert had remarked more than once. "The whites point and say I've got Negro blood, and the slave children say I'm not a real black boy."

"You are who you are," his mother said. "So what if they point at you? You best just let 'em point. Pointin' ain't whipping. Pointin' don't mean a damn thing."

Why does every man's finger point at me? Same way they stick their finger at an outsider?" he asked. "I feel like a stranger in my own town."

"A stranger sure enough," she said. "My people came from the Guinea Coast to this place and the whites came from England," Lydia said quietly. "All of us come from somewheres else. Strangers in this world. Little man, we stay here on earth for just a short while, then, in a blink, our soul's gone and on its way up to heaven or down to hell. Right now all we got is each other and the Lord, and that should do for us."

There were times when Robert even reached the point of despair. "Mama, I want to just disappear. I don't fancy living here, but I'm not pining for heaven neither," he said. "It's something else I want, but I don't rightly know what it is. All I know is every day here they point and talk, and every day they try to make me cry."

Lydia had looked across the room into her son's brown eyes and said, "You're my child and my only family here. You can't allow no pointy fingers make you cry. You gotta let those fingers make you strong. Life's too short to be worryin' about a few pointy fingers." Then she smiled and wagged her bony black finger at him in jest. Their laughter filled their little room, as tears of joy and sadness wet their faces. Robert remembered it like it was last night.

It had been a long time since he let the finger-pointing bother him, but he always remembered what his mother had said about it making him strong. But nothing made him as strong as did the memories of Lydia. He tried to picture what it might have been like for her to taste freedom for the first time, but his imagination failed him. It was all too unbelievable.

In the months to come, Robert received no news about his mother. There were few *Charleston Mercury* articles about Beaufort, but he did hear that his wages should now be sent to Henry McKee at a different address – one farther inland. Hannah had received occasional fragments of information about Beaufort from her family members, but nothing from Lydia.

Finally, in January, there was a letter. It had been smuggled in from

Beaufort by an Episcopal Church courier who managed to get it to Robert at the Ancrum's address. Composed by his mother, the words had been scribed by a white teacher who had come down from Boston to teach the slaves to read and write. Hannah read it to him slowly and carefully.

Dearest Son Robert,

I am safe in Beaufort, so you should have nary a concern for me. I still live in our old place and I make coins cooking for blue soldiers, who now stay in the big house. Some folks cane down and built a school for Negro children. Leena and me made them let us in, too. How about that? Miss Lorena Brennan is our teacher and she is writing this down for me. Teacher says I will be writing you letters myself soon, so you best learn to read like me. The McKees went inland to live with Henry's people. They said they would be coming back and that I still belong to them, but the bluecoats say I am free and don't even have to go back to slaving. Most of our people are poor and in need of most everything, but the Lord provides. I pray for you like I promised. I truly hope you and Hannah are well. I hope this letter gets to you.

Your mother,
Lydia Polite

Robert listened carefully as Hannah slowly read each word, only stopping her whenever he needed to wipe his tears. The words penned by this Brennan lady didn't sound exactly the way Lydia talked. There were however, an odd cluster of letters scribbled at the bottom of the page.

"Look," said Hannah. "Your mama wrote her name right there in her own hand." Robert burst into loud tears when Hannah pointed out where his mother had signed her own name.

"God is good," he whispered over and over again as he touched the place where the rough ink marks had been made on the page. "He's so good! My mama's learning to write." Hannah showed Robert the *L* from Lydia and the *P* from Polite – the first two letters he ever learned.

As he dried his face, Robert breathed a great sigh of relief and joy. His mother was not only safe, she was beginning to savor her first tastes of a new and amazing life – the life of freedom. With every piece of news that was smuggled in from Beaufort County, his heart was encouraged and he tried to imagine what this new Promised Land was like. It appeared that things were changing rapidly in Beaufort. The Charleston papers didn't say much, but Hannah read to him every piece of news that came.

Chapter 29
Liberation

When the Yankees liberated Beaufort in November of 1861, the city and its inhabitants had been quite unprepared. The more prosperous whites were united in their desire to leave town for inland regions still held by the Confederacy. In most cases, they departed in haste, taking only their savings and a few things that could be easily carried. Keepsakes, gold, art objects, and clothing also went with them, but furniture, tools, and most of their slaves were left behind.

What had started as a systematic migration of wagons and persons soon degenerated into an unregulated stampede. Mothers scolded their whining children while their husbands shouted blasphemies at one another, at the bluecoats, and at their inept Confederate government. The few whites that stayed behind, silently slid themselves into a few remaining nooks and crannies, hoping they might not be noticed. It was a sad and challenging time to be a master and a good time to be invisible.

Robert's mother's last contact with the McKees occurred on a Thursday afternoon. Missy Jane was urgently packing up the last pieces of clothing from the wardrobes in their big bedroom. Mister Henry busied himself pacing back and forth, never for a moment assuming that elegant 'pose' he had favored so much. Lydia persisted in asking what she might do to help, but Jane seemed to be intentionally ignoring her. Robert's mother couldn't remember ever seeing so many tear tracks on white faces.

Henry McKee had slammed the front door angrily as he returned from his final visit to his father's grave at Saint Helena's. Lydia had noticed wet places on the knees of Henry's breeches where he had obviously been kneeling on the damp grass of the cemetery.

"Lydia, what are you staring at?" he shouted into the now empty rooms of the front parlor area. "By tomorrow, the Yanks will most surely have taken the town. There won't be enough food to feed all our servants, so I suppose you'll have to figure out how you will live."

Lydia hadn't understood what he was saying, but neither, she reasoned, did he. Henry had so often launched into these lengthy and virulent speeches that she wasn't confident his words held any logical meaning at all. At this point, she was still reluctant to even speak of manumission, but like every other Negro in Beaufort, she sensed she stood on the very threshold of freedom.

"What do you require of me?" she asked. It was a familiar question she had asked every hour of every day for the past 52 years, but it felt strange now. It was even stranger not to get a reply. By now, her masters were frantic and sweating and were too urgent to care about Lydia's trivial assignments. Their lives, like the lives of every prominent family in Beaufort, were presently crashing down like the walls of old Jericho. Lydia empathized with their sadness but inwardly swelled with a personal urge to clap and sing.

With the departure of the masters, all of Beaufort County was swarming with a distraught and energized throng of freed Negroes. These were slaves who had previously labored – unseen for the most part – out in the fields and back in kitchens. Now, tens of thousands paraded through the streets of town. Groups of them gathered by the wharves and in the front yards of the big houses along Bay Street. Most were hard-pressed and hungry, yet even from a distance, one could hear the sounds of celebration – loud talking, laughing, and lively church music. Lydia, like most house servants, had not realized there were so many of her race, but without her son and the master's family, the old McKee house seemed frightening and empty.

Unsure at first, Lydia did her best to live off of whatever foodstuffs were left behind. In her mind there was a chance that the McKees might be back soon, the fortunes of war being what they are. But as the pantry supplies ran low, she wondered what she would eat. Not knowing what to do, Lydia decided to just keep doing what she was used to doing. For a while, she did her best to keep the big house just as the McKees had left it. But she soon got restless and bored, since there was little work to do. There was also no money.

If there was any thought of selling items from the big house, these were soon dismissed. Around town, everyone was trying to sell such items but there was no one wanting to buy anything, and no money to buy it with. Looted house decorations were all but worthless. Everybody just wanted something to eat.

In the first weeks, Lydia took walks downtown almost every morning, moving in stunned silence through the hoard of rowdy and unfed freedmen, whose number grew daily. Their elation was matched only by their universal neediness. There were no designated leaders and no clear direction as thousands roamed the county in search of food, friends, and a future.

What she remembered most was the ever-present sound of singing and prayer. Once, she heard a group of them sing the same lyric, over and over, for most of an hour.

Oh, bye an' bye, bye an' bye
I'm goin' to lay down my heavy load...
I'm troubled, I'm troubled,
I'm troubled in mind
If Jesus don't help me
I surely will die.

Despite the slaves' ordeal of confusion and want, there had been almost no crying among them. The needs of most were met through handouts they received from others who had somehow come by edible provisions, clean water, and clothing. Union soldiers were also distributing food and supplies down by the old armory.

As a pious woman, Lydia had to look the other way when items were looted from the abandoned food supplies in the big houses. She had been taught to view stealing as an evil thing, but like most of the others, she reasoned that the Good Lord was providing a blessing of restitution for his oppressed children. Their sudden liberation by 20,000 uniformed angels in blue had brought them the long-anticipated year of Jubilee. The white folks' food would have eventually gone bad anyway.

Lydia herself had remained in the slave quarters long after the McKees had departed. For days she had wrestled with the idea of moving herself into the big house of her masters, but a lingering fear kept telling her to stay where she was for a while. When it became clear that the masters would not soon be coming back she was soon driven by necessity to enter the kitchen to get food for herself and the McKee slaves that found their way to Prince Street. Lydia remembered that she could hear the beating of her own heart as she walked. The guilty conscience of a slave lives on long after the day of freedom comes.

By the second week of December, Lydia finally ventured to move some of her things into the McKee's bedroom. The masters had taken with them most of the kitchen utensils and smaller furniture. Any foodstuffs or supplies had already been removed to be distributed among the displaced Negroes of the county.

As she looked down at the large bed which consumed the greater part of the master's room, Lydia could make out the twin impressions where Henry and Miss Jane had slept for 30 years. She could discern the sunken indentations of a man and woman on the flatness of the big feather mattress, left there like footprints in soft ground or like sunken places in an old graveyard.

The bigger cleft on the left side had obviously been left by Henry, and perhaps by his own father John who had slept in that same bed in the years before his death. As Lydia stroked her fingers across the white satin of the bedcover, the fabric felt strangely cold, and she wondered if white folks would ever again return to this house and the life they once knew. She then rubbed her hands together, as if she had been wiping off some sort of stain.

That same night was the first and only time Lydia tried to sleep in that bed. At first she had reveled in the amazing softness of its luxurious fabric, which was a welcome change from her musty straw cot in the servant quarters. But as she lay in her owners' bed, her eyes refused to shut and her mind couldn't find rest. She was startled by every little sound and was beset by every passing notion. She didn't belong there, at least not quite yet. She thought she might try it some other day, but she never got around to it.

Before an hour had passed, Lydia was back in the uncomfortable but familiar confines of her own shack, sleeping on the hay-stuffed tick where she had passed every night for the past 57 years. Her bed was no more than a pallet really, a small rectangle of weathered slats that had been used by whatever slave woman had come before. Lydia had always assumed it would serve as the lying down place for the next slave girl who followed after she left this world.

It had sufficed as her bed, her sitting bench, and her folding table for the laundry. It had offered rest to her sore bones after each day's labor and had even provided the place for Robert's birth. Lydia had always supposed she would one day die in this same bed, but now her future was any man's guess. Her heart rejoiced, but trembled, too.

She wasn't even sure whose house this was now, but that's the way things were everywhere in Beaufort. She reckoned that it would be sufficient to house her and the few other McKee slaves who remained, at least until somebody in authority decided who owned what, and who owned who. Everybody would have to walk with the Lord, and on eggshells, until then.

Lydia and the remaining Prince Street servants lingered unsupervised on the grounds of the big houses for about two weeks before the men in blue coats came. These soldiers had been sent on an official visit to expel them, but soon learned that these Negroes had been slaves in these houses. Lydia and most of the others were invited to stay on as employees of the Union Army. They would be helpful in serving the needs of the officers who would soon be occupying these homes. So much for Freedom Land. There would be no milk and honey distributed anytime soon, but they wouldn't starve either.

Despite Lydia's insistence that Jane Bold McKee had told them to guard the house, the stone-faced soldiers kept reciting the same words over and over. It was a memorized sentence saying that "all Negroes in Beaufort County were henceforth to be designated as contraband of war." He said they were being freed, but that they must nonetheless do what they were told. It didn't sound like they would set foot in Freedom Land quite yet, and the slaves were presented with no better choices.

"You coloreds must leave for an hour or so," the officer with the biggest hat said. "After that, you can come back and we will hire you,"

"What if we just sit right here where we are?" asked Lydia, always the sensible one.

"Yes, that would seem to make sense, wouldn't it?" the man said, smiling. "But this is the United States Army, ma'am, and Uncle Sam does his best to make things as confusing as possible. We can't just take possession of you. They say it would appear too much like slavery, but if you come back in an hour, we can start over fresh and new, hiring you all back as free men and women."

"So if we're hired folks now," said Lydia, "How much money we get?"

"Well," the big hat man said, "That's a good question, and yet to be answered. Keep in mind there's a few thousand coloreds in town that would line up to do it just for the meals and housing."

"So it's pretty much like slavery," said Lydia.

"Yes, ma'am," said the man. "I suppose so, at least for now, but with some hope for better times ahead. That's all I can offer you."

"Well enough," Lydia said. "I suppose we'll be back to see you after a while."

"Exactly," the officer said. "Just don't tell no one else, or we'll have every darkie in Beaufort County flocking over this way." Then the white soldiers pointed rifles at them and chased them off the McKee estate to wander Bay Street with the throngs of other displaced blacks.

As they left, Lydia kept glancing back toward the big house to see what the bluecoats would do. Within the space of a minute, the soldiers had finished writing in their ledger books and started saluting one another and such. When some bugle boy tooted a little tune a long way off, most of the blue men scurried off down the road toward the music.

After an hour, Lydia and the others snuck away from the big crowd on Bay Street and gradually made their way back to the big house. Two child-faced officers served to assign each of the servants to their duties, which were pretty much the same duties they had done for years as slaves. But the words of the big hat man proved true. Times started to get a bit better after that.

Lydia took note that each day there were fewer and fewer blacks wandering the streets. Some of the McKee servants began making weekly visits to a place at the north end of the waterfront, where there was said to be food and help. Word was, provisions, clothing, and educators were being sent down from up North. If freedom was incomplete, at least some help was on the way, and for this they were grateful.

Lydia and everyone in town still felt a touch of uneasiness as their future continued to unfold. Even their sleep was uneasy, for at night they could hear the sound of breaking glass as roaming bands of former field hands broke into the abandoned businesses of town. This looting was often accompanied by gunshots as the bluecoat patrols tried to protect property and preserve order.

In the mornings, the Yankees would regularly display the dead bodies of offenders who had been shot the previous night. There were mostly males, some females, and even a few children among the corpses. The bluecoats almost always placed a written sign on the chest of one of the dead to clarify his crime and to send a warning to others. It was a rare Negro who could read what these messages said, but it wasn't hard for any of them to get the message.

After enduring almost three months of chaos and privation, a semblance of order began to take shape among the former slaves of Beaufort County. Provisional shelter gradually became available for individuals and families. Bulk shipments of food and supplies were delivered from ships arriving from up north. But the brightest ray of hope came in the form of a small black woman named Harriet Tubman, who everyone called Little Moses.

Before the war, this ebony crusader had made a name for herself by delivering hundreds of southern slaves to freedom through her underground railroad. She fed the hungry, comforted the sick, and generally put fear into any man, white or black, who dared to stand in her way.

Harriet Tubman did and said the things Lydia had always dreamed of doing and saying. There was no back-down in her, but her heart somehow still overflowed with the love of God. It was as if each of the slaves was her child, brother, sister, or mother. The sea island blacks had laughed at her accent at first. Having lived so long lived in isolation, they had only been acquainted with Gullah speakers. But her hard work and open heart soon inspired their trust.

In Port Royal, Harriet risked her own life nursing the victims of the 1861 smallpox epidemic. She fed the hungry daily and encouraged everyone just about all the time. When she preached at church, she urged folks to prepare themselves for heaven, but Little Moses also worked to build them a washhouse to keep them clean in *this* world. In this washhouse, black women also earned money doing laundry for Union soldiers. In a time of turmoil and discouragement, Miss Tubman was the light of inspiration and the tender touch of divine love.

Chapter 30
The Notion

Despite the besetting hardships of war, life up in Charleston continued to bustle. For Robert and Spider, moments of unsupervised leisure were few and far between. A slave was always obliged to be in some particular place at some particular time doing some particular thing. Before Sumter, they had been pretty much free to move about the city, but now there was a growing fear of Yankee subversions or slave uprisings. Now there always had to be direct supervision or at least paper authorization for slaves to walk the streets, and this was only during daylight hours. And as it had been back in Beaufort, Robert could now mark every sundown by the sound of Charleston's big curfew bell.

Opportunities for rest or socializing were rare, and pretty much had to be stolen. Winks of leisure might be snatched in situations where slaves waited for orders, or if by chance, they were on the way somewhere. Like most blacks in Charleston, Robert and Spider had mastered the art of taking the long way to almost anywhere.

Their circuitous errands often permitted them to take walks down the Battery. The long row of cannons there had been in position since the nation's earliest days, when General Benjamin Lincoln had repulsed the British fleet. Through the years, the original guns had been replaced with new ones of course, but this symbolic show of force was a source of security and pride for the citizens of the city.

The best people of Charleston made sure to own houses along The Row, a street of large columned mansions with dozens of rooms. They could be seen from quite far away and were the first homes seen by visitors coming in on the ships. From their second floor windows, residents and servants could watch the sun rise each morning, if they were up by then. Out in the harbor past the wharves and ships, the distant rectangle of Fort Sumter stood, a well-armed Gibraltar between them and the blue waters of the Atlantic.

The cobblestone sidewalk along the waterfront was lined with a thousand blooming plants – azalea bushes that blazed in spring, roses that bloomed all summer, and various camellia bushes that displayed their splendor in both spring and fall. Every yard and East wall was festooned with colorful foliage and buds. From mid-morning until dusk, a synchronized parade of black maids walked fair-skinned children down the promenade, to chat and take in the sun that crept through huge boughs of the moss-laden live oaks.

The scene had become so familiar, that no one paid any attention to Robert and Spider as they laughed and walked together along the southernmost end of the Battery. Captain Relyea and General Ripley had sent them on a run into town for provisions, but the boys were taking a less than urgent stroll back to the wharf. Their relaxed meandering looked nothing like a run.

As they approached the first cannon, Robert noticed that Spider was smiling as if he was preparing to say something outlandish. He put two fingers to his lips and turned to his ever-eloquent friend. "Shut it, Spider," he urged as they felt the soldiers' eyes upon them. "Watch your mouth."

A platoon of grim-faced rebel boys stood beside each of the Battery's twenty artillery pieces. Others were quietly rubbing down the big cannons with oiled rags. These were similar weapons to the ones that had blasted out the first shots in the name of the Confederate cause.

As they passed the battery of cannon, Spider smirked at Robert and whispered under his breath, "Them gray boys sure do prize them big guns." Spider then made a serious face at Robert and began to make profane genital gestures. "White men always envy long guns. Big black guns."

Robert nearly busted his cheeks as he restrained laughter. "You're bad as the devil," he whispered as they quickly walked on.

"This mouth of mine's gonna get me killed someday," Spider said.

"Yes," Robert said. "I may just kill you myself." As they headed back toward the wharf, Spider chattered the whole way with his usual barrage of questions and banter. Robert paid little attention until his friend touched on a subject near to his heart.

"You think we gonna die slaves?" Spider asked as the two men moved down the boardwalk toward the South Wharf. "Is it gonna be like this all our lives, sneaking the long way through the Battery just so we can talk and have a joke?"

Robert had often wondered the same thing ever since he had first confronted the fences around the McKee house in back in Beaufort. For most slaves, the dream of freedom was a recurring one. For Robert, it was a constant thing.

"Stop here," he said, pointing out toward the hazy shape that was Fort Sumter. "You see out there? A year ago there was a whole garrison of Federal soldiers in that fort, men who might be inclined to fight for our freedom. They got all dressed up in their blue suits, strutting like roosters and singing their marching songs. But when the gray men on this side commenced to fight, shooting cannons at them for just one night, them Unions surrendered and ain't come back since. T'ain't expected to come back for some time. Maybe never."

"You ask if we're going to die slaves?" Robert continued. "That's a good question, friend. I can tell you one thing – no gray-coat, no blue-coat, no dazzle-coat angel from heaven's glory is going to come down here to *make* us free men. We're gonna have to do it ourselves, and I've been doing some thinkin' about how we might do it."

Spider for once, didn't have a word to say, but only stared at Robert in silence as they made their way down the walkway to Pier Number Six where the *Planter* was moored. Suddenly the moment was interrupted by a shriek from Captain Relyea.

"My Lord Jesus. Joseph and Mary!" he shouted. "Where have you fools been all this time? Robert, get on this boat! Your chores have been crying out for you. And Spider, the General's at the house, ready to skin you alive!" At once, both Robert and Spider nodded submissively and went to their tasks.

As Robert boarded the *Planter*, he tossed a sack of vegetables to Lieutenant Sam. Turning, Robert looked straight at Spider and whispered, "We'll finish this later." Robert noticed that the whites of his friend's eyes were swollen wide. Robert hoped it was from excitement, but suspected it was fear.

"Later," Spider said as he walked away toward Ripley's place. "I'll be waiting." Then he looked up to heaven and added, as quiet as a child's prayer, "Amen."

Robert added his own silent Amen to their decision. In his mind, he had already begun to fan a spark of an idea into flame. It was little more than a wish at this point, just the tiny germ of an idea. But there was a brave and unstoppable notion in his heart. They were going to escape.

He eagerly threw himself into his duties as the *Planter* prepared to shut down for the night. Robert's muscles flexed with sweat as he watched Captain Relyea down his flask, trying as always to drown his troubles. For Robert, there was no whiskey, but his mind was nonetheless cheered, dreams so often being the intoxicant of slaves.

Both slaves and sailors pass their days in two different but concurrent worlds. While their bodies endure arduous hours of backbreaking labor, they permit their minds to voyage elsewhere, distracting their souls with thoughts of better days and better things. Such was the case with both the boys that day as they worked on their respective sides of the wharf.

Across the way at Ripley's house, Spider was stowing vegetables and other provisions into the General's food pantry, and as he sorted the various beets and grains, his mind reached for his oldest imaginations of liberty. As he watched his drops of sweat hit the kitchen floor, Spider's mind went down a well-worn path. He asked himself what he might do if he was able to escape. A familiar daydream. There were always three blessings he could picture in his mind.

In the first, Spider dreamt of marrying a pretty wife of his own choosing. She would cook him bacon every morning and love him with a hungry heart every night. Since they were free, she would be his forever and could never be sent away. She would bear him a nest of strong sons that looked just like their daddy.

In his second dream, he traveled up to the free states. He'd been told that up there, a black man could live the high life, dress finely and own his own house. Spider envisioned himself strolling down some big street, with the other men tipping their hats to him, and with young men calling him Sir. He would never tire of walking down such streets.

Finally, there was a third dream – to enlist as a Union soldier. He'd get himself the bluest blue uniform and the longest rifle the army allowed. He would kiss his pretty wife farewell and then he'd march all the way down to Charleston. He'd strut right up to Lieutenant Zerich Pitcher with a smile, salute him politely, and then he'd shoot a big hole through the middle of Pitcher's forehead. "Thanks kindly for everything Lieutenant," he would say. "You can go to the devil now!" These were just dreams of course, but just the thought of them brought cheer to Spider's heart as he labored to finish his tasks.

On the other side of the wharf, Robert was on the foredeck of the *Planter*, dreaming dreams of his own. He was envisioning a day when he could read books as little Liddie McKee had done. His wife and children would sit around a fire at story time as he read selections from *Robinson Crusoe* and the *Holy Bible*. And when his mama quoted some sharp-bladed text from the Good Book, he could look it up to make sure she wasn't adding any words of her own.

He could also see himself owning land one day, with a big house like the McKees. He might even command his own ship. These visions were only a slave's daydreams, but just the notion of such things pumped life into Robert's tired muscles and soothed his blistered palms.

Robert always thought Spider's dreams were more inspiring than his own. Spider's visions were amazing and vivid celebrations of limitless victory. Robert's were usually more like battle plans. While Robert had occasional flashes of fancy, his thoughts were more inclined to things in the real world. Pipedreams of Paradise might offer fleeting comfort, but only as a surplus of liquor does. Robert preferred to busy his mind with plans by which Freedom Land could be effectively seized in the here and now.

So as Spider rattled on and on about all the things he would do when Paradise arrived, Robert concocted practical maps for getting there. He wanted a Freedom Land he could set his boots on. And he wanted it in *this* life. He wasn't foolish enough to think it would be easy, but if his cause was right and his plans sound, he was confident the Lord would grant success.

Robert knew of only three instances when slaves had tried to escape. The first was the case of a Beaufort slave named Drake Mayfield who had reportedly run away from his master and set out across the sweet grass swamp toward the mainland. A few days later, young Robert had seen the corpse of this man dragged feet first through the town. Folks said Mayfield had gotten himself killed by cottonmouth bites in the marsh, but Robert always wondered if the whites cooked up this explanation to discourage other blacks from running too.

A second story involved a Charleston slave named Maylah Routs who was actually the aunt of engineer Dark John. This woman Maylah was a house slave and had been sent by her master to buy goods on East Bay Street, but lit off with the money bag, hoping to somehow buy passage north. Within a week, she was caught hiding in a boxcar, then was brought back home, bloody and in shackles. Her masters sold Maylah to some men from Summerville who put her out in the sugar fields as a chopper. They say the slave bosses whipped her every day until she went up to glory a year or two later.

The third tale involved Hannah's own uncle. His name was Robe Mills and he fled after killing his plantation foreman. Hannah said he stabbed the man in his sleep right before daybreak. Robe got away scot-free and ran free for twelve whole days until men with dogs caught up with him in a patch of woods near Hinesville, Georgia. The trackers claimed they'd killed old Robe by stringing him up by his neck, but them that knew the truth say Mills had already done himself in with his own noose, suicide-style. Robert had always thought Uncle Robe had come out the best of the three.

Robert had long-ago resolved that if he ever got a notion to escape, he wouldn't just run willy-nilly like some broom-whipped dog, only to be trapped and killed. It might take some time, but he would prepare a flawless plan and always stay a step or two ahead of the masters.

Chapter 31
The God of Faithful Fools

Robert, of course, was not the only slave to have contemplated escape. Truth was, it was never far from any of their minds. Slaves' thoughts had to be monitored as closely as their whereabouts. White masters presided over a tenuous world where four million Negroes were dry tinder, and notions of freedom were the match. It was universally acknowledged that the twain must never be allowed to meet.

Before the war, newspapers and books up North had been saying much about the need to put an end to slavery. Songs were written about the subject, mostly catchy tunes and military marches. Sales of Uncle Tom's Cabin were only exceeded by those of the King James Bible. Organizations, both political and religious, were formed to champion the emancipation of the Africans. A growing circle of statesmen in Washington spoke in support of the idea that Negroes should be free, calling themselves abolitionists, as if it were a religion like that of Methodists or Baptists. And like other great causes, abolition was aflame with passion and theory. It was something to die for. Incendiary talk it was, but it was all talk for the most part. There were however a few men like John Brown for whom discourse was not enough.

Even from afar, Southern slaves had caught wind of the idea that freedom might be on its way. As a child serving in the big house, Robert had often heard Henry McKee and his friends conversing about emancipation, in less than affectionate terms of course. In his own mind, Robert resolved to keep his hopes in check. For while it was encouraging that somebody was talking about his freedom, he knew that when all was said and done, there is always a whole lot more said than done. He had served enough tea on Southern porches to know that white folks could talk everlastingly without any appreciable result.

Robert had long ago concluded that words seldom change anything in this world. He had seen piles of logs neatly stacked in a yard. Season after season, they could sit there until they rotted to mulch. It took a man, perhaps cold from winter or hungry for a cooked meal, to get up and chop those logs. Educated men could make their nice speeches about the best way to cut them, he might even pray for a fire, but in the end, he'd still be cold and hungry.

Robert had come to think of the slaves like that pile of firewood. The whole big stack of them would lie there rotting in their assigned place until some brave soul got a notion to swing an axe and put a torch to the thing. Robert always figured one day he would get such a notion. He wanted to be the man with the axe and the torch.

Things had taken a turn on a particular Sunday back in the spring of 1859. It was the day Robert stopped going to slave church. Charleston's Negro churches there were much larger than the ones back in Beaufort, and their sermons went much longer. Hopeful words can inspire some folks, but they were always too long for Robert's taste. He had always been a good Christian, and he loved the Lord dearly, but Robert decided that he'd had just about enough. Every screaming thought in his mind told him it was time for action.

The tension in the city was becoming too much to bear. Even on the Lord's Day there were whites who stood behind the slave gatherings, watching them. Some of the whites were just there to enjoy the beauty of their music, but others were there to listen for something else. Since the Vesey Revolt of 1845, there had been a growing fear that the blacks here might somehow organize themselves.

White ears were attuned to any words hinting of conspiracy, and not just in the sermons. Even colored prayers and praise had to be carefully monitored. The slang and Gullah dialect of the slaves presented a sinister puzzle to the whites, and it took sensitive and suspicious ears to discern what was being thought, said, and sung.

There were songs about heaven, of course, but there were other unfamiliar songs, more cryptic to Caucasian observers. These were old African and island tunes, and odd lyrics were always being added. Secret messages and code words. These spoke of safe places for runaway slaves, checkpoints on the way to the North, and places where food and assistance might be found by those escaping to freedom. The sublime beauty of their hymns was like a lid over a bubbling cauldron of dangerous ideas. All in all, their worship was a mystery to their masters, and intentionally so. As enigmatic and duplicitous as a slave's smile.

As a child, Robert used to love church. He had liked the music, the energy, and the comfort of being surrounded by his own kind. Everything seemed to be electric with the presence of God. But now in his impatient twenties, he could no longer endure it. They had endless songs, sermons, and prayers about the Freedom Land, but no one really expected to ever get there, except perhaps in the next world.

Their spirituals described the arduous road to liberty, a lonely road, a long hard climb, but no one ever thought to actually set foot on that highway. The longing to *Fly Away Yonder* burned in their hearts, but in the end, they all just sat there. Robert listened as prayers, cries, and Amens were sent up every Sunday, but the next day everyone just went back to their chores. It had gone on this way for years. Too many years, to Robert's way of thinking. As much as he loved to worship, Robert just couldn't sit though slave church anymore, where every congregant was inspired, and paralyzed, by dreams.

He did not judge them for their inaction, for slaves had much to be afraid of. Robert recalled his years growing up in the cottage behind the McKee house. Between the slave quarters and the big house there was a path, with a short rail fence that ran along the full length of it. This row of split rails marked the Southern boundary of Henry McKee's property, and slaves could not go beyond it unaccompanied or without orders. There would be hell to pay, and hell was paid.

Where the fence neared the big house stood a flat gray headstone with a name roughly carved on it. Every slave had heard the story of Uncle Jimmy, a house slave who was brought in to do heavy work for John McKee in the early days. It was said that Jimmy got mad one day and had words with old John out in the yard. When told to shut up and kneel down, Uncle Jimmy kept upright and just looked John McKee eye to eye. Jimmy took a notion and slowly hoisted his leg up and onto the top of that little rail fence, right there in front of everyone. Then, stubborn as you please, he hopped over that little rail fence and commenced to run off somewhere.

Well, some say he was shot, while others said he was hung up in the town. In any case, folks said Jimmy's body was buried right there by this fence, and that stone was put there, not so much as a memorial but as a warning. After that, slaves who lived behind Prince Street walked past it every morning and every evening. Some suspected Uncle Jimmy wasn't even buried there, but it didn't matter. Though none of them could even read the inscription, everyone knew what it meant.

After that, no one gave much thought to lighting out for Freedom Land. Their hopes and dreams, thus deferred, became mere lyrics in a church song. Inspiring, but forever out of reach. Like the other slaves, Robert's notions of freedom were gradually pushed to the back of his mind.

So when he first began to entertain the idea of escaping, stifling fears filled his heart. Two hundred years of scolding, whipping, and lynching conspired to quench even the spark of such a dream. Though occasional notions of freedom entered his mind, he was obliged to hide and guard the secret. Like a house cook keeps the home fire burning, Robert never abandoned the tiny flame that was hope. Any fear of punishment was overshadowed by his growing disgust for slavery.

On a cloudy morning in the early summer of 1861, heaven sent a sign, a small event that set bigger things into motion. Robert was finishing his last sips of morning coffee on the foredeck of the *Planter* when he heard the sound of a man shouting. Cursing actually. A moment later he heard boot steps running along the boards of the dock. The whole incident was almost comic.

Hank MacDougall, a large and muscular Scottish stevedore, was yelling loudly that somebody had taken his chickens. He was looking every which way, not so much for the thieves exactly, but for someone to complain to.

"Damnable scoundrels!" he screamed. "I'll kill 'em all!"

"Who?" a yawning lieutenant Sam asked as he came up from below decks.

"Hell if I know," Hank said. "Some little thief stole all six hens and my best rooster. I'll break him in half!" It made sense for Hank to suspect some *little* thief, for just about every man who worked the wharves was smaller and less muscled than Hank. MacDougall could outsize and out-lift any man in Charleston.

"Anyone see anything?" Sam asked.

Robert and Spider, mouths shut tight, just shook their heads. The rest of the men who had gathered around began to hobnob with each other, but nobody saw a thing.

"You want we should put up a wanted poster or something?" Spider said. "I can draw chickens pretty good. It tickled him greatly to see white boys in such a fix.

"Hell's bells," Hank said. "Ain't nothing *to* do. Them hens are likely sold or stewed up by now. Had no tags on 'em or anything!"

"Gone to Freedom Land," whispered Spider to Robert.

"Flown to the bosom of Abraham," Robert added with a chuckle.

"Abraham's stew-pot, most likely," Spider said as he smiled and went back to his morning chores at Ripley's.

As the boys went back to work, a single thought began to roll over and over in Robert's head, planted there like a tiny mustard seed of an idea. Somebody had up and stolen MacDougall's best hens. Here was a huge man that no one could lick, and any man would have been a fool to try. Hank's figure was so menacing that he didn't even have to leave his chicken pen locked, for no thief was strong enough to whip him or brave enough to try. But some 'little thief,' as Hank called him, had snuck in under the cloak of darkness to do the deed, and had managed to get clean away. Robert's mind was on fire with a brave notion.

If a man could snatch chickens, maybe he could also snatch freedom. If liberty would not be surrendered by those in power, perhaps it could be stolen. Robert had often dreamed up plans to fight his way out, but the sequence of events he imagined in each scenario ended in an almost certain death. The power of the whites was so great that all frontal attacks were doomed to fail. Freedom could not be fairly won through bravery and strength. Vesey's and Nat Turner's rebellions had recently proved the truth of that.

History also bore witness to what happened to those who just broke off and ran. There were simply too many whites to sneak past, and too much territory to cover. Lone blacks stood out wherever they went in the South, and a Negro on the move would be even more conspicuous. Traveling alone, they were likely to lose their way, and if they escaped as a group or cooperated with others on the way, the potential for errors or loose words was just too great. There would be alarms sent out, pursuers dispatched, and always a pack of keen nosed hounds. Running was suicide.

But even though no slave was going to fight his way out, maybe it could be accomplished through trickery? What if, instead of following the expected roads through the Confederate heartland, they escaped east. Out to sea? If they could somehow got away in a ship, there would be no masters to chase them – no marshals, no hounds, and no trail. Robert was a helmsman and his friends were experienced sailors. Such a plan might actually succeed.

There certainly would be the possibility of failure, but it was just a possibility, not a likelihood as with a land escape. What they lacked in power they could make up in stealth. They could steal the CSS *Planter* the way some little thief had taken MacDougall's birds. All through that day, Robert's mind was filled with something even better than a dream. He had begun to concoct a detailed plan for action.

Though it only existed in his head, the escape plan became Robert's most precious possession. For the next weeks and months, it had to be kept as a guarded secret – like family gold, or like baby Moses hidden down in the bull rushes. The biggest challenge was to maintain silence. Though he could conspire, he could not yet speak. If he did venture to speak, it could only be to the few friends who had earned his absolute trust. This would have to be a very short list. Confidants must be prepared to take the secret to their graves, for the grave was a distinct possibility for any of them whose tongue was loose.

Being Robert's best friend, Spider would be told first. As servant to General Ripley, he was privy to valuable information about military doings in the harbor. Spider was an adventurous soul, and his energy and ingenuity would prove valuable in carrying out the plan. The hardest thing would be to keep Spider's mouth shut. A very hard job indeed.

Deke and Dark John must also be included. As engineers, their skills with the boilers and engines would be indispensable, since maximum steam would be needed to get out of the harbor. This would be especially true if any Confederate boats endeavored to chase them down. Seven miles of water and five checkpoints stood between Pier Six and freedom.

"What about Allston, Chiz, and the other boys?" asked Deke. "We can't leave them behind."

"We'll have to," said Robert. "Four of us are sufficient to run the *Planter*. I can trust four men to keep a secret. Any more than that, we'd just be multiplying the danger. Each man we take along ups the odds that we'll be found out. Young bucks like David and Will are loose-minded and mouthy. We can't take the chance."

"And you don't think Spider is mouthy?" asked Deke as Spider walked over to join their conversation.

"He was the first one I told," said Robert. "And he's already sworn on his mama's life. He's my best friend and I trust him."

"The Lord Jesus trusted his friends too, and one of them sold him out," said Deke.

"I'm ain't no Judas," said Spider, "and anyway, I'm already in on this thing. I've already picked out my seat on the boat."

"So the four are in, the others are out," Robert said firmly. "Ain't no more to be said about the matter. My mind's set like stone."

Even as he spoke, William Morrison and David Jones walked up the gangway. "What are you talkin' about so sneaky-like?" they asked.

As Robert looked into the callow and eager eyes of Will and David, his heart softened. Could he really leave these boys behind? Robert just shook his head. "Good God," he whispered, "This is gonna be too hard." Deke and Dark John had to restrain themselves from smiling as Robert went ahead and spilled every detail of the plan to the two boys. He concluded by making them swear an oath on their lives, "You must keep this secret to yourselves at all cost. You'll need a strong mind."

"Yeah," said Spider with judgelike sternness, "Your mind must be like Robert's. Set like stone." Robert just pursed his lips and gave Spider his best dirty look, but love was in his eyes. "I knew you couldn't leave nobody behind," said Spider. "There's a smile behind that frown."

"Gallows humor," smiled Robert. "I suppose it's proper that we all perish together. Wouldn't do to leave good friends behind." He looked around at the conspirators who now numbered six. "Well I guess we'll need to tell all the others," he said. "The whole bunch of us can fit in one big grave, I suppose."

"Don't worry about no grave," offered Spider with a smirk. "It'll probably just be nooses for all of us. And Charleston's got plenty of big live oaks."

"… And dogs," Robert said, grinning now. "Packs of long-toothed tracking dogs," as he wrapped his arm around his friend's shoulders. "But something tells me it'll be all right, my brother, if God is the God of faithful fools!"

As they all went back to a full day chores, a new sound now filled the air. For the first time in his stint on the Charleston waterfront, Robert heard men whistling. Was this the confident music of bold dreamers, or just frightened boys whistling in a graveyard at night? Only God and time would tell.

Chapter 32
The Great Fire

As he headed home that evening, Robert's steps were quick as he made his way through the city. He was so wrapped up in the hope of escape that he was oblivious to all else. But as he walked, he became aware of the clicking of his own boots on the cobblestones of Bay Street. Where was everyone? During his days as a lamplighter he could tell time by the comings and goings of the crowds in the various parts of Charleston. The sun was almost down now, and it outlined the dark steeples of the church district. A quaint and lovely place, he expected to find scores of people enjoying the milder temperatures of evening, but the streets were almost deserted.

As the last hints of sunset disappeared to the west, Robert began to notice another, unexpected glowing off to his right. It was too early for it to be the lamps of the city. Only after a hurried ten-minute walk did he see the shocking horror of what was happening. Charleston was on fire.

Up ahead he came upon hundreds of people, some standing, some running, and some lying dead. Robert could see no flames but there was smoke everywhere, all of it turned a dull orange by the sunset. In the distance, Robert could hear the hushed crackle of the flames. There was also a hissing sound as volunteers doused the blaze with bucket after bucket of water from nearby wells. Most of the noise, however, was not from the blaze but from the crowd. Fire bosses shouted orders to firemen and to anyone else who seemed interested in helping. Even children and slaves were pitching in.

"Mind your footholds, the stones are slick!" the man warned. "Move back or you'll pass out!"

When three little boys and their nine year-old sister got too close to the workers, the fire boss screamed at them to get back. "Where are your parents?" he bellowed.

"Somewhere that way," the girl said, pointing toward the distant holocaust. "They told us to run, but they haven't come to fetch us."

"Well you can't stay here," he said as he pointed his hand down Blake Avenue. "Go that way."

"But Granny's back there, sir," the girl said. "I fear she might be dead."

"Well, you can't go back," the marshal said. "You best follow those people there. Keep walking to where you can see the sky. We'll do our best to send your people out, but you must clear out."

"You've got to save Granny," the girl said. "She's bed-bound and needs someone to tote her."

"Sorry, little darling," he said, "but the folks are mostly all dead up that way. Those not burned have been done in by the smoke."

At this, the children began to cry uncontrollably. The younger ones just sat down on the pavement. "I've got this, sir," Robert said as he took them by the hand and pulled them toward clearer air and safety. "Hold on to each other's hand," he said. "Your folks will come after you when they are able." The little white girl's hand felt incredibly soft in his, and he could feel it trembling.

"My papa's a sergeant," she said, "with big gold stripes right here." She pointed to Robert's sleeve. "He's a brave man like you. His name is Thomas... and he's white," she added.

"Yes, it's good to know that," Robert said with a smile. "I'll do my very best to find him, little sister. I'll send him and your mama to find you and your little brothers."

At the place where the smoke cleared was a large crowd, which from a distance, appeared to undulate like angry waves in a storm. Just as soon as one cluster of people ran back to get some air, others pushed themselves back in, undoubtedly trying to rescue loved ones or valuables in the buildings that had been swallowed by the rampaging flames. The only people not screaming were the coughing ones who were choked up with soot. The whole panorama roared like the thunder of battle or the chaotic blazes of everlasting hell.

After taking the youngsters to a safe spot outside the African Methodist Episcopal Church, Robert returned to help the bucket brigade that was trying to save a three-story brick building on Calhoun Street. He saw one elderly man screaming from a third story window, but there were no ladders to help him. Even from the street, Robert could discern the man's words. He was saying the Lord's Prayer. At his feet, Robert noticed a sandy-haired woman who was attempting to wake a man who had passed out from the smoke. "Somebody!" she cried. "Somebody please help me with my husband!"

"Here, ma'am," Robert offered. "I can carry him for you."

"Oh, thank you," the woman said. "He's out cold from the smoke. I think I can manage to lift my mother."

Robert noticed the small body wrapped in a blanket at the woman's feet. It was covered by a gray uniform coat that had the stripes of a Confederate sergeant on the sleeves. This must be Granny.

"I think I just met your children," Robert said. "They all safe, but they were worried about you all."

"Thank God," the woman said, lifting up the tiny bundle that was her mother. The sergeant was a medium-sized man, but Robert had little trouble hoisting him up and across his broad shoulders. He had loaded heavier cotton bales in his days as a stevedore. As they staggered through the smoke and away from danger, the wife was coughing loudly and seemed hard-pressed to carry Granny. By the time they all reached the church, both Robert and the woman were breathing in deep and ugly gasps.

As Robert laid the sergeant down on the lawn of the church cemetery, the husband began to wheeze as he regained consciousness. As his wife held his head against her heaving chest, he suddenly turned his head away and coughed up some sooty phlegm, laced with blood. His rattling breath reminded Robert of drowning sailors he had attended to at sea. The grandmother was still unconscious, and appeared to be near death.

Having some distance between them and the smoke, the cries of, "Mama!" soon came from across the lawn. Robert wept to see the little ones embrace their parents. Robert found some water cups set out on a table in the churchyard and he brought some to each member of the family. By now, the sergeant had put his gray jacket back on and the grandmother was sitting up now, alert enough to complain that she'd been brought to the front yard of a Negro church.

"You saved us," said the white man, still struggling to catch his breath. "We're truly in your debt."

"It was my pleasure, Sergeant," said Robert. "I'm just glad everyone's all right. In the heat of things, I forgot to salute you. I'm the helmsman of the *CSS Planter.*"

The sergeant just smiled back at him. "Oh, these stupid stripes," he said. "They don't mean pig squat at a time like this. Ain't no call to salute a dead man."

"Well, it was your stripes that helped me find you," Robert said. "I didn't want these babies to lose their papa, you know. I'm a father myself."

"Well done, in any case," he said. "My family thanks you."

"And he saved Granny too," the daughter said.

"Well, sir," said the sergeant with a grin, "I suppose I should forgive you for saving my mother-in-law." They both chuckled. "Alive or dead, I suspect the old bitty would've woke up in some place fiery place, here, or in the next world."

"Well, I brought her to a church in any case," Robert said, looking around at the monuments in the cemetery, "even if it *is* the graveyard."

"Perhaps she'll take the hint," the sergeant laughed, reaching out his hand to Robert. "My name's Carson, Thomas Carson," he said.

"Robert Smalls," he replied. "Glad to help." It was the first time he could remember getting a respectable shake from a white man's hand, not even his father's. It was, however, not yet time for celebration,

By now, the area around the church was becoming an overcrowded madhouse. Everywhere one looked, there was crying and despair. Husbands endeavored to comfort family members whose homes had been consumed by the blaze. A dozen clergymen of various denominations said prayers with the injured and bereaved. Here and there, folks of all ages and classes reclined to receive fresh air, comfort, and information. As mothers shrieked over the loss of their little ones, old men argued loudly about who was to blame.

In the distance, Robert could hear the explosive sound of snare drums. Columns of Confederate regulars and South Carolina Militiamen were trotting toward the factory area, where the blaze was believed to have had started. Robert overheard that the fire was suspected to be the work of Yankee saboteurs. Similar acts of subversion had recently taken place on the Matthews plantation on Bear Island and some at buildings out near Green Pond.

Later evidence indicated that the blaze had begun somewhere on Hasell Street near the Atlantic Wharf. By the time it was extinguished, it had scorched a mile-long path through the very heart of the peninsula that was downtown Charleston. Confederate troops 14 miles away on Johns Island could see the flames from their camp.

No one ever discovered with certainty how what came to be called The Great Fire of 1861 started, though the *Charleston Mercury* said it began at Russell & Company's Sash and Blind factory. Others insisted the first sparks came from Cameron's Machine Shop near Russell's. And as people are prone to do with suspicious catastrophes, blame was assigned to various unloved groups – slaves, Southern turncoats, or other arsonous agents of the enemy.

If the origins of the fire remained obscure, its effects were not. Hundreds of people who had burns were receiving aid from military nurses who had come over from the various forts that guarded the harbor. In an open field beside the church, the dead were laid, all in parallel rows. At first the bodies had been tightly wrapped in white bedsheets, but they did not stay covered for long, as friends and family members made frantic efforts to identify and claim the remains of their loved ones.

Robert was alarmed, but not altogether saddened by what he saw. He was actually a bit cheered at the thought that Charleston, this safe and smug haven of slaveholders, was forced to taste the bitterness of this war it had started. On the other hand, it was painful to survey the charred remains of what had once been beautiful buildings and good people.

The old Circular Church was gone, as were a hundred townhomes and most of the biggest shade trees along Reeves Street. Also destroyed was South Carolina's Institute Hall, which had been the site of the Democratic National Convention back in April of 1860, when Stephen A. Douglas had been nominated for President. Feeling that Douglas was too moderate on the slavery issue, 50 militant Southerners, ironically called fire-eaters, had stormed out of that convention in protest.

'They've brought this down upon themselves,' Robert thought to himself. But in his heart, he felt no feelings of celebration. The rampaging destruction of this war was swallowing up everything and everyone in its path. Folks north and south, slave and free. In the end, there would likely be nothing left for anyone, if indeed there ever would be an end.

"It's the judgment of Jehovah," said a voice from behind him. Through the lingering smoke, Robert could make out two familiar figures walking towards him. Spider Jefferson, normally the smiling jester, now stood there stone-faced, his usually shining features painted dusty gray by ashes. Deke Gradine stood beside him.

"Divine wrath," Deke said in his resonant preacher voice. "It's the Day of the Lord, it is."

"It's just a fire," said Spider as he looked around at all the destruction, "but a pretty big one. I doubt God had much to do with it. He seems to have turned his back on South Carolina."

"This fire will be put out, but I doubt it'll be the last," said Robert as the last light of day was disappearing in the west. "I'm beginning to wonder if it's ever gonna be over for good."

"Ain't nothing to be done anyhow," said Spider.

"We've gotta keep on praying," said Deke. "It's truly in the Lord's hands. We must wait on him. Bible says those who wait upon the Lord will renew their strength."

"No," said Robert. "You can wait on the Lord all you want, but I suspect the Lord's been lookin' down from heaven waiting on *us*. The whole world may be in God's hands, but the spark that started this wasn't dropped from heaven. Some man struck the match."

Deke had no answer to offer, and even Spider for once seemed too dismayed to speak. The three stood there, gazing at the smoldering skeleton of what had been their bustling city. The victims, the shopkeepers, bankers, and customers, tried to restore things, but there was almost nothing left of the downtown streets that had so recently jingled with coins and enterprise.

"We need you boys to make your way over there," an old man said, pointing toward the AME churchyard. "Some girls from Saint Anne's are trying to move some bodies."

Robert and his friends were tired, but still ready to help. It wouldn't be seemly for slaves to look idle today, when folks were dying and a thousand white masters were seeking to assign blame. Without a word, they walked back towards where the man had pointed. It was almost dark now, and it was hard to move about without stepping on someone, dead or living. Approaching the light of two oil lanterns, they found the group of uniformed seminary girls who were doing their best to drag burned corpses, one by one, into their assigned rows.

"Men here, women over there," one girl said, "and the two rows over there are for the children." Robert and his friends quickly jumped in to assist them.

"Thank you, gentlemen," said another girl. "You are so good to help." This girl was heavy-set with hands that had been blackened by the greasy char of the bodies.

"No problem, Miss," said Robert, cheered that someone had called them gentlemen. "We're happy to help."

"Were your homes burned in the fire?" another girl asked, as they positioned the last body, this one so burned they couldn't be sure if it belonged in the men's or the women's row.

"No ma'am," said Robert. "We're just sailors from the harbor." Before their conversation could continue, a loud call came from across the churchyard.

"Get a move-on, girls!" the young woman's voice shouted. "They want us to clean up now." Robert that he knew this voice from somewhere. Looking out through the darkness, he could only make out the thin silhouette of the female supervisor who now stood between him and the lights of the church's big stained glass window. The dark shadow of her hair was outlined like a glowing halo of auburn. He would know that red hair anywhere.

"Robert, is that you?" she said. As he drew nearer, he made out the familiar features of Liddie McKee. Twenty-three now, her voice was no longer that of a young girl. She spoke the firm words of one in command. As she moved into the lamplight, Robert smiled to see her warm smile again and, of course, those freckles.

"Yes, I'm still kicking and breathing," he said. "What are you doing in Charleston?"

"My folks fled inland once Beaufort fell. I'm here at Saint Anne's Academy now, finishing my training as a nurse. These six girls here are mine," she said, pointing to her troop of novices.

"Well done," he said. "I always knew you had a gift for bossing. I've got a crew of my own anchored down at Pier Six."

Liddie smiled. "I'm not surprised," she said, "and if I know you, it's probably a pirate ship."

"That ain't all that far from the truth," he said. "But it sounds like they need you to be heading back to the school."

"Yes," she said, "but come by and see me when you're able. I want to hear about everything."

"I'll do my best," he said. "I've got a good-looking white Lieutenant I want to match you up with. I'm pretty close to making an abolitionist of this boy, and I'm gonna need you to take him dancing one of these nights."

"I'm all ears," she said. "You and I still have a blood oath to settle up, you know."

"Oh, I ain't forgot," he said. "But it may have to wait until my time gets freed up. They haven't made me General of the Harbor yet."

She just laughed as she turned to go. "It was a surprise to see you," she said, "a real nice surprise."

Robert just nodded as he walked back into the darkness. "Just don't be shocked when I show up at Saint Anne's. God be with you, Liddie."

"And you," she said as she waved goodbye.

Over the next hours, Robert and a hundred others did their best to assist those who continued to put the dead, the town and the facts into some semblance of order. When he finally made it back home just before midnight, he was weary from an eventful day. In just one day he had initiated a conspiracy to steal a boat, saved lives in a fire-scorched city, and renewed a connection with a long-lost friend. All energy now spent, he sensed that the end of the world was coming upon them. And if all hell was presently breaking loose, maybe the Day of Redemption was not far behind.

Chapter 33
Conspirators

To a man like Robert, decisions came quickly and without long deliberation. It never took him long to jump on a task, sell a thing, or buy it. In a special situation, he might even venture to take a swing at another man. Back in 1856, once his desire had become clear, he was prompt to ask Hannah for her hand and had straightway gone to seal a deal with Samuel Kingman. Once a course was mapped-out, Robert despised delay.

Back in December, the theft of MacDougall's hens had sparked the notion to steal the *Planter*. The idea had kept him awake all that first night and by noon the next day he had gotten every one of his crewmembers to pledge their lives to the endeavor. As usual, Robert was impatient to get things moving. He would always remember the events of the following day.

A cool breeze had been blowing in since dawn. Men all along the waterfront were celebrating the successful arrival of the British side wheeler *Lady Seymour,* which had somehow slid through the Union blockade the night before. Now, a red sky was hinting that some kind of storm was on its way. Later that night, the crew would have their first opportunity to flesh out the details of an escape plan. It would be an evening none of them would ever forget.

A thick fog had rolled in ahead of the bad weather, weaving itself between and around the flickering gas lights of the city. Folks all over Charleston were hurrying to get home before the worst of the storm made landfall. Deke had graciously volunteered his small shack to be their meeting place.

An uneasy Robert arrived early, which only gave him more time to pace back and forth. "You're as jittery as a whore at a revival," Deke said. "You're gonna wear out my floor boards with all your movin' about." Robert had to force himself to sit down, but even then he began to click his fingers rhythmically on the arms of his chair. With his nose pressed against the glass of Deke's only window, he nervously watched as one by one, Spider, Dark John, and the others entered through the alleyway behind Dornley Street. It was unlikely anyone could have seen them through the mist, but the slave laws, and the nature of their meeting, made it necessary for them to take precautions.

As the first strong breaths of the storm began to blow in, the boys squatted down in a circle on Deke's floor. They recounted the frustrations of their workdays, cracked a few jokes, and made chit chat about this and that, everything but the matter at hand. These old friends did not bring their usual smiles, whiskey, and playing cards. Tonight, for the first time, they were gathering as conspirators.

The room was almost completely dark by the time the last man arrived. Robert lit a single small candle and placed it on the floor in the middle of their circle. "Deke, ain't you got any curtain for that window?" asked Robert. "It wouldn't do for all of us to be seen together after nightfall."

"Ain't nobody'll be looking in unless they climbed up onto the rooftop," Deke said. "Anybody with any sense is curled up at home tonight out of this wet mess."

"Well enough," Robert said. "I suppose it won't hurt to break one more law, seeing what we're here to talk about." The men all tried to chuckle, but no sound of laughter came. Everyone hunkered their heads down so as not to be seen through Deke's second floor window.

The time for idle conversation was over. They could hear the first heavy squalls pounding on the roof, but they could see little through the dark window. Lightning flashes threw shadows across the faces of the nine men who were now sitting in patient silence.

"All right then," Robert whispered, quietly scanning the eyes of each of the eight other men in the circle. "I feel like I'm at the Last Supper or something," he said. "Except we got just nine men, and none of them are holy apostles."

"And you ain't Jesus," Spider added.

"But we do need the Lord right now," Robert said. "We should all pray. Deacon Gradine, you're a preacher, you'd be the best choice to lead us."

Deke just shook his old head. "I was a minister, Robert," he said, "but now I'm just a former preacher, being de-frocked and all."

"Now look here," said Robert. "All of us are fixing to sail off for good. Former preacher, or former slave, it don't matter no more."

"You talk like we is about to depart this world," Fish said. "Like we're dead men."

"Well," said Robert. "Dead or alive, we're all about to be a former something-or-others. We've all got places and folks we're leavin' behind. Any life we know is about to come to an end... and to start up all over again. Frocked or de-frocked don't matter. I'm asking you right now if you want to be a preacher or not?"

"Well," said Deke. "Since you put it that way... yes, I believe I *do*."

"Then, Reverend Alfred Gradine, consider yourself re-frocked," Robert said. To a man, the crew all smiled as Robert added, "Let's all get down on our knees so this man of God can let fly." Closing their eyes and bowing their heads, they tightened their circle and joined hands as Deke lifted their hearts toward heaven.

"Almighty and gracious God," he began, "Your humble servants are bowing before you tonight. Here,in a wild storm. Here, in the dark of the night. On our knees, Lord, we beseech Thee!"

At this point the lips of each man voiced an, "Yes, Lord!" or "Good God!" as Deacon did what Deke did best, doing what years ago God had called him to do.

"Lord Father, we have set our hearts on the prize. In this big storm, we cannot see the way. Thou art up in heaven, but we're down here, so blind on this foggy night that we can't see. You sit in splendor of Thy golden throne, but we're lost in a dark world of sin. Though we cannot see Thee and can't draw nigh to feel the healing touch of Thy hand, through faith we reach out our feeble hands. We stretch out the tips of our fingers toward Thee. Oh Please, Father God! If Thou wilt just let us touch the hem of Thy garment, we shall be content. If we could hear just one holy whisper of Thy tender voice, it shall be enough for us, for even the darkness is as daylight to Thee!"

By this point, their Amens blended into less articulate moanings as Deke put into words the deepest longings of each man's soul. The wet tears-spots on the floorboards told Deke that he was, once again, under the anointing of God. By the time he closed his prayer in Jesus' name, all the men in the room were weeping, but none felt any more fear or confusion. The room was quieter, but filled with the power of God and energy of hope. Like Israel's pillar of fire, the Lord was in their midst and was about to guide them from this darkened slave shack all the way to the Promised Land.

The prayer being complete, they raised their heads, knowing that it was time to sit down and make plans. Occasional strokes of lightening illuminated the bare sticks of a tree that swayed just outside Deke's window. In the gusts, the black branches scratched against the blurry glass like malevolent hands. A moment later, they were surprised by the sudden sound of the branch piercing the glass, with pieces flying in every direction. Every man ducked down, as the moist wind blew into the room, blowing out their candle.

"God A'mighty!" whispered Fish. "It's the cold breath of the devil."

"Or maybe angels," Deke offered.

"I suspect all the ghosts of Charleston know what we're planning," said Abe Allston.

"Those ain't ghosts, just a tree limb," Robert said. "But if there are any spooks around, they're likely wanting to book passage on any boat headed out of this hell-hole, too." Robert raised himself up and stuck his head outside, just in case something more dangerous than trees might be looking in. The rain was really coming down now, and even through the mist, he could see that the streets were empty. "Just sit low and be still," he said. "This storm's a blessing, the best kind of night for a meeting like this."

"Yeah," said Spider as he lit the candle again. "We're the only ones daft enough to be out in a hurricane."

"The storm's an omen, don't you think?" asked Chisholm. "Could be the stars are against us."

"Nonsense," said Robert. "It's just some wind and rain, and you can't even *see* the stars. This weather rains on black men and white men alike. Every one of us gets soaked wet all the same. Now looky here," he implored, pointing his finger in turn at every man in the room. "Look around this circle for just a minute. What do y'all see? Some of us are Christians and some ain't, some married, and some not. In this circle, we got just about every kind. Deke's a preacher and he fears the Lord. Chisholm, he's a sailor who fears omens and stars. Dark John's a quiet man who don't like talking. Spider's a crazy-headed man who's can't shut himself up. Some of us fear we're too old for what we're about to do and some are afraid they're too young. Well, you know what? I'm afraid too. Maybe more afraid than I've ever been of anything in my life. We might get caught and it's likely we'll fall short somehow. I fear what they might do to my family. But you know what I fear most? I'm afraid we'll lose heart. I fear one of us will back down or back out. I fear we'll forget the one thing that unites us all, the dream of freedom. You want a sign, Chiz? Abe, strip yourself of that shirt and show them the scars on your back. Look close, men. There's your sign."

They all gazed at the shiny, horrific gouges that marked the entirety of Allston's back. "William, you and David are just boys and don't have no marks like this," Robert said. "Not yet in any case, but in time you will. Pray to God or trust the stars, I don't care. All I know is we all got scars of one kind or other, and we've got just one boat... and just one chance. I say we pipe down about all our fears and reasons. Brothers, let's *do* this thing. Let's steal their damnable boat. Who's with me?"

At this point, Robert had to take a big breath as sweat poured from his forehead and tears ran from his eyes. His bold speech had surprised even himself. They all gathered around him with confidence and joy in their eyes. "I believe we've got us a natural-born preacher," said Deke. "The Holy Ghost done spoke through you tonight." They all nodded eagerly.

"All right then," Robert said, not whispering anymore. "Light up a couple more candles and let's plan this thing."

It was assumed by everyone that, as helmsman, Robert would be in command. He would have all the details of the plan in his mind and would keep possession of the small piece of paper that would provide the only written record of their conspiracy. Like most of them, Robert couldn't read. He had, however, become proficient in interpreting the drawings and symbols of the ship's maps. Right there on Deke's floor, Robert spread out a wrinkled piece of blank paper. On it, he had scribbled the simple elements of their escape.

There was a rough map of the wharf area, the harbor, and the forts that they would have to pass. One small rectangle at the bottom of the page represented the *Planter*, and on it, he drew stick figures to represent him and the crew. A curved vertical line was the waterfront, and it ran all the way up to the Atlantic Wharf where the *Etowah* was moored, another rectangle. On it he added more stick figures to stand for Will Morrison, Hannah, and the others.

"You bringing the women and children?" Allston asked. "Ain't that a bit risky?"

"Got no choice," said Robert. "If they get left behind, the Rebs would likely come down on them pretty hard. And I ain't running to freedom without my family."

"Well, I've got my Suzanne too," said Dark John. "I'd surely die not to take her with me, either of a broken heart... or she'd kill me herself." They all smiled. "And you need to add in our baby... and Suzanne's sister Serenade."

An exasperated Robert took up his pencil and slowly drew in three additional stick figures on the *Etowah*. "Is that it?" he asked.

"Well," said Fish. "We need to take my Lavina too. I already promised her she could go... and David's told his Annie as well."

"Good Lord in heaven!" said Robert. "I thought we all swore an oath of silence."

"I know, but I broke it," said Fish, "but I done asked God to forgive me."

Robert shook his head as he picked up his pencil once again and drew in more figures next to Hannah. "What else?" he asked with a frown. "Did anyone remember to invite the whole Confederate army?" He only frowned for a moment, and once he smiled again, a moment of welcome relief fell over the room.

"Now that we've got every soul in South Carolina on board," Robert said, "Let's figure out what everybody's job is."

"I say you should be the captain," Deke said, and all of them nodded in agreement.

"I don't fancy no title," said Robert. "Lettin' me be the helmsman. That's enough."

"Fine with me too," said Spider. "Long as I don't have to salute nobody. I always hated captains anyhow. A helmsman's a man I can sip a drink with."

"Well, I'm a Baptist, you know," said Robert. "But I might be persuaded to tip one back when this thing's all over, all to God's glory, of course." Relaxing now, Robert proposed a list of everyone's duties.

Deke Gradine and Dark John would need no training to run the engines, but it was thought best that Fish and Allston would bring in a fresh supply of pulpwood to stoke the *Planter's* boilers up as quick and hot as possible. These men would have to be the first to arrive at the boat, around four bells on the mid watch, it was decided. The other crew members would come around five bells, or 2:30 am.

William Morrison, being the only one of them who could read and write, asked Robert, "Do you want me to be writin' all this down?"

Robert had to stifle his laughter. "No thanks, Will," he said, "Other than the Rebs, you're the only one who could read it. We're gonna need you to take charge of the women and children on the *Etowah*. You know your way around the Atlantic Wharf and have free access to that boat. You'll hide our people below decks until we fetch you. Remember, you'll have our families in your hands." All through the night, they went around the circle making assignments, reviewing every detail of the plan.

No one knew exactly how long their trip might take, so they would have to arrange for provisions to be hidden in the *Planter's* supply closet. Allston and the boys would load the howitzers, in the event some conflict arose from Confederate ships. Timing would be everything. A Friday or Saturday would be best, as those were days the officers were mostly likely to go into town. They would escape by night, of course, but would probably do best to leave at a full moon to better discern the channels of the harbor. These, and a dozen other contingencies were discussed and agreed upon.

Hard experience had taught Robert that the plans were the easy part. The real world would not be so predictable. All would be lost if any one of them missed their mark, so it made sense to throw a bit of cold water on their enthusiasm.

"Let's look at anything that's likely to go wrong," he said. "Where's the devil in these details?" One by one, every man in the room held up a hand to answer him.

"Damp boilers," said Dark John.

"Oversleeping," said Deke.

"Rebel patrols," said Chiz.

"Maybe a storm," said Allston.

By this time, Robert found himself staring at such a sea of raised hands that it seemed wise to shorten this discussion. "I suspect we could go on all night like this," he said. They all lowered their hands and nodded, all except Abe Allston.

"Betrayal," he said. "One of us might sell us out." The room got deathly silent for a long minute as each a began to look around at the others.

"We'll have none of that talk," Robert said. "Good sailors don't never betray sailors, and I trust every man here."

"But all these ain't sailors," Abe said, looking across the circle at Spider. "That one right there is a fast-takin' house boy." All the others just sat in silence, waiting for their helmsman to speak.

"Truth is," Robert said. "Spider's neck's on the same block as ours. Any one of us could bail out in a moment of weakness. Man, woman, or child, every one of us needs to pray for strength not to let the others down." At that point, there were no more raised hands or words. The die was cast.

Before they knew it, it was dawn. Robert spread their plan in front of him and looked deep into the eyes of every conspirator in the circle. "Look," he said quietly as he took out his pocket knife and drew the blade across his thumb. "We're all in on this thing now," he said as dark drops of blood began to roll down his hand. "Ain't no turning back now, so come cut yourself and each man put his spot on this here paper. It's a blood oath... to God and to all of us."

One by one, each man moved closer to make his mark and swear. As Deke made the final red spot, the first sliver of morning light slid in through the open window, illuminating Robert's penciled map and reddening the nine bloodstains at the bottom that represented their word of honor. As he folded up the paper and put in his pocket, he looked around at the others and whispered, "Here's to brothers in life or death."

"Brothers in life or death," they all repeated.

"In Jesus' name," Deke said, "Amen."

The streets of Charleston were still wet from the storm as Robert made his way home, carefully staying in the shadows of Charleston's back alleys. It was not a dangerous thing for a black man to roam the streets after dawn, but this morning was an exception. In his inside coat pocket he carried the wrinkled piece of paper upon which their plan had been scratched. As the dripping trees struck his hat and shoulders, Robert could swear he could feel heat coming from the folded plans in his pocket. By the time he got to the Ancrum's stable, he couldn't wait any longer.

He lit a small candle and sat down in the darkness between the horse stalls, unfolding the conspiracy plan across his lap as if it had been the Holy Bible. In the flickering light, he gazed down at the coarse images that had been hastily scratched on it. Here were no words or letters to confuse, only simple pictures.

His eyes were drawn to the dark rectangle that represented the *Planter*. On top of it, eight stick figures were drawn, all holding hands. The crew. A dashed line led to the *Etowah* where there was another row of black stick figures – Will Morrison, five women, and five children. Another line curved down the page through the maze of checkpoints to the far right side of the page where a row of Union ships were anchored below a roughly-drawn American flag. Robert brought the paper to his mouth and kissed it, leaving his moist lip prints on the flag.

It suddenly seemed silly to have written all these things onto this tattered piece of paper. None of the boys would ever need to look at this drawing again. They could no more forget this map than they could forget the face of their own mother. This pencil-drawn map was the distillation of their life's dream. It was, in a very real sense, their heaven.

Robert held the corner of the drawing over the candle and watched as the flame slowly burn it to ash. The smell of the burning page was as majestic and sweet as Episcopal incense.

Chapter 34
Telling Hannah

The next day was a Thursday and, all the next morning, Robert's mind was consumed with dreams of freedom. His thoughts blazed like pine in a boiler box until Spider arrived to throw a sizeable splash of cold water on them.

"What did Hannah say when you told her what we're doing?" he asked.

Robert was not in the mood for such a question, so he decided to lie. "She was fine with it," he said. Robert, of course, hadn't said the first word to his wife about their conspiracy and Spider noticed that his friend's eyes were blinking nervously. He was quick to spot a lie, and Robert hated him for it.

"You coward, you didn't tell her!" Spider said. "I suspect she'll have quite a bit to say."

"Maybe," Robert said as he turned and tried to walk away. Last night, he and his comrades had passionately sworn allegiance to the plan, exchanging smiles, tears, and even blood as they pledged themselves to be free or die. Today, Robert's woke with glorious visions of liberation. But now the thought of telling Hannah loomed like a thundercloud that threatened to rain on his parade. Her common-sense words would likely be a harsh slap in the face. Suddenly, the strong words of last night seemed like idle chit-chat, as if his crew had been some group of boys volunteering to climb a tree. Long speeches and blood spots wouldn't be enough for Queen Hannah when there were yet so many mountains to climb.

"Oh, she'll be sure to have a suggestion or two," Robert offered, "but she won't have no problem with it." Having spoken these words out loud, Robert's heart trembled at the thought of facing her. Hannah most certainly would have something to say. As Spider was about to open his mouth again, Robert held his hand up. "Hush," he said. "I plan to let her speak her piece. I'll just listen."

"Listen?" said Spider. "If you listen, you'll lose for sure. You always listen, and you always lose the argument. I know your Hannah."

"No. This time I won't give in," said Robert. "I can't. All the men have put their blood on it and I'm obliged to put my foot down."

"Well, be careful where you put down that big man-foot of yours," warned Spider. "She's likely to chop it off. This is Hannah we're talking about."

Robert wasn't dissuaded. "Look here," he said. "I'm the man here and she knows I'm the head of the house. The Good Book says wives must live in subjection to their husbands."

Spider just laughed. "Holy verses ain't a big enough stick where Hannah's concerned," he said. "You might want to bring a gun along."

"Well I'm sorry," said Robert. "It ain't her choice. She's my wife and the children are my children. The choice is mine and she'll just have to obey."

"Hold your horses, General Washington," said Spider. "Hannah's no wisp of a girl. Folks call her a queen, and she's used to bein' one. This ain't like asking for collards instead of peas. You're asking her to risk her life and the lives of her babies. She'll want a big say in this."

"I'm fine to give her a say, but either way, she's still got to go along," he affirmed. "I'm doing all this for her and the children."

"Fine, but I just think you best use your gentle voice," Spider said. "You know she can whup your butt if she's a mind to. And she may bring your mama up from Beaufort to help her thrash you."

After Robert walked around in a few angry circles, he calmed a bit and he muttered to Spider, "I made a big mistake not to tell her before this. You think she'll go along?"

"Might be mad, maybe so mad she won't want to go with you," Spider said.

"She has to go," Robert whispered. "I'd sooner stay a slave than to run off without her, and I could never, ever, leave my children. I've gotta make her understand."

"Fine then," Spider said. "But use your loving voice, not your helmsman voice."

Robert nodded soberly. "Say a prayer for me... and for my backside."

Spider, always needing to have the last word, just grinned and said, "I'll pray... and I'll also have some bandages ready when you get back. Good luck, brave brother." All the rest of that day, Robert labored in dread of the conversation that waited for him at home.

He whistled nervously as he left the dock area after work. Robert was impatient to tell Hannah of his decision and take his punishment. All the way up East Bay Street he was thinking about how best he should say it, preparing his words the way generals prepare their troops for battle.

By now he was convinced that his wife would scoff at the idea of stealing a Confederate warship. For men like Robert and his crew, making the decision was all of it. That's the way the mind of a man works. Once the die is cast, their course is clear. A man's dreams are like great birds rising in the sky, free to fly anywhere they have a notion to go. But Hannah Jones Smalls was no flitty bird, she was a woman. Women have questions, women want details, and Hannah was a strong-minded woman. She knew dreams don't just need wings to fly, they need feet to land on. 'My God,' he thought to himself, 'she'll poke every flaw. Hannah's gonna roast me like a chicken on a spit.'

His head was flooded now. Would she call his decision foolish? Would she be willing to go? Making the choice to steal the boat had been so quick and simple, but his woman would want more than a notion. Robert's mouth was so dry he stopped his whistling. As he turned from the cobblestones of the waterfront and strode up the last gravel stretches of East Bay Street, Robert had two pictures flashing back and forth in his mind.

In one, he saw Hannah, calm and smiling as she welcomed the news that they would be free. "I'm so proud of you," he could almost hear her say, as she and the children embraced him. Then they would all sit down to the best supper he had ever tasted. But another scene came into his mind, a less pleasant one.

In this vision, a perturbed and resolute Hannah greeted his news with cold silence and a frown. "You decided this? Just you?" she asked. "Was I not to be consulted at all?" He could almost see the dark wrinkles in her brow. "Have you even once considered that we all might die in this fool scheme of yours?" In this second vision, she just ranted on and on. Robert was unable to say a word. God alone knew how it would all turn out.

Both of these scenes rolled over in his head, and after a few minutes, the vision of soft Hannah began to fade, and all he could envision was trouble. 'Oh God,' he thought to himself, 'I should have told her right away.' By the time he mounted the narrow stairs to their apartment above the stable, he felt like a condemned man climbing the gallows.

As he shut the front door behind him, he was met by smiles and an embrace from little Elizabeth. "Hello, Papa!" she said, "Mama, Daddy's home." As his daughter raced back across the room to take hold of her mother's apron strings, Robert saw that Hannah was busy at the stove preparing supper. The aroma of bacon rinds and greens filled the kitchen. It was a good smell and a good omen, he thought.

"Smells like heaven in here," Robert said. "How was your day?"

As his wife turned to him, her face was stiff and her brow was pinched with angry lines. His blood suddenly ran cold. This was not the calm and smiling Hannah. It promised to be a difficult evening.

"You took your sweet time getting here," she said. "I hope you were having a better time than I did today."

As Robert reached to greet and comfort her, she pushed his hands away, not so much to reject him, but to free her hands to gesture. It always scared him when Hannah needed both hands to talk. She held both her arms out in front, all her fingers spread out stiff and wide. He sensed a hurricane of female words was about to make landfall. Now Robert had seen scores of windstorms at sea, but this type of turbulence was the worst. He had only asked, "How did your day fare?" It occurred to him that this might not be the best evening to tell her about the plan. The married brothers on the dock had come to call this a woman-storm.

But as all of them sat down to eat, no storm of words came. Robert was not altogether comforted, quiet storms often being the worst. Looking across the table into the sullen face of his wife, he noticed that young Elizabeth was tending to Robert Junior. Hannah had placed their dinner in the center of the table. Never in his life had he been so discouraged to see a roasted hen on a spit.

Robert had wanted to ease into his planned speech, but instead he just blurted out the truth. "Me and the boys have resolved to steal the *Planter*," he said. "We're gonna get us all out of this hell hole. We drew up a plan and done made our marks with blood."

The room suddenly fell as quiet as a white church, and Robert knew his wife well enough to know that this was not a good sign. It was not the quietness of peace but a crushing silence. Hannah said nothing, but Robert never forgot the look of cold defiance in her eyes. Her pupils spread out wide, like those of an infuriated bobcat in torch light.

"My Lord above!" she said. "Just let me sit myself down and take this in."

Hannah leaned back in her cane chair and turned her face to the ceiling and began an imaginary discussion with God and his imaginary jury of angels. "Dear Lord above, this boy you call my husband marches in here," she said, gesturing toward the rafters. "Lord, he's bringing me some whopper of a tale saying he's got some kind of man plan. Like some story-book child, he says he's done sold our cow for some magic beans, only we don't own no cow... and he didn't get no beans."

Hannah then turned to address the girls and the baby. "He says all this brilliance is gonna save us all," she said. "And his wife, and all his friends, even his own blessed little children are going to put their lives on the line for this fool notion of his." The children's eyes were wide with fear by this point.

"I'm over here, Hannah," Robert said. "The Lord already knows about the plan. You need to be talking to *me*. Saint Paul says, "the husband is the head of the wife," you know, "as Christ is head of the church." It's my decision, my call to make."

Hannah did her best to hold back, but Robert's words had gotten her blood up. "So let me get this clear. You tell me you're the head of me. Over me like Lord Jesus is over his church. Fine, but you don't sound like any Good Shepherd to me. You say you got a plan for getting away from the masters and that you're doing all this for freedom. But what about my freedom? Are you the only one free? Don't I get no say in this?" she said. "Near as I see it, you're lordin' your way to some kind of male Freedom Land while still wanting the women to be your slaves. If you're inviting me to freedom, that's well enough, but it had better be freedom for *all* the slaves. Women included. Robert Smalls, I'll walk through the valley of death by your side, but I'll burn in the devil's hell before I'll live under your thumb."

He was stunned and inspired at the same time. Hannah had just said things Robert had never thought about in all his life. "You're right, of course," he said as a long and silent moment of recognition took hold in his mind. "If we're headed for freedom, we'd better all be free, both men and women, free to make our own choice. I just couldn't bear the thought of leaving you behind."

For one of the rare times in her life, Hannah could muster no words. Finally, she raised her face to Robert, and for a brief moment he could only stare at the tip of her nose, wondering if she was about to nod it up and down in approval or perhaps shake it side to side. She did neither, but only stood in frozen silence.

The icy quiet was broken when she slowly raised her clenched right fist and from that fist emerged a single index finger. Snapping it toward heaven, she gritted her teeth and snorted from both her flared nostrils. "Yes!" she said. "By God, *yes*." The 'yes' ended in a hiss so loud that

Robert feared it might be heard by every citizen in Charleston. "We're gonna be on that boat!" she exclaimed. "We're all going to Freedom Land together." Robert just looked at her, in awe of his wife's words as her face gradually turned from rage to resolution.

"What a piece of work you are!" he said with a tender smile, his eyes locked on hers now. "What a wise wife God has given me!" he said. Taking her into his arms, he kissed her cheek and neck. "Please, please," he said, "Forgive this poor boy, this simple fool that I am."

"You're no boy and you ain't no fool," Hannah said. "I believe I may be married to the only real man, black or white, in all of South Carolina." She stepped back from him and folded her hands softly across her aproned chest. "Robert Smalls, I will be quite happy to go with you, come what may. Like sister Ruth said in the Good Book, 'Where you go, I will go, and where you die, I will die.'"

Robert pulled her to him and they held each other more tightly than either of them could remember. Slowly sinking to their knees, they all knelt down together to pray, thanking God and asking his blessing on the brave thing they were about to do together.

"You married a crazy man, you know," he said.

"And a brave one," she said, "Brave enough for all of us."

As Robert held her in his muscular arms, Hannah imagined she heard the angels rejoicing from the courts of heaven, and Robert himself believed he heard the voice of Jehovah himself, summoning chariots of fire for the battle that was to come.

Chapter 35
Preparation

By the next day, Robert's faith had floated back to earth. A misty drizzle soaked his hair and clothes on his way to the wharf and the whole dock area stank with the smell of a big catch that had come in yesterday. Fish heads and entrails were strewn everywhere and he almost slipped on the bloody boards of the dock. About a dozen boys were still busy gutting what remained of two tons of bluefish.

Robert had overflowed with confidence after Wednesday night's meeting, and his hopes were bolstered even more last night as Hannah was won over. But, now, just one day hence, he had awakened in a cold sweat, and all morning he was beset with stifling fears. *'What have we done?'* he asked himself. He reasoned that they might have just signed their own death warrants.

Generations of scolding, whipping, and lynching were conspiring to quench every spark of hope. Robert's mind was drowning in doubts as he completed his morning chores on the *Planter,* simultaneously watching as a thousand fish were beheaded along the dock. He had heard the frightening tales of slaves who met death while trying to run. Robert had always taken these with a grain of salt, since masters were prone to embellish such accounts so as to forestall escapes. He told himself not to give in to fear, but not all his fears were unfounded. He had seen enough with his own eyes.

In his childhood, he once passed a live oak that had the remains of two black men hanging from its branches. His mother explained that these two slaves had lit out from the cane fields three weeks earlier, only to be apprehended by white men with whips and dogs. Lydia recounted the details she'd heard from those who had been there to see it.

These runaways were bound up with ropes, and then a team of horses dragged them in a big circle around a plowed field. This went on for a whole half hour while all the other slaves were forced to watch. The victims screamed until they could do so no longer, but the slave women and their children continued to weep after that.

At the end, one man was dead and the other one was still breathing, and this live one was shot through the head. It was said that both bodies were stripped down to naked. The men's privates were severed with a shovel blade to be tossed to the dogs. What was left of them was strung up in the big tree and left there. The punishment was over, but the lesson was lasting. By the time young Robert came upon them, decay, insects, and the birds painted a picture that was much more dire. For runaways, failure came inevitably, and at a frightfully high price.

Such scenes were not common, but these lynchings served to bolster the horrible rumors that circulated amongst the slaves. Robert reasoned that the details of such stories had been embellished with each telling, but there was truth enough at their core. Successful escapes were rare, and those who fell short should expect no mercy at all.

Now nine black boys had a notion to steal a gunboat, and that right under the nose of General Ripley, whose home and headquarters were just across from Wharf Four. To fail would bring something worse than death. Their punishment would make hell's lake seem like a parlor fire and everyone in South Carolina would be watching.

As slim as the odds seemed, there was no turning back now. The conspiracy was too well underway. Nine men, five women, and four children were already involved. Even if any of them decided to back out, the dream had already filled the hearts and minds of all the others. The cat was out of the bag now, and a scary beast she was.

Success would require flawless execution of a perfect plan, and this only with the constant aid of Almighty God. As Robert looked up from the *Planter's* bridge, he saw only an empty gray sky bereft of angels and chariots. It would take more than faith to get them free, it would require hard work and a lot of luck.

It occurred to Robert that most slave escapes failed not for lack of courage but lack of planning. No slave, or group of slaves, could ever overpower or outrun the masters, they would have to out-think them. The whites' underestimation of African intelligence was a constant insult, but it might also provide a delightful point of weakness. The Rebs might think a slave capable of running or even violence. They would not, however, expect a plan of strategized brilliance, and a brilliant plan it would have to be.

For the period between mid-January and the end of March, Robert's mind was a storehouse for a hundred schemes and details. He couldn't read and write, so nothing could be put down on paper. This was probably good anyway. Whites might stumble across written checklists, timetables, and maps, but even their watchful eyes couldn't see the plans of a black man's mind. Nevertheless, it all presented a daunting task. Required actions must be laid out in proper sequence and pristine detail.

Each conspirator must prepare to do his or her part, to be in the right place at the right time. Each must have their assigned duties perfectly committed to memory, and they couldn't take action until each of them carried in their brain an inerrant copy of the plan. During the next forty-six days, each waking moment became a mental classroom, where every move had to be memorized and rehearsed. Their whole enterprise could be undone by a single mistake by any one of them, and to fail was death.

They would also have to communicate with each other regularly, but always secretively. It wouldn't be wise for them to converse in public or meet as a group. If some adjustment to the plan was needed, they would all have to agree and understand. No one was free to act on their own.

If there arose any need for all of them to meet, there was no easy way to call such a gathering. For each conspirator, there would be long periods without contact with the others. In the rare opportunities when they did see each other, their words had to be few and brief, tidbits of distilled information, spoken in code. Faint whispers, subtle nods, and sly winks conveyed orders, answers, and most of all, hope. Those whispers were life, as they continued to refine their battle plan. Day by day, each detail was meticulously pressed into place, like the multicolored glass shards of a cathedral window.

Bigger issues concerned how they would guarantee the proper timing of things. Being late to their marks could be fatal, and they dreaded the thought of leaving anyone behind. Generalities like "sundown" or "midday' would not suffice. They would need to know the precise time.

Hannah and Will Morrison were the only ones among them who could read the hands of a clock, so Hannah taught the women and William the men. None of them had watches, and most of them lived in places with no visible or trustworthy timepiece to discern minutes, not just hours. William carried around his neck a family watch his father had left him, but it hadn't worked for years. Each conspirator had to scout out places around town that had working clocks. Hannah would use the one in the lobby of the Baines Hotel. The dry goods seller beside William and David's quarters also had a clock that could be seen through the front window. It was first thought that the boys who slept on the *Planter* could set time by the bells that were sounded on the South Wharf, but its chiming was too infrequent and unreliable. Various whims of the guards caused bells to be rung at irregular times and sometimes not at all. Spider, always the schemer, came up with the idea of using Captain Relyea's spyglass. With it, the boys could read the minute hand of the clock on the tower of the town hall, which was visible from the prow of the *Planter*. Even at night, they could see its movements by the streetlights of the square. At the top of every hour the big bell would ring loud enough to be heard throughout the city.

Robert and Spider said they should all be sure to awaken by one o'clock on the morning of their departure. This was an easy goal since it was not likely any of them would sleep that night anyway. The men who worked the *Planter* would plan to arrive by one-thirty to make final preparations and would begin firing up the boilers by two. By three a.m., the ship should be ready to cast off.

Hannah would watch the lobby clock at the hotel and depart by two a.m. to gather the bags and the children. The plan was for Suzanne, Serenade, Annie, and Lavina to meet on the corner of Elizabeth and Chapel Street and then sneak through the back alleys to the *Etowah*. The women would travel in pairs so as not to arouse the suspicion of the constables. All of them would arrive at the end of the North Wharf by three o'clock, hiding in the steamer *Etowah* which was tied up at pier number five. Will Morrison would be there by two-thirty to unlock the hold of the boat and hide them all safely below decks until the *Planter* was able to come their way.

The children had to be trained to maintain silence whenever necessary, and mustn't be told the details of all that was happening until after they got safely to the boat. It was risky enough to ask adults to hold their tongues. Little ones could only be trusted to keep secret what they did not know. There could be no mention of what they were planning – no winks, no hints, and absolutely no words about it – even in their family prayers. And their prayers were increasingly fervent and frequent as the day of departure approached. As they filled their brains with plans, they hoped that the Lord Almighty was busy apprising his angels of what help would be needed, and given.

Even routine errands through town took on new meaning as they gathered information as to which street corners were patrolled, which gaslights got lit and by when, and which gates got locked after dark. They became concerned about things that had once been trivial details. Which Confederate guards were habitually late or early? Which thoroughfares had the lightest traffic? Which ones had and the longest and darkest stretches of shadow?

Robert and Spider even counted the number of footsteps through the back streets between the Baines Hotel and the North Wharf. Hannah would need to have a general idea how long it would take her to pick up the children and to cover the distance to the *CSS Etowah,* where the *Planter's* crew would gather them and take them to freedom.

For her part, Hannah was in charge of her own doings and the movements of the children. Robert knew better than to try to interfere too much. Since her comings and goings at the hotel were not monitored closely, it would be a simple thing for her to steal away at the proper time. No one would ask her any questions, since she was always the one with all the answers. The women did inquire as to what clothing and personal belongings they might take along.

"Just what you're wearing," was Robert's answer. "You came to South Carolina naked and will likely not have much more when you bid it farewell."

"I understand," Hannah said. "But it'd be a pity to leave my best things behind."

"No, we've gotta leave everything," Robert said.

Hannah had the idea of having a street sale to liquidate their belongings to make a bit of money to take with them. Robert said no. "We gotta just walk away from all of it," he said. "A neighborhood sale would alert everybody that we're fixing to run off." They couldn't even *give* their things away. If they started handing off all their worldly goods, folks would start asking questions. "Those folks can likely divide our possessions after we're gone," he said.

"Like they do for dead people," Hannah said.

"Trust me," Robert said. "I'm trying to keep you alive."

"Maybe I could take our new down pillows though," she said. "Wouldn't hurt nothing."

"Look at me," he implored. "Freedom's the thing, the only thing. Pillows ain't worth dying for."

"Well maybe," she said. "But them's fine pillows. Can't I just stuff 'em right here under my blouse like this?"

"Flower pie, Robert said, "If you stuff them things in your shirt like that, we'll have every lusty buck in Charleston sniffin' after you, you pretty thing."

At that, Hannah offered a sweet smile and he could feel in his heart that she was with him. She still couldn't resist making just one more request. "And Miss Ancrum just got her a nice French petticoat made of fine white silk. I figure I could snatch it from her closet before I go."

Robert looked sternly into her eyes. "We ain't gonna run off with other people's belongings," he said. "We gotta pack light and move fast. We ain't risking our lives for no underwear."

"But," she said, "You ain't *seen* this petticoat." Robert just shook his head.

As the details were gradually forged into a workable strategy, Robert could see a measure of confidence growing among the women and the crew. What was confusing became clear, and fear was replaced with faith. Though it cheered Robert's heart to witness their increased excitement, there were other thoughts that prevented him from completely sharing their joy.

Each of them was preparing to do their part to escape the city, but Robert, as their leader, wrestled alone with certain questions that still remained. Between the North Wharf and the Federal fleet lay a difficult labyrinth of obstacles. The first challenge was to navigate the maze of channels from the piers to open water. There had always been dangerous currents and shoals, but a year ago the Union had complicated things by blocking the harbor with ships filled with granite which were sunk in a row between Sullivan's and Morris Island.

In addition to the shallows and sunken hulks, there were hundreds of floating mines that had to be avoided. Some mines floated, but others were submerged, and any one of them could sink the largest of ships. All these would be difficult to negotiate in daylight, but would be even trickier in the darkness.

Their escape would require light. The big bow lanterns would help them to clearly see the channels ahead, but they would also signal their presence to the checkpoints. Robert had always joked that he could navigate Charleston Harbor with his eyes closed, but it was just a joke. Total darkness was not an option. The *Planter* would have to burn her lights all the way out, and if they were noticed, so be it.

Once up to steam, there were five guard posts and forts to pass, and since the war came, these checkpoints were both alert and well-armed. Any one of them would sound an alarm for any unauthorized vessel that attempted to pass.

The first checkpoint was the tower at the end of the South Wharf, the pier where the *Planter* had its mooring. Though this guard post was only lightly armed, it was perhaps the most dangerous, since it was the first one they had to pass. Any alarms from it would surely alert every cannon and gunboat in the harbor before the *Planter* could get up to speed. Robert was familiar with the guards who stood the night watch there and knew them to be easygoing men who weren't likely to blow any whistles.

The channel from there to the Atlantic Wharf was tricky and lined with buoys, but there was no checkpoint once they reached the wharf. After gathering Hannah and the others from the *Etowah*, they would have to turn around and return through the same narrow channel they had navigated to get there.

Once underway, there was likely to be clear sailing until they came upon a small fort called Castle Pinkney, about a quarter of a mile into the harbor. This was a brick parapet usually staffed by just a handful of soldiers. Though it had a few cannons, it was primarily dangerous because its channel was lined by floating torpedoes, which Robert had assisted in installing earlier that year. The tower at Castle Pinkney would also require them to give the proper code to pass. These codes, which were changed weekly, were usually a special combination of whistle blasts and bells. Captain Relyea, like every other Southern commander would always keep the current code written in his logbook. Relyea always kept that book in the ship's safe, which was usually left unlocked.

As they took a southern course across the harbor, there was another checkpoint where the channel took the *Planter* past the guns of Fort Ripley. This battery, named after Charleston Harbor's military commander, served as part of the second level of defense against vessels that might succeed in getting past the bigger forts at the entrance. The small fort had been built only recently and was positioned strategically on a sandbar in the very center of Charleston Harbor.

Their next test would be a big one. The mines of the channel, and the sunken ships left by the Union would force them to pass just under the guns of Fort Johnson on James Island. Robert knew these were some of the biggest cannons in Charleston Harbor since, on the *Planter*, he had delivered the big guns himself last year. The rows of floating torpedoes were arranged so as to funnel all passing vessels to within two hundred yards of the fort. An improper signal here would almost certainly get the *Planter* blown to pieces.

Fort Sumter of course, presented the final and most formidable challenge. From the Charleston waterfront, the fort appeared as a hazy sliver of brick on the horizon, but Robert had often had occasion to see it up close. Built following the War of 1812, Sumter was a pentagonal structure, with masonry walls that rose an imposing fifty feet above the waters of the harbor. Each of its five sides bristled with cannons, each of which could precisely hurl a 42 pound projectile that could destroy any target within a two mile range. Like the other forts, lines of sunken torpedoes compelled every ship to pass just under Sumter's biggest guns, the Columbiads. To arouse the wrath of these cannons would be sheer suicide.

Sumter's checkpoint was the last one a ship had to pass before they could head out to blue water. Because of this, the guards here had the most stringent procedures of any post in the harbor. In addition to the code signals, there would usually be verbal interrogatories exchanged to ascertain the name and nature of the vessel, its orders, and its destination. Robert would need to stand ready to answer such questions. There were even times when, at the discretion of the guards, a military boat might need to be searched. Robert doubted that there was anything he, a black boat thief, could say in such an event. Prayer was his only reasonable preparation for such a contingency.

"What exactly is our plan if we get caught?" asked Chisholm. "Do we surrender ourselves or do we try to fight our way out?"

"In that case, there is no plan, unless you consider heaven a military plan," said Robert. "If we get caught, they ain't gonna put us in no jailhouse, and they won't send us back to slaving neither. They'll likely just slaughter us all – men, women, and babies. If we try to fight, there's a chance they'll take some of us alive, and we don't want to find out what would follow that."

"So then, what?"

"We best just blow the boat up and ourselves along with it," Robert said. "But most likely, the boys in the forts will assist us in taking care of that. I don't want the Rebs to get their hands on any of the munitions we have on board."

"Then I suppose we'll just have to succeed," said Chiz.

"I figure it'll be all right in any case," said Robert. "We'll either be glad-handing each other or glad-handing the Lord Jesus by day's end."

Once they were past Fort Sumter, there was nothing but blue water between them and the Federal fleet. In his mind, Robert had more than once daydreamed about what it would feel like when Sumter was safely out of range. He once started working on a speech he would give to whatever Union ship greeted them first, but with all the worries and plans buzzing in his head, he thought it best to devote his energies to executing the escape. He would leave it to others to make the fancy speeches.

For the month before their departure, Robert took every opportunity to review the captain's maps of the harbor. He committed to memory every fortress, checkpoint, and every possible channel they might take in escaping. Having passed these checkpoints before, Robert knew the guards would have a relatively clear view of the *Planter's* bridge and were likely to look for Captain Relyea personally. He was familiar with the kinds of greetings that might be exchanged between the pilots and those on the fort's walls. As a helmsman, Robert had sometimes waved to them himself. If this happened, he hoped they wouldn't be able to see his hands trembling.

The possibilities soon became too numerous to consider, and by mid-April, he reasoned that he would just have to wait and play some cards as they fell. If nothing else, the situation helped Robert's prayer life. And with every new day came new possibilities, questions, and fears.

One arose on a particular Tuesday, as Robert was making his way down Market Street. From the bottom of the hill, he saw a familiar figure standing in front of the general store. Here was Abe Allston, holding a sack of paw paws and staring through the window at a display of rifles and pistols.

"You reckon we'd be wise to get hold of some guns?" he asked, "Just in case Johnny Reb turns up at the wrong time? I think the boys might rest easier having us some rifles."

"You might want to think about that for a spell," said Robert. "Weapons give comfort but I venture they'd also make good flags. Whites seem to get touchy when slaves come around totin' guns. We're trying to lay low here."

"I'd reckon nine black men with rifles would be pretty hard to explain away," Allston conceded.

"And if any shooting starts," Robert said, "There ain't enough muskets in South Carolina to shoot our way out of this place."

"So no guns," Abe said. "Then the plan's got to work, I suppose. If we fall short, we'll all be in the hands of the enemy."

"And in God's," added Robert. "He'll be with us."

"Better be," said Allston. "Gotta be."

Robert put his arm around Abe as together they walked back toward the *Planter* to polish off what remained of the day's work. In the distance, they could see a black man running towards then from the gate to the wharf area.

"They're calling for Negroes to help."

"Tell 'em we're working," Allston said. "We're busy enough right here."

"They're paying a dollar," said the man. "Cash money for just an hour."

Robert was never one to pass up a dollar, and he reasoned they might be able to pick up any stray rumors that were circulating around the harbor. Any tidbits of information might prove helpful in their escape to freedom. Up ahead, a big crowd had gathered at the Atlantic Pier.

"Oh my Lord!" was all Robert could say as he and Abe drew nearer. They arrived just in time to see Confederate soldiers winching up an ominous iron cylinder from the water. It was Hunley's submarine, wet, rusty and dripping with seaweed.

"Get back!" the officers yelled. "Clear out, fools!" The underlings, all enlisted men, ran backwards as the higher ranks pushed closer to the *Hunley* as its metal hull clanked, wobbled, and grinded to rest on the cobblestones. Two Rebs used a crowbar wrench to open what must have been the hatch of the vessel.

"Good God," the older one said, as he stuck his head into the hatch opening to look inside. "I ain't about to touch none of this," he said. "Get those darkies over here and clean this thing out." He was pointing to Robert and Abe.

As Robert held the hatch open, he could see the ghastly faces of a half-dozen drowned crew members. Their heads had been jammed together as they had simultaneously tried to escape the vessel through the 26-inch opening. Each wide-eyed dead man wore a tortured expression. As the vessel had filled with water, they had obviously battled one another for a chance to get out.

"I can't even get in there," Robert said as he tried to take a gulp of fresh air.

"Step back, boy," the old man said. "They bunched themselves up this way last time, too." He pushed his black boots into the hatch opening, roughly kicking the heads of the dead men down into the vessel. "Now you boys crawl down in there and pass these brave sailors out."

No dollar on earth would have sufficed to pay for such hideous work. One by one, the cold wet bodies of eight men were extricated from what the Rebs came to call the *iron coffin*. Two of the victims appeared to be in their teen years. Some were found in one another's embrace while the man who was dressed as captain was found clutching a candle in the bow of the ship. Robert later learned that the submarine had already drowned three different crews, all this before ever seeing real action at sea.

As a crowd of colored dock workers looked on, the waterlogged bodies were pushed up from below. Each corpse popped up head first through the hatch opening, rising to almost full height before toppling over in sequence like cut logs at a sawmill.

"What are you gawking at?" the old Reb barked at the crowd. "These heroes don't need no cotton pickers staring at them in their honorable death. You best get back to wherever you were."

Robert and Abe were careful to avert their eyes as they worked, but couldn't ignore the awful thud of the wet bodies as they smacked the pavement. The sound reminded Robert of fresh-caught groupers being tossed from a boat. Today's was a grizzly catch indeed.

"Don't weep for these warriors," said the officer in charge. "They're heroes, they are." Coming over to the last body on the end, he leaned over and straightened the dead man's collar. "This one here's H. L. Hunley. He's the man who designed and built this damnable thing."

"Damnable for sure," Robert said to Abe. From the farthest end of the wharf, they could see a column of eight recruits marching in their direction, all in identical uniforms.

"Looks like the next batch of sardines is lining up to be put into the can," Abe said.

"Just pray we all can escape easier than these dead boys," Robert said. "Win or lose, I doubt we'll see any kind of death worse than this." Robert and Abe hurried back to the *Planter,* not even bothering to collect their dollars. It was almost sundown now, and their day was far from over. Robert remembered that he and Spider were slated to escort General Ripley and Captain Relyea into town that night. None of today's duties were the kind he looked forward to.

Chapter 36
Calves of Gold

If Charleston's Battery Promenade was a place people went to be seen, there were plenty of other parts of town where men went to be invisible. The district around Water Street, mostly empty during daylight hours, stunk of evil after sundown. It was said in jest that the district became *dark* after dark. Men's baser spirits emerged as liquid spirits flowed, and unfettered wickedness filled every street and heart. Here good Presbyterians and Episcopalians, divided on Sundays by the doctrines of Calvin and kings, were united in the fellowship of debauchery.

Scores of white men hid under their widest straw hats. The brims were pulled low over their eyes so as not to look at each other or to be looked at. As they savored the charms of strong drink and weak women, each pretended to be someone else, or perhaps no one at all. Inflamed with lust, yet shy as schoolboys, they made inquiries in the third person, as if they were speaking about someone else. "Where can a man get a drink?" or "Would one of you ladies be willing to accompany a gentleman upstairs?" Every person present had learned to play along with the charade, and play they did.

The younger men, driven by the more powerful demons of youth, showed no subtlety in their pursuit of sin. Drinking openly in the streets, they displayed no reticence to curse in the presence of the deacons, priests and choir members who populated the anonymous shadows. Fathers urging their sons to go home might themselves be told where to go.

Evil was both pursued and overlooked here, where every man existed as both perpetrator and witness. Each was complicit in this brotherhood, where sin reigned, and where forgiveness and confidentiality were a mutual obligation.

Captain Relyea and General Ripley were infrequent visitors to the district, but when they did show up, they were welcomed as lifetime members. While the masters tasted forbidden fruit, slaves like Robert and Spider had to stick together, enjoying as escorts a special fellowship of their own.

"Brother, you've got it all right here," Spider said. "All things a wayward man might crave. Every sin in the Bible, you might say."

"Yes," smiled Robert. "Both Testaments. Old Moses might have to run back to get him another stone tablet or two."

Spider grinned back at him. "I fear I'm beginning to have a bad effect on you, brother. A very good bad effect."

Robert just smiled, "When I was a boy," he said, "Mama would pray for God to send an angel to guide my path, but I doubt if she had you in mind."

"Every guiding angel has a purpose," Spider replied. "Good and evil, light and dark. Men need both kinds to be truly human. Folks say angels and demons argue from both our shoulders."

"The bad angels seem to speak louder," Robert said. "On Saturdays at least.

"These fellows come to this place to be men, but the more they carouse, the more they become just a bunch of little boys," said Spider, "trying to live like they did in their youth, or how they wished they had lived in their youth."

Robert just nodded. "They drink to remember who they were," he said, "and to forget who they are."

"To forget what they do," Spider added, "and what they can no longer do."

"It's a kind of church meeting for them," Robert added. "Here you've got singing, rejoicing, and a better heart of brotherhood than they ever had at Saint Helena's. What a shame."

"They're in the spirit all right," said Spider. "But it ain't the Holy one." Robert's friend stopped to admire the exposed legs of the bad girls who were lined up along Water Street like so much ripe fruit. "Look there," he said. "The Hebrew children are bowing down to all them golden calves!"

Robert just shook his head, but Spider wasn't finished. "Let us pause to kneel and worship, my brother!" he said.

Robert chuckled, trying to avert his eyes. "You're the angel of death, you know."

"Always ready to serve," said Spider, "firmly perched on your left shoulder."

"Like scripture says, 'a *never* present help in time of need.'" Robert concluded. The boys took their time walking back toward the place they had left the General and the Captain. No slave had ever been chided for tardiness in collecting his master from such an evening.

"Does it ever vex you?" Spider asked Robert. "These white fools get drunk while we have to be their keepers?"

"Folks say it's our place... and their prerogative," Robert said. "But I'm beginning to think it may be part of some bigger plan of God."

"A sad plan, I think," said Spider. "And only you would try to see God's hand in this nastiness."

"No, in the midst of all this, God may be offering us an open door," Robert said. "Do you believe he ever sends signs?"

"I keep watching, but I don't never see nothing but beer signs," Spider said, "Just white boys livin' the life, while we've got to stay sober and walk 'em home."

"Yes, but keep your wits about you. Perhaps God will show us some crack in their armor," Robert said. "Their privilege may be their prerogative, but it may also be their weakness."

"What are you saying?" asked Spider.

"Just this." Robert said, "While they're losing their minds here, we're talking sense. While they're drowning their reason, we're plotting our escape. We've gotta hit 'em where they're weak and when they're weak. Ain't no way we're gonna steal the *Planter* by force, and we certainly won't get all the officers off the boat by smooth talk. They're not stupid men, but we might find some way to make them stupid. We can't force 'em off the ship, but just maybe we can *entice* all three men into town. We've gotta make them stupid, and sin's always strong enough to make a man stupid, even a good man."

"Then," Spider answered. "It will surely have to be on a Saturday, the a day of sin."

"You might be right," answered Robert, "but we may have to make them stupid enough to fall into sin on a Monday or a Tuesday."

"My Lord!" Spider said. "I doubt that even white boys can be that weak-minded."

"Well, just you wait," Robert said, "and wait upon the Lord. He'll send us a sign."

Just then, the tavern doors swung open and their intoxicated masters emerged from their revelries. Captain Relyea was wearing some woman's hat with flowers on it. General Ripley's sweaty hair was falling in his face and his shirt was gone. Robert and Spider just looked at each and nodded in silence. A horsey blonde woman soon came out to snatch her hat from Relyea's head, then walked back inside.

"Sorry it took us so long, boys," the Captain said. "And we regret you have to see us like this."

"No worries, sir," said Robert, looking over at Spider, "We're very much encouraged by what we see. We're glad you've had a pleasant time."

As Robert and Spider escorted Relyea and the General back home, their spirits were greatly lifted. Many details of their plan were still unclear, but they were now confident there would be a way to get all three white officers off the boat. "God is a wise and good God," Robert whispered. "Even on the Street of Sin, his angels are showing us the way."

"You'll make me a convert yet," smiled Spider.

"You should buy yourself a Bible," Robert laughed.

"Or maybe just steal one," said Spider, smiling a hypocritical grin. "Praise the Lord."

Robert chuckled to himself, looking up toward heaven as they walked on. God had revealed a sizeable crack in the masters' armor. Even now Robert was beginning to plan their next steps on their clandestine path to freedom. Tomorrow was Sunday, and Robert decided it was time he went back to church.

Chapter 37
The Graveyard

As spring arrived, Charleston's languishing economy and the stress of the war conspired to turn up the heat for everybody. Plantation owners, sailors, and slaves all found themselves in the same sad stew-pot. Robert was discouraged to hear that the McKee family had exhausted almost all of their wealth, and even rich men like Samuel Kingman were not exempt.

Back in the summer, Kingman had been forced to liquidate two of his larger plantations, and by the end of the year, he was forced into the more dire action of selling his Charleston townhouse. By May of 1862, he was calling in markers from everyone who owed him anything or had anything. It was a cool Wednesday when Kingman stopped by Wharf Six to speak to Robert.

"How's my girl these days?" the old man asked. "Hannah fairs well?"

"She does," Robert said, a bit suspicious of Samuel's pleasantries. "What's this about?"

"It's concerning our arrangement," he said. "In five years you've paid in less than three hundred dollars of what you owe me for Hannah and your daughter. Now I hear you've just had another baby come."

"Yes, sir," Robert said, "a little boy who bears my name."

"The boy," Kingman said, "is yours in name only, of course. The court would say he was mine."

"He's my son, my blood," Robert said, "I'll buy him from you like I did the others."

"That brings up why I've come," said Kingman. "The document says I can call in full payment after five years, the whole lump sum, and that's what I'm here to do."

"You can't hit me like this all at once," Robert stammered. "I'll need more time."

"I got no legal reason to extend you any more time," said Kingman. "I need the outstanding balance of the original seven hundred, plus a hundred more if you want Robert Junior. Give me full payment this week, otherwise I'll be taking Hannah and the children with me when I move inland. That's all there is to it."

"But you can't do that," Robert said. "I've paid you steady every month. You can't just up and take my family."

"Hate to do it, but I can and I must," said Kingman. "Blame me or the Yankees if you will, but times are dire. There's nothing more to be said."

"Dear God, how much?" Robert asked. "How much, and by when?"

"Four hundred ninety-five by next Wednesday," he said, "or I'm bringing the court officers with me. The minute I get cash in hand, you can tear up our agreement and have your people free and clear."

"It ain't enough time," Robert said. "Ain't enough time and you know it."

"I know nothing of the sort," said Kingman. "That you darkies are bad planners is no concern of mine. You owe me four hundred ninety-five. I venture I can sell Hannah and your children for a sight more than that." Kingman waved his long piece of paper up for Robert to see. He couldn't read a word of it, but he fully understood what the flat gold seal at the bottom of the page signified. Men waving that seal had the law on their side.

"Then I suppose that's how it's got to be," he conceded. Robert thought about calling Kingman a dozen evil names, but the Holy Spirit and his better judgment held his tongue in check. "You'll have your money," he said. "Payment in full."

"Good then," the old man said, "But I won't be put off, not even an extra day. The Yanks are tightening the noose around all of our necks and it's not my fault if you're feeling it too."

As Kingman turned to walk back towards town, Robert was saddened to see yet another white master scrambling for coins, but only a little bit saddened. Kingman's own greed had just kicked things into motion. He would have to steal the *Planter* in the next seven days. By next Tuesday morning, both Samuel Kingman's dollars and his slaves would be in Robert's possession and sailing their way out of Charleston Harbor. The old skinflint would never see his money or his slaves again.

With Kingman's deadline, there was no longer any possibility of turning back. If Robert needed a reminder that time was short, it was provided by the big courthouse clock as it struck four o'clock. At the final echoing strike of the bell, his heart trembled with sober fear.

Everything would be happening quickly now.

Robert felt all alone as he walked back toward the waterfront, trying to gain composure. It was a beautiful and balmy day in the harbor, but he found himself staring down at his jittery hands. Eight men, five women and five children had entrusted their future to an illiterate 23-year-old slave-turned-helmsman. Most of them were probably off praying somewhere to a God who hadn't made a significant appearance since the raising of Jesus. Robert's faith was drowning in trepidation. Only his reason was left to him, and his reason told him their lives were hanging by the thinnest of threads. The torments of slavery would seem like paradise if they fell short. As he rubbed his hands together, his mind began to focus on the punishments that might await them if they failed in any way. Suddenly terrified of facing his crewmen, Robert battled an unrelenting storm of dread that swirled in his skull.

Though it was approaching sundown, he set off in no particular direction. Any place more peaceful than the waterfront and the Market District would do. He took his normal route towards home, but instead of cutting over to East Bay, he just kept going, speaking to no one as he went, not even stopping to look into the store windows.

He had made this walk many times, but today it was taking an unusually long time to blow off steam. During his days as a lamplighter, Robert had lit the wicks along most of these streets, but after a half-hour of walking, the thoroughfares became signless and unfamiliar. It had never taken him this long to calm himself.

By the time he reached the north edges of town, the cobblestones had turned to gravel paths. He tried humming church tunes and after that, counting the blue doors and shutters of the houses, but nothing worked. Soon the spaces between the houses became larger. After that, there were only barns, tall trees, and open fields, but he still wasn't ready to turn back toward his troubles. God seemed to be leading him into his own private wilderness.

His steps led him to a vine-laden gateway with an impressive wrought iron arch over it. Robert didn't have to read the sign to know it was a cemetery. Covered with low brush and weeds, only the tops of the markers were visible through high grass. Robert stopped his walking then, not so much out of reverence, but to decide whether to go on. He was already fleeing from his fears, and he doubted that a graveyard would help. The path was about to take him through the very center of the graveyard, and his only other choice was to turn back.

He wished he had some friend with him now, for the place was noticeably quiet. Even Spider's blatherings would have been welcomed. The number of visitors to Charleston's cemeteries always diminished as evening approached, but this overgrown place looked like no one had visited these dead for a long time. Robert had no particular dread of dying, but he was not anxious to linger in this eerie place. He moved briskly and he resolved to focus his mind on cheerful or trivial things. But as he stepped past row after row of headstones, he couldn't help but to slow down and look.

Unlike the well-manicured graves in the Saint Helena's Churchyard, these stones were neither straight nor clean. A few of them showed signs of care, with clipped grass or even flowers over them. Most graves, however, were choked by weeds, and some were barely visible. He could see that the rows of monuments did not stop where the open area met the forest, but rather continued into the bushes and trees. This was an ancient place, no doubt dating back to the very beginnings of the colony.

Some markers, large and ornate, marked the resting place of noteworthy individuals. In most other places there were many rows of stones, all of uniform size and color. Here and there, headstones were organized in plots, families being laid to rest side by side in eternal togetherness. In some of these, there were larger stones for the patriarchs and matriarchs. Around them were smaller markers for their descendants, and even empty spaces. Likely reserved for family members who had not yet departed this life.

Though Robert couldn't read the words, he could discern the purpose of the inscriptions. The larger letters at the top were almost certainly the name of the dead one. In some cases, there were additional words carved in smaller, often italic letters. As a child he had been told these were words of comfort or endearment like *Rest in Peace, Beloved Mother* or perhaps lines from poems or scripture.

Just below that, they always put numbers connoting the dates of birth and death. Robert was good with numbers and knew how to cypher, so as he walked, he began to subtract the numbers to figure out how long each person had walked on earth. There were some who had lived well past 80 but also babies that had passed way so quickly that there was just a single date inscribed. Most folks seem to have lived only fifty years or so.

Robert walked respectfully. Stepping carefully between the mounds of earth, lest heaven's citizens see him dishonor their places of rest. His heart was touched by pairs of graves bearing the same last name –

married couples resting here just as they had slept in their earthly beds. Mostly the men seem to have outlived the mothers of their children, and many of the men had more than one woman buried beside them. Surrounding them were the smaller stones of their children, many who had died in infancy. Occasionally, a spouse was buried with a blank stone next to them, reserved for some wife or husband who was yet to pass, or who had moved on to other cities or family connections.

Robert wished he could read and understand every one of the words, being as they were, the only remaining record of these precious lives. He supposed that most of these stones would soon be obscured by weeds, then bushes, eventually to disappear into the forest. Holy anonymity. Robert began to wonder how long he would live and what might one day be written on his stone. Would he even have a headstone?

His attention was soon drawn to one conspicuous monument near the center of the cemetery, a sizeable arrangement of white marble blocks with carved trim and inscriptions everywhere. Up on top stood the bearded statue of some famous white man, but Robert had no idea who he might be. Some city founder perhaps, a philosopher, or maybe one of the saints of God. Robert ran his fingerers through the chiseled grooves of the man's name and then down to the dates below. 1741-1804.

Robert was a young man, but even now he knew most of what would be on his own monument. Robert Smalls would be inscribed at the top, and under that will be April 11, 1839, the day he was born. He reasoned that the first part of his legacy was already settled, literally carved in stone. It remained for his dreams or Confederate cannon to fill in the rest.

Perhaps God would be gracious; maybe they would succeed in escaping. Robert might go on to live a long life, dying as a gray-haired freedman with grandchildren all around. Grandchildren with story books under their arms. Would all the longings of his boyhood be realized? 'Not likely,' he thought.

As Robert mused over what his death date would be, he became more sober. There was a good chance he'd be caught and killed in the next few days, a 23-year-old boat thief swinging from one of the big live oaks on the waterfront. Some stonecutter would inscribe May 13, 1862, and that would be that. The smooth marble now felt cold to the touch as he remembered the great odds that stood between him and freedom. He suddenly deemed gravestones to be fleeting things. Hadn't this gloomy place and these overgrown monuments once been the very center of Charleston's life? These dead had dreamed of a colony that might become a town, and a town a great city. They fought battles, some won and some lost, and prayed to make some difference in the world. Did these slabs of marble comprise their only mark? Had their years and strivings boiled down to these stone note-pads, each bearing eight numbers. Robert recalled the ancient words of Saint James.

What is your life?
It is even a vapor
that appeareth for a little while,
and then vanishes away

His eyes were moist as he scanned the far edges of the graveyard, now obscured by vegetation. The aspirations of all these departed ones had returned to dust, their legacies rendered unreadable by time. Their resting places, once cleared, was now disappearing again into the eternal forest.

As his fingers again stroked the two carved dates on the marble, his spirit was suddenly lifted by the refreshment of recognition. The first number was unchangeable and the second date, in God's hands. 'Every man, black or white, will have a birth and a death date,' he thought. It occurred to him that that little nick in between was what makes us somebody or nobody. He put his finger on the tiny chipped hyphen that was flanked by the two dates.

He remembered the words his mother spoke when she showed him the blank spot on their old doorpost so many years ago. "That smooth space is hope," she had said. "How it's cut, that's between you and the Lord. Hope's the only little piece of this world that God has put in your hands."

In his heart, he said a sober but wordless prayer, then began to make his way through the graves and back toward the city. Soon he whispered out loud to himself, to God, and to any angels that might happen be listening, "I will not shrink back," he said. "I will be free, my wife will be free, and my children will be free."

As the final glowings of sunset sank behind the towering pines, Robert walked with refreshed steps through the heart of the bustling city. It was time to get busy. In his head, he could almost hear the courthouse clock ticking and in the distance and he imagined the sound of the *Planter's* engines as she waited at Pier Six. The growing darkness didn't bother him at all, for he knew by heart every one of the well-marked steps that lay before him.

Chapter 38
The Ticking Clock

On Saturday night, Robert stood silently at the wheel of the *CSS Planter* as she made her way back toward the South Wharf, chugging into an unusual outbound breeze. As the orange and lavender brush strokes of sunset faded behind the marshes, he negotiated the final labyrinth of buoys that defined the safe margins of the channel. Beneath the surface of waves lurked tricky shoals, rocks, and even more dangerous torpedoes. Far ahead on the docks, Robert could make out the dark figures of stevedores and dock hands, silhouetted against the glow of carriage lights that were just now blinking on along the Battery Promenade.

For the white citizens of Charleston, Saturday evening was a magical time – when families dressed, dined and chatted over card games. Friends who strolled the flowered streets would drop by for good conversation, inspired by wine, spirits, and news from that morning's *Charleston Mercury*. As the evening breezes cooled the town, the life of the city emerged, butterfly-like, from the warm cocoon of the Carolina afternoon. But for the African servants, these evenings held no promise of repose.

For slaves who worked in the big houses, the evening brought additional work after an already long day of subservience. Blacks who had labored all day in the shops or on the boats were now responsible for added hours of cleanup and preparation for the next day's tasks. If a boat-slave was somehow able to finish his work before bedtime, the pleasures available to him were few, usually conversation with his cohorts or perhaps an occasional song. Suffering ruled a slave's nights as it did his days.

As the colors of sunset faded before him, Robert turned around to look at the water one last time before they went ashore. He watched the stern lantern of an outbound dispatch boat shrink into the hazy distance. It felt good to be done with today's trips. Two blasts from their whistle signaled the dock hands to prepare to catch the ropes that would bind the *Planter* to her moorings. Those who owned pocket watches looked at them now, for everyone was anxious to finish up for the day.

Standing beside Captain Relyea, Robert spoke no words as he steered the boat toward the tie up. It was customary for slaves to do their work in silence, a practice which led most whites to assume that their servants had no interest in their conversations. Some slaves liked to listen though, and Robert always listened. Tonight was one of the rare times when there was truly something to hear.

When the dock officer James Wales jumped aboard, he quickly climbed up to the *Planter's* wheelhouse. It was his custom to check the log and sign any cargo receipts. Robert noticed the young man was breathing hard.

"You better read this, Cap," Wales said. "There's some important work headed your way." He went on to inform Captain Relyea that on Monday, the *Planter* would be receiving a full load of armaments for transport to Fort Ripley the next day. Robert pretended to watch the rope men on the pier, but he was straining to hear the whispered details of the officer's conversation. "Cannon, shells, and powder," were mentioned. It became clear that this week, Sunday would not be a day of rest.

Robert did his best to remain expressionless at the helm, but the news had just sent his mind spinning, always arriving at the same conclusion. The escape would have to go down Monday night. All the tedious months of talking, planning, and praying were about to end. In the dark hours of Tuesday morning, they would steal the Rebel's flagship and steam off to freedom or death.

The Lord had brought them nothing but pleasant surprises so far, so pleasant that it scared Robert a little. Every detail was coming together, if anything, better than planned. The *Planter* was about to be filled with fresh fuel and a valuable load of Confederate armaments. The crew and the women had rehearsed their parts and memorized the timing of things as if it had been Holy Scripture.

Samuel Kingman's deadline was unexpected, of course, but had only served to move things along. Robert smiled at the thought that the old Samuel would never see a nickel of the money he would show up to collect on Wednesday. By then, all the conspirators would be long gone and free.

The clock was ticking now for sure, and there was a long list of things to be done if they were to be ready by Monday night. Robert had to get the word out to everyone. They had set in motion a plan by which each man would tell another, who would then pass the message along to the next one. This was simple in theory, but it might be a challenge to contact all eight crewmen. God alone knew what they might be up to their elbows in.

The women would likely be thrown into a tizzy by the short notice, but they'd have to get over it. Getting away from their chores might require some forgivable lies, but Robert knew them to be courageous and ingenious souls. They would no doubt succeed in rounding up the children and getting everyone to their hiding place on the *CSS Etowah*.

Robert would get the Captain's harbor maps and current whistle codes from the drawer safe on the *Planter's* bridge. He reasoned that if necessary, he could navigate the harbor channels without the maps, maybe even with his eyes closed. The codes were another matter. These would be essential for them to get them past the checkpoints between Pier Six and blue water. On top of all this, they would have to keep an eye out for the various guards and officers that, willy-nilly, roamed the docks. These unpredictable idiots were likely to turn up at the most inopportune times. The more Robert thought about things, the longer his prayer list became, and the more his head hurt.

That night, he was almost too disturbed to sleep, and in the wee hours of the morning, his childhood nightmare returned. It had been many years since he'd been visited by the foggy vision of the McKee's yard, but every character and detail was still there – the children calling his name, the angry constables in pursuit, and the old black man with the scars on his back.

The end was the same as before. The black man stepped over the split rail fence and went off to God knows where, and, as always, Robert woke up with his heart pounding and his bed soaked with sweat. As usual, he woke before he could find out whether he followed the old man or not. He just remembered himself standing like a statue, staring down at the rail fence.

In the shadows before dawn, Robert lay in his bed and tried to sort things out. He marveled that all the details of his silly nightmare were still waiting for him in his head, like the familiar books from his childhood. It was like some question that never got answered. A question that might never be answered. Robert glanced across the blanket at his sleeping wife, who was quite unaware of his troubles. He thought about waking her, but reasoned that a man has to wrestle with certain nightmares by himself. It should suffice that at least someone in his bed was enjoying peace.

The next morning, Robert arrived at the wharf too early even for mess hall or coffee. Tired and nervous from a sleepless night, he distracted himself with trivial duties – refilling lanterns, tightening ropes, and such. He couldn't keep his mind from drifting back to thoughts of tomorrow night's escape.

To sail the *Planter* to freedom would be a sweet victory and would constitute a painful blow to the Confederate cause. The Rebs would curse the loss of their flagship and its valuable cargo, but the thought that it had been stolen by a pack of slaves would twist the dagger in their heart. Robert only wished he could be there to see their shocked faces.

By now, the sun was peeking over the corner of Sullivan's Island, and Robert watched as Spider made his way from General Ripley's house. Robert was always glad to see his friend and the hot cups of coffee he brought each morning.

"Morning, brother," Robert said. "I was hoping you were on your way."

"Waitin' for my handsome smile, I suppose," Spider said.

"I was thinking about the *coffee*," Robert smiled. "But I'm fond of you, too.

As Spider sat down with him on the dew-soaked planks of the wharf, the first rays of sunlight illuminated the steam rising from their cups. One by one, the other crew members began to arrive, pitching into their morning chores. Spider knew something was up when his friend reached down and pretended to inspect the rope that secured the ship to its moorings. It was the kind of thing Robert did when he was nervous.

"I know you're sittin' on something," Spider whispered. "Spill it."

"It'll take a minute," Robert said.

"The old man's sleepin' off whatever happened last night," Spider said. "I've likely got all day."

Robert shook his head, and with the twitch of one finger, he pointed out to the far side of the harbor. "Try not to get spooked," he said, "but it looks like tomorrow night's the night, brother. We're going."

"Going?" Spider said. "Really going? Like *going*, going?" He scoffed out a doubtful breath as they both became so quiet they could hear the waves kissing the posts of the pier.

As two young patrolmen walked past, Robert and Spider quickly shut their mouths and lowered their eyes. The pimple-faced guards looked to be no older than boys, donning baggy gray uniforms that had been sewn for larger men. But they did have pistols, badges, and worse than that, ears.

Robert and Spider kept sipping their coffee and did their best to look busy as they pointed out into the harbor at nothing at all. After the guards were beyond earshot, Robert looked up with a cool look in his eyes. Grasping Spider's arm firmly, he drew his face close enough to smell the coffee.

"I'm serious as a snake, brother," he whispered. "We go tomorrow night."

With each second that passed, Spider was losing more of his smile. He pulled back and vigorously shook his head. "Tomorrow?" he said. "A Monday?" He didn't even make eye contact with Robert now, swinging both his legs out to dangle them over the edge of the dock. "You're out of your mind. We're out of our minds," he whispered. "Stark plum crazy."

"Captain and Pitcher are planning to head into town tomorrow, and I've got a plan that'll get Sam Smith to go as well. The thing's *on*," Robert said. "I done told Hannah, and everybody."

Now Spider was the jittery one. He began to nervously rub his dark hands together. "So we're going on a work day," he said. "Very same day the grays are fixing to take them guns out to Fort Ripley."

"So you heard about that too," Robert said. "We're gonna steal them cannons when we go."

"You're dreaming," he said. "You best pick some other tomorrow to be your big tomorrow."

Robert just kept tying and untying the ropes while he stared at the distant speck that was Fort Sumter. "No joking, Spider, not anymore," he said. "We'll stoke her up by three and be gone by four. Tomorrow night we're crossing Jordan."

"Preacher talk. Foolishness," Spider said in an unexpectedly belligerent tone. "You say tomorrow, but you been saying that same thing just about every day for two months straight. We ain't no closer to freedom than we were yesterday."

Robert slapped his fist into his hand. "Look at me," he said. "Ain't no turning back now. Waiting time's up." Robert was now speaking into his own clenched fist, squeezed so tight Spider could see the veins in Robert's forearms. "We're close now, brother. Close to freedom."

"And death," Spider said. "Close to death."

"Yes," Robert said. "But by this time Tuesday morning, it's sure to be one or the other. Every night I've been dreaming about it. In some dreams, I die at the end, but in some I live. I've done already tasted death a dozen times. If I die tomorrow, it won't be my first time."

"But," Spider said. "Those were dreams. This death's gonna be real. This one's gonna be your last. You ready for that?"

Robert just nodded. "We done waited, but we can't wait forever," he said. "Tomorrow's as good a time as any."

Spider couldn't look Robert in the eyes any more. He turned and glanced back over his shoulder at the buildings and church spires of Charleston. "You've got to understand," he said. "That town there, that's my home. You've got your ship, your wife, and a mama back home in Beaufort. But this city, she's my ship, my wife, and my mama, too. I know every step of her streets. I can play her like an easy mark in a card game, and all my life I've been able to get most any pleasure I want from her. I know her ropes, her good side and the evil one too. Charleston's my home."

"Your prison, you mean," Robert said. "She may seem like some easy mark, but at some point you've gotta ask yourself, 'Who's playing who?'"

"I can't help it. This is what I was born to," Spider said. "Ain't no sin to be a slave and ain't no sin to stay alive." Spider now smiled a broad grin like he always did when he was uncomfortable. Robert wasn't about to take any more of this. He rose and pulled both of them to their feet.

Picking Spider up by the collar, Robert jacked him up against the timbers of the wharf gate. "Wake up," he said out loud, not even caring if anyone could hear him. "Bein' born slaves was our misfortune, but may God damn us if we let it be our destiny." As Robert pushed him away, Spider just smiled, calmly picking up the empty coffee cups as if to leave. But Robert could see that Spider's hands were quivering.

Robert pointed at the buildings that lined the waterfront. "That ain't home, Spider, that's *hell.*" With his left hand, he slapped the cups from Spider's fingers so hard that they flew out across the boards of the pier. With his right fist, Robert hit him with a clean blow across the face. On wobbling legs, Spider was still smiling that pitiful, frightened grin as he wiped the blood from his lips.

"For just once in your life, stop grinning like a jackass," Robert said. "Your jokes may buy you a few laughs, but one day you'll look over to the world of free men and you'll wish to God you'd gotten on this boat."

"That's enough," Spider said, straightening his clothes and continuing to wipe the blood from his split lip. For the first time in their friendship, he turned his back on Robert and walked away, all without a single snide word. Robert just stood where he was, making no effort to go after him. Though he didn't regret a word of what he said, Robert felt like crying. He might have just lost his best friend.

Robert resumed his duties, but was mostly just going through the motions. By the time the crew sat down to have breakfast, he wasn't hungry and he didn't feel like talking. He just kept remembering every detail of his encounter with Spider. 'I shouldn't have hit him,' Robert thought to himself.

Neither Relyea nor the lieutenants ever arrived to give the crew any work assignments. Normally, this would have been good news, but the hours of idleness left Robert too much time for regret. He told the boys about his tiff with Spider, but they all agreed with Deke that Spider would cool off and come to his senses.

By three bells, Robert had been sitting so long it was only intense sadness that kept him from falling asleep. It was then that Deke finally broke the silence. "I told you not to fret," he said. "Look yonder. It appears your Prodigal boy has returned."

Robert looked up just in time to see Spider making his way from the far entrance of the pier. At first, Robert's heart leaped with joy, but his friend's face still had the stern look he'd worn during their altercation. Though he wasn't yet sure what Spider was thinking, he felt a small measure of relief when, instead of going into General Ripley's house, Spider turned and came towards them. Robert's heart had burned to make things right, and it soared when Spider finally broke into his familiar pearly grin.

"It wouldn't do for me to miss my own funeral," he said. "If you can play the part of a dead helmsman, I suppose I can play along as a dead sailor." Spider then gave Robert his best comic version of a navy salute. "Count me in... *sir!*"

Robert just shook his head and smiled. "I was afraid I might be forced to kidnap you at gunpoint," he said.

"I'm glad you didn't try it," Spider said. "Kidnapping's a serious crime, almost as wicked as stealing a gunboat." They both chuckled as they hugged each other's neck.

"I shoulda left you, you know," Robert said as his eyes flashed both ways down the wharf. "Shush," he said as he motioned for Spider to follow him down below decks. "I want to show you something."

Robert led Spider down into a supply room off the main hall, to a small room where they usually kept the buckets and mops. From a dimly lit closet, he pulled out a large wardrobe trunk that he opened with a key from his back pocket. Robert pulled back a layer of old burlap rice sacks to reveal a full store of food and water. "See this?" Robert whispered. "These here will be enough for all of us, even if we have to sail ourselves all the way down to Hilton Head. He pointed a big finger right in Spider's face. "We're going through with this."

"Holy pissin' saints," muttered Spider, staring down at the stowed items. "Looks like you're really gonna do it."

"No, *we're* gonna do it," said Robert, confirming his promise with a single word, breathed out like some holy benediction at the end of a prayer, "Tomorrow."

The two friends just stared at each other in silence. For the first time Robert could remember, neither one of them could think of a word to say. Finally, Robert was the first to speak. "You're in this now," he whispered.

"In," Spider said. "It's such a little word."

"Yes, but it can change a man's life," replied Robert.

"Or end it," whispered Spider.

At that point, they just stared into one another's eyes and giggled the way young boys do when they're taking some scary risk. If either of them were not yet properly afraid, the next moments would ensure that they were.

From above them, they heard a man shouting something, immediately followed by heavy footsteps on the deck. There wasn't time to put the things back in their hiding place. The black boots that stepped quickly down the steps were familiar. It was Zerich Pitcher. Before Robert could move, there stood the lieutenant, gazing down at them with those malevolent eyes of his. The boys stood up quickly and tried to look at Pitcher calmly, but their hands were shaking. Robert stood at attention, saluted, and blurted out the only thing he could think to say. "Sir!"

"Don't 'Sir' me, you black idiot," Pitcher barked. "What is all this?"

"I can explain," answered Robert, trying to buy a few seconds so he could come up with some plausible explanation for this trunk of foodstuffs. He reasoned that pigs had drowned in shallower slop than he and Spider were caught in.

"I see your hands shaking," Pitcher shouted. "You're up to something. You'll give me the truth and you'd better do it fast."

"It's for…" Robert began, but he had never been a skilled liar. Spider Jefferson however, was more gifted in that regard.

"You weren't supposed to see this, Lieutenant," Spider said. "The Cap done warned us."

"Warned you of what?" he asked. "Spit it out."

"The big surprise," Spider said. "The big supper we're fixing to cook up. It's a celebration for you 'cause Cap's gonna raise you up a rank next week. No more Junior Grade Lieutenant for you, Cap told everyone on the wharf you're getting a new stripe. I heard him telling old Ripley about it just this morning."

Then Robert, mustering up his best worried look, pitched in. "Cap's gonna kill us if he finds out we told," he said. "You ain't gonna tell him, are you sir? You can't let on to nobody."

For what felt like a full minute, Robert silently prayed to heaven, waiting for the axe to fall. "Dear God, please make this man as stupid as he is mean." For once, even Spider prayed. It was then that Pitcher's ever-stern face softened into a faint smile.

"Up a rank, you say," he said to himself, straightening his uniform. "Promoted. I won't say a word to the Captain or nobody. We'll just leave it as a secret." Pitcher proudly touched the place on his sleeve where the new stripe would soon be sewn. "You boys had best hide all this food where it was. Don't want to spoil the surprise."

Having completely swallowed their lie, Pitcher wore a big smile for the first time the boys could remember. He saluted them and quickly vanished back up the stairs. Spider and Robert did their best not to choke on their laughter. Neither of them was able to take a full breath until they heard the last sounds of the Lieutenant's boots leaving the boat.

"Tomorrow's the day," Robert said, "if God is with us."

"And it looks like he is," said Spider to Robert's amazement. Realizing that he had momentarily veered from the paths of unbelief, Spider locked eyes with Robert as he mounted the stairs to go above. "Praise be." he said with mock piety, "Hallelujah."

"Like I promised," Robert said as they reached the foredeck, "All the pieces are coming together." He spread his ten fingers out and then meshed them together like pieces of a puzzle fitting together. "Click… click… click," he said.

Spider didn't nod however, but only stared stone-faced towards the entrance to the harbor. "There may be a few too many pieces that still have to click," he said. "Every wildcard's got to fall just right. Too many, I think." Both men became quiet for a minute after that, so quiet they could hear the chirping of the birds in the trees on the shore.

"We've always known we'd be taking a chance," Robert finally said. "I doubt Providence will ever grant us a chance as good as this one. If we delay, we might surely be waiting forever."

Spider was not as confident. "No, brother," said Spider, in a voice more serious than Robert had ever heard him use, "We ain't nearly ready to pull this thing off. I was there when you first posed this thing. I assumed we might take a few risks here and there. But not tomorrow. Not a Monday. We should wait for something closer to a sure thing."

"You want a sure thing?" Robert said. "Being a slave forever, that's the sure thing."

"But," Spider said, "There'll surely be better opportunities coming along."

"We've already *been* waiting. I've been waiting, my Mama's been waiting, a million of us have gone to our graves waiting. But not me, not no more. The boys will be at the boat by two tomorrow night and they'll have the boilers fired up by three. Hannah, Annie, and the others will slip away and be waiting for us with William on the *Etowah*. The bones have done been rolled, brother."

"Then we're dead men," Spider muttered, his emotions having finally raced past all logical arguments. "Oh my sweet, blessed Lord! We're stone cold dead men."

"Don't waver on me," Robert said, not asking this time but ordering. "You have to come."

"I don't *have* to do nothing," he answered. "I ain't your crew and you ain't my master."

"All right then," Robert said, "No more orders. But I'm not leaving without my best friend, and we could surely use your help." Then, Robert looking once more into his friend's eyes. "Come," he said.

"I'll need a chance to do some walkin' and think," Spider said, "but I expect you oughta save me a place on the boat,"

"No," Robert said, "I know you. If you walk off now, you'll talk yourself out of it."

Spider turned his face away, then suddenly looked back and locked eyes with Robert, his pupils wide with anger. "Now look here, moonlight," he said, "Don't be pushin' me now. It's my neck ... and my call."

"Fine," Robert said, "You decide. But decide or not, the whites will most likely string you up when they find out you've been in on this thing. Pitcher saw what he saw, and the Rebs will have no trouble adding up two and two. You don't have a choice here. You come or you die."

Spider's reply came, in a faint whisper now, "Sounds a bit like slavery," he said. "I suppose I've got no druthers."

"I'll pray God will give all of us good courage," concluded Robert, "We'll surely need it in abundance."

"I doubt any amount of prayer will put courage into my heart," Spider said.

"Well, if you won't have faith in God above, maybe I can find you somethin' else," Robert said. In a flash he scurried up to the bridge and came back down with something in his hand. "Here," Robert said. "I brought you something maybe even you can believe in." It was the little American flag he had brought with him from Beaufort. "Just don't wave it at any Rebs 'till we get past the forts," he laughed.

Spider managed a smile, but still looked afraid. "You know you're my only real friend," he whispered. "The only one I'd die with, the only one I'd die *for.*"

He and Robert walked together up the pier with sober hearts and closed mouths, tenuously carrying tomorrow night's dreams like pockets full of stolen coins. As the courthouse clock bell announced sundown throughout the city, Robert was reminded that time was short, but his mind was not concerned with slave curfew. Under that familiar old gray hat of his, he was cyphering the number of hours until they launched.

Chapter 39
The Day of Deliverance

The next morning, each of the crewmembers pursued his normal routine, as if it had been a day like any other. Faces were washed, eggs were cooked up and eaten, and work clothes donned. Throughout the unfolding hours of the day, each of them was amazed that their duties were dispatched in such an ordinary and uneventful fashion. The only thing noteworthy was the slowness with which the hours passed.

"I feel like Joshua," Deke said to the boys. "The Lord has surely stopped the sun in the sky."

"I feel it, too," said Robert, "But we should be happy for such an unremarkable day."

"I've never felt such an itch to toss a log into the boilers," said Dark John. "All this waitin' is about to kill me for sure."

Robert put a finger to his lips as Captain Relyea walked past them. "Hush it, John," he whispered. "We can joke of death after we get past the forts."

Monday was ordinarily a quiet day along the wharf, but today things were bustling with the anticipated arrival of the big guns. All through that morning, Robert imagined he could hear the distant ticking of the big clock at the courthouse downtown. Once Captain Relyea arrived at seven, the pace of the ticking seemed only to speed up.

"Holy wrath of God!" the old man said as he stormed up the gangplank. "I do believe old Rip's trying to capsize us. This vessel was built for cotton," he complained. "If we get one more cannon on the starboard side, it'll likely flip us."

Robert just smiled as he saw the freight wagons arriving with the big artillery pieces. These cannon, a Dahlgren smoothbore, three Parrot rifles, and a 12-pound howitzer were damaged equipment which had been taken when the Yankees surrendered Fort Sumter. These had been refurbished and were now ready for deployment to the Fort Ripley Battery at the center of the harbor.

As usual, Robert paid close attention to the work of lifting and loading the cannon barrels, each of which weighed a ton or more. It was also important to make sure they were properly positioned and secured, but today he was mostly concerned with the order of things. If the ship left too soon, conspirators might have to be left behind. If they were late in casting off, the whole group would likely be caught red-handed, and with hell to pay.

As the cannons, projectiles, and powder were delivered to the dock area, stevedores jumped on their work like starving men at supper. Everybody wanted to get this done quickly. Tempers flared and sweat flew as muscles were flexed to their breaking point. One Irishman even got his hand crushed during the hasty loading.

Chisholm, Fish, and the others worked even faster than the whites. Their very lives depended on getting the ship loaded and their officers cleared out by nightfall, but from the beginning there were problems. As always, there was a delay in setting up the cranes. A broken block and tackle put them further behind. Robert, however, counted it a blessing. Today, it was probably good if things took longer than usual. They would need some excuse for the *Planter's* crewmen to stay late.

Rules said there always had to be white men present to supervise and control Negroes, but it became routine to let the crew-slaves finish up so the white officers could head into town for the evening. Though this arrangement was unofficial, everyone knew the drill.

One by one, each white officer would leave, telling the blacks that one of the other officers was in charge. Later on, the other officer would himself depart, saying that some other one was in charge. Eventually all the whites would be gone, and the crew would be left to their own devices, and everyone on both ends of the deal would be happy. It would be conveniently difficult to figure out who was to blame.

Robert's plan was predicated on the assumption that his men would be left to themselves on this particular Monday night, and things seemed to be happening according to plan. By the time evening approached, the loading was mostly done and the cargo secured. Relyea would be inclined to let the boys sleep on board tonight because he had to get an early start the next morning. With their hold full of guns and ammunition, the Captain would need his crew to be well rested for a full day's work. It normally would have been good news that their duties had been finished by five, but it made Robert a bit uneasy. It had to look like there was still some work left to do.

According to their plan, everyone but Robert, Deke, and Dark John had to clear out at sundown. The curfew bell would signal the time. Cap and his lieutenants would likely be nervous if too many of them stayed around without white supervision, and things needed to seem peaceful enough for the officers to head into town.

Robert made sure there were still a few logs to be moved and stray ropes to tie. Like actors in a play, time and timing was everything. And this was serious drama. As the sun sank snail-like down the western sky, Robert watched it as if it had been the hour hand of a clock. He thought the Captain would never leave.

The crew lingered aimlessly on deck as the sun inched closer to the horizon. "What are you smiling about?" Fish asked Robert, who was just now coming down the spiral steps from the bridge.

"I'm laughing at all of you," he said. "You're standing around like cooks waiting for a pot to boil. We've got another nine hours to go."

After what seemed like an eternity, the big clock downtown finally signaled sundown. "What now?" Chiz whispered. "Cap and his boys are takin' their sweet time about leaving."

"No need for you to linger till they're gone," said Robert. "You've gotta leave before the patrols hit the streets at seven."

"I'd feel better if the officers had already cleared out," Chiz said. "You think they're on to us?"

"Naw," Robert said, "You're thinking too much. They'll clear out, you just do your part." Everyone was acting strangely and it was wearing Robert out. He reasoned that the hardest thing for men to do was to act naturally.

As Chiz, Allston, Fish, and the others left for the day, Robert was watching their every move. Their steps seemed obtrusive and awkward as they made their way down the long pier. 'What a painful comedy,' he thought. He didn't relax until the boys finally stepped off the dock and onto shore. Robert didn't think he could take nine more hours of this.

"So will there be anything else?" he kept asking the Captain, hoping to somehow pester the old man on his way. As Robert watched the birds flying off toward the west, they seemed to move as slow as a painting. "My God, they're so slow I could count them," he said.

"I suspect I could count their feathers," Deke laughed. "But everything happens in God's good time." Deke put his big hand on the back of Robert's neck and tried to soothe the tension there. "Just be still," he said in his big deep preacher voice. "Everything will be all right."

Sure enough, sometime after six thirty, Relyea said his goodbyes and headed into town for supper. Robert had heard that Cap and General

Ripley were meeting for drinks later on. "I'll leave you boys to mop up," the old man said. "We'll fire her up at four bells of the morning watch, and depart by six."

"Aye sir," said Lieutenant Sam. "We'll have her stoked and ready."

"The boys will be early," promised Robert, with only a bit of a smile on his face. Early indeed. Out of the corner of his eye, Robert could see Zerich Pitcher standing at the stern rail. The Lieutenant had been secretly watching for the captain to get out of sight so he too could leave for the day. As Captain Relyea stepped onto the cobblestones of South Bay Street, Pitched clapped his hand together as if he had just rolled a seven in a crap game.

"Finally," he said. "I thought he'd never leave. I want to get an early start on my drinking tonight." None of them said anything in response to Zerich's words, but everyone felt relief that Pitcher was leaving. It was always one of the high points of their day. Once Pitcher was out of earshot, Sam Smith was free to speak his mind.

"That fool is cross-eyed by seven every night," he said. "I'm not sure what an early start on drinking would look like." They all chuckled.

"Well, he didn't leave us with a lot of work in any case," Robert said. "I'd be happy to stay closed-mouthed if you chose to leave, too."

"I kind of figured I would," Sam said. "I'm meeting a sweet thing tonight at nine."

Robert pretended to act surprised that the lieutenant was meeting a girl, but on this night he knew exactly which girl Sam was talking about. "You must promise me that it'll be just *one* girl," Robert joked. "This ain't some professional woman, is she?"

"To be honest, I'm not sure," Sam said. "She's been following me around for a week now." The lieutenant made one more slow tour of the deck before he stepped down the gangplank.

"Behave like a good Christian," Robert said as Sam was walking away. "Me and the boy's will take care of things here."

"All right," Sam said. "I'll try to at least act like a back pew Christian." He and Robert both just smiled. It occurred to Robert that these were likely the last words he and Sam would speak to one another. 'Good luck, my friend,' he said in his heart.

As Robert turned back to the boat, everything suddenly looked different. Deke and Dark John joined him on the bow, and they locked arms as they surveyed the long expanse of the *CSS Planter*. The whites were gone, and the empty length of the ship stretched out before them.

Fully loaded, yet unsupervised, the boat belonged to them now. From now on, the dark-skinned men who sweated on these decks were no longer an anonymous cadre of slaves. They were fellow-sailors and comrades, conspirators in blood. Each one had a face, a story, and a heart full of dreams. Robert loved these men and would happily give his life for any one of them, and he had no doubt they would do the same for him.

With just the three of them on board now, the waiting got worse. When the clock bell rang out seven times, the last slave curfew bell they would ever hear, Robert rejoiced that they were an hour closer to casting off. But he had to wonder if the rest of the boys had made it off the streets in time. Tonight, a night in the calaboose would mean a lifetime of slavery.

All the preparations were done now, and darkness had begun to creep across the clouds. If Robert felt any relief that evening had come, it was diminished when he realized he could no longer see the sun move. All day he had followed its slow journey across the sky as if it had been the hand of God's big pocket watch. The night that was falling upon them now promised to bring with it the biggest test of their lives.

The first part of the evening passed like an eternity, and the waiting was pure torture. Robert, Deke, and Dark John agreed not to talk about any of their fears or worries, so they just stood together, in silence for the most part. From the bridge, they could see the lights blinking on in the pubs and brothels along the waterfront as the hushed cadence of the waves lapped the sides of the *Planter*.

"Tick, tick, tick!" John said. "Just like the slow drip of rain through a roof leak. It's enough to drive a man insane."

"Just standing around quiet don't help none," Deke said. "It's like a bland sermon with no Amens. It just seems to go on and on."

"It best that we move around a bit," said Robert. "Maybe you boys could go below and rearrange the logs or something. We're supposed to be working, you know."

By the time Deke and Dark John left the bridge, the whole waterfront was dark. From the distant end of the Battery, Robert watched as, one by one, the street lamps were lit. No doubt some greenhorn was moonlighting for some extra coins tonight. He remembered back to his early days in Charleston. Robert lit a small lantern and mounted the bridge, taking the smooth spokes of the ship's wheel into his hands. The rhythm of the waves against the hull marked the passing of each tedious second between them and liberation. He became aware that that both his palms were sweating as they gripped the helm.

He even tried to pray a little, but his thoughts kept twisting and clawing in his skull like a hundred pent-up stallions. The plans had been drawn up, the assignments made. Standing alone in this darkness, he sensed that control had now passed out of his hands now and into the Lord's. But it wasn't the Lord he was worried about. It was those eighteen uneducated and temperamental slaves. "Guide, guard, and direct us all," he prayed.

Though his faith told him to turn it over to God, he could feel his human hands tightening their grip on the wheel. His soul may have been reaching towards heaven, but his eyes kept scanning the farthest corners of Charleston Harbor... for shoals, for ships, and for floating mines. His heart kept returning to the feeling that all the chaos of hell was about to break loose.

The tension of the moment was broken by the deep voice of Deacon Gradine from below. "Hey, Robert," he shouted, "Looks like Jackson left us some grub down in the mess." Robert wasn't hungry in the least, but was gladdened to hear this news. It would be good to just relax and eat something.

With most of the crewmembers gone, the mess table seemed too large. Robert, Deke, and Dark John spoke of their future as they enjoyed some boiled peas and cornbread.

Tonight the die would be cast and the arrival of this night unleashed every pent-up thought and dream. It was hard for any of them to believe that this night had finally come. No longer simple boys, they all felt like men, like officers, even heroes. But they also felt afraid.

"This is more than just a bunch of slaves running off," said Dark John. "It's an ugly slap to the master's face, and a hard slap at that."

As one would expect, Deke saw it through more spiritual eyes. "It's the Exodus, it is, the Glorious Year of Jubilee.

Robert said it was their standing-up day, their Declaration of Independence. Equally moved, William said he'd be quite happy to lay his life down for the others this very night.

'You may very well get your wish, young brother," spoke Dark John, rarely one for words. "We got us a bunch of pretty plans, but a whole lot of things gotta happen just right."

"God'll be with us every place we set our foot," Deke said. "We're on our way to Canaan's Land."

"And crossing Jordan in a stolen boat," Robert laughed. "We still got work to do, but remember, tonight we're working for ourselves." They all clasped hands with the others, and Deke prayed for God's blessing on their success.

After cleaning up, they all made their way back to the deck. Their chatter on the stairs was put to silence by the huge full moon that was just now rising over Sullivan's Island. "Just look at that thing," said Deke. "Ain't that something." For a quiet moment, arms around each other, they watched it climb up into the low clouds of the dark horizon. Each man in his own way was touched by the beauty of God's big world and of their brotherhood. Each one also reflected on the avalanche of events that were about to be set into motion.

"Whatever happens," Robert said. "I'm proud to be alongside you men." He surveyed the smooth expanse of glassy water which would soon be broken to froth by the *Planter* as it sped toward the Union fleet. Robert could almost hear the alarms, shouts, and pistol shots that would soon ring across the now quiet harbor. In a few more hours, his fate, and that of his family and friends hung in the balance, tottering atop a mountain of unanswered questions.

Would all the boys arrive so they could embark on schedule? Would the women and children manage to get to the right place at the right time? One careless word, one unexpected sentry, one misread hand of a clock – any small misstep might bring death to them all. Would any of the officers return to the boat early for some reason? Would their off-schedule firing of the ship's boiler arouse suspicion? A cyclone of questions spun around in his head, with each thought and each doubt coming faster than the last, returning again and again.

His misgivings mostly had to do with human frailty. Who could predict the behavior of fallen man? All it would take would be for just one of them to make a single mistake, just one. He, Deke, and Dark John were already in place on the boat and seemed to have things under control. Ample food and provisions were stowed in case their escape run became a longer voyage. There was enough wood to fuel the boilers for a trip of many days. Robert was altogether confident in his ability to navigate through the harbor, down the coast, or out to sea. But, as always, the people were the wild cards.

The women and children were a matter for special concern. Robert had seen Hannah and Suzanne give sway to their emotions at times, and the two were wont to bicker with one another over the smallest of things.

For their part, Annie and Lavina were usually compliant, but they were dull of mind and might forget the time and place where they were to meet the others. Worst of all, the younger children would be hard pressed to keep silence as they traversed the back alleys of the city on their way to the Atlantic Wharf. How could they not arouse suspicion if anyone took notice of them on the streets at such an hour? He doubted that this motley entourage would move with any measure of speed. Was it not madness to suppose that the odds of success were in their favor?

And what of Spider? With his impetuous spirit and loose tongue, he had gallivanted off to God-knows-where. By now he might be in some pub in town, half-drunk and running his mouth. Or maybe even turning them in. No one could say whether Spider would make a timely appearance or any appearance at all.

Among the hundred other details that had to fall into place, there would surely be one that they missed. There would no doubt be some unpleasant surprises. Spider had probably been right when he said they had needed more time.

Just then, Deke's voice was heard from the deck below. "Hoy, Robert," he said in a guarded shout. "We've been stacking this same stack of wood over and over. What's next?"

"I believe all's in place," Robert replied, feigning the cool head of a commander. "You boys just sit tight until it's time. We've got a few hours until our steam needs to be up. We'll cast off at three thirty."

Noticing the trembling of Robert's hands, Deke's eyes showed a trace of fear. "You all right, brother?" he asked in a whisper.

"No. I don't know of any problems at all," Robert said confidently. "But there are just so many things to get right. Everything's here in my head, but my thoughts are a hailstorm right now. I think I might go mad."

"It'll be all right," offered Deke. "The Lord will help us."

"Will the boilers be ready?" asked Robert.

"The steam should be up with no trouble, and we've got all the wood we need," he answered. "The boys should start showing up around two, but they'll likely be cutting it close like always." Robert was not encouraged by these words.

"I suspect this will all go smoother than we dreamed," Robert lied to himself, "I suppose I worry too much. By this time tomorrow, we'll all be free."

"It'll be quite a relief," said Deke, "when we finally get past the big guns at Sumter."

"Amen," replied Robert, folding his hands together.

Deke broke into a big grin as he gazed straight into Robert's eyes. "I can't believe this is finally comin' to pass. Won't the masters be surprised when we're free and clear!"

'And I'll be surprised too,' Robert thought to himself. It would be nothing short of a miracle.

"We should toot the whistle and ring the bells once we're out to sea," said Deke.

"Why don't we wait till we're clear before we make too much commotion?" Robert cautioned. "Those Columbiads on Sumter can hit an outhouse at two miles." At these words, the corners of Robert's face took on a more serious and thoughtful look. Deke had mentioned the sounding of the whistle and bell.

"We'll need the proper signals," Robert said, almost as if to remind himself. As he reached down for the knob of the door of the Captain's drawer safe, he pulled but it wouldn't budge. "Holy saints!" Robert said, "This thing's *never* locked," He did his best to rattle the knob. "What a fix!" he said. The logbook was locked inside and only the officers had keys.

"Pull harder," urged Deke. "Maybe it's just stuck."

Robert yanked and tugged and even began to thump the iron knob with the heel of his boot, but it wouldn't budge. "I should've known something like this would happen. It's locked up tight. We'll need that key to get the logbook."

"Cap's got one," said Deke as he noticed that Robert's hands were shaking again. "Maybe you can go get it."

"It wouldn't do," he said. "Cap'll know we're up to no good. I'll have to go into town and find Pitcher or Sam. Maybe I can finagle the key from one of them." Just then the old town clock rang out 10 times.

"May God be with you," said a stone-faced Deke. "I'd look for Sam first. Pitcher's as bad drunk as he is sober."

"Pray for me, boys," Robert said as he sped away. "All ain't lost, but we'll need those codes."

Chapter 40
The Keys to the Kingdom

On his way into the city, Robert wanted to run, but such would only arouse suspicion. In a place like Charleston, a hasty Negro was cause for alarm. Despite his urgency, he would have to proceed with a natural pace, unworthy of note. Behind him, he could feel the full moon looking down at him like some silent critic as it climbed up the eastern sky. It appeared they were all going to die and it was Robert's fault.

"O God, help me," he kept whispering as he made his way up Water Street. Pitcher would likely be with some harlot by now, and Robert didn't fancy walking in on that. Sam Smith was probably in one of the livelier taverns. "Lord guide my steps to the drunk man," he prayed. It felt strange to be soliciting divine help to find a house of sin.

He only glanced briefly into the first few pubs he passed. One had a big clock over the front doors and Robert made the mistake of checking the time. Past 10:30 already. He needed to make haste. He suspected Sam would be in a place called The Fat Porgy, a two-story tavern on the east end of the sin district. This was a place the lieutenant often spoke of, and even though it was a Monday night, it was pretty crowded by the time Robert arrived. He knew better than to step through the doors. Colored men were required to stand outside if they sought someone at the bar.

"I'm looking for Lieutenant Sam Smith," Robert said to a young man at the door. "It's an urgent Navy matter, sir."

"I don't know your man," said the greeter. "Do you see him anywhere?"

The place was dark, and looking around, Robert didn't see Sam. "He sometimes talks about something called the big porch," Robert said.

"Yes, that's upstairs," said the man, pointing to some dimly-lit stairs behind him. "I've got to stay down here, but you're welcome take a gander if you like. Just make it quick."

Robert tried to walk unobtrusively through the white crowd. The place smelled of bourbon, tobacco, and old perfume. At the top of the stairs he found the porch Sam had spoken of. It was the rooftop, and dozens of men and women were standing and drinking along the second floor railing. Most were laughing at other drunks who stumbled around on the streets below.

At the far corner of the big porch he saw Sam, who was embracing a young lady who held a drink in each hand. At the table nearest him, Robert noticed a gray jacket with lieutenant's bars that was hung over a chair. Robert marveled at his luck. As he fumbled through the pockets of Sam's coat, he kept praying the key was in here somewhere, there was nothing. Sam probably had it in his pants pocket.

"Wonderful," Robert whispered to himself. This was frustrating, but things were about to get more awkward. Lieutenant Sam Smith had left his girl at the porch rail and was presently walking toward the table.

"What the hell?" said Sam. "You're supposed to be on the ship." Sam had the smell of sweat and rye whiskey about him.

"Sorry, sir," said Robert, making sure to cast his eyes down. "I hated to interrupt. The ship's fine, but Cap came by to get your key to the safe. He's misplaced his at the moment and he wants me to bring him his charts."

Sam just glared at Robert for a moment. "Dang, Robert," he said. "You're the master of bad timing. I'll have to come with you now, as I'm sworn not to let that key out of my sight."

"Now just one second, Sam Smith," said a woman's voice from across the room. "I ain't about to let you run off with anyone right now." Robert knew that voice well.

Here came Liddie McKee, waltzing across the porch in the fanciest, lowest-cut dress he had ever seen. Robert had arranged for this, but when he laid eyes on her in that dress, it was all he could do to restrain himself from laughter. She took hold of Sam's arm and nuzzled her face against his shoulder.

"You're not gonna leave me unchaperoned, are you?" she cooed in a voice Robert had never heard a Christian girl use before.

Sam glanced deeply into the bright blue eyes of the red haired damsel on his arm. "Oh, God," he said, reaching deep into the front pocket of his breeches. "Forget the rules. Take the key," adding, "I'm gonna want it back tonight."

"But I thought we were dancing tonight," sang Liddie, stroking Sam's arm. "I was planning to keep you occupied." Robert was both delighted and aghast. Little Bible girl seemed to have turned into

Potiphar's wife.

The lieutenant glanced down at the sultry peach next to him and said, "I suppose you can give me the key in the morning."

Taking the still-warm key into his palm, Robert offered his most humble nod, saying, "Thank you, sir. I'll be careful with it." Sam turned to flag down a barmaid who was proffering a fresh tray of drinks.

"Yes," said Liddie, "Do be careful." As her azure eyes met Robert's, she winked and whispered words only he would understand. "Blood oath."

"Blood oath," he whispered back as he turned to go. "I hope to see you again." At these words, their eyes locked on each other's and saddened a bit as Robert slowly made his way toward the staircase.

Walking back to the boat, Robert could no longer sense the intense pounding of his heart and he began to breathe normally again. Even the clock on the courthouse was quiet now as his fears subsided and the spark of his faith grew brighter. The plan was back on track. He slowed his steps now, feeling that the Jordan had just been crossed and that the key to the Pearly Gates was warm and safe in his right pocket. His heart was filled with but a single thought, 'God is good.'

Approaching the wharf, Robert was encouraged to see that the dock area was completely dark and quiet. With no frantic guards and no alarms. The crew had kept their lamps below decks as he had instructed, and he could now hear the faint sound of their conversation, but there was no one within earshot who might pay any attention. Far behind him, the big clock struck one. In a little more than two hours, they would be underway.

"Evening, boys," said Robert as he mounted the *Planter's* foredeck. "It's a relaxing night, isn't it?" The men said nothing, but just stared at Robert in nervous anticipation, hoping he was joking. After a long and deliberate silence, like some amateur magician, he reached down into his pocket and produced the small brown key. The all stared at it as if it had been made of solid gold.

"Praise God Almighty!" exclaimed Deke, immediately covering his mouth so as not to be heard. "Let's get them codes."

Robert stepped quickly up the stairs to the wheelhouse, with Deke and Dark John following closely behind. Kneeling before the safe, he twisted the key and peered inside. From the dark confines of the iron box he took papers, maps, and even a small envelope of currency, but nothing else. Deke pushed his lantern up closer to the safe, but here was no log book to be seen. They stared at one another like boys lost in a deep woods.

"What now?" Deke asked.

"We die now, that's what," Dark John said. "Without them codes, we're all dead men."

"No, said Deke. "We can't give up. That book's got to be somewhere."

"Oh, I think we know where," said Chiz. "Only one place it *can* be. Cap's got it."

"Holy saints," Robert said. "The old boy's surely in his bed by now, stone drunk likely. If we wake him, it's over."

"Well," said Deke, "It's over for sure if we don't try. We can't get out of this harbor without those codes. We'll have to go get that book somehow, even if we have to kill the old man."

"No," said Robert. "Just one of us. I'll sneak in and get it."

"Amen," said Deke. "Steal it to the glory of God."

"You boys sit tight," Robert said, "and hang on to Spider when he shows up so he doesn't come looking for me."

To make it to Relyea's house and back before three, Robert would have to move quickly. Running though Charleston at this time of night might rouse every whistle-blowing constable in town, but there was no other choice now. Robert needed to run, so he ran with all his might. Desperate times called for desperate measures.

Chapter 41
To the *Etowah*

Sitting in the lobby of the Baines Hotel, Hannah heard some fast footsteps outside, but she paid no attention. She was watching the wall clock at the hotel, and there were times that night that the hands seemed not to move at all. From time to time, guests would come downstairs to ask for something from Reynolds at the desk, but as they approached, Hannah had to step around the corner to hide herself. Tonight, she was not on duty.

The whole evening, she had prayed fervently that no one would ask her any questions. She needed to stay close to that clock, for it measured out the last hours and minutes of her slave life. Two a.m. would signal the time for action, and she was filled with excitement and just a sprinkling of dread. She kept reminding herself that tomorrow she would be free, but there were times that evening she felt like a prisoner awaiting a noose at the strike of dawn. Her mind kept reviewing her checklist for action. A small bag waited for her in the alley behind the hotel. In it were a few items of clothing and two boxes of honeyed hardtack for the journey. Clara and Charlotte were watching Elizabeth and Robert Junior at home and would be waiting for her to gather them at 2:15. She had wisely stolen some street passes from the hotel desk. After so many years at the hotel, Hannah could scribble a pretty fair rendition of Joshua Reynolds' signature. These might help them if their presence on the streets were challenged.

Suzanne, Serenade, and the others were to wait at the corner of Queen and State Street. Hannah had reminded the women of their duties so many times that they had almost come to blows. Her concern was that they might waver in their resolve. They were good hearted but timid souls, and there would be no time to go looking for them in the dark alleys of Charleston. 'They have to come through,' she thought. To leave them behind would be unbearable.

"How long are you going to wait?" asked Reynolds. "It's beginning to look like your husband's forgotten about you."

"No, sir," Hannah answered. "Robert will be here to walk me home when he gets done with his work at the dock. I best keep waiting."

"Well, why don't you at least sit down," he said. "All your pacing around is giving me the heebie jeebies."

This seemed like a good idea. After a long day at the Baines, the cushions of the maroon couch felt wonderful on her back. She quickly reclined and put both of her feet up on the footrest. Hannah told herself that she mustn't close her eyes, but she was soon overcome by fatigue. Sleep came over her, and with it, a dream.

She dreamt it was an early morning. Her girls were standing together, all dressed in pastel church clothes. Robert was there too, looking strong and handsome in the borrowed suit of clothes he had worn at their wedding. But in this dream, it soon became clear this was not a wedding, for all her friends and family were encircling a freshly-dug grave. They were all repeating a single word, over and over again, "Freedom." A squad of young men were lowering an open pine coffin, and as it went down, every eye looked to see the dead woman inside.

It was then that Hannah saw her own face in the box. She was dressed in hew white bridal gown, but had a hemp noose tied around her neck. In this dream, the people wept, and continued to shout, "Freedom!" Glancing around, she could see that every family member and every one of her friends had a noose around their neck, too. "No!" she cried. As her heart pounded, a warm rush came over her and she woke, still reclining on the big couch in the hotel. Hannah's eyes were wide open now, and she was soaked with perspiration.

"No? No *what*?" Reynolds asked from the front desk. "I didn't even ask you anything!"

Hannah was alarmed that she had dozed off and quickly looked up at the clock. The short hand of the clock was at the two but the long one was all the way at the bottom. She told herself it couldn't be, but it was 2:30 and she was a half hour late. Springing up, she ran out without a word. She had told the girls to wait for her, but only until 2:30. If she hadn't arrived by then, they would go by themselves to the rendezvous point, and then to the wharf. This had been the plan, but Hannah figured their plans were in the wind now. Bag in hand, she ran as fast as her sore feet could carry her.

The streets were dark and her thoughts darker. By now, the children had probably panicked. They might already be wandering the streets or waylaid by the constables. Hannah hoped they had been late in leaving. "They've got to be here," she whispered as she scurried up the back stairs that led up to their apartment over the stable. Clara and Charlotte had never been on time in their life. Hannah wanted to be hopeful, but her instincts told her everything sounded too quiet. By the time she had fully opened the door, her worst suspicions were confirmed. The girls were long gone.

Strangely, Hannah's first impulse was to be angry that they had left their dirty dishes on the table. 'What will Mrs. Ancrum think when she finds all this?' she wondered. It amused her that she still had the urge to scold them for the mess they had left. But there was nothing to be amused about now, and no reputation to worry about. She had to find those children and get everyone to the boat somehow.

On her way to Queen Street, Hannah stayed in the shadows, walking as fast a slave could walk without arousing suspicion. At every intersection, she looked back and forth for any sign of the girls and the baby, but there was nothing. She gained speed with every step and by the time she reached the rendezvous point, Hannah was at full gallop, panting audibly. But the corner was empty.

Had her children already met the others and gone to the boat, or had Clara and Charlotte just left when no one had come at the appointed time? There was no time to search for either group. Hannah had to trust that everyone had followed directions. She just had to get herself to the ship.

East Bay Street ran straight to the piers from here, but in the evening fog, it was impossible to see if anyone was between her and the docks. "Dear Lord God!" was all she could say over and over. She figured the angels would have to fill in the rest of her prayer. In the urgency of the moment, emotions overcame caution. "Clara! Charlotte! Elizabeth!" She shouted. "Are you there?" A voice came from out of the fog, but it was not a girl's.

"You there," a man shouted, "Stop at once!" It was likely a constable on night patrol, but Hannah didn't stay to find out. Though she had street passes in her skirt pocket, she gave in to every slave's natural response to such commands. She ran.

She could hear whistles behind her as she turned down a sidewalk that ran between a long row of red brick buildings. The fog was so thick she couldn't even read the street signs. The boot steps behind her were getting closer as she meandered through the maze of alleys. She was trying to head in the general direction of the North Wharf, but only God knew what street she was on now. As a nearby patrolman blew his whistle, Hannah wondered how far she had to go, and she feared she might not have the energy to make it. Suddenly, between some trees, she caught a glimpse of twin gaslights ahead. The gate to the wharf.

By the time she reached the catwalk to the *Etowah*, she was comforted by the fact that she heard no more sound from behind her. A loud whisper came from the dark shadows of the ship, "Here! Up here!" it said. It was William Morrison. "Hurry, Hannah!" he urged. Morrison tossed her bag aboard and, grasping her waist, shoved her down into the hold of the boat. Here, huddled around the tiny flame of a single candle, were her children. Behind them stood Suzanne, Serenade and the others.

"You never showed up," Charlotte said. "We got worried."

"You're so late, Mama," Clara said with a stern face that resembled the one Hannah herself always showed when she was angry. "Real late."

"Well, you're right," Hannah said. At these words, the mouths of the girls fell wide open. The had never heard their mother offer anything this close to an apology. They didn't know what to say, and thought it best to say nothing.

"I almost got us all killed," Hannah said, "but God's been good to us tonight." They all closed their eyes and embraced each other so tightly that, even after a half-hour of huddling, they were still too scared even to pray. The waiting seemed to go on forever. Hannah figured this was how the Hebrew children had felt as they waited in silence for the Angel of Death to pass over.

"I sometimes sing when I'm scared," said little Elizabeth. "I think we should sing." From outside, nearby police whistles could still be heard echoing along the waterfront.

"Singing will bring the gray men, baby," Hannah said. "There'll be time enough for singing once we cross Jordan." She pulled her babies to her chest and held on for dear life. Their soft breath touched her cheeks like the tender breezes of Freedom Land. She hoped they also had been praying for Daddy, who presently needed his own share of divine intervention.

Only a few blocks away, Robert was running toward Captain Relyea's house when he heard the faraway echoes of police whistles along the waterfront. "Dear God," he prayed. "I hope they're not after my people." In any case, the constables were the least of his worries, he had to get his hands on that log book.

The windows were dark at the Relyea house. Robert reached up over the doorsill to see if Captain's door key was in its regular hiding spot, but it was gone, which meant the old man had already gone inside for the night. To sleep it off, no doubt. Robert was considering how to sneak inside when he was startled by a familiar figure walking towards him. It was Spider.

"Wait," Robert whispered, "You should've been at the boat by now."

"You hear those whistles," he said. "We're all enjoying a grand game of hide-and-seek."

Robert had no time for Spider's foolery. He pulled Spider's face near to his own. "Can you just shut up, for once?" he said. "You gotta get to the boat."

With a sudden flailing of his arms, Spider slithered from Robert's grasp. "Get your damned hands off me and don't you dare tell me what to do! You were just a skinny little boy when I found you, right on this very street if I remember. And I made you something. Now all I ask is that you steal your stupid boat and leave me alone."

Robert stepped back, trying to catch his breath. "I can't. Not without you," Robert said. "You're part of me."

"Get it through your half-white brain," Spider said, "I ain't you and I can't do the things you do."

"Don't waver on me, Spider Jefferson," he said. "For once in your life, I don't need you to be witty, I need you to be strong."

"But that's just it," he said. "I'm not strong, at least not like you. I'll never be more than a smartass."

"Well," Robert said, "You're just gonna have to be a brave smartass. I was twelve when you found me on this street, and you made something out of me. Now it's time to made something of yourself."

Spider had tears on his face as he finally nodded in agreement, doing his best to smile a nervous smile. "You'll be the death of me," he said.

"Well, that's *one* of the two ways this night can end," Robert said. Right now, I need you to steal a damn gunboat."

As Spider ran off toward the docks, Robert turned back toward Relyea's house to somehow come by the precious codes that would save their lives. By now, police whistles were tweeting on a dozen streets between them and the waterfront. Four blocks away, after all the waiting, the courthouse clock, after so much waiting, finally rang three times.

Chapter 42
Crossing Jordan

As the echoes of the clock's third strike reached Wharf Six, the *Planter's* crew was feverishly preparing the boat for launch. Dark John was stoking the boiler fires now, tossing in anything that might possibly burn quicker and hotter than the hardwood logs. He threw in cooking oil from the galley, sealing pitch, and every scrap of pulpwood in the kindling boxes. They needed to get the steam up in a street whore's hurry. The dozen mooring lines that had secured the port side were mostly untied or at least slacked. One knot each at the bow and stern were left until the last moment. There wouldn't be much time once Spider and Robert returned.

As Samuel Chisholm gazed out across the dark harbor toward the distant beacons of Fort Sumter, he was suddenly aware that the feverish activity on deck had ceased. He turned just in time to see the wide eyes of the deck hands looking up at two gray-coated Rebs. The soldiers were pointing a spot lantern toward them and the sight of Confederates hit like a blow to the belly.

"You boys are starting pretty early, ain't ya?" the older soldier asked, not seeming to be in any state of alarm. "Who's in charge of this here boat?" he asked.

The terrified slaves stood in silence, each one hoping that one of the others would offer some plausible answer. There was growing impatience on the whiskered faces of the guards. They expected an answer, but there was no way the truth would do. A pack of slaves was getting ready to steal a gunboat and none of them had any snappy words on their tongue. They wished Robert or Spider were here.

"Something's amiss," said the older one. "You boys seem nervous about something. Why is no white man on deck to supervise?"

Fish Turno knew somebody had to say something. The younger guard had begun fondling the bosun's whistle that dangled from his neck. One toot from that thing and the world would come crashing down on them like the walls of Jericho.

"Sir," said Fish, motioning for the older man to come aside with him privately. "If you please sir, I've got to tell you something, but I don't want to make trouble for the masters."

"What are you talking about?" the man answered gruffly. "We need a straight answer." At that point the other guard came over to join the conversation.

"You see, sir," Fish began, "We're doing what the lieutenant told us, but he's been below decks for some time now." Then Fish lowered his voice to a whisper. "All them officers done ate a mess of hot pepper gumbo in town. It's that stringy stew they serve at Bleeker's. It sometimes goes bad. Real bad, if you know what I mean. The bosses have been lined up to use the head all day, havin' a time of it. Throwing up and, you know, the *other* thing." Fish pinched his nostrils. "You're welcome to go below to talk to 'em, but I wouldn't really advise it if you've got a weak stomach."

The guards smirked at each other but tried to maintain military dignity. "You wanna go below and speak to 'em?" the older guard asked.

The younger soldier just shook his head and smiled. "We should let these boys get back to their work," he said, turning up his nose with an expression of disgust.

"Back to it, boys!" the old guard shouted. "And tell 'em to steer clear of that Gumbo."

Chiz and the others had never in all their lives been so happy to be ordered back to work. They must have saluted those guards about twenty times each as they left. After this unforeseen visit, the crew was now behind schedule. Sweat poured from their faces as they prepared the *Planter* for departure. They secured the ropes, lit the bow lamps, and restocked the bridge with fresh tobacco and water. They had, it turned out, no reason to hurry as there was still no sign of Spider or Robert.

Their relief gradually melted into a grim nervousness. Robert and Spider should have come by now. The boys treasured last precious remnants of night time as they waited for dawn. Their work-sweat that had just dried was now being replaced by the perspiration of worry. "O Lord, be near us," Deke prayed as his eyes looked up into a dark heaven that made no reply. "And help us steal the white man's ship." They all smiled and said a quiet, "Amen."

The waves became smoother and came slower now. It was as if the ocean's clock was slowing down to give Robert more time, but every man on board was inwardly burning. Today's duty list had been hell, but all this waiting was worse.

"What do you suppose is keepin' them?" Chisholm kept asking. "We're loaded up, fully fired, and ready to cast off."

Their nerves became increasingly raw as, minute by minute, they drew closer to seven bells of the middle watch, which had been designated as their time to push off. In an hour or so, Captain Relyea should arrive to oversee the *Planter's* departure to the forts. By then, of course, their chance for stealing the boat would be over. And, in truth, their lives might be, too.

"The time's flying," Fish said.

"You think maybe they caught 'em?" asked Allston.

"It don't help to ask. We still got a bit of time before dawn breaks," answered Deke. "Just wait. He'll be here."

Abe Allston finally opened up his heart. "I've been wondering what they might do to us if them alarms sound," he said.

"Brother," said Chiz, "You don't want to start wondering about such things. If them bells strike, then the soldiers come. If the soldiers come, ain't nobody knows what they'll do to us. Not you, not me. We surely don't want to find out."

"Only God knows, I suppose," said Dark John.

"What they do to us might just be hotter than God's hell," offered Deke.

"A scourgin' and jail time, you suppose?" asked Fish.

Chisholm raised himself up and said in a strong voice, "Looky here, boys. This ain't like sassin' back or being late with the firewood. Whippings are for slaves, but what we're doing is worse than an act o' war. A captured soldier goes to Andersonville. Black soldiers will surely dance on the end of a Rebel rope."

"Lordy mercy," whispered Fish as he stared down the foggy pier toward shore, "Make haste, Robert. Please make haste."

There was no breeze now and the humid darkness of the harbor enveloped the seven men as they circled the flickering light of their lone deck lantern. Just days ago they had sworn an oath to each other in bold words. They would lay down their lives like heroes, and wouldn't stop until they had seized their freedom. They had prayed in Jesus' name and all made their marks in blood.

But now, after all the bluster, planning and sweat, they were beginning to feel like the slaves they had always been. The intrepid band of conspirators wondered if, in the end, they were just a nervous circle of work boys. Staring into the trembling wick of their lantern, they waited passively for larger forces to reveal their fate. To God in heaven, they must certainly have seemed small and inconspicuous, their lantern a mere firefly in the dark expanse of Charleston harbor.

As they listened for their helmsman's approach, their ears could hear things their eyes could not see – the chirps of a thousand insects, the grunts of toads from the shore, and the hushed hiss the distant Atlantic. Their nervous hearts thumped heavily, like the cadent rhythm of the waves against the hull. Even their spirits were drowning under the stifling blackness of the waterfront. Where was Robert? Where was God?

When a nearby rooster squawked out a pre-dawn greeting, the men all raised up on their haunches. "The cocks are crowing now," said Fish. "It'll be daylight soon."

"Naw," responded Dark John. "Roosters crow any time they please, even at night."

"It was night time when Saint Peter heard his rooster," whispered Deke.

Chiz just laughed. "As I recall, that didn't end so well for old Saint Peter." Before any man could say anything else, there was the hint of a distant sound. Footsteps on the planks at the gate.

"Somebody's coming," whispered Allston. "Everybody be quiet and mind to your work. And pray hard."

"Pray that it's Robert or Spider," whispered David.

"Pray it's Robert," said Allston. "We can do without Spider." The boys resumed their pantomime of activity, trying to look busy while at the same time being quiet enough to hear what was coming.

"I think we'd better make a little bit of noise," Fish whispered. "Somebody might get the idea we're stealing a boat."

"Shhh," said Chiz.

As their hands pretended to wash rails and tie ropes, their eyes were focused far down the pier. Through the mist they could discern that someone, only a distant shadow at this point, was moving past the two large gaslights that flanked the wharf entrance.

"Maybe it's just Mattox," Chiz said, referring to the belligerent dog that roamed the South Wharf. "I brought a stick of salt pork for him if he comes this way."

"Ain't no dog," said Allston. "Unless it's wearing boots. Listen!"

The men all stopped their work and cocked their heads to hear. Sure enough, there were clear sounds of boot heels on the planks. When a black silhouette crossed between them and the lights, they gasped in unison. This was no dog. For good or ill, a lone figure was slowly and deliberately walking their way.

"It's Robert, I think," Chiz offered. "I know his walk."

"You don't know nothing," Dark John said, shading his squinting eyes with a flat hand as if it had been noonday. "Whoever it is, he's moving slow, and stands up straight like an officer. What I'm seeing don't move nothing like Robert."

"Should we be running then?" asked Chisholm.

"Run where?" Allston replied. "If that man's trouble, then trouble's surely coming our way. You gonna run across the waves like the Lord Jesus?"

"Saints and angels!" said Deke, "Look busy! Keep your wits and say nothing. We don't know nothing and we ain't seen nothing."

Each of them nodded and stayed hunched over whatever task he was pretending to do. All they could do was watch. The next hundred feet of the main walkway was unlit to the place where the next gaslight was hung. There the dock split off toward the section that led to Pier Six, where the *Planter* was moored.

Lit only by moonlight now, the mysterious figure was slate gray and indistinct. It kept moving until it suddenly faded into the dark stretch of boardwalk that led to them. For a long moment the men held their breath, hoping that the man would keep moving down the main dock and not make the turn toward Pier Six.

They all flinched when the peace of the dock area was broken by the distant clanging of two bells, the signal that some captain had arrived to cast off a boat. They all knew which captain and which boat.

"We're dead men," whispered Sam Chisholm. As the unwelcome bell rang out across the waterfront, every member of the crew longed to stifle it with wet towels, anything to quiet the sound. Its knell fell heavy upon their hearts. Like the very sentence of death.

As the officer approached the fork to Pier Six, a soft voice was heard. Chiz was whispering a prayer to himself with rapid breaths, "Lord, no, no, no, no..."

But the approaching figure did not move past them. Turning right, the silhouette headed straight toward the *Planter*. Whatever fate was to befall them was about to happen.

"O my Lord, Lord," groaned Deke. "I see the devil walking to and fro upon the earth."

The blurry figure was more than a shadow now. Every fifteen yards there was a lantern, and even from a distance the limping, but unrelenting steps were unmistakable. They trembled at the sight of the wide straw hat, commander's coat, and longpipe. They were so close now they could see the puffs of smoke. There was now no more need for guessing. Captain Relyea had come early, and with his arrival, their long-awaited day of deliverance had suddenly become Judgment Day.

Like condemned prisoners, every man kept his eyes down now, and no one ventured any words. They might have whistled if they had enough spit to do so. In what seemed like an eternity, those by the gangplank watched the Captain's polished boots as they walked up to mount the foredeck. Deke's downcast eyes were glued to the bare iron rail that was now just inches from his face. His old heart was twisting like a knotted rope in his chest.

When a hand finally gripped the railing, Deke got the surprise of his life. It was a brown hand with brass rings on every finger, Robert's hand. Negro skin had never seemed more beautiful than it was to Deke at that moment. That hand could not have been more welcome if it had been the luminescent hand of the Son of God.

"Oh my Lord and God!" Deke blurted, his heart almost exploding with joy.

"It's a sorry crew that won't salute its captain," Robert laughed. "I suppose you men can start your hearts to beatin' again."

Deke grasped a small lantern and slowly raised it up. The crew's eyes followed the light as it illuminated the familiar face of their dark helmsman. Robert was grinning, his bright teeth beaming out between his closely-cropped black whiskers.

"I do believe you're the angel of the Lord!" Deke said as they all gathered around Robert and embraced him. Their tears of joy spoke louder than any words they could have uttered at that moment.

Puffing out a cloud of tobacco smoke, Robert spoke in his best imitation of Captain Relyea, "Atten-*shun!*"

As they enthusiastically scurried to line themselves up, the full moon cast a line of dark images on the foredeck. Robert remembered thinking their shadows looked just like the stick figures he had drawn on their conspiracy plan. Abe Allston led them in a group salute, and after returning it, Robert said, "It's a fine morning, men. How 'bout we steal ourselves a ship?"

The crew could barely restrain themselves from dancing, shouting, and hoisting Robert on to their shoulders, but everyone realized that the

Rebs were near, and that time was short. Their long-awaited dance with the devil was underway, and it was Robert's tune to call.

"Deke, I need your best miracle prayer," he said. "This black slave is about to turn into a white captain."

From his coat pocket Robert produced a pair of snow white gloves, which he methodically put on the same elegant way Relyea liked to do. The shout-hatch to the engine room was cracked open a tad, and the boiler fire cast a flickering blade of light across the steps that led up to the bridge. In the wink of an eye, Robert stepped across that line and climbed the spiral steps up to the wheelhouse. Taking the helm, his blood raced hot like lightening in his veins. He was as born-again as a man baptized in a crystal stream.

With his European uniform and broad hat, he was the very image of the Captain. "O dock-mastah!" he boomed, stringing out the final syllable in his best British voice. "The CSS *Plan-tah* is prepared to cast off!" The crew almost burst out laughing.

After a long moment, the tower's reply was returned through the darkness as a long blast from a foghorn. Taking the logbook from the inside pocket of his coat, Robert sounded the precious harbor code. One long whistle blast , two bells, and four short blasts.

In a short moment that seemed like an hour, there was an answer from the tower that echoed the one they had received. One long, two bells, and four short. After the last of these, they could hear another sound. The sound of the crew exhaling.

"Prepare to cast off!" Robert screamed to the boys below. "Full ahead! The *Planter* is underway!"

As the paddlewheels began to churn the dark water to froth, the crew scurried about the decks, untying the ropes and manning their various positions on the ship, doing real work this time. "Hoist the anchor! Shed the ropes!" Robert shouted. Each man in turn replied, "Aye," or "Aye, sir," as each hustled about his respective tasks. They had never obeyed any man so joyfully or willingly.

Some of the boys wondered whether the harbor master recognized the voice as that of Relyea or Robert, but it didn't seem to matter. Any member of this crew would have gladly followed that commanding voice into the very gates of Hades. To freedom or to death, they were finally on their way.

Chapter 43
Farewell, South Carolina

Above them on the bridge, Robert stood as still as a statue. His gloved hands cocked the wheel with a ease and resolve. The monstrous roar of the twin engines rang out a clanking song from below decks.

"Dark John's got her singing for us tonight," Robert said to Chiz, who had come up to assist with the whistle and bell. Captain Smalls opened his logbook to double-check the code. "Stand by with the signal Chiz – one long, two bells, and four short." Chisholm took note and nodded as he grasped the whistle lever and the bell rope.

As they neared the end of the South Wharf, Robert could almost make out the face of the harbor master in the light of a lantern above. It appeared to be Boyd Pierce, the youngest of the Rebs that served on the tower. To act naturally at this point was the order of the day, and act he did.

"*CSS Planter* requests to depart!" he shouted. "Hooo...aye... yah!" With a nod of his head, Robert ordered Chiz to give the departure signal. A single blast of the whistle was followed by two clangs of the bell. After another four toots of the whistle, everyone on board held their breath. As the engine continued to chug along, it was quiet enough for them to hear the waves kissing the *Planter's* bow.

"Permission to clear the wharf!" cried a voice from the tower, followed by a second voice saying, "Pass the *Planter*!" As a foghorn sent a single, prolonged reply of approval echoing across the harbor, Robert's men could scarcely restrain their elation. The code signaled their freedom, at least for now. To them it rang out like Gabriel's trumpet, proclaiming their welcome through the Pearly Gates.

Robert smiled under the shadow of his big straw hat, but there was little time to savor the moment. He kept looking back to the empty berth at Pier Six. Before long the real captain would be walking down that same pier to discover an empty space where his flagship used to be tied up. It behooved the *Planter* and its crew be long gone by then.

Robert's last glance along the waterfront was slow and deliberate.

The glowing row of street lights reminded him of his early stint as a lamplighter, when morning and evening he climbed a hundred poles to light and then extinguish the flames. It suddenly occurred to him that he might never again set foot on his native South Carolina. As a half-turn of the helm urged the ship north toward the Atlantic Wharf, he waved a farewell to Charleston. It seemed strange to him that he could shed sentimental tears while simultaneously spitting in defiance. "Farewell, South Carolina. Burn in hell, Confederate States of America."

For the first time in his life Robert found himself alone at the bridge, without orders from any man. Looking down at his hands as they gripped the wheel, his thoughts, like the ship, were all his own. "Thanks to God," he whispered to himself. "You're the only one who can tell me what to do now."

Robert scanned the dark foredeck, trying to verify that every man was properly about his business. Even from the bridge, he could hear Deke and Dark John shouting at one another in the engine room. Fish, Chisholm, and Abe Allston stood at the bow of the boat, waiting for orders, but mostly watching for torpedoes and Confederate patrols.

"Keep an eye out when we near the North Wharf," Robert said. "William will have two lamps hung on the tips of the *Etowah*."

"Aye, sir," they said, almost in unison. "The way looks clear. Just keep her in the center of the channel."

Away now from the lamps of the Southern Wharf, the dark foredeck of the *Planter* was illuminated by the glow of the big moon that by now high in the sky. Robert glanced down to his boots, the Captain's, firmly planted where old Relyea had always stood. As he gripped the wheel, it all felt familiar but also strangely new to him. It took him back to the day when Mack Lyle had given him his first chance to steer a ship. But this time the helm was not his for a brief moment, today his hands would not release their grip until the arrival of freedom or death.

The big twin paddles were at full spin now, churning a moonlit furrow of foam through the black smoothness of the harbor. Robert began to feel more peace in his heart as he barked orders to Abe Allston who stood on the starboard rail. "Better raise our flag, Abe," he shouted.

"Aye, sir," came the reply. "What flag shall we fly, sir?"

"I suppose we should remain patriotic Confederates until we're clear of Fort Sumter," he replied.

"Aye, sir," Allston said. "Just don't ask me to salute that damned thing." Abe ran off toward the stern where the Stars and Bars would fly one last time to guarantee their safe escape.

In a few minutes, Fish Turno came up to the bridge to offer Robert some hot coffee. "Here, Cap," he said. "I figured you might need a fresh jolt of wake-up."

"Thanks for the thought," Robert said, "But my heart's still beating like a snare drum. Been so since yesterday. You seen Spider?"

"Not topside," Fish said. "He might be helping Deke and John down below."

"Well," said Robert. "Send him up to me, if you would."

"Aye," said Fish, but after a few minutes he was back to the bridge. "The boys ain't seen Spider tonight," Fish reported. "He never showed."

The news hit Robert like a fist in the gut and he slammed an angry fist on the bridge rail. "Damn that fool," he said. "I should have noticed. He promised he'd be here by eight bells of the dog watch."

It just like Spider to come up short when it counted most. If there were tears to be shed, they would have to come later. Robert had spied the two lights on the bow and stern of a distant ship. It had to be the *Etowah*. By now, the women and children would be hiding there with Will Morrison, waiting to be picked up. Robert had no time to worry about Spider.

As the *Planter* was completing her final stretch between the Southern Wharf to the *Etowah*, Robert was growing impatient. He popped open the shouting hatch and screamed down to the engine room. "Have our fires gone out?" he bellowed, more as a complaint than an actual question. "Feels like we're dragging both anchors."

"She's cranking full steam and more, sir," Deke replied. "We're doing a good twelve knots at least, even into the wind. Be patient, Robert. We're on course and right on schedule."

Robert was about to yell something else, but stopped himself. "Well,' he said, "Just maintain course and keep feeding those fires." Just then, Deke stuck his sweat-drenched head out through the shout-hatch.

"You all right, Robert?" he asked.

"I'm sorry to scream at the men," he said. "It's Spider. He never showed and never sent word. He's gone off to God-knows-where."

"You did your level best," said Deke. "The boy's a flighty one, but I thought he'd man up and show himself."

"Well," said Robert. "It's too late in any case. I just hope he hasn't sold us out."

Deke stretched his right arm all the way up through the hatch and grabbed Robert's hand. "You've gotta have faith," he said. "You said yourself that Spider's no Judas."

"I guess my heart's just broke," Robert said. "Spider looks to be a dead man now, I suppose. Zerich Pitcher will surely connect the dots and know Spider was in on this thing. He's my best friend."

"The Lord Jesus told us to put our hand to the plow and not look back," Deke said.

"I just wish he had at least said goodbye," Robert said.

In the hazy moonlight, Robert could just now make out the slender figure of a man running along the foredeck of the *Etowah*. William was waving to them as the *Planter* drew near. "Hoy there!" he cried. "You're a welcome sight! The dock patrols have been buzzing around at the far end of the pier, and they'll be headed back here right soon." A ragged huddle of women and children were just now emerging from the hold of the *Etowah*.

"Hey, baby!" Hannah shouted. "I told 'em you'd come." She staggered uneasily on the foredeck of the boat, holding little Elizabeth by the hand and carrying Robert Junior under her other arm. "I knew you'd be right on time."

"She's a liar," said sixteen-year-old Clara, who was clutching their big tote bag. "Mama's been sayin' you was a dimwit and that you weren't coming." Little Elizabeth nodded in agreement.

"So I had a moment of weakness," Hannah said. "But praise God, you got here." There was no time for hugs or any more words as they all managed to climb aboard the small skiff that took them over to the *Planter*. Down the Atlantic Wharf, the beam of spot lanterns could be seen scanning back and forth across the piers, looking for where the sound of voices was coming from.

"Hurry now," Robert implored. "We've got to get out of here."

The *Planter's* engineers had been standing ready and didn't even need a command from Robert. Once the women and children were safely below decks, the main hatch was slammed shut. With a loud blast of steam, both engines engaged and the ship lurched forward. Both side wheels splashed up a fountain of froth as the *Planter* chugged away from the dock.

In the shadows behind them, Robert could see the dock guards, lanterns in hand, running back and forth along the length of the wharf. It only took the *Planter* a short minute to fade into the anonymous darkness. Robert's heart was now beating along with the urgent drumming of the engines, his eyes straining to discern the channel through the hovering mist on the water.

"We're free!" young Charlotte cried. She and Hannah had snuck up from their hiding place below. Her dark eyes sparkled as she gazed up at Robert. "How long till we get there?"

Robert immediately flashed a frown towards his wife. "Hush her," he scowled, "and get all these women and children below decks. We've got four more checkpoints to get past."

Hannah sent Charlotte below, then she looked Robert square in the face. "What is all this?" she asked. "Why you snappin' at everybody?"

Robert was about to give her a piece of his mind, but then thought better of it. She was right. His brain was about to boil over like a hot stew pot. "I'm sorry," he said. "I ain't myself."

"Well," she said. "Whatever's stuck in your craw, you best set it aside. We need you to keep your head."

Robert just nodded in silence and exhaled deeply. "I think I've been holding that breath since we cast off. Spider missed his mark," he said. "He never made it back to the boat."

"I'm sorry," she said. "You think he caved in to the Rebs?"

"Maybe," said Robert. "But I haven't heard any alarms on shore. He and I had it out, but I thought things had gotten resolved."

"You best let it go, baby," she said. "We still got miles to go to till we're safe."

"Aye, my Captain," he said to her, smiling now. You and the children will have to be enough for me." Hannah touched his arm gently as she passed by to go below.

"I'll pray for you," she said softly. "Be strong."

Just then, he became aware that Charlotte and the other children had all come back up on deck. He wanted to scold them, but instead turned loose of the helm for a moment and gathered them into his arms, kissing each one, then pulled them all together for one big embrace. "I love you all," he said with big tears rolling down both his cheeks. "The Lord has been gracious to us. Your daddy's gonna take you to freedom!"

"Don't your father look special in that fine getup!" Hannah said, urging the children back toward a safer place belowdecks. "Let's let Captain Daddy mind his steering or we'll be steaming up the center of Meeting Street."

Robert was eager to make headway, but this first stretch of channel was well-lined with explosive mines. "Back off that throttle," he said. "Take us down to half speed." Any careless veering could blow them all to kingdom come. "God, watch over us," he prayed as they chugged in their slow and deliberate course towards freedom.

Just minutes later, Chisholm was seen running up the stairs to the bridge. "Robert!" he said, "Have we got a working spot lamp on board?" There was something looming in the neck of the channel up ahead.

Robert could see the urgency on Chiz's face. "Deke's got one in the engine room," he said. "Inform me as soon as you can see anything."

'What now?' Robert thought to himself. It might be a stray torpedo, or maybe a patrol vessel. He gripped the wheel tighter than he had ever grabbed anything. "Prepare to reverse our engines," he shouted. Things were getting sticky and they weren't even to the first fort.

"Appears to be a boat," Chiz shouted, "A launch or smaller." Allston was leaning out over the bow, doing his best to shine the lamp on whatever lay ahead in the channel.

"Prepare to fire," Robert commanded. "It may be a patrol."

Chisholm and Fish looked uneasy, but took charge of the forward gun. With a burning wick in his hand, Chiz aimed the small cannon it in the direction whatever lay ahead.

Peering through the darkness, Robert Suddenly had second thoughts. "Hold fire, boys," he said. The Confederates wouldn't be sending a skiff to stop a gunboat, and any shot would alarm the whole harbor.

"Something's moving, Robert," Abe said from the bow. "Looks like just one man in a boat... and he's waving something in his hand."

"Reverse engines!" Robert shouted. "Stop us!"

"Oddest thing," said Abe as he looked straight ahead. "Somebody appears to be waving a flag."

Robert wondered if it might be a fisherman, but quickly dismissed the thought. The Rebs had outlawed night fishing over a year ago. Only a drunk or a fool would risk floating in the middle of the harbor after dark. Just then, Robert heard a familiar voice in the distance. A fool to be sure.

"Ahoy, Captain Smalls!" the voice shouted. "Ahoy!" As the *Planter* chugged nearer, Robert could make out the smiling face and lanky limbs of Spider Jefferson in the cloudy beam of the spot lamp. He was waving the small U.S. flag Robert had given him.

"Lord above!" Robert exclaimed as they pulled his friend aboard. "I can't believe it."

"And *you're* supposed to be the believer," Spider said. "Sorry to be tardy, but some constables had apparently saved me a seat in the calaboose. I had an old street pass in my pocket, but it took the best speech I ever made to slide my way out of this one."

"I was going to kill you for missing your mark," Robert said as he embraced Spider's soggy neck, "and for breaking my heart."

"Sorry to wet down that dandy getup of yours," said Spider as he tried to brush the moisture off Robert's captain's coat. "Oh, but you do look white!" Spider began to paw over the elegant coat, vest and trousers Robert was wearing. "You even look like the captain," he said.

"If you want to command, you gotta look like a captain," Robert replied, "and I do look the part." he smiled. "Captain Relyea won't miss it 'cause he ain't got a ship no more."

"Can't believe a Christian would do such a thing," Spider joked, "Theft being a sin and all."

"The church would say I stole it," Robert said, "but in the Navy we just say it was *appropriated*. And look," he added. "I got all *this* too." He then put on his broad sweetgrass hat and lit up his long briar pipe.

Spider put his hands over his mouth at the thought that a slave had gotten away with the old man's things. "Cap was snoring the whole time I was ransackin' his closet," Robert said. "The old goat won't be pleased at sunup, standing naked in the pale light of dawn."

"It looks better on you anyhow," said Spider. "You were born for it."

"Full ahead," Robert shouted as he puffed out a cloud of gray smoke. Urging the boat back toward the center of the channel, he smiled as he stroked the spokes of the wheel. "You know, Spider," he said, "Paradise wouldn't have been as sweet without you."

"Nor hell as hot," Spider joked. "It's sweet when the pieces of a good plan come together." Spider then spread his dark fingers out and meshed them together like Robert had done. "Like you said before, "Click, click, click."

"You best scoot down to the engine room," Robert said, "and get you some dry clothes." Spider gave his best version of a salute, and then thumbed his nose at Robert as he left.

"And I prayed for this," Robert chuckled to himself as he rolled his eyes toward heaven. "Heaven has returned my wicked angel to me."

Chapter 44
Passing the Forts

As they made their way across the harbor, the haze was clearing a bit and, but even from the bridge, Robert could barely make out the long line of channel buoys. He squinted toward the east, trying to catch sight of their next checkpoint.

Castle Pinckney was out there somewhere. As usual, the mist was thickest near the North end of the harbor, and with limited visibility, Robert had to scale back to half speed for this part of the trip. The eyes of everyone on deck strained to catch the first glimpse of the fort.

"Relax, boys," Robert said. "Pinckney's gotta be out here somewhere. The tide's coming in and is slowing us down a little."

Suddenly, there came the sharp sound of a fog horn. All of them grabbed the rails and ropes as a voice came out of the fog. "Hail there!" it said. "What ship is that?" To the port side they could barely make out the dark outline of Castle Pinckney.

Robert stood stiffly behind the helm. "Chisholm, get ready to signal," he said. Then, in a well-rehearsed bluster, he shouted, "The *CSS Planter* requests to pass!"

"Now?" asked Chiz.

Robert just nodded. "One long, two bells, and four short," he said. Chisholm quickly sounded the code. They maintained their speed as they came near the fort.

"Clear the *Planter!*" came a high-pitched voice from the tower. "Pass the *Planter!*" echoed another from the tip the wall. They were safely through. The channel opened up at this point, but there was still cause for concern. Back in December of 1861, the Yankees had tried to close Charleston by sinking old ships full of stones across the entrance to the harbor. The Federals called this the First Stone Fleet, and by the end of January of 1862, they had sunk 29 of these hulks in place. Strong tides soon began to move them around a bit, leaving narrow channels that ran right under the guns of Forts Moultrie on the north and Johnson on the southern shore.

"How's our speed?" Robert shouted.

"Currents are swirling," Allston said. "Near as I can tell, we're only doing around ten knots right now."

"The tide's a river, and the wind's in our face," said Robert. "We're headed right into the teeth of it."

Just then, the shouting hatch flipped open from below. Robert expected to see Deke's sweaty head emerge, but it was Hannah instead. "Where are we now?" she yelled, trying her best to be heard over the clanking of the engines. Robert kept his eyes on the channel ahead and pretended he didn't hear her.

"I see you not seeing me," she said. "I know you heard me."

"Yes ma'am, Captain," Robert said sarcastically. "You'll know we've arrived when you hear the champagne corks poppin'. Otherwise, keep yourself below, and don't be telling John and Deke how to do their work."

"You're beautiful!" he smiled as he slammed the small hatch shut in her face. Robert looked up at Chiz and Allston. "Remind me to buy a lock for that hatch when we're done," he said. "We got a few too many captains in this slave's Navy." They all smiled.

Now past Castle Pinckney, there was almost a mile to cover before that had to pass under the guns of Fort Ripley, a recently-constructed battery situated in the middle of the inner harbor. Having been slowed down by the incoming tide, they were falling behind schedule. Robert reckoned it was after four o'clock by now, but it would serve no useful purpose to ask what time it was. They were racing to beat sunrise. Once daylight came, the forts could send and receive signals, and every ship and cannon in the harbor would be mobilized to stop them.

As they made their approach, Fort Ripley was curiously dark. This particular fortification was a new addition to Charleston's defenses, having been hastily constructed on a strategic sandbar at the beginning of the war. It had been put there to shore up the central section of the harbor's inner circle of defense. Robert had been at the helm of the *Planter* when she delivered the first cannons to the fort. He sincerely hoped he would not instigate any action by which he might be killed by guns he had delivered himself.

"What do you make of it?" asked Chiz, scanning the fort's tower for any signs of lights or personnel. "You reckon they're asleep?"

"I suspect they'll shout out a challenge soon enough," Robert said. Like Chiz, he was focused on the tower and the top of Ripley's ramparts.

Neither man spoke as they approached the place where the south channel came within 200 feet of the cannon's muzzles. All they could hear was the churning of the paddle wheels and the growl of the engine below.

"Should we slow the boat?" shouted Abe Allston from the foredeck. "I don't like the looks of this. It's too quiet for my taste."

"Fort Ripley may look dark to us, but we're pretty dark to them too," Robert said. "I always figured that when a man gets uneasy, he should just keep going. Folks tend to let you alone if you look like you know where you're headed."

Robert's words reassured the men, but his heart was thumping an erratic rhythm inside his chest. The *Planter* was sliding past the fort like a man tiptoeing past a sleeping lion. In a whisper, Robert began to sing to himself an old lullaby his mother used to sing as he drifted off to sleep.

Hush baby sweetcakes, don't say a word,
Mama's gonna buy you a mocking bird.

He broke into a grin as both Chiz and Allston softly chimed in.

And if that mocking bird don't sing,
Mama's gonna buy you a diamond ring.

The men finished the whole rest of the song, hoping the guns of the fort would continue to snooze.

As the full moon silhouetted a lone guard who stood atop the wall nearest them, Robert nervously raised his gloved hand and waved. After a brief moment, the small figure waved back. There would apparently be no official signals exchanged between the *Planter* and Fort Ripley tonight – no whistles, no bells but best of all, no cannonade. It looked like everybody in Ripley was catching up on their rest.

The mood wasn't so restful for the boys on the deck of the *Planter* as hints of dawn were now beginning to tint the Atlantic horizon. It wasn't nearly time to exhale. The checkpoints at Forts Johnson and Sumter still stood in their way, and Robert knew there would be no dozing watchmen there.

"We've got another mile to Fort Johnson," he said to Chisholm. "Get below and see what they need. I suspect the women and young'uns will be craving some water down there."

As the boys left, Robert's mind was busy estimating the minutes until sunrise. To the west, the amber disk of the full moon was already crawling down the ladder of western clouds. Soon it would disappear into the spires of the city. He recalled those old story times back in the McKee's parlor when little Liddie had begged to read *Cinderella*. He remembered the suspense as the palace clock chimed out midnight, when Cinderella's charmed life would revert to what had been before. Here at the *Planter's* helm, all dressed up in his best charade of a captain, darkness was life. Any breaking of the spell would prove fatal. "Slow down," he whispered to the moon. "At daybreak I'll turn into a black man again."

His solitude was interrupted when a beam of light slid out through the hatch from the engine room. Hannah's sweat-soaked head once again emerged and shouted up to him, "You doin' all right, baby?"

"Just praying," he said. "Looks like the Lord may need to stop the sun from rising. Are you folks all right?"

"Pretty much," she said. "But it's hot as hell fire down here. We've been boiled soft like beans in a stew pot."

"Sorry about the heat," he said. "By the looks of your hair, you may need a bandana before we meet Mister Lincoln." Hannah just stroked the perspiration from her head and gave Robert a bemused but nasty look.

"Just get us there," she said. "We can spiff up first thing when we get to Freedom Land." Hannah huffed her chin out at Robert just before she slammed the shouting hatch. This ordeal was wearing everyone down to the nubs.

The last beams of moonlight illuminated the line of buoys that marked the south channel that ran straight from Fort Ripley to their next checkpoint. Johnson was a big fort and had been guarding the harbor since the first ramparts were constructed there in 1708. Through the years and the wars, many of its walls had been repaired and expanded so that by the time of secession, it stretched all the way along the northeastern point of James Island. It was from here the Confederates had fired the first shots of the war. Robert sincerely hoped to see no more shots fired from Fort Johnson today.

As the *Planter* drew near, Robert was careful to discern the channel and to watch for any loose torpedoes that might have drifted from their positions. Back in November, a Rebel harbor tug had been sunk here by one of these wayward mines.

"Chiz, I'll need you on the bridge," Robert said. "Those boys at Johnson's tower will want that code."

"Aye," said Chisholm as he climbed up to the bridge. "One long, two bells, and four short."

"Aye," said Robert in reply. He was confident, but he still looked down to the logbook to verify the proper dots, dashes and circles that spelled out the signals. Noticing how carefully Robert verified the code in the book, Chiz nodded in approval. With so many lives at stake, being careful was no sin.

Robert was feeling the stress and the effects of not having slept or eaten in 24 hours. "Give me strength." he prayed as he tried to discern their course through the haze. "Just two forts left."

"Would it help if I slowed her down to half-throttle?" Chiz asked.

"Keep us full-on," said Robert. "We wanna look like we know where we're headed."

He took Captain Relyea's spyglass from the bridge drawer and tried to make out the personnel in Fort Johnson's western tower. Near as he could tell, there were three men watching the *Planter's* approach. Soon they heard an extended blast from the fort's big foghorn. Robert knew this to be both a safety warning and a request for a clearance code. "Play our song, Chiz," he said. Chisholm nodded and quickly sent out the request for passage. One long, two bells, and four short.

Robert stood obtrusively on the bridge and waved vigorously to those in the fort. "Good morning, gentlemen!" he bellowed in his best rendition of Captain Relyea's voice. "*CSS Planter* requests to pass outbound!" he bellowed. Robert then sucked some smoke from his longpipe and blew it out the way the Captain always did.

The *Planter's* crewmembers did their best to look busy, but all of them were holding their breath as they moved slowly under the huge guns of the fort. These Rebel cannon now inspired the crew to do something Deacon Gradine had been trying to get them to do for two years. They all prayed.

"Good morning, Captain Relyea!" a gruff voice shouted from the upper level of Fort Johnson's tower. "Code received! Pass the *Planter!*" he shouted.

In the depths of their hearts, the crew gave thanks. Robert was so elated he wanted to continue his verbal impersonations of Captain Relyea, but wisely restrained himself and didn't even venture to wave this time. Something told him it was safer to get out of this game while he was ahead. And alive.

"Just one more to go," said Chisholm. "One fort more to freedom."

"Hush," urged Robert, holding his fingers over his lips as if something unlucky had been spoken at a game of craps. "Hold your tongue 'till we're clear."

"I thought you trusted the Lord," said Spider, who had just now joined them on the bridge. "Now you're gettin' superstitious on us."

"I trust God," he said. "I just don't want us to be overconfident, that's all."

"Well," said Spider. "We may need both God and a few lucky demons to get us past Sumter."

Robert wanted to chide him, but by now the first blazes of dawn were beginning to glow from the east horizon. "I hate the look of this," he said. "We've got a mile before we clear Sumter, and there's a red sky coming on."

"Red sky at morning," Chiz whispered. "Folks say it's an omen."

"Sailor talk," said Spider. "Anyway, it looks mostly pink to me. Pink don't mean nothing, as far as I know."

"Shut up now," Robert said as he squinted into the still-dark channel before them.

"I was just saying," said Spider, "that most of the time..."

"No! Shut up!" Robert said before Spider could finish his sentence. Robert's face suddenly froze with the look of absolute terror. "Reverse engines!" he screamed as he let go of the wheel and jumped to the front rail of the bridge. "Stop the boat!" He was frantic about something he saw up ahead of them.

With a thundering of boot heels on the stairs and deck, everyone was coming topside to see what Robert was pointing at. About a hundred yards ahead, the last beams of moonlight were glistening off a row of dark objects that were bobbing in the water all across their path.

"My God!" Robert said, "They must've drifted loose."

"Buoys?" asked Chiz.

"Not buoys," Robert replied, "Torpedoes. All armed and ready to blow us to glory." The string of floating mines blocked the whole width of the channel.

"What now, Robert?" asked Chisholm.

"I don't like our choices... or our chances," said Robert. "We could backtrack and take the North Channel past Fort Moultrie, but it'd be broad daylight by the time we got there. The *Planter* would be a sitting duck. We might try veering from the markers, but we'd likely run aground and be captured. Or we could just try to plow straight through the torpedoes."

"Holy God," Chiz said. "None of those sound very promising."

Though crowded, the *Planter's* foredeck had become dead quiet now. The boat was at a dead stop and even from the wheelhouse, Robert could hear the rhythmic slapping of the waves on the bow, ticking off the seconds before dawn arrived. "We can't linger," he said. "Where's Fish?"

As Fish Turno came up the stairs, Robert put his arm around him. "Gabriel," he said, "I think this might be a good morning for a fish to swim." Robert was smiling like a man who had something in mind.

A few minutes later, the whole crew, along with the engineers, women and children from below, were gathered together on the foredeck, watching Fish as he lived up to his name. As smooth as a dolphin, he dove headlong into the dark water and made his way toward the distant string of mines. Taking hold of the rope that was attached to the mine on the far end of the row, he waved back to those on the boat. They all cheered.

"Now double it back," Robert shouted. "See if you can fold the whole line of 'em back on itself."

Everyone prayed and held their breath as Gabe slowly dragged the mines to one side of the channel, tying the rope to the nearest unarmed buoy. They wanted to clap their hands for him, but they quieted by fear. Even after the mines were repositioned, there remained only a narrow opening for them to slither past.

"Can we get through?" Chiz asked.

"We've got no choice," Robert said, "But it's gonna be tighter than threading a needle."

"A needle lined with death," added Spider.

Robert urged everyone to move back to their posts or below decks. What ever happened, it might be easier if a crowd wasn't watching. But all of them, men, women, and even the children, disregarded Robert's orders and stayed right where they were. Some stayed to watch, others stayed to help. Many of them stayed because they didn't want to die separated from their loved ones.

"Deke, take us all ahead slow," Robert shouted. "Fish, you stay in the water at the prow and try to fend off any torpedoes that get too close. That one on the end will be a tight squeeze." Robert's heart was greatly encouraged that Fish said nothing, but simply and willingly carried out his orders. 'The boy's a brave sailor,' Robert thought to himself.

As the ship crept forward, his hands guided the spokes of the wheel softly with the tips of his fingers, like the way his mother used to carry clusters of fresh-laid eggs. As the next minutes unfolded, the prayers of their hearts showed their faith, but every face showed traces of terror.

"We can't see a thing," said Hannah, who nervously stood on the deck with the women and children. "Is he doin' it?"

"Well," said Robert. "You'd surely hear a loud sound if he wasn't. We need prayers more than we need questions, right now."

After about ten minutes, the good word came. "Fish has got both hands on the torpedo at the end of the chain," Chiz said. "He's gonna try to hold away it while we slide past."

They all leaned over the starboard gunnel now, watching and praying as Fish held the mine at arm's length. With his back pressed against the hull, inch by inch, he and the bomb slowly glided down the full length of the ship.

"Hold the pegs where the chains are attached," Robert said. "Any small tap on the sides will set it off."

"I feel like I'm dreaming a nightmare," said Fish. "Waltzing with a fat mermaid."

"Well," Robert said, "Be gentle and hold that gal away from you... and for God's sake don't let her *kiss* you. I suspect she's got quite an explosive temper."

Robert didn't fully exhale until the whole string of mines, along with Fish Turno, bobbed harmlessly in the dark water behind them. Everyone was smiling and celebrating now. They were free of the mines, with only Fort Sumter standing between them and freedom.

"Now pull that young hero back aboard," Robert said, "and put some dry duds on him." Everyone patted Fish on the back for saving them and Deke led everyone in a prayer of thanks. As they all shouted Amen, a roar was heard from below as Dark John cranked the engines up to full steam. "Let's clear these decks!" Robert commanded. "We're underway!"

As Robert gripped the helm, he breathed a sigh of relief, but his hands were still shaking. Having come so far, he knew he should have felt more relaxed, but his mind was throbbing and his normally-strong heart had begun to skip beats. They were one step from the Promised Land, but he knew the Confederates had saved their most intimidating weapon for last. Fort Sumter, that intimidating monument to Southern secession, stood between them and freedom.

With the luminescent background of the morning sky behind it, the fort loomed like some mythical castle before them. This was, in fact, how the Rebs wanted Sumter to be viewed. A grotesque monolith, its formidable ramparts were on display at the entrance to Charleston Harbor like a huge stone fist being shaken at the world. Even the most powerful navies on earth were afraid to come near.

Robert had seen the worst of Sumter with his own eyes. Its Columbiad cannons were mounted on the *barbette*, which is what they called the fort's upper level. These were the largest guns in South Carolina, and they made a thunderous sound that could deafen a man. With a full charge of powder, these could propel a 225 pound shell almost two miles, and anything within one mile would be like shooting fish in a barrel. Incredibly, the *Planter* would have to pass within two hundred yards.

"I got a bad feeling about this," said Spider. "There are just too many guns on top of that wall."

"With the channel arranged as it is," Robert said, "I can't see that we have a choice."

"But what if we exit the channel and make a run for it... out to blue water?" Spider suggested. "If we stick to the main channel, they're sure to destroy us."

"If we skedaddle, they'll open fire on us for sure," Robert said. "It's certain death, and a coward's death at that."

"Then I'm gonna shut up, and just pray for a miracle," Spider said. "You're the Cap."

Robert couldn't help but smile. "It surely must be a day for miracles," he said. "I just heard Spider Jefferson say he was gonna shut up... and that he was going to pray."

"Well," Spider said, "You'd better write it down, for those are likely to be my last words."

Robert had often dreamed about this moment, anticipating that his heart would be filled with terror. But oddly, it was not fear that he found inside him now, and neither was it confidence. It was a growing anger that surmounted his fears and blew away all his doubts. He stared at the ominous walls and threatening cannons that seemed to darken the whole harbor and he spoke out loud to the fort. "Enough," was all he said.

Some on board who heard him now waited for him to continue, but that one word said what a hundred other words could not have embellished. *Enough* was all that he felt like saying and all that he needed to say. Just as his people had been terrorized by Beaufort's whips, curfews, and rail fences, Sumter now loomed as slavery's final affront – one remaining plantation master guarding the path out of South Carolina. This bully protected an entire world of oppression and servitude. Everything outside was the realm of free men.

No further words were needed; the matter was settled. They would stay the course and pass right by the fort, trusting the code and God to get them through. It seemed better this way. Robert concluded that even quick death would be a sort of victory now.

When they came within a thousand yards, Robert could hear the distant sound of Charleston's courthouse bell ringing out four o'clock. Up ahead, he saw three men running along the forts south wall towards the watchtower that faced Morris Island. The *Planter* had been sighted and now the only question was whether it would be codes or cannon. A twist in the current was now trying to push them off course, and the *Planter* had to make a half-turn, laboring into the teeth of a stiff Atlantic breeze. Their passage past Sumter would not be a quick hello.

"Spider and Chiz, come here," Robert commanded, "I need you to strut around a bit on deck. Flash your lanterns about, then come up to the bridge and salute me once or twice.

"Sounds stupid, if you ask me," said Spider.

"It may feel stupid, but it looks *Confederate*," Robert said. The Rebs on that wall are watching us, and we must do our best to do what they expect."

"Then *stupid* it is," Spider laughed. "I can look stupid in my sleep."

At two hundred yards, the channel was bringing them right alongside the fort. Robert could see a man on the tower looking them over through binoculars. Robert wondered how he looked from that distance. Not knowing what else to do, he adjusted his straw hat, puffed his longpipe, and waved vigorously. Chiz and Spider did a convincing job in their assigned parts. In a moment, there was the sounding of a foghorn – the customary request for the code.

Robert turned to bark orders, but Chiz already knew the drill. By now as adept as a musician in an orchestra, he pulled the whistle cord and sounded the bell like a virtuoso. One long, two bells, and four short. Everyone hiding below decks heard the whistles and bells, and then the dead silence that followed. They held hands and prayed to God.

"Captain Relyea requests to pass the *CSS Planter!*" Robert shouted.

The engines chugging loudly as they slowly made headway under the big guns of the fort, "Now the hard part," Robert whispered to Chiz. "Try to keep *breathing*." For almost half a minute there was no answer, then finally there were words came from the guard on the tower.

"Code received!" the man shouted, and then he uttered the most beautiful words Robert had ever heard in his life. "Sentinel, Pass the Planter! Give 'em hell, Captain! And keep your eyes peeled for torpedoes and Yankees!" Sumter's tower bell signaled their official approval to exit the harbor.

Robert considered a number of clever replies he might have thrown back to the fort, but it seemed best to let the Rebels have the last word. As before, he simply waved, convinced that the best thieves never trumpet their own success. They were finally headed for open water.

As soon as the word reached those in the engine room, Robert could hear the muffled shouts of joy and celebration coming from the folks below. Almost out of the harbor now, the bigger sea waves were striking the *Planter*'s bow at the rate of one every second. Deke and Dark John were overstoking the boilers to maximize their speed against the tide. Robert estimated it would take them about 300 more of these wave slaps to get them out of the range of those big cannons. He also figured the counting the waves might keep him from total lunacy.

Once he had passed 250 slaps, Robert began to count out loud and the boys on deck gathered around to listen. By the time he got to 300, all the crew and family members had made their way to the fore deck. He smiled down at them and nodded, but kept on counting the waves just to be on the safe side. Only when he hit 350, did he feel safe enough to hand the helm over to Abe Allston. It was time to celebrate.

Those on deck would never forget how Robert looked as he grandly made his way down from the wheelhouse. Tossing Relyea's pipe and that ludicrous hat into the sea, he grinned like a saint who was finally strutting through the Pearly Gates. His eyes were wide and bright as the sea wind blew the wisps of his beard in every direction. His crew and family members recall that he shouted over and over, "Praise God, We're free!" One by one, he grabbed each man, woman, and child and looked straight into each one's eyes, repeating louder and louder, "Praise God, We're free!" Most of them were too overcome, even to speak.

As they followed him around to the aft deck, they all began to sing, clap, and dance. Some pointed or waved toward the city, while others took the opportunity to spit astern, pronouncing their final curse upon their slave masters. Soon, they were inspired to form a big circle, with Spider in the middle, dancing like a madman. It was pure elation, the year of Jubilee.

With dawn finally breaking and only open water in front of them, Robert was free to look back at the wharves. The Confederate ships still slept at their moorings. There were no bells or alarms to be heard. Even if the Rebs could manage to signal Fort Moultrie or Battery Gregg, the *Planter* was well out of range now. Past the Atlantic horizon, Tuesday's sun was beginning to sparkle a thousand diamonds off the endless whitecaps. They, with God's help, had done it. They were free.

Chapter 45
The Unthinkable

Charleston's waterfront was just waking up as the first bells rang out the alarm. All along the Bay Street, a thousand sailors and soldiers were roused, still blurry from their sleep. Even without their usual jolt of coffee, every officer and the enlisted man was wide awake, buzzing about like a hive of tormented hornets. The Confederate flagship was missing and its colored ship hands with it. The unthinkable had happened.

At first some hoped the boat had departed earlier than usual to deliver the armaments to the batteries in the harbor, but after Captain Relyea and the *Planter's* two white officers were located, the worst was confirmed. As one by one the guards and reported to their superiors, things became clearer. The gunboat had been stolen some time during the early morning hours. The eight Negro crewmembers, some of whom were known to sleep on the boat, were nowhere to be found.

At first, one officer suggested that an attachment of Yankees might have sneaked ashore and led the raid, but interviews with the guards at the wharves and the nearest checkpoints made no mention of Union troops. Patrols confirmed that the *Planter's* black crew had worked well into the night. A few witnesses swore they had seen Captain Relyea wave to the gate guards sometime around three that morning. Just after that, two seamen on the *CSS Sullivan* had seen the Planter leaving the South Wharf. Everyone insisted they had followed military protocol. Nonetheless, there was an obtrusively empty space at berth Number Six.

Later interviews certified that the ship had followed the South Channel through the harbor and had successfully navigated past all five checkpoints on their exit, each time giving the proper signal code. The unimaginable truth was becoming clear, and it hit them like the explosion of a ship's boiler. A group of illiterate slaves had, right under their noses, sailed off with their flagship. No one doubted that there would be hell to pay – enough holy hell for everybody.

Nervous men scurried about, mustering crews and untying ropes, feigning some plausible attempt to apprehend the long-departed thieves.

For nearly an hour there was cursing, sweating and fist-pumping, as they came to recognize the bitter truth. There was nothing that could be done now. They had no vessel up to steam and, even if they had one, there was no hope of overtaking the *CSS Planter* as it became a shrinking speck on the horizon.

Those in roles of responsibility began quickly to point fingers of blame. Word soon traveled to the very top of the chain of command. General Robert E. Lee himself advised that those responsible for the lapse in security should be held accountable. *The Charleston Mercury* recommended that the wharf guards should be court-marshalled, the *Planter*'s officers should be imprisoned, and that the negligent sentries at every checkpoint should be shot at once. An unabated torrent of public suggestions were similarly draconian.

Every military man pointed toward someone lower in rank, but most civilians cried for the heads of those at the top. High-ranking officers and politicians shouted and shook their fists at each other, while most underlings maintained anonymous silence, pretending to be ignorant, or occupied with some duty or other. When noble necks are on the block, humble men find comfort in the shadows of their betters. It was a good day to be nobody.

Black dock workers and stevedores also tended to their own affairs, doing their best to keep their thoughts to themselves. It was a time to maintain silence and look industrious. Slaves made sure to avoid eye contact with any white person, and if they happened to exchange glances with another black, they were sure to hold back any word or expression.

Each of them, of course, understood the exuberance that now swelled in every one of their hearts. Colored men had stolen the Rebel's prize. Amidst all the uproar, each slave kept a single image in the corner of his eye – the empty place at Wharf Number Six. Where yesterday a 147-foot Confederate gunboat floated, today there was nothing but dark water and five untied, floating ropes. The void between the boats moored at wharves five and seven was glorious to them, as eloquent and miraculous as if it had been the empty tomb of the Lord Jesus himself. Eight slaves had gone to glory, and for once they hadn't had to perish to get there.

The whites, of course, wanted immediate revenge. Huffy townspeople began to opine in vivid detail what Old Testament-styled punishments should be meted out to these African scoundrels. Hanging, burning, and dismemberment were proposed, with many people suggesting various combinations of these. In its evening edition, the *Charleston Daily Courier* would recommend public torture, but such recompense, though longed for, was never to come.

Never had a city felt so despondent at sunrise. All through that day, people met to vent their anger at public meetings. More spiritual souls sought comfort at prayer services – as if they had been mourning the loss of some dear loved one. General Ripley, whose home was only a hundred feet from Pier Six, at first contemplated suicide, but instead fired eleven of his subordinates.

The waterfront was crowded all morning, as it seemed everyone in Charleston had come out to help, to grieve, or to hear the latest rumors of what happened. Reporters interrogated witnesses, politicians made speeches, and hawkers sold hundreds of apples, biscuits, and sandwiches to the onlookers.

Lieutenant Sam and Liddie McKee were among them, still holding hands as they had all night. As they watched the excitement along the waterfront, Sam was more jovial than Liddie would have expected. "Well, it looks like I won't be getting my key back," he chuckled. "I'm likely to be in a bit of hot water for this."

"You'll be punished?" she asked.

"Probably, but not killed. Not with so many heads on the chopping block," he said. "I suspect they'd have to jail half the soldiers in Charleston, officers first."

"How far do you think the thieves will get?" she asked.

Sam scanned the horizon, shading his eyes from the growing brightness of the dawn. "If I know Robert, they'll get as far as he's got a notion to get," Sam said. "He was my first black friend, you know."

"But not your last, I expect," she whispered. "A new world's coming." Sam just nodded as he put his arm around Liddie and led her through the chaotic crowd. "I don't think you have to worry about being on time for work this morning," she said. "Let's get some breakfast."

"Sounds good," Sam said as he turned to take one last glance down the South Wharf. Past the frantic crowds, he noticed the dark silhouette of a man who was looking out to sea.

Alone, and almost unnoticed at the end of the pier, stood Captain C. J. Relyea. Hatless, in baggy house-pants and a faded nightshirt, he was almost unrecognizable. Now bereft of his resplendent uniform, his longpipe, and his wide hat, he appeared to be just another old man in the crowd. He might well have considered such anonymity a blessing. The flagship of the Confederate fleet was gone, and his mind could imagine no scenario in which he would not be blamed for the entire debacle.

Relyea just stared toward Fort Sumter, too stunned to talk, and too much a man to cry aloud. His mind was filled with a single vision. Somewhere in the far reaches of the harbor, a 23-year-old slave boy now donned his uniform, smoked his pipe and commanded his ship. The *CSS Planter* and its dark helmsman, along with the captain's hopes for personal glory, were presently steaming out toward blue water and the dark row of ships that were the Union fleet.

By now, a score of freed slaves had gathered on the foredeck of the *Planter*, and not one of them was looking back. Standing in the wheelhouse above them, Robert inhaled deeply as he surveyed the brightening horizon, wishing his ship might exceed its maximum speed of 13 knots. With the wind and tide in their face, progress was slow, but every wave-slap on the bow took them another fathom farther from slavery.

Above the sound of the engine and the sea, he and his friends could hear distant echoes behind them, as every bell, horn, and snare drum in Charleston announced that the unimaginable had happened. All on their own, a pack of lowly slaves had stolen a gunboat, and the flagship at that. Robert's only regret was that he could not be there to witness the anger of the Confederates. They were furious at the loss of their best ship and, most of all, at the Africans who had hoodwinked the best military minds of the South.

The victors cared little about the consternation of Charleston, or anything else they had left behind. They were too busy laughing and embracing one another, reveling like Irishmen at a rich man's wedding. They sang mostly hymns, for their joy was in every way a spiritual celebration. *Swing Low, Sweet Chariot, Steal Away to Jesus,* and *I'm a-Rollin'* were all songs about departure, about traveling, and about the Promised Land. And for the first time in their lives, they sang of a land that was not far off. Faith had become sight.

Freedom Land waited half a mile away in that line of Union boats. Here on deck, eloquent hands were pressed against sweating foreheads, raised to heaven, and then waved to and fro. God's name was glorified as a hundred kisses were blown toward the highest reaches of the blue sky. Men, women and children, some unshod, danced to ancient tunes and deep rhythms that swelled up from centuries of pain. A fountain of tears came too, and flowed as each one in turn glanced back one final time at the fading horizon of South Carolina. Farewell, slavery. It all seemed like the happy ending to some long-suppressed dream. They were finally free, and with a brave black Moses manning the wheel.

"Stoke her fine, boys!" Robert shouted to the men below. "Make her blaze! The Yankees are gonna want to get hold of their new prize."

Even in the darkness of the engine room, the sooty faces of Dark John and Deke Gradine glowed with bright smiles. Robert knew, of course, that the boilers were already fully fired, but he nonetheless liked the sound of his voice shouting orders for a change.

They were almost there. Robert squinted into the rays of the rising sun as stiff morning breezes and salt spray blew against his face. The orange brushstrokes of dawn lined every far-off cloud to the east, and a row of Federal vessels were sketched against this backdrop, looking infinitely prettier than the stick drawings they had scribbled on their escape plan.

Hearing the shout hatch snap open, he looked down to see Deke's sweaty head looking up at him. "How far we got to go?" he shouted.

"Not far," Robert replied. "We've got a bit of tide and wind in our face, but nary a ship on our tail. How's our steam holding?"

"Holding well," Deke said. "Got hell fire in our boilers and heaven on our mind."

Robert smiled as he scanned the far horizon, bobbing his head urgently like a child waiting for something sweet. As the shout hatch slammed shut, he now heard a faint and unfamiliar sound. For the first time Robert could remember, Deke and Dark John were singing boisterously together. The ebullient music of free men. He never knew they could sing so well.

As full daylight arrived, those on deck began to congregate along the bow railing, wanting to catch their first clear look at the Union ship and the sailors who would welcome them to their new life. Their song became louder as the words of *Steal Away*, familiar to all of them, rang out.

Steal away, steal away, steal away to Jesus,
Steal away, steal away home.
Ain't got long to stay here.

But a thousand yards away, the sailors on the bridge of the *USS Onward* could hear nothing. A sentinel ran to inform its commander, Lieutenant J. F. Nichols, that an unknown vessel was approaching. They had seen its lights leave the harbor in the darkness of pre-dawn.

"It appears to be heading straight for us," the ensign said. "We figured it would turn at Fort Sullivan, but it just keeps on coming."

Nichols' hands were steady as he looked through his long eyeglass at the *Planter*. "It's a gunboat for sure," he said, "And she's making straight for us."

"Your orders, sir?" the boy asked, "Shall we prepare to fire?"

"Sound the general alarm," he commanded. "All men to their posts! Prepare to fire at my order!" the captain shouted. The pounding of snare drums and the blast of a bugle called every Union sailor into action. The sound quickly reached the distant wheelhouse of the *Planter*.

Robert's smile turned suddenly cold as, all along the side of the Union vessel, gun ports began to pop open. One by one, the ominous barrels of cannon began to emerge. "Dear God," he said. "They're afraid of us!"

Against the sunrise, Robert could see the dark silhouettes of Union sailors scurrying on the decks and up the rigging of the *Onward*. A lone figure of an officer stood atop her aft rail, his arm pointed toward the sky, but this was not a greeting. He was preparing to signal a broadside.

"They think we're the enemy!" Robert shouted. "Clear the deck!"

Songs of praise suddenly turned to wails as the women and children dispersed in every direction. Some flattened themselves on the deck while others knelt down where they were. Others grabbed children and ran toward the aft deck. "What's happening?" Hannah asked, holding the baby tight to her bosom. In a short moment, the bliss of heaven had turned into Armageddon.

In the distance, Robert saw the bright flash of a cannon from the bow port of the Federal ship. The boom of the gun arrived two seconds later, just after a splash was seen about 100 feet off the *Planter*'s bow. Uncontrolled shouting and crying came from those gathered on the aft deck. Deke and Dark John came topside to see what was happening.

"It's a warning shot!" Robert shouted, "Get down behind the bulkheads!

His mind was frantic. Had they come all this way just to be blown to bits? Below him, the mothers were doing their best to comfort and cover the crying children as they all clung to each together. None of them uttered a word, but Robert could feel their eyes on him, and from all those eyes he could feel fear mixed with accusation. He felt like Moses at the Red Sea. Had he rescued his little flock from slavery only to see them all swallowed up by the gaping jaws of death? He had to do something, but what?

Suddenly, it was Deke who shouted, "Look up!"

"Ain't time to pray!" Robert screamed.

"No," said Deke. "Look!" He was pointing to something up over Robert's head. The flag. They were still flying the Rebel stars and bars on their wheelhouse pole.

"God in heaven!" Robert shouted. "Get that flag and bring it down!"

As David Jones scrambled up to the base of the pole, Robert's heart pounded in double-time, like the piercing sound of the snare drums that now echoed from the Yankee ship. As the Confederate insignia crept snail-like down the flagpole, we wondered if the Union sailors be able to see. The next silent moments felt like an eternity.

"Stand up, everyone!" Robert screamed as he spun the helm to starboard. "And wave your hands so they can see we mean them no harm." He waved both of his own arms and prayed to like he'd never prayed before. The *Planter* had drawn within 500 yards now, and Robert's eyes were glued to the raised arm of the Union commander. If that hand dropped, it would be the end of them.

He could now hear the voice of the *Onward's* commander.

"Prepare a full broadside!" Lieutenant Nichols shouted, "and hold ready."

Robert turning to those on deck, Robert's eyes racied from face to face. "A white flag!" he shouted. "We've gotta raise a white flag or we're all dead!"

"We don't have nothing like that," said Chiz, his face streaming with sweat and his wide eyes blinking with fear.

"Find us something white." answered Robert.

At 300 yards now, he could now clearly discern the muzzles of the twelve cannon that were primed to put an end to all their dreams. It was then that Hannah appeared on the bridge. Her arms to her side, she was moving quite strangely, reaching for something under her long brown dress. Her face was set firmly, in that all-business way of hers.

"Here," she said, offering him a large, silk petticoat. "Don't be mad, baby. I stole it from Eliza Ancrum's dresser last week."

"Oh you beautiful, clever, thief!" Robert said, handing the garment to David, who hurriedly sent their opulent flag of truce up the pole. Hannah twisted the young man's ankle firmly and chided him, "You take care with that petticoat!" she implored, "I'm gonna want it back."

David's hands fumbled nervously as he secured the corners of the garment to the rope and yanked it up the mast as fast as he could. As its sumptuous silk unfurled in the breeze, Robert broke into a grin. But it wasn't time for smiles yet. Within 50 yards now, a loud voice could be heard from the deck of the *Onward*.

"Ready," he shouted, "Aim…" They were close enough to hear the clicking of the lanyards as the *Onward's* number four gunners grasped the trigger cords tightly. They were seconds from blowing the *Planter* out of the water.

Robert's people were frantically jumping and waving their arms, but by now they sensed it might be too late. Almost in unison, they were saying, "O Lord! O Lord!" In a moment that seemed to last forever, they closed their eyes and waited for the thunder of the cannons, but the only sound that came was the hushed hiss of the wind and the slapping of the waves against the hull. In that dead silence, some would later say they heard the voice of God.

"Hold!" shouted Commander Nichols. "Hold your fire!" Though his spyglass, the lieutenant could now clearly make out the people on the deck of the *Planter*. "These are not Rebs!" he screamed, "only coloreds. They seem to be surrendering."

At his words, the sailors on the deck of the *Onward* gave a sustained cheer, but it was not nearly as loudly as the celebration on the *Planter*. Men, women, and children, all now free, were jumping, leaping, and praising God with a joy that must have rocked the gates of Heaven. Spider had embraced and lifted up Robert, carrying him round and round on the deck, almost dropping him over the port rail at one point, all in the irrational madness of liberation.

In the minutes that followed, Lieutenant Nichols ordered the *Onward* to be brought alongside the *Planter*, dispatching an ensign and twelve Union sailors to take charge of the vessel and its passengers. Robert Smalls, his family and his friends were to be taken aboard the Union ship and then transported down to Union Headquarters at Hilton Head.

"Good morning, sir," Robert said as he was brought eye to eye with the *Onward's* commander. "I'm helmsman Robert Smalls, and I've brought you some of the old United States' guns."

"How many people have you got with you?" the Lieutenant asked.

"I've got eight other crew members, five women, and five children. All of us slaves," Robert said. "Or *former* slaves, I should say."

Nichols seemed at a loss for words. "You must forgive me if I appear a bit surprised," he said. "Your arrival was unanticipated."

"Well," Robert answered with a smile, "our *survival* was also a bit unanticipated. I'm still pinching myself."

"You know we came close to killing you, don't you?" asked Nichols. "It's lucky you got that white flag up in time."

"I know, sir," said Robert. "but we've gotten pretty accustomed to dancing with the devil. My heart was pounding."

Just then a young officer came in to report to Lieutenant Nichols. "We've searched the ship, sir. We've found no Confederates on board sir, only these coloreds. They've got some heavy ordinance in the hold."

"Refurbished guns from Sumter, sir," said Robert. "They were being dispatched to Fort Ripley, but we *diverted* them, so to speak."

"Well done," said Nichols. "This is an encouragement for our side. How on earth did you get the notion to pull this thing off?"

"Well, sir," Robert chuckled. "You might say it started with some stolen chickens." He then proceeded to recount the details of their conspiracy and escape, blow by blow. The longer Robert talked, the more Nichols was amazed. The whole tale was still pretty amazing to Robert, too.

"Well," said Nichols, "I'm not sure where things go from here. You've done an extraordinary thing, and I suspect you'll provide some very useful information about the harbor and its defenses. You'll be sent to meet with Admiral Du Pont."

"If you'll permit me, sir," Robert said. "Would it be possible for me to have a word with my crew before we're dispersed?"

"Yes, of course," Nichols said. "My ensign and his men will accompany you back to your vessel."

On the foredeck of the *Planter*, the sun was now beating down hot on all of them as they gathered around to hear whatever words Robert had for them. The Union ensign stepped to the side, waiting with a squad of well-uniformed men along the starboard gunwale. Robert's friends stood in a circle, and for once, even Spider held his tongue.

"The good Lord has delivered us to freedom," Robert began, "and now he's the only one who knows where we'll end up. But I suppose that by now we've got ourselves used to the idea of jumping into the dark. For some reason, God saw fit to bring us into this world as slaves. Some of us like Chisholm, Jackson, and Turno got scars on their backs from that life. Some like Abe Allston saw their families stole from them, and others like Deke were stripped of their professions. Slavery hurt Dark John so bad that he hardly says a word, and it hurt Spider so much that all he does is chatter like a jaybird." They all chuckled, but everyone was still arm in arm.

"But some time back," Robert said, "just a few months ago really, God put a different sort of notion in our heads. The dream of stealing a boat and sailin' to safety. Whites would've said it was a crazy notion that didn't belong in a slave's empty head, but the notion came nonetheless. Time and time again they came close to stopping us. Truth is, there were days we came pretty close to stoppin' ourselves. But in the Lord's good time, and with a little help of our engineers and a twitch of the helm by yours truly, we managed to take a nice little boat ride together." They all smiled at this, many wiping happy tears.

"What we did together was something special, but if white men keep writing all the books, I doubt we'll find any place in history. But that's all right, because it's now just a little ripple of water in our wake. We didn't risk our lives to get in some book, we did it to get free. Free with our families, free to have a say-so, and free to chase whatever good dreams we've got a mind to chase.

"The world didn't just hand us our freedom, and we can't guarantee what the future may hold. God's done put the helm in my hand... and in yours. All I want to say is that it was an honor to risk my life alongside you good people. Heaven has set our feet on a good path. Let's vow to make the best of it."

At this point they all burst into cheering and crying. Hugs, tender words, and congratulations were passed all around. Even the squad of sailors from the *Onward* applauded with enthusiasm at Robert's speech. None of them, white or black, would forget this day as long as they lived.

Chapter 46
Boy to Man

The slaves' capture of the *Planter* was not good news to white Southerners, so it wasn't surprising that the story was not widely publicized. Even on the Union side, details of the exploit were closely guarded, as the Navy sought to use the boat, and the intelligence information provided by the crew, for military purposes.

By the end of the summer, the report that Negroes had stolen the Rebel flagship had reached Beaufort. The Federal soldiers there, and especially the newly-freed slaves, were greatly encouraged by news of the theft, but most folks were doing their best just to stay alive. Robert's mother Lydia was particularly dismayed by an announcement that came to her on a cloudy Monday in August.

"It looks like you'll have to leave this place, Miss Lydia," said a young Union soldier. "Word is that the McKee house is scheduled to be auctioned off."

Lydia had long expected this axe to fall. Federal officers had been roosting in the McKee house since Beaufort fell, but everyone knew it would be sold off at some point. After surviving six decades of slavery, she had learned to roll with the punches, but it was a bit unnerving that she didn't know who the buyer would be. She hoped the new owner might still require her services. Now 66, she didn't fancy having to look for a whole new way of life. Her little shack behind the McKee's had been her home since she was thirteen.

"I reckon somebody will need deep pockets to pay the piper for this place," she told the young soldier. "Think they'll be Union people?"

"Oh yes, ma'am, I would reckon so," the boy said. "Wouldn't do to have slavers take back what we took from them fair and square. My captain says some buyers are coming down to make bids."

"Well, tell 'em I'd be proud to serve them," she said. "I ain't keen on the prospect that I might be put out on the streets."

For the next weeks, Lydia busied herself with cooking for the Union officers, but when the bluecoats began to clear out of the big house on

August 24th, she began to pray a bit more than usual. She knew it wasn't right for a Christian to worry, but it seemed to her that a bit of worrying was called for in this case.

Her friend Leena had a special way of walking when she had news, and on the 27th, she came scooting up Prince Street with that walk. "Well, it's a fine kettle, it is," she said.

"What?" said Lydia.

"They done nailed up the list of the auctions," she said. "The McKee place is one of the twelve, all right."

"How long we got?" Lydia asked.

"Just a week," said Leena. "They set the sale for the second of September. We can find you a bed down my way, if you like."

"Well," Lydia said. "The Lord said, 'Foxes have holes and birds got nests.' I guess I've got myself pretty attached to this little nest of mine. The Lord's will provide another, I suppose."

Lydia had trouble sleeping that whole next week. Pray though she might, her heart was filled with fears. She made up her mind to walk down to the armory the day before the auction was to take place, just to look around. She wanted to pray.

Like every other slave in Beaufort County, she hated this place. It was quiet and empty now, of course, but the auction block was nonetheless populated with ghosts. Old homes and furniture had been sold off here, along with many of her slave friends. Lydia had seen the whippings here, and her mind echoed with the memories of the gavel-hits that sent her people to the sweltering fields of the Sea Islands. Most of these folks were dead now, praising God before his throne in heaven, but she sensed their spirits still lingered in this despicable place.

Lydia kept telling herself it was different now. She was, at least on paper, emancipated. Since the Yankees came, she was liberated. 'Liberated for what?' she asked herself. Since being freed, she was only free to do what she had been doing for the past sixty years. Her free tasks were identical to those her ancestors had done, cooking, cleaning, and toting things, all for white people who had more money and less sense than she did. And now, here she stood, again at this auction block. The very place where her ancestors had stood, waiting to find out who they would serve next.

Black folks in Beaufort kept reminding each other that they were free and that they earned their own wages now. But all of them knew well, that after paying for their food and the roof over their head, most of them were even less well off than before, still slaves in most respects.

But this time they were slaves to poverty rather than to some white family. Lydia wasn't sure which was worse.

Now her highest hope hung on the possibility that the new owner of the McKee house might keep her on. If not hired, she would be homeless by tomorrow night. If her best dream came true, she could finish out her final years cooking for the new folks, living in that little shack behind theirs. Hired servant or slave, it was all just about the same.

Trudging slowly home, she resolved to take her mind off of her poisonous and ungrateful worries. She reasoned that she should be thankful. The crepe myrtles were in bloom, and even the abandoned houses had persistent geraniums and petunias popping up here and there in the flowerbeds. She told herself that every day of life in God's big world was a blessing.

As she walked up the last little section of New Street, he could feel the warmth of the setting sun on her back. Behind her she could hear the distant horn-blast of a steamship coming into port. The boat had likely brought in some rich folks for tomorrow's auction. As always, things were in the good Lord's hands.

The next morning, she woke early. Though Beaufort's auctions no longer included the sale of human beings, Lydia still counted them among the most depressing events a body could witness. With the hard times brought on by the war, families here had been selling just about every precious thing they had ever owned. Almost every week there were homes, goods, and horses lined up for disposal. Perhaps more touching were the children's garments, family paintings, and various personal keepsakes. Anything might be sold off for a greenback dollar – even pints of corn meal or a tin of salt. These auctions were the hell-side version of judgment day.

A crowd of perhaps a hundred people had turned out for this one. They were mostly white folks, but some blacks, too. Many of the wealthier folks had come with large rolls of U.S. currency, since most sales required cash rather than useless bank paper. Lydia, of course, was not there to bid but to watch, and sad entertainment it was. She felt something like a mourner, but also a little bit like a vulture.

At first she paid little attention as various work animals and objects changed hands. There were so many! It seemed strange to Lydia that, after every sale, the crowd clapped loudly for the winner. No one acknowledged the tragedy that there was also a loser, who went home with a few coins to compensate for the loss of their life's dreams. Even sadder were those whose valuables got no bids at all, and boxes of keepsakes had been carried to auction that morning, felt even heavier on the sad trip home.

Lydia quietly prayed as the time drew near for the McKee Mansion to be sold. In these house sales, the auctioneer never mentioned any family by name, simply announcing, "Up for bid: the property at such-and-such Street in Beaufort, South Carolina." By the time 511 Prince Street hit the block, she could feel herself breathing shallow, rapid breaths. She even imagined that there was the sound of a drumroll or of foot-stomping, but it was merely the racing of her own heart. "The Lord is my shepherd," she kept saying to herself.

"What is offered?" the man shouted. "Who will bid me five hundred? Do I hear five?" After a moment, a heavy-set man in the front tipped the brim of his hat, signifying his bid. "Five!"

"I have five hundred!" the auctioneer said. "Who's prepared to give me five-fifty? Do I hear five fifty?"

Robert's mother was not accustomed to hearing such large sums mentioned out loud, but it seemed to her that the house had to be worth far more than this. She reasoned that all the really rich folks had stayed up north.

She couldn't say that she blamed them. Since all these mansions had been confiscated by the Union, no one seemed to be very concerned with making a profit. Beaufort was a buyer's market and the government just wanted somebody to take these places off their hands. How Lydia wished she had the dollars to make a bid!

"Five-fifty," came a shrill voice from the other side of the crowd. This was Gerrit Lafayette, a local who had recently lost all his land and slaves in the Union occupation. He was one of the few white kingpins who had refused to run inland. Lafayette was known to be miserly in his dealings, and was a harsh slave master. It was said he had killed more than a few of his own field hands. Lydia gasped at the thought that he might end up being the high bidder on the house. 'I'd rather starve on the street,' she thought.

"We have a bid of five-fifty," the barker shouted. "Will anyone bid six? Six hundred dollars for this fine place!"

Next to Lydia, a white man leaned over to his wife, "This is robbery," he whispered. "Henry McKee would be outraged."

Lydia could not disagree. Surely some good man would be pleased to buy such a place for so little.

"I'll do Six!" shouted the fat man in the front row, forgetting to tip the brim of his hat this time. "Six hundred!" And so the bidding went, as Lafayette and the big man duked it out.

In less than a minute they had run the price up to eight hundred, and the crowd was beginning to get excited. Lydia was no longer praying silently but whispering out loud now, "Oh Lord God," she pleaded. "Please be with the fat man."

The heavy-set man was ahead now, having bid eight twenty-five, but after a long silence, Gerrit Lafayette's ugly voice barked out, "Eight-fifty! My final offer." Lydia, the auctioneer, and everyone else let out a huge sigh. Then their eyes flashed up to the front row, but the fat man just lowered his head and pulled his hat down over his face. He was done.

The auctioneer scanned the sea of faces for anyone who might have been waiting for this moment. "It's a sizeable mansion, folks!" he said. "And there's one last chance! Do I hear nine?" But for what seemed to Lydia as an eternity, no voices came. Lafayette stood up and began to receive smiling congratulations from his cronies.

"We've an offer of eight-fifty!" the auctioneer shouted. Do I hear nine? Eight-fifty going once! Eight fifty going twice!"

Suddenly, there came a deep voice from the very back row. "Nine!" the man shouted.

At that, the place went quite, but immediately started buzzing. Lydia couldn't see who had made the big bid, but she had heard an audible sigh and a murmuring through the crowd. There was chatter, and then a rising roar from across the room. People were moving aside for whoever it was as he made his way through the crowd toward the front. Who was this?

"Quiet now!" the barker shouted. "I've got a bid of nine!" Everyone in the front was looking back at Gerrit Lafayette, but he just shook his head, wanting no more of this action. "Do I hear nine-fifty?" the auctioneer asked, but the crowd was dead quiet. I've got nine hundred! Nine once! Nine twice!" For good or ill, it was all over. "Sold!" he screamed. "Sold to, sold to..."

"To me," the buyer's voice shouted. "Robert Smalls!" Lydia thought her poor old heart was going to stop dead. Had she heard right? Before her disbelieving eyes, the crowd continued to part as Robert made his way to the table to make his mark. Folks, even the white ones, stepped back on either side, standing like the walls of the Red Sea. Up to Beaufort's old auction block came her own son, dressed now in the dark blues of a Navy Commander, a roll of United States dollars in his hand.

Some of the white onlookers turned and walked away, complaining audibly among themselves as they went. Blacks in the crowd were wise enough to hold their applause, but every one of their hearts was overflowing with amazement and joy. Former boy and troublemaker Robert Smalls had just purchased the McKee mansion where he had served as a slave. Having received a reward of half the value of the *CSS Planter*, Robert was not only a war hero but was now a rich man to boot.

As the last few people exited the armory area, Robert stood with Hannah and the children at the auction block with the legal papers in both his hands. The only other person left was his mother, who stood by herself in the back, silent and unmoved from the place where she had been standing. She wanted to walk over to where her son and his family were, but her feet seemed frozen to the cobblestones beneath her.

"I'm coming, Mama," he shouted, walking towards her, handing the paperwork to Hannah. "It's ours now, Mama," he said. "Ours, free and clear."

"So you're the one," Lydia said. "The one they've been callin' the boat thief."

"I hoped you'd be proud," he said, embracing her as tightly as a grown man can hug a woman of her age. "I know you taught me not to steal, but I confess. I took that warship from the Rebs, and today, I pretty much stole the McKee house as well. Your Christian boy's been doing a lot of thieving."

"Well it ain't the McKee's no more," she said. "It's your house now."

"No, Mama, it's *ours*," he said. "Bought and paid for."

They exchanged kisses they would never forget, and some chit-chat none of them would remember. All rational thoughts were drowned in a sea of joyful tears. The familiar streets of town stretched out before them, dreamlike as they walked towards Prince Street. The myrtles were bright with blooms and the first green pecans were just now appearing in the trees above.

Halfway up New Street, the town bell rang, calling black children to their afternoon arithmetic class. Robert stopped everyone in their tracks.

"Is that slave curfew?" he joked. "We best hurry on back to the big house before we meet up with trouble." All the adults laughed, but little Elizabeth couldn't understand what was so funny.

At the top of the hill, they stopped again as Lydia pointed to where the setting sun's rays illuminated the distant shore of Ladies' Island. "That's the place I called home when I was little," she said. The children had a hundred questions for her, and she hoped she would live long enough to tell them every detail of her life's journey. This day was just one moment in a long story, but it was a precious moment, marking as it did, both an end and a beginning.

The big house looked the same, but felt altogether different. The women went inside to make some supper, but this time it wasn't for a master but for them, and for the family they loved. When Lydia and Hannah opened the swing-doors to the pantry, the shelves were for the most part bare.

"Not much to pick from," Lydia said, shaking her head. "Soldiers' grub. We're gonna be hard pressed to make supper from this little bit of nothing."

"Be thankful, Miss Lydia," Hannah said. "Just look at all this empty space you've got here." Hannah then proceeded to rub her hand over the pristine emptiness of each shelf. "An empty shelf's a beautiful thing," she said. "Just stand before these shelves and close your eyes. This ain't Jane McKee's kitchen no more, it's yours. Keep them eyes closed and tell me what you see."

"Well," old Lydia began, timidly at first. "First of all, we won't have no jars of that awful raisin sauce Missy Jane used to put on everything. And none of that fatty potmeat Henry McKee fancied."

"Good," Hannah said. "Now you're talking."

Lydia then raised up her hand and pointed with her old black fingers. Her eyes were still closed and her hand was shaking nervously. "Right up there, all along that whole top shelf, that's where we're gonna keep the vegetable preserves – yams, butter squash and blackeyes. Lots of blackeyes."

"And big full bags of onions, taters, and cornmeal," said Hannah. "Where we gonna put all of 'em?"

"Here, down below," Lydia said with a smile. "Down low on the floor. We ain't gonna have no slaves to lift 'em down from above. For good or bad, this is my kitchen now. We're gonna make things better from now on. Gonna set things up right."

Hannah moved up close now, wrapping her strong arm around Robert's mother. Lydia opened her eyes now and saw that there were tears rolling down both of Hannah's cheeks.

"What's wrong?' she asked. "Why you crying, child?"

"I lost my mama a while back," Hannah whispered. "Never got to say goodbye or hug her neck at the end. She'd have died to see this big kitchen, but I'd give it all up for just one chance to kiss her cheek again. I surely miss her."

"I ain't never had a daughter," Lydia said. "But I'd be pleased to be just a little bit of a mama to you. And a grandma to your girls."

At that moment, Hannah no longer felt like the queen of the Baines Hotel. Her eyes welled with unashamed tears as she held Lydia to her breast. At 38 now, she was once again somebody's little girl. "I love you, Mama," she said, staring face to face into the old woman's eyes.

"God has showed his love on us," Lydia whispered.

"But I've gotta warn you," smiled Hannah, "I *do* like to run things."

Lydia just nodded with a mother's smile on her lips. "The Lord smite us if we can't get along in a big place like this."

From the kitchen window, the women looked out across the back yard. The flowers of summer spread their Edenic blooms through every corner of the garden. In the distance, Robert and the children were just now kneeling at the entrance to the old slave cottage. He had taken out his pocket knife and was busy carving a new notch on the gray wood of the old doorpost.

"What on earth are they up to?" Hannah asked.

Robert's mother brought two fingers to her lips and closed her eyes. "Boy to man," was all she whispered. "Boy to man."

An Epilogue

It should surprise none of us that Robert Smalls went on to do great things. The theft of the *CSS Planter* was only the first of his noteworthy exploits. A longer and more detailed account is even more astounding, and would include:

- In 1862, a resolution of the United States Congress named Robert Smalls "the first hero of the American Civil War," for his theft of the Confederate ship. He and his crewmembers received recognition for their bravery and cash rewards totaling half the value of the *CSS Planter*.

- After the loss of their ship, the Confederates put a price on Robert's head, but no punishment even fell upon him. A court martial sentenced Captain Relyea, Sam Smith, and Zerich Pitcher to fines and imprisonment, but their convictions were overturned on the grounds that a military court had no jurisdiction over contract employees.

- Robert's knowledge of Charleston Harbor and Confederate military secrets proved to be invaluable in helping the Union cause. He provided intelligence that allowed Federal forces to seize fortifications around the Stono River, which became a base of Union operations against Charleston for the duration of the war.

- In late 1862, he traveled to Washington and had successful meetings with Abraham Lincoln to urge the formation of African American regiments for the Union Army. Black units like the 54th Massachusetts Volunteer Infantry (featured in the 1989 movie *Glory*) were sent to spearhead Union attacks around Charleston in 1863.

- In 1863, The *Planter* was taken to Philadelphia for repairs and refitting. During his seven months there, Smalls hired two tutors who taught him to read.

- Robert was eventually assigned to return to Charleston where he served as helmsman aboard the *Planter* again. Over the next two years, he won acclaim for heroism in 17 separate military engagements of the Civil War.

- In one of these battles when the *Planter* was ambushed by Confederate cannon fire, the Union captain abandoned his post (and was later demoted for cowardice in battle). Robert assumed command, fought his way out, and saved the ship. As a reward for his bravery, he was promoted to be captain of the *Planter*, making him the first African American to command a warship in the U. S. Navy.

- With the money he received for stealing the boat, Robert purchased the Prince Street mansion where he had served as a slave. He and Hannah had five children together and remained married until her death in 1883. Robert and members of his family lived in that house for the next 90 years.

- After the surrender of the Charleston in 1865, Robert Smalls returned to Fort Sumter in the *Planter* to watch as the American flag was once again raised there.

- Smalls served as commander of the *Planter* until his discharge from military service on June 11, 1865. At war's end, he was sworn into the South Carolina Militia and was assigned the rank of Major General.

- Upon his retirement from military service, Robert was granted a full captain's pension.

- Henry and Jane McKee were left impoverished by the war and received ongoing financial assistance from Robert and Hannah. Their relationship was always a friendly one. Henry McKee passed away in 1875.

- Many years later Jane Bold McKee, elderly and with dementia, was found wandering the streets of Beaufort. Robert took her in and allowed her to live out her years in her old bedroom in the big house. He played along, allowing her to believe she was still the mistress of the house until her death in 1904.

- Elizabeth Jane (Liddie) McKee went on to marry and have children with a man named Edwin M. Bailey. She remained friends with Robert and resided in Beaufort until her death in 1924. Liddie lived long enough to see women finally receive the right to vote.

- In his post-war years, Robert Smalls was recognized as one of the leading citizens of Beaufort County, South Carolina. Robert served for two years (1868-1870) in South Carolina's House of Representatives, and from 1870 until 1875, he served in South Carolina's State Senate. He participated in drafting the new constitution for the state in which he had been a slave.

- In 1875, Robert Smalls became the first African American to represent South Carolina in the U. S. House of Representatives, where he served five terms (1875-79, 1882-87). During his five terms in Congress, Robert Smalls championed the civil rights of African Americans and those of mixed race.

- In his later years, Smalls establish a successful business in Beaufort, a general store for freedmen. In his later years, Smalls served as U. S. Collector of Customs in Beaufort.

- Robert Smalls died in his sleep at his Prince Street home on February 23, 1915. He was survived by his two daughters and a son.

- In 1975, his house at 501 Prince Street was designated a National Historic Landmark by the U. S. Department of the Interior.

- In 2004, the U.S. Army commissioned the *Major General Robert*

Smalls, the first U.S. Army vessel named for a Civil War hero and the first to bear the name of an African American.

- Camp Robert Smalls was a part of the Naval Training Station at Great Lakes, Illinois, where African American recruits underwent basic training in 1942.

- In Beaufort, South Carolina, there is a Robert Smalls Middle School and the Robert Smalls Parkway. Many other public landmarks still bear his name.

- Though Robert Smalls has many living descendants, none of them have the last name Smalls. His first son, Robert Junior, died in childhood. Robert's second son, William, had only one son, Robert, who had no male offspring.

- Robert Smalls' list of descendants includes many people of note. His great, great grandson, Michael Boulware Moore, has been selected to head the new International African American Museum in Charleston, SC.

Other Books About Robert Smalls

Captain of the Planter: The Story of Robert Smalls by Dorothy Sterling, Pocket Books, New York, 1958.

From Slave to Civil War Hero: The Life and Times of Robert Smalls by Michael Cooper, Rainbow Press, 1994.

Fragments of the Ark: A Novel by Louise Meriwether, Pocket Books, New York, 1994.

Gullah Statesman: Robert Smalls from Slavery to Congress 1839-1915 by Edward A. Miller, Jr., University of South Carolina Press, Columbia, SC, 1995.

Robert Smalls Sails to Freedom, by Susan Taylor Brown, Millbrook Press, 2005.

Yearning to Breathe Free: Robert Smalls of South Carolina and His Families by Andrew Billingsley, University of South Carolina Press, Columbia, SC, 2007.

Robert Smalls the Boat Thief by Robert F. Kennedy, Jr, Hyperion Books, 2008.

Seven Miles to Freedom: The Robert Smalls Story by Janet Halfmann, Lee and Low Books, 2008.

The Wheelman: How the Slave Robert Smalls Stole a Warship and Became a King by Marshall Evans, Land's Ford Publishing, Spartanburg, SC, 2015.

2

CPSIA information can be obtained
at www.ICGtesting.com
Printed in the USA
LVOW10s0624250517
535771LV00009B/121/P

9 780998 493701